FROZEN Heart

HELENA NEWBURY
NEW YORK TIMES BESTSELLING AUTHOR

Foster & Black

Cover by Mayhem Cover Creations
Main cover model image licensed from (and copyright remains with) Wander Aguiar Photography

Second Edition
ISBN (Paperback): 978-1-914526-27-5
ISBN (Ebook): 978-1-914526-26-8

ALSO BY HELENA NEWBURY

All my books can be enjoyed as standalone titles, but I've grouped them by theme here so you can find things easily.

Russian Mafia

Lying and Kissing

Kissing My Killer

Kissing the Enemy

The Double

Frozen Heart

The O'Harra Brothers

Punching and Kissing

Bad For Me

Saving Liberty

Outlaw's Promise

Brothers

Stormfinch Security

No Angel

Off Limits

Guarded

Capture Me

The Sisters of Invidia

Texas Kissing

Kissing My Killer

Hold Me in the Dark

Other Titles

Alaska Wild

Royal Guard

Mount Mercy

Captain Rourke

Deep Woods

Fenbrook Academy (New Adult Romance)

Dance For Me

Losing My Balance

In Harmony

Acting Brave

1

BRONWYN

I STILL REMEMBER the exact moment Radimir Aristov marched into my bookstore. I had no idea who he was. What he was. Or that, eight weeks later, we'd be married.

I just *sold him a book.* And then everything just kind of...spun out of control.

It was past seven in the evening and outside the store's big glass windows a blizzard was raging. A real Midwest special, the kind you only really get in Chicago, where the wind screeching between the buildings makes your ears ache, the cold slices straight through your clothes and the snow forms deep, crunchy drifts that soak the ankles of your jeans.

But inside *All You Need Is Books* it was warm and snug. I *cannot* let it get cold because cold means damp, and damp turns books into swollen, misshapen monsters no one wants to buy. That's my excuse for running the heating full blast, despite the bills...and okay, yes, also I hate being cold. And my customers appreciated it, as they quietly wandered the aisles, reading blurbs and piling up books to bring to the register.

It's not a big store. And if you look too closely at where the vanilla-milkshake walls meet the sky-blue ceiling, you'll see the edges are messy because I was balancing on a stepladder to paint it. But it's mine.

I looked around and smiled to myself. I was beyond exhausted: the store was losing money, so I'd started opening for twelve hours a day, eight till eight. Sometimes, my best friend Jen works a shift to help out but today I'd been on my own the whole time. Between serving customers, I'd sorted and shelved new stock, swept and tidied and fixed a leaking pipe that could have turned the romance section into papier mâché. I still needed to make a costume for the kid's story time session I'd organized and bundle up some books for a local reading charity. I'd been on my feet all day and my joints had thrown a hissy fit: it felt like someone had poured burning hot sand into my knees and ankles. But in calm, quiet moments like this, when I could look around at all the readers engrossed in their new read, or hunting for their next one, it was worth it.

Then the door opened, and my life changed forever.

The howl of the wind shattered the silence. Freezing air flooded the store, making people shiver and curse and sending snowflakes all the way to the Biographies section in the back. Everyone looked up.

A man was standing in the doorway, scowling. His eyes flicked over the wooden shelves, the books, the people, and his jaw tightened in suspicion. The wind was shrieking around him so fiercely it made me hunch my shoulders in sympathy, but the cold didn't seem to bother him. It was our strange world of warmth and comfort that he didn't trust.

He stepped into the light, and I got my first good look at him. *Big,* well over six feet, with shoulders that almost brushed the doorframe and a broad, hulking chest. He had the build of a firefighter, but he was wearing a three-piece suit and an overcoat, like he'd come from a board meeting. He was looking down, dusting snow from his waistcoat, so all I could see was soft curls of glossy black hair. Then he looked up and—

Oh God, he was gorgeous. People talk about *classic looks*, and suddenly I knew what they meant: he was like a statue of some ancient leader brought to life. He had high, sculpted cheekbones that made me think of somewhere distant and cold: I could imagine him standing on a frozen battlefield, commanding thousands of troops. That hard, dispassionate upper lip: that was made for snapping out orders. And that soft, sensuous lower one...that was made for kissing willful barbarian queens into submission.

He gave the bookstore another suspicious glare. Then he tugged the bottom of his waistcoat to straighten it and joined the line of people waiting to be served.

A guy in his twenties backed towards the door, staring fearfully at the man, and slipped out. Then an old guy did the same. It wasn't just that the man looked so scowly and intimidating, it was like they recognized him. *Who is this guy?*

He definitely had money: his overcoat looked like cashmere. So why was he here, in a neighborhood realtors optimistically called *up-and-coming,* instead of at one of the fancy bookstores downtown? He was still scowling and whenever the line stopped, he'd start tapping the toe of one polished leather shoe, like he had somewhere else to be. Busy. Powerful. Someone who never normally stood in line for *anything.*

I scanned and packed up a stack of romances for Melissa, one of my regulars, then stole another glance at the guy. There was something about the way he stood, the way he carried himself. Most people mess with their phones while they're waiting, they sort of turn inward. But he had his head up and was glancing around, taking everything in. It was more than just confidence. It was deeper than that, stronger than that. The whole store seemed to echo with his presence: it felt like everyone was too scared to make eye contact with him. *I* was scared. But I couldn't stop myself from sneaking peeks at him.

The next customer in line had pre-ordered a new fantasy novel the month before. I ducked down and grabbed it from under the counter, rang it up and handed it to him with a big smile. Now the scary mystery guy was next-but-one in line. And as the line shuffled forward, he looked at me for the first time.

I went stock-still. His eyes were the pale gray of a winter sky, so breathtakingly cold that looking into them made my chest hurt. There was no kindness there, no trace of caring, and the way he scowled down at me made my stomach drop. I almost looked away. But there's a part of me, way down deep, that's always been stubborn, or stupid. My grandmother called it *our Welsh ancestor's fighting spirit.* It made me keep looking.

And something happened.

For a second, his eyes narrowed. Then I saw the tiniest hint of warmth creep in, like faint sunshine breaking through frozen trees in a forest, and it was heart-stoppingly beautiful.

Then the warmth expanded, accelerating outward, and the cold gray turned scorching, blistering hot. His eyes flicked down my body, back up, and locked with mine again. They glittered, molten diamonds. He'd seen something he wanted. He was going to take it.

I swallowed, my face going hot. A deeper, darker heat raced down my body and detonated in my groin. I'd never felt so...*wanted.* Men don't look at me that way, especially not men like *him.* I'm not all tanned and toned and blonde haired. My skin's the sort of milky white that makes me fry if I step outdoors after May, I'm all boobs and ass and my hair is red. And I don't mean a delicate strawberry-blonde or a sophisticated auburn, I mean long waves of bright, coppery red: with my curves, I look like a farmer's daughter, like I should be fetching water from the well or guiding a plow.

And yet he was looking at me, the heat so intense it was like a physical touch. His gaze traced along the line of my jaw, over my lips, down the soft, sensitive skin of my neck...

"Um..." said the woman standing in front of me.

I snapped out of it, red-faced, and quickly served her. I kept my eyes on the books she was buying, on the numbers on the register, on her credit card...anywhere but on his face. *Did that just happen? Did he just look at me like he wanted to bend me over this counter and—*

I bagged the woman's books, thanked her, and she left. And *he* stepped forward.

I kept my eyes on the counter, but I could feel him looming over me. I was flustered and breathless, my skin was throbbing under my clothes and deep in my core there was a slow pulse of heat I couldn't control. It wasn't just the look he'd given me. It was the way I was reacting to it, the way I was reacting to *him.* He was big and intimidating and scary as *fuck,* but he was also gorgeous and...*different,* in a way I couldn't describe. *Dangerous.* It pulsed from him, a vibration I could feel. Like I and everyone else in the bookstore were deer and he was a wolf.

That should have made me run. But that vibration strummed through my body and some deep, dark place inside me sang like a tuning fork.

I lifted my eyes slowly. His waist came into view, his stomach flat and tight, hugged by an immaculate gray waistcoat. My eyes climbed higher, to where the twin slabs of his pecs pushed out his snow-white shirt. He seemed even bigger, up close, his chest wide enough to block my view of everything behind him. And *tall:* I'm 5'6" but I had to tilt my head way back to see more of him. Up past the knot of his blue silk tie, up past his shoulders...

Up into those amazing, pale gray eyes. The scalding lust was gone. Wait: no. Not gone. *Controlled.* Locked behind bars of ice. And he was frowning at me, demanding to know how I'd made his control slip.

I shifted from foot to foot, feeling small and vulnerable...but in a way I wanted more of. I wanted to drop my eyes to the floor but at the same time, I couldn't look away. I pressed my fingertips against the wood of the counter to anchor myself. Then I took a breath and forced my voice almost level. "Welcome to *All You Need is Books*. How can I help you?"

He glowered down at me. God, glowering was *invented* for this guy. Scowling, too. With those dark brows and the gray eyes and the way those gorgeous lips tightened...it was pure sex. A memory scratched at the back of my mind. I'd seen him before, somewhere.

"I need a book," he told me.

I blinked. Normally, I would have made some crack like *well, you're in the right place* or *unfortunately, we don't sell those.* But I was busy dealing with his voice. The words were heavy and cold as hunks of ice. And they'd been cut from a glacier by his accent, a silver axe that left the edges of the words wonderfully rough in places and silky smooth in others. I wanted to rub my mind against his voice. His accent fitted his cheekbones: somewhere cold and distant, but I couldn't place it. "For yourself?" I managed.

"A gift for my cousin's daughter. She's fourteen."

I nodded. "Well, okie dokie." *What? Since when do I say* okie fucking dokie?! I flushed all over again, then rallied. "I'm sure I can suggest something. What does she read?"

This time *he* blinked. He glanced around the store, then back to me. "Books."

I stared at him. *He doesn't read!* For him, this must be like when I went to a sports store with my former boyfriend and they had two hundred badminton rackets that all looked identical. I tried to imagine what it would be like to not love books. To never have the glorious anticipation of taking a new book home, desperate to start it. To never open a book to chapter one and let your mind sink into the story.

He was scary, rich, and intimidating...but I felt sorry for him.

I forced myself to focus on the task. Luckily, recommending books is what I'm best at. There's nothing I love more than pointing someone at a book and then a few weeks later having them come back into the store, grinning and floaty, having devoured it. I turned and marched over to a bookshelf, ignoring the pain in my legs. I plucked out a white-and-gold hardback and held it up. "*This* is a great book. It's about a girl who finds out she only has six months to live..."

His lips tightened. "I want to give her a birthday gift, not traumatize the child."

"No, no, it's okay! Because she finds a portal to the Fae world, and time passes more slowly there, so she can live out her whole life." I walked back to him, running my fingers lovingly over the embossed title. "And then she meets the Fae king, and they fall in love, and she learns how to shoot a bow and fights in a war, and—" I'd started grinning and couldn't stop: I always get this way when I talk about books I love. "It's got everything, adventure and emotion and romance—I mean, teen appropriate but it's *so good*. She'll love it."

I looked up. He wasn't looking at the book, he was looking at me. Watching me get stupidly carried away. I felt the heat start to creep into my face...

But then I saw how his eyes had softened.

He tore his gaze away and nodded. "I'll take it."

I nodded and scanned the book's barcode. He moved closer and I caught a hint of his cologne. It was like nothing I'd ever smelled, citrus and vanilla but with an undertone of something darkly intoxicating, and I couldn't get enough of it. If there was a magical, dark amber fruit that put you under a spell with just one bite, it would smell *exactly* like him.

He held out a glossy black bank card and I grabbed the card reader and went to tap it against the card...

And that's when I read the little silver letters that said *Radimir Aristov.*

My stomach plunged like an elevator with its cables cut. I suddenly knew where I'd seen him before. On the TV, tugging his waistcoat straight as he told a reporter that his property company was a legitimate business, and that he was a legitimate businessman. I knew why two of my customers had fled when he'd walked in: because they were *fucking terrified* of him.

Radimir Aristov. Some said he was the city's most powerful criminal since Capone. That nothing happened in Chicago without his say-so. That the foundations of his buildings were dug extra deep, because that's where he put the bodies.

His aura made sense to me now: dangerous and irresistible. *Power.*

I looked up at him. Now that I was looking for it, I could just make out the shadowy shapes of tattoos under his white shirt. *A Russian mob boss. A Russian mob boss is in my store.*

His eyes hardened again. He knew I'd recognized him; he could see it in my face.

There was a shrill electronic *beep* as the card reader accepted his card and I jerked and nearly dropped the thing. I kept my eyes on the counter as I put down the card reader, picked up the book and put it in a bag. Except my hands were shaking and the bag wouldn't open and every time I tried to push the book inside, it caught on the edge and—

His hands came into my view and closed around mine. I stared at the backs of his hands, my heart hammering. His hands dwarfed mine, his fingers strong and thick. *He could kill me. Just wrap them around my neck and—* But he was surprisingly gentle as he guided my hands and slid the book into place.

He released me and picked up the bag and I tentatively met his eyes again. He nodded to me, his expression unreadable. "Goodbye." Then he hesitated. "Miss...?"

"Hanford," I managed.

"Goodbye, Miss Hanford."

It was strangely, wonderfully, old-fashioned: I felt like I should be in a corset. I was so off balance, I gave it a go. "Goodbye...Mr. Aristov."

He headed towards the door. I closed my eyes and my whole body slumped in relief. *It's over. He's going.*

But as he walked away, I felt an...*ache.* That heat he'd lit in me, the memory of how his eyes had softened for a second. And the ache tugged at me.

I felt my mouth open.

Don't be an idiot, Bronwyn. Just shut up. In a few seconds, he'll be gone.

He put his hand on the door handle.

"Mr. Aristov!"

Everyone in the bookstore *except* Radimir turned to look at me, and it went utterly silent. Then Radimir turned, one eyebrow raised, as if no one had ever dared to shout after him like that before. He tilted his head a fraction of a degree: a warning.

What are you doing, Bronwyn? He's a freakin' mobster.

I swallowed. "It's—It's a trilogy. So if she likes the first book..."

For a moment, he just stared at me, as if willing me to weaken and drop my eyes. But when I choose to dig in, I can be stubborn. I lifted my chin and stared right back.

I thought I saw the faintest hint of a smile play across his lips, as if he was impressed with me. Then he nodded curtly, and he was gone.

2

RADIMIR

IT STARTED WITH A WEAKNESS.

I was on my way to a meeting with the mayor and I'm *never* late. But it was Lina's birthday in a week and she's one of the few relatives I have left in Russia. So, when I'd seen the little bookstore's window lit up bright, I'd told Valentin to pull over. *Two minutes,* I'd told him. I'd be in and out and still be on time to meet the mayor.

Except...it hadn't worked out like that.

I cursed under my breath and marched out of the store's orange glow and back into the darkness. The wind hit me full force, gusting under my coat and up my back, but I ignored it. Whatever cold America threw at me, I'd known colder.

I walked faster but it didn't matter. However fast I walked, I couldn't leave her behind. She was *there,* in my mind.

Tight green ribbed sweater, the lines arcing and curving as they traced the shape of her breasts.

Blue jeans that hugged the ripe curves of her hips.

Copper hair that fell in soft waves past her shoulders, gleaming gold and scarlet as it caught the light. A shock of color in my gray, cold world.

None of that mattered. Lust was lust, a need that could be sated with any of the women who circled our family like lipsticked, long-legged spiders. What mattered were her eyes. Big and liquid and the soothing green of a virgin forest. So welcoming, from the moment she saw me, despite me being a big, scary bastard. So warm, no matter how hard I'd glared at her.

So *innocent.* I was...*drawn* to her. I didn't understand it, but just the memory of her had my cock swelling in my pants. She was so...*good.* The mirror image of me. She'd genuinely wanted to help me find the right book. And I could tell she was a hard worker: the floors of the bookstore were spotless, despite all the customers tracking in slush from the snow outside.

A good-hearted, honest woman. It had been a long time since I'd met one of those. It made me want to shove those tight blue jeans down around her ankles along with her panties, baring those milky-white thighs and the soft pink lips of her pussy. Press her up against the counter and bury my cock in her, just sink balls deep into that innocence and fuck the good right out of her, in front of all her customers. Until she was sopping and slick around me, until she was clutching me, eyes screwed shut, screaming my name.

The part that made me hardest was knowing she wanted it just as much as I did. I'd seen it in the way she flushed, in the way her breathing quickened when our eyes locked. There was a part of her that needed my darkness as much as I needed her light.

I reached the street and scowled left and right, waiting for a gap in the traffic.

There was something else. The way she'd gotten so damn *happy* when she talked about that book. She'd gone off into her own little world, grinning and bright-eyed and...in Russia, we would say *Voskhititel'nyy. Adorable.*

Adorable has never been my type. And yet, when she talked about that book, about fae kings and girls with bows...I could have listened to her for hours.

I wondered what it must be like, to believe in happy endings.

A gap opened up in the traffic and I stalked across the street to where Valentin was waiting. "That was a lot longer than two minutes," he said mildly as I climbed into the car.

I knocked the snow off my shoes, then pulled the door closed. "There was a line."

Valentin turned slowly around to stare at me from the driver's seat. "You waited in line?"

I felt my lips tighten. Valentin notices every little thing. It's what makes him such an effective killer but right now, it was infuriating. It made me ask uncomfortable questions: why *had* I waited in line? That wasn't something I'd normally do. But the store had felt like her little world, and I'd been a guest there.

I glowered at Valentin. With anyone else, that would have done the trick. But Valentin just raised a questioning eyebrow. He and my other brothers are the only ones who'll stand up to me.

Wait...that's not quite true. The woman in the bookstore...even after all my scowling, even after she realized who I was, she'd called after me. *She'd* stood up to me, even though it made her legs shake.

Innocent. Adorable. And brave.

"Drive the car," I ordered. "We're late to meet the mayor."

Valentin reluctantly turned around and started the engine. I glanced out of the window at the orange glow of the bookstore across the street. *Miss Hanford.* Even her name was honest and upstanding...

Then I turned to face front and rammed those thoughts down deep. They were childish weaknesses, soft pink ribbons that I crushed between efficient, icy cogs.

There was no room for a woman in my life. Closeness makes you vulnerable. And there was no place for *warm* or *adorable* in my world. Those things would get snuffed out in a heartbeat.

She was the good-hearted, sweet princess, safe in her castle. And me? I was no prince. I was the monster who eats people like her.

But as the car surged away, I watched the store in the rear-view mirror until it faded into the darkness.

3

BRONWYN

I CLOSED the store at eight but, by the time I'd cleaned up, re-ordered stock and locked up, it was closer to nine. After being on my feet all day, my joints were swollen tight and every step felt like bone grinding on bone. What I really wanted was to soak in a long, hot bath, with some candles and maybe some caramel crunch chocolate. But she needed me.

So I bundled up in a coat, scarf and gloves and set out into the blizzard.

The subway train was packed so I had to hang from a strap, which meant that each jolt and sway of the carriage whip-cracked my body, pulling my joints in all sorts of interesting ways. There was a priority seat, but it was occupied by a big guy in a suit who reeked of alcohol, and I wasn't going to get into a fight with him. Even if he gave up the seat willingly, I'd have to deal with everyone else in the carriage. *Why do you need the seat anyway? Look at you, there's nothing wrong with you!*

Climbing the stairs that led up to the street nearly killed me: I had to stop twice and take a breath of freezing air before I could push through the pain. But then I was at the top and I put my head down and just went for it: along the street, through the doors of the care facility, past the nurses's station and into her room—

My grandmother, Babette—she's always insisted I call her Baba—is 5'8" and built, in her words, like a dockworker. When she was a nurse, she could heave even the biggest patients onto gurneys and more than once she punched out some drunk guy who tried to grope her. But now, nestled in a drab, high-backed chair, she looked tiny.

I pasted a happy smile on my face even as my heart broke inside. *"Hey!* Sorry I'm late." I hurried over and hugged her. Her right arm gave me a weak little squeeze...but *only* her right arm.

It had happened three months ago. She'd been carrying a bag of groceries in from the car when she staggered sideways and just crumpled, hitting her head on a wall as she went down. The paramedics rushed her to the hospital and the doctors confirmed she'd suffered a massive stroke.

She was out of danger, now, but she wasn't recovering as the doctors had hoped. And I knew this place was part of the reason. The room, with its cracked, faded yellow paint, felt more like a cell. Baba needed physiotherapy and stimulation to help her brain regrow all the connections it had lost. But the staff barely came into her room. Her plates from breakfast and lunch were still sitting in the corner and the puzzle books and word games I'd bought were in an untouched stack on the shelf. I wanted to scream in frustration but there was nothing I could do: Baba needed twenty-four-hour care which I couldn't give her at home, and this place was the best I could afford.

I blinked hard: I'd save the crying for when I got home. "Have you eaten?" I asked. Both of us glanced sadly down at the plate of rubbery tubes in watery sauce that the care facility called pasta. "Can't say I blame you," I deadpanned. "Why don't I run down the street and get you something?"

I brought her some hot food and helped her eat. Then I read to her until the nurses told me I had to go.

~

I hadn't eaten all day so when I got back to my apartment, I dug around in the refrigerator and made myself a sandwich. Maybe I'm weird but sandwiches have always been my comfort food: there's no other food where you can customize it to your exact mood. Right now, I need pastrami and cheese and extra pickles, and chips, lots of chips. I layered it all into a huge, bursting-at-the-seams sandwich, poured a glass of milk and then huddled in bed to eat it because it was too cold anywhere else.

But even when I was full, and I'd stopped shivering, I couldn't sleep. I kept thinking about my bank account, which had been dropping deeper and deeper into the red each month. The tiny salary I paid myself barely brought it back into the black before bills and the cost of Baba's care facility slammed it down into the red again. I was barely able to afford groceries: luxuries like new clothes were a distant memory. And then there was the store, a whole different level of worry.

It wasn't always like this. Once upon a time, there was a bouncy eight-year-old who loved swimming, board games and, above all, books. My parents had always been big readers, and they got me reading early. I'd lie for hours stretched out on my stomach, chin propped on one hand, utterly still apart from the slow turning of pages. I was a princess, a starship commander, a farmer with a family of talking mice...

And then one day, I came home from a weekend with Baba and my own story just...stopped, like someone had torn out the rest of my book.

I remember Baba clutching me to her chest as I sobbed into her dress. She was struggling not to cry herself: she'd just lost her son and daughter-in-law. "We'll get through this," she told me. "The two of us."

Suddenly, at fifty-eight, Baba had to become a mother again. I moved into her tiny apartment, and we did our best to make it work. She put in long shifts at the hospital to pay the bills and I helped where I could. I'd always had a weird, analytical brain, obsessing over tweaking systems and making things mesh: that's why I liked board games so much. I put it to work organizing rotas, meal planning and clipping coupons. College was out of the question so when I left school, I got a job working in a grocery store.

The place was fascinating to me. There was something about the complex flow of it that suited my brain: seeing how all the staff, product lines and store layout worked together wasn't too different from figuring out board games, or meal planning. I soaked up all the knowledge I could and after a few months I started making timid little suggestions, like *maybe we could widen the baby food aisle, because then it would be easier for parents pushing prams.* And when profits went up, my boss noticed. Over the next seven years, I rose slowly up the ranks. But when my dream job, a store manager post, opened up, my boss took me aside and gently explained that I wasn't in the running. "You're great," he said with feeling. "You could run a store. But there's no point even putting you forward. These days, they want a college degree."

That night, I was one of the last ones in the store, checking around before we locked up. I shut off the lights...and then I just sank down in the darkened vegetable aisle. It hit me that *this was it.* I was going to be stuck at this level for the rest of my life unless I did something.

What if I opened my own damn store?

And as I sat there on the cold tiles, I suddenly knew exactly what I'd sell: books. Books had helped me through the death of my parents, my teens, they'd been an escape from the daily grind of work...I wanted to share that and help people to find books they'd love.

So I enrolled in a business course at the local community college. It was exhausting: I was working shifts at the store by day, then classes in the evening and then reading books on bookkeeping and finance until I fell asleep. But slowly, very slowly, I started to shape my crazy idea into a workable business plan. I saved as much of my paycheck as I could for the startup costs and Baba insisted on throwing in a chunk of her retirement savings to help.

And then Nathan walked into my class. Plaid shirt rolled up to show chiseled forearms dusted with golden hair. Ocean-blue eyes that twinkled when he smiled, and he smiled a lot. He flopped down in the seat next to me without asking if it was taken, then leaned over. "You look smart. Can I copy off you?"

I flushed and nodded. I'd been single for over a year: I hadn't had time to meet anyone, and guys weren't interested in the pale, curvy girl who lived with her grandmother. But at the end of the class, Nathan asked me out for coffee.

A few hours later I knew all about his plans. A wife, two children (a boy and a girl), a Jack Russell (his family had always owned Jack Russells) and, when his planned chain of organic smoothie stores was successful, a fancy apartment in a nice part of Chicago and holidays in Europe. I'd never met anyone so sure of what they wanted, before. Two more dates and we were having breathless, up-against-the-wall sex at his place. A month later, I met his parents. And eight months after that, as we walked through showers of pink cherry blossom in Jackson Park, he went down on one knee and asked me to marry him.

I stared down at him, open-mouthed. Ever since I was a kid, I'd had daydreams about someone riding in to rescue me. Some handsome prince who'd carry me off and marry me, complete with a big, fairytale wedding. *This is it!* I felt my throat closing up. *"Yes!"*

We booked a trip to New York for the following weekend to celebrate and I ran home to tell Baba. She'd always been a little hesitant about Nathan, but she hugged me tight and told me how happy she was for me.

I'd been getting twinges of pain in my joints, and I didn't want it to spoil our trip to New York, especially because we'd be spending a lot of time walking. So I talked to my physician and he sent me for x-rays and tests. The day before we left for New York, Nathan and I sat down with a specialist.

I had early-onset rheumatoid arthritis. My body was attacking the lining of my joints, making them swollen and painful. It could be managed, but it couldn't be stopped. And it was going to get a lot worse.

I grabbed for Nathan's hand and he squeezed mine reassuringly.

But when he turned to look at me, it was like he was seeing me for the first time. And when we stumbled, dazed, out of the specialist's office, we looked around at the other patients in the waiting room, most of them with some form of arthritis. Some were as old as Baba, some as young as me. Some had to use sticks to walk, some couldn't walk at all. I was staring at my future.

The next day, I was lying on the grass in Central Park, my head cradled in Nathan's lap as he sat against a tree. The sun was shining, a string quartet was playing, and the diagnosis seemed like a bad dream. *Everything's going to be fine,* I told myself. "When we get back," I said gently, "should we start looking at apartments?"

"Mumm." He was right there, stroking my hair. So why did his voice sound so far away? "Let's do that."

A week after we got back, he said we should maybe slow things down a little.

A week after *that*, he split up with me. That picture he had in his head of his perfect life. I no longer fit. He didn't want a wife who was flawed.

In the kitchen of our little apartment, Baba hugged me tight while I cried my heart out. I'd had break-ups before, but I'd never been left feeling so utterly worthless. So *not enough.*

"I don't know what—what I'm going to do," I sobbed. My bookstore plan had been risky. Now it felt impossible.

Baba squeezed me harder. "I do," she said. "Our ancestors were Welsh. Celt warrior women who lived in the forest and when the Romans invaded and tried to take their home, they fought. That's what you're going to do, Bronnie. You're going to fight."

And so, three months later, I opened *All You Need Is Books* (my grammar-nerd friend Luna had argued that technically it should be *Are Books,* but it was my store, dammit). Baba was right, I had to fight. Fuck Nathan and fuck arthritis.

The first few months went well: every store gets a boost when it's new and people are curious. But now, six months on, the store was losing money each month. Baba's care facility bills meant I could barely afford food. I'd almost burned through my startup money. If I didn't figure something out soon, I'd have to shut down...and Baba would have lost the money she gave me.

I rolled onto my back, wincing as my aching joints flexed, and stared up at the cracked plaster of the apartment's ceiling. I had no idea what I was going to do. And there was no one I could go to for help: my parents were gone, Baba was sick, the man I'd thought I was going to marry dumped me... I was twenty-seven and, suddenly, I was all alone. I had some great friends, but they had problems of their own and they weren't the same as family. I felt like I was adrift on an endless black ocean with no one else in sight.

I could feel my mind tumbling downward, faster and faster, and I knew I had to think of something else, *now,* or I wasn't going to stop until I hit bottom—

Radimir Aristov.

My mind stopped with a jolt, like a falling rock climber grabbing a handhold. *Radimir Aristov.* He was definitely unique enough to distract me. I wrapped the memories around me to shut out the cold dark. That accent, shaping each syllable until it was deliciously rough ice. That name, *Aristov,* like the whisper of a silver dagger being drawn. The swell of his pecs under his soft white shirt, just a hint of dark tattoo peeking through. The way he jerked his waistcoat to straighten it. The warmth of his hands when they'd touched mine...

And something happened. I'd only meant to distract myself but once I started thinking about him, I couldn't stop.

It was that power that throbbed from him, like a drumbeat too low to hear, a vibration that shook my whole body. It resonated right to my core and bloomed into heat. I've always been built out of steel, like Baba, but the heat just melted me into taffy. He felt so utterly different to every man I'd ever met. Like he'd stepped into my bookstore from a shadow world that was colder, harder, *realer* than the one I knew.

After he'd stalked out of my store, I'd run over to the door: I couldn't help it. I saw him climbing into a big, black Mercedes that whisked him away. What would have happened if he'd taken me with him?

I closed my eyes and imagined. I could feel the shocking cold of the night air as he pulled me across the street, my sneakers skidding in the snow. I felt something *drop* inside me, dark and deliciously hot. Like the feeling you get on a rollercoaster when you tip over the first hill and plunge.

He threw me into the car and I sprawled on my back on the back seat. He climbed on top of me, a knee pressing between my thighs, and the door *whumped* shut. The sound of the street dropped away instantly: we were in *his* world, now, hidden by tinted glass. The driver started the car and I rocked on the seat as we roared away.

I stared up at him, our faces only a foot apart. "What do you want?" I managed.

He was lit by the streetlights whipping past, his face alternating between light and shadow. "*You know what I want,*" he rumbled, those gray eyes blazing. He pushed me down on the seat, my legs kicking towards the ceiling, and his lips came down on mine.

He was hungry, aggressive, forcing me open and making me his. The first touch of his tongue against mine sent an electric shock through my body: my back arched off the seat, my hair sliding on the leather as my head rolled back. I could feel myself reaching up, not to push him away, exactly, just to maintain some control. But at the same time, it was like I was falling backwards into pink bliss. The hard press of his lips, the slow grind of his pecs against my breasts...why exactly did I need to maintain control, again?

His hand traced down my side and then up, underneath my sweater and vest top, and I groaned in shock as his fingertips skimmed over bare skin. He smoothed up my side, the warmth of his hand shocking, and then his hand was sweeping around to the front.

He slid his hand under my bra and suddenly my breast was in his hand, being rolled and softly kneaded, my nipple rasping against his palm. I swallowed, panted, and groped upwards, blindly, too far gone to open my eyes.

A hand closed around one of my wrists. Then it captured the other one and pressed them both down to the soft leather above my head.

I got that roller coaster *drop* again. I wasn't in control anymore. *I should be scared.* A part of me *was* scared.

But I didn't want him to stop.

The kiss changed, a slow grind of his lips against mine as his tongue sought me out and then freakin' *owned* me. I was breathless, urgent in a way I'd never felt before. However hard he kissed me, I wanted it harder. I felt weak, damsel-fainting-in-a-corset weak, and all I could do was kiss back, like whispering into a hurricane. But every time I brushed the tip of my tongue against his, I felt his whole body go rigid. His chest vibrated as he full-on *growled.* The more he felt me lose myself in the pleasure, the more turned on he got.

He suddenly rammed my sweater and vest top up around my neck. My bra fought valiantly for a second to keep me covered. Then he grabbed it and pulled, there was a sudden snap, and I was completely bare. He lowered his head and licked at my nipple, bathing it in warmth and bringing it to quivering hardness. Every flick of his tongue sent a new wave of hot, tight pleasure strumming through my body. I tried to reach for him...but he still had my wrists pinned, and his grip was like iron.

That dark, forbidden *plunge* inside me. I went floaty and breathless. I pushed against his grip again, a little harder, this time. My wrists lifted a fraction of an inch off the seat. Then his hand pressed them down even harder, and a dark ribbon of heat twisted straight down to my groin and made me crush my thighs together. *God, what is this?*

Radimir suddenly lifted his head. I blinked hazily and saw him staring down at me, his eyes molten. His hand stroked down my body to the waistband of my jeans...and he paused. He was giving me a chance to say *no.*

But my pulse was like a bass drum crashing inside my head, drowning out anything else. I panted, staring up at him, and stayed silent.

I thought I saw his eyes gleam. Then he grabbed the front of my jeans and pulled, *hard,* and I felt the buttons on the fly pop open, and with a second jerk he dragged them down over my ass and hips, down around my knees. I felt the cool air of the car against my pussy lips and realized he'd pulled my panties down with them. I flushed as his eyes swept over me, drinking me in. Then he was unfastening his belt, shoving his pants down one-handed as his cock sprang free. He spread my knees, and I cried out as the head of him parted my slickened lips and plunged deep into me—

Everything blurred, becoming frantic flashes of sensation. The silken stretch of his cock inside me, the pleasure making me arch my back—

The weight of him between my thighs, pinning me—

The silky rasp of his expensive shirt against my nipples as he thrust—

Him flipping me over and pulling me up onto my hands and knees, then fucking me from behind, even harder, holding my wrists behind my back *OH GOD YES*—

I bucked and trembled as an orgasm rolled through me, waves of pink pleasure that tumbled me into delightfully dark depths I hadn't known were there. I finally surfaced, panting, and opened my eyes. I was in my bed, one hand in my soaked panties.

My heart was still slowing. *What the hell was that?!* I fantasized plenty but never about some random guy I'd only met for a few minutes. Sure, Radimir was hot as hell, but he was an actual, real-world gangster. If the stories were true, he'd killed people, or at least *had* them killed. Why was I fantasizing about being whisked off in his car while he... I reddened.

It had been so real. My wrists still felt warm from where he'd gripped them. And what was *that* about? I'd never wanted it rough before. Or at least, I'd never been conscious of it. But I couldn't deny how the fantasy had taken hold of me. And now I felt gloriously floaty and relaxed, like the orgasm had wrung all the stress out of me.

I closed my eyes and felt myself sinking into sleep. But as I drifted downward, reality crept back in.

Baba was still sick. The store was still losing money. And I was still alone.

When I was a kid, I'd thought that someday, a prince would come and rescue me.

I'd thought Nathan was that prince. But all he did was make me realize the truth.

There are no princes.

4

RADIMIR

"YOU NEED TO GET YOURSELF A WOMAN," Valentin told me.

I reluctantly looked up from my phone. My brother was leaning over the VIP room's balcony, looking down on the crowd below. Three hundred of Chicago's young and beautiful bounced to the thumping bass and there was no shortage of tanned, leggy women in flimsy dresses.

I scowled. "Why on earth would I want a woman?"

"She might make you a little less..." he imitated my scowl.

I sighed and rolled my eyes. I didn't mind him making fun of me: he knows not to do it when anyone's around. Valentin is the youngest of us and the most casual. He was wearing a tight white T-shirt and midnight blue jeans and blended in with the club goers much better than me, in my three-piece suit. Only his long black leather coat made him stand out. I knew there'd be at least three knives hidden somewhere under it, maybe a gun, too. We were here for a polite, good faith meeting and in theory that meant no weapons. But the people we were meeting wouldn't obey that rule and so neither would we.

"*You* find yourself a woman," I told Valentin. "I don't have time for a relationship." And it was true. My brothers and I ruled half the city, but when you have the throne, you have to fight to keep it. A new group had moved in from Armenia and were trying to take our territory. The mayor wanted my help to keep the lid on a scandal and I had my job as CEO of Aristov Developments, our property company.

But that wasn't the reason I stayed single. Valentin knew it, and I knew it.

I checked my phone for the tenth time and my foot started tapping irritably. "Where are they?!"

"They're not late," said Valentin calmly. "You made us get here early."

I had. I refused to be late for things. But I also hated waiting: it was inefficient. And I hated this club. It was wildly overpriced and too cool for its own good, with its black-walled VIP room and glass tables that seemed to float, and its DJs from Iceland and drinks served in light-up glasses. It didn't even have a name, it had a *symbol,* a squiggle you were supposed to pronounce as *Indigo,* which was the stupidest thing I'd ever heard. "At least when we meet the mayor, she does things properly," I grumbled, jerking my waistcoat straight. "What's wrong with a deserted construction site? They only picked this place to show off."

"You're in a foul mood, brother," said a voice behind me. My head snapped around and I saw Gennadiy emerging from the shadows. He'd been almost invisible in his charcoal suit and dark, open-neck shirt. He sprawled next to me on the blinding-white couch and poured himself a shot of vodka from the bottle we'd ordered: at least this place had the good stuff. "Perhaps you need to get laid."

"That's what *I* said!" said Valentin.

I turned and glared at Gennadiy, who gave me one of his infuriating smirks. He's the middle brother, older than Valentin but younger than me. What happened to the three of us—we just refer to it as *Vladivostok*—affected us in different ways. It left Valentin haunted. It made Gennadiy hard-hearted. And me? It taught me that love makes you weak. *That's* why I'd never allow myself to fall in love.

The door swung open and Mikhail, our uncle, strolled in, leading his dogs. "Sorry," he muttered, waving his hand at them. "The bouncer."

Dogs, of course, are not allowed in nightclubs. But Mikhail doesn't go anywhere without them, as the bouncer probably found out to his cost. I petted one of the four enormous Malamutes, and my bad mood lifted just a little. Mikhail has trained them since puppies and they're superb attack dogs. But to members of our family, they're just adorable fluffballs. Mikhail gave each of us a hearty embrace. "What are we talking about?" he asked.

"How Radimir should find a woman," said Valentin before I could stop him.

Mikhail punched me playfully on the shoulder. "You *should* find a woman! I keep telling you to think about an heir!"

I huffed and scowled. "Everyone stay the fuck out of my love life!" I had enough to worry about, holding this family together after everything we'd been through, without worrying about starting a dynasty.

Mikhail settled on the couch, and we waited. The entire Aristov family lined up.

Valentin is our hitman. He spends most of his time up on Chicago's rooftops, watching his targets, before descending to slit their throats in the night. Gennadiy handles the day-to-day running of most of our illegal operations. Mikhail, he's our link to politics and power. He makes the introductions and handles the bribes: everyone who's anyone in the state of Illinois knows friendly Uncle Mikhail, or *Misha,* as he insists they call him.

Then there's me. I'm the CEO of our legitimate property business, make the decisions and hold everything together, bound by the promise I made my brothers and Mikhail all those years ago: *family first. Family, always.*

And as we sat there together, my mind did what it always did, as soon as there was a second of quiet. It slid to *her.*

It had been a week since I walked into that bookstore, and I hadn't gone an hour without thinking of her. I'd be at the office, and I'd imagine her magnificent, denim-clad ass raised in the air as I bent her over the photocopier, or her copper hair tossing and pale legs kicking as I fucked her on the conference table. I was starting to obsess over what her pussy looked like: light pink or dark pink lips? The curls of hair red or brown, or shaved completely? I had to know.

The lust wasn't the thing that unsettled me, though. There was a craving I couldn't seem to get rid of, a little *lift* in my chest when I thought about seeing her again. I scowled. *What's the matter with me?*

One of the club's waitresses appeared at the door. The club makes them wear this ridiculous outfit, an indigo dress and knee boots and a platinum-blonde wig. "Your guests are here," she told us, looking shaken. And the Nazarov brothers strolled in.

The Nazarovs are Russian, like us. Spartak was first, a giant of a man, almost as tall as me but much wider. He used to wrestle back home, and he was good at it. He's an old-school, vicious bastard who likes to wrap his enemies in chains and drown them in the river. I only deal with him because I have to: he runs most of the drugs in Chicago, as well as some bars and a sleazy nightclub.

Behind him followed his brother, Borislav. Bald, leaner than Spartak but just as big and unpleasant, Borislav acts as muscle. He rides his brother's coattails and spends most of his time drinking and partying.

"Do you need anything else?" asked the waitress. Her eyes never left Borislav, and she was holding her silver tray across her chest like a shield.

I stiffened, furious, and scowled at Borislav. He has a reputation in the city. He's assaulted or raped several women, but only two have ever reported him, only one led to charges being filed and that case was dropped when the woman suddenly disappeared. Everyone hates him but no one can do anything because he's Spartak's brother. My guess was that Borislav had slipped his hand up the waitress's dress on the way upstairs and if there's one thing I can't stand, it's men who mistreat women. "No, thank you," I told the waitress. "We don't need anything else." She hurried away, leaving Borislav looking disappointed.

The door closed and we settled down to business. Our families have managed to maintain a grudging, fragile peace for years, an agreement brokered by the *Vosem,* "The Eight," an unofficial sort of high council of senior Bratva members back in Moscow. I don't like working with lowlifes like the Nazarovs, but peace is better for business and disobeying The Eight would see our family isolated and quickly wiped out.

The Nazarovs were just leaving when my phone vibrated with a message from Lina. She calls me Uncle even though she's my cousin's daughter because I'm the closest thing she has to one.

LINA

Uncle Radimir, could you please get me the next book in the series?

Already?!

You read that book in five days?!

No, in two days. YOU HAVE NO IDEA! She didn't know the king was in love with her but she just found out ARGH please please!

I felt a rare bloom of warmth, deep within my chest. The innocence of childhood, when just a book can make you happy. It should probably have made me nostalgic for when *I* was like that. But my childhood was nothing like Lina's.

I could still make *her* happy, though.

Yes, Linyushka, I will get it for you.

Thank you, thank you!

I felt a trace of a smile touch my lips. I'd pick the book up that afternoon—

At the bookstore. Something unfamiliar unfolded in my chest, expanding to fill me. *I'll see her again!*

I froze, glaring at a spot on the floor, careful to keep my face a mask. I stamped on the rogue feeling hard. Then I carefully analyzed it, like a scientist putting a new and possibly dangerous insect under a microscope. I hadn't felt it in so long, it took me a moment to identify it. Excitement.

"Bullshit," I said aloud. My family all turned to look at me. But I was their *Pakhan,* their boss. I didn't owe them an explanation. And I certainly wasn't getting giddy over seeing some woman. I wanted to fuck her, that's all it was. I wanted to plunge my tongue between those soft, pink pussy lips, feel those milky thighs clamp hard against my ears as she came.

That's all it is.

~

Later that day, Valentin parked the car opposite *All You Need Is Books.* It wasn't snowing today but it was still bitingly cold. "I'll be two minutes," I muttered as I climbed out.

"Don't wait in line, this time," Valentin told me helpfully.

I ignored him and stalked across the street, the wind making my overcoat billow out behind me like a cape. *She might not even be there,* I told myself, mentally shrugging. *Or she might be so busy with customers that we'll barely speak.* It didn't matter. It didn't matter *at all.* I was relaxed. Casual. So why had my chest gone tight?

I pushed open the door, repeating nonchalantly in my mind: *she might not even be here, she might not even be here...*

I froze in the doorway. A woman with ash-blonde hair was behind the counter. *She's not here?!* I'd been repeating it, I hadn't thought it would *actually happen!*

The tension in my chest shifted to raw panic. *Where is she? Does she work a different day? A different shift?* And then a horrible possibility hit me. *What if she doesn't work here anymore? What if she never worked here, what if she was just filling in for one shift on that day I came in and now I'll NEVER FIND HER AGAIN?!*

My woman stood up from where she'd been ducked down behind

the counter. She was holding a silver-and-black hardback. "I saw you pull up. I'm guessing she wants the next book?"

I stared at her. I was panting like I'd just run three blocks; my eyes were wide and... had I just thought of her as *my woman?* I took a deep breath and walked slowly forward. "Miss Hanford."

She pursed her lips and looked up at me through her lashes. "Mr. Aristov." She was scared of me. But there was just a hint of humor, too, gently making fun of me for being so formal, and that daring teasing made my cock instantly swell in my pants. I wanted to seize her by the waist, lift her over the counter and mash my lips down on hers.

I took another deep breath. My heart was still pounding from that moment of fear when I thought I'd lost her. *What the fuck is happening to me?* "*Yes,* please, the next book." I swallowed, trying to make my voice coldly impassive. "My cousin's daughter said how much she liked the first one."

She grinned, innocent and happy, and it made her whole face light up. Suddenly, nothing else existed but those sparkling, forest-green eyes. She almost reminded me of a librarian: smart and sexy and *good*, shut away here in her snug little world of books. "Would you like me to gift-wrap it, this time?" she asked.

I knew something was wrong. I wasn't acting like myself. But my brain wasn't interested in investigating, right now. All that mattered was that gift wrapping meant more time with her. "Please."

"It's three dollars extra," she said apologetically.

"Fine." Three hundred would have been fine.

She gave me another one of those grins and I felt my chest...*lift.* I fought to focus, to try to be analytical. She cared about every sale, every extra, far more than if she just worked here.

"This is your store," I realized.

She nodded, entirely focused on smoothing the creases on the gift wrap. She was using expensive, delicately stenciled paper and scarlet ribbons: she couldn't make much money, even at three dollars per book. She was doing it *right,* not ruthlessly cutting corners for profit.

A good woman running an honest business. The polar opposite of me.

She expertly cinched the ribbon tight and tied a bow, then held out the package. And now I'd calmed enough to see that *she* was breathing fast, and her cheeks were flushed. Excited. Nervous. Not completely in control. I held my card out to the card reader, and it beeped, far too quickly.

"I'll keep a copy of the third book for you, Mr. Aristov."

I wasn't walking away without knowing her name. "Radimir."

She swallowed. "Bronwyn."

Bronwyn. It sounded faraway and magical, like she should be walking through a misty forest, and it suited her perfectly. I nodded, then turned and walked out.

On the sidewalk, the freezing air slapped me in the face and my steps slowed. *What just happened?* The way my stomach had plunged when I thought I'd never find her again. The way I tried to spin out the encounter as long as possible. Something about her made me lose control and I'm *always* in control.

I stopped in the middle of the sidewalk and stared at the gift-wrapped book in my hands. *This is dangerous.* Feelings make you weak.

Then I shook my head and marched across the street with long, determined strides. *Ridiculous.* Of course I didn't feel things for her. I just wanted to fuck her, and I'd been disappointed when I thought she wasn't there, and of course I'd wanted more time with her so I could gaze at the swells of her breasts under her sweater and the ripe curves of her hips under those tight, tight jeans.

Feelings make you weak. And that's why I never felt anything for anyone.

~

Life went back to normal for a few days. But then I started to get this...itch. I could feel a certain street on the west side with a certain, warmly lit storefront calling to me. *No. Not until Lina asks for the next book.*

A week came and went but Lina didn't message. By now, the itch was more of an ache. *What's taking her so long?*

Two weeks passed. I started checking the messaging app every few hours to see if Lina had messaged. This time, I'd paid extra to courier the book to Russia in twenty-four hours, so she'd had it for over twelve days, now. *What's the matter with kids today? Don't they read anymore?*

Then my stomach knotted. *What if it wasn't any good?* What if the author had gone off the boil and the second book wasn't as good as the first?

What if Lina doesn't want the final book?

After sixteen days, I couldn't take it anymore and I messaged Lina.

Have you finished the new book yet?

She messaged me back immediately.

Haven't started it yet. I have exams.

I kicked my desk so hard I bruised my foot.

It was three days after that, still with no word from Lina, that my assistant, Irwin, poked his head into my office. He's a civilian, like all the workers at Aristov Incorporated, and doesn't know about our illegal activities. He's nervous and awkward, with a slender build and thick glasses. But he's an excellent assistant and he's a lot less distracting than some gorgeous woman in a short skirt and high heels.

Bronwyn. She'd look amazing dressed as an assistant. With that red hair all piled up and pinned tight, so I could have the fun of *un*pinning it when I pulled her across my desk. And an indecently short skirt, and four—no, *five-inch* heels. And she'd call me *Mr. Aristov* in that soft, slightly teasing voice and—

I shook my head and forced myself to focus. "What is it?" I asked Irwin.

"Your brothers are here."

I sighed and ran a hand through my hair. "Send them in."

Gennadiy and Valentin strolled in, followed by Mikhail and his dogs. Gennadiy made sure the door was closed, then stalked over to my desk, his face grim. He glanced at the ceiling, the walls, then raised a questioning eyebrow. *Are we safe?*

I nodded. "I swept for bugs this morning." I leaned forward in my chair. I knew it must be urgent: we don't discuss family business at my office if we can help it.

Gennadiy leaned close. He looked shaken and it takes a lot to shake him. "I had a call from The Eight this morning. They want us to end someone."

I nodded, confused. It didn't seem like a big deal. We'd kill the person and then—

"Brother," said Gennadiy, "it's *Borislav Nazarov!*"

I froze, horrified.

"It will start a war, Radimir," said Mikhail. "One we'll lose."

He was right. The peace deal with the Nazarovs had allowed us to move into legitimate business and mainly white collar crime. But the Nazarovs had used the peace to build up their drug empire. Spartak was in business with a drug cartel in Mexico and sold their product all over Chicago. Plus, somewhere in the city—no one knew where—he had a factory churning out hundreds of thousands of pills. The money from those two operations had bought him a lot of soldiers and a lot of guns. If it came to war—and Spartak Nazarov would absolutely go to war with us if we killed his beloved brother—we'd be wiped out.

"Can we refuse?" asked Valentin.

I shook my head. You don't say no to The Eight.

"Why would they ask us to do this?" asked Gennadiy. "They were the ones who got us to make peace!"

"They must have a good reason," I said, steepling my fingers. "We all know Borislav's reputation. My guess is, he's raped another woman, or killed her. Some district attorney has finally gotten serious about putting him away. And The Eight think a trial would put too much attention on the Bratva." I looked at each of them in turn. "I have no problem killing the piece of shit, after all the women he's hurt."

"But Spartak will declare war on us," said Gennadiy.

I cocked my head to one side. "Only if he finds out it was us."

"It's his *brother!*" said Gennadiy. "Spartak won't stop until he finds out who did it."

I thought. "Then we make it look like an accident."

"I can do it," said Valentin.

I shook my head. "This one I'm doing myself."

Valentin's eyes widened. "It's my job. It's *what I do.*"

I nodded sympathetically. Valentin is our hitman, and he really is good at his job, one of the best I'd ever seen. Only a guy I used to know in New York was on the same level. "It's not that I don't trust you, brother," I said gently. "There's just too much at stake. If this goes wrong, I want it to be on my head, not yours."

Valentin nodded unhappily and I showed them out, taking the opportunity to give Mikhail's dogs ear scratches as they passed. *I better get this right,* I thought as I watched them leave. *Or we're all dead.*

At that moment, my phone buzzed with a notification. I was so distracted, I had to read the message a few times before the implications sank in.

LINA

I read the second book in A DAY! OMG they're going to make her Queen but the King's missing and there's a traitor!!! Please next book please thank you you're the best!

Borislav and Spartak were instantly forgotten. I marched out of my office and loomed over Irwin's desk. "Move up my afternoon meetings," I told him. "I have an errand to run after work."

That evening, Valentin parked opposite the bookstore for the third time. "Maybe next time, you should just buy all three books at once."

I caught his eyes in the rear-view mirror and gave him a sharp glare. *Did he know?* If he did, his face showed no trace of it. *So what if he does know? So I want to fuck the bookstore owner. So what?* There was nothing wrong with lust. It was feelings that were the problem.

As I crunched through the snow towards the brightly lit store, it sank in that this was the last time. The series was a trilogy: once she finished this one, I'd have no reason to go back. *Maybe she can recommend another series for Lina. A nice long one...*

I pushed open the door and stopped dead in the doorway. *What the fuck?*

Bronwyn was behind the counter, working through a long line of customers who all clutched thick stacks of books. Not surprising when hand-lettered signs offered 25%, 30%, even 40% off. A banner hung overhead: red paint on what looked like a white bed sheet. CLOSING DOWN SALE.

I marched past the line to the counter. Bronwyn looked even paler than usual and thinner, as if she hadn't been eating. "What's going on?"

Her shoulders sank as if every time she told the story, it drained something, and she had nothing left. "I was losing money already," she told me. "I thought maybe I could turn things around, but then..." She shook her head. There were dark circles under her eyes. "Things changed."

"*What* changed?" I knew I was being snappy and terse but I couldn't help it. I was worried.

She sighed. "It's nothing that can be fixed." She looked at the floor and in that second she didn't look like the confident businesswoman I knew. She looked...*broken.*

Without thinking, I reached out and gently lifted her chin so that she had to look at me. "Bronwyn," I asked, my voice soft but firm, "*what?*"

Big green eyes blinked up at me. “The guy who owns the building wants to sell it so it can be turned into apartments. He has to get rid of the businesses: me and the coffee shop next door. So, to force us out, he used a loophole in the lease to double the rent.”

I stiffened. A storm cloud started to form in my chest, blacker than midnight and shot through with lightning.

Bronwyn inhaled and it was shaky. “There’s n—no way I can pay so—” She broke off, unable to continue. She gave a brave little *well, that’s life* shrug and even managed a weak smile. But those forest green eyes were shining.

I watched them fill, the storm cloud in my chest billowing outward, expanding exponentially...

A single tear escaped and ran down her cheek.

I tugged my waistcoat straight. “This,” I said, my voice tight, “is *unacceptable.*”

And I turned and marched out of the store and across the street. I climbed into the car and slammed the door.

Valentin saw my face and immediately knew it was no time for jokes. “Home?” he asked quietly.

“No. Back to the office.”

When I walked in, Irwin was lounging in his chair, feet up on his desk, playing a video game. He looked up, saw me and almost fell off his chair. “Mr. Aristov! I thought you’d gone for the day!” He scrambled to clear the screen.

“I’ve decided to expand our property portfolio,” I told him, taking off my coat. “Find me the owner of 302 Wychwood Avenue. Who he is. Where he lives.”

Irwin scrambled to take notes. “Yes sir. No problem.” He glanced at the clock: by now, it was well after six. “I’ll get on it first thing in the morning.” His eyes flicked up and he saw my expression. “I’ll get on it *right now,* sir.”

An hour later, I was climbing the stairs to the top floor of a huge house in the Gold Coast. The building's owner was called Lewis Van Peterson, and he'd had his maid show me up rather than come down to answer the door himself, just so I knew how important he was. He didn't realize that I wasn't in the mood to be fucked with. On the drive over, that black storm cloud in my chest had swollen until I was almost shaking with rage.

He was waiting for me on a little balcony that overlooked the city, a balding, flabby guy in his sixties with an accent that was firmly Chicago old money. "Mr. Aristov!" He pushed his plate of steak aside but didn't bother to get up. "I don't normally take visitors at this time of night, but I'll make an ex—"

"You're selling the building at 302 Wychwood Avenue."

The ice in my voice cut through all his posing. "Yes?" he said uncertainly.

"You're going to sell it to me."

He gave a short, sharp laugh. When I just stared at him, his smile collapsed. "I already have a buyer."

"I know. And I know what they're offering. I'll pay the same."

He balked. Then he thought and I could almost see the dollar signs appear in his eyes. "Clearly you really want this building. I'll consider it if you offer five percent more."

The anger in my chest was still swelling, my fingers twitching with the need to let it out. But I wanted to settle this peacefully if I could. "Take the offer," I advised quietly.

"No!" he said, petulant as a child. "In fact, I want seven percent."

And the rage exploded outward, taking control.

I marched over, picked up his fork, and slammed it down into the meat of his hand, hard enough that I buried the metal prongs in the table. He screamed, but I'd already clapped my hand over his mouth.

It's about respect, I told myself. *Making sure people know they can't fuck with us.*

But I knew that wasn't why. *He made her cry.*

I pulled a thick sheaf of paper and a pen from my coat pocket and dropped them on the table. "Sign."

He stared at me over the top of the hand gag, terrified. But he didn't pick up the pen.

I picked up his steak knife and traced it over the fingers of his pinned hand. "You need one hand to sign," I warned. "You don't need both."

5

BRONWYN

"OKAY," I mumbled to the mirror. "I may have underestimated on the seashells."

A half hour curling my hair into soft waves had given me definite princess-of-the-sea vibes. And the thrift store dress Jen and I had covered in giant sequins made a pretty good mermaid tail. But it turns out, seashell bras work better in cartoons, especially when the mermaid is big up top. However much I tugged at the cardboard shells, there was a lot of sideboob or underboob or just *boob*boob.

Jen put her head around the door. She's been my best friend since middle school. She's curvy, like me, but with ash-blonde hair and a gorgeous, golden tan, and she consumes detective fiction like I consume romance and fantasy. She's always eager to work a shift in the store because her acting gigs aren't enough to pay the bills, and I love working with her. I'd take her on full time if I could afford it. "They're all ready for you," she told me. "About twenty kids."

I sighed. In an hour, I'd be closing the store forever. I wanted to sob in a corner, not be happy and upbeat. But I wasn't going to disappoint the little ones just because some hedge fund prick decided to put me out of business. "How do I look?" I asked, turning to face her.

Her jaw dropped and she came into the room. "Like The Little Mermaid started an OnlyFans."

I swatted her arm, then took a deep breath. "Okay, I'm going out there." I started shuffling towards the door: the dress trapped my legs together but at least the tiny steps were easy on my joints. Goosebumps were rising on my skin: I had the heating on but seashell bras are not designed for January.

Jen opened the door for me, looked outside and quickly closed it again. "It's *him*."

I felt my skin flush, and my heart rate shoot up like someone had stamped on the gas pedal, and I wasn't even sure if she meant *him* him yet. *God, what is this?* "Who?" I checked, trying to sound casual.

"The eight-foot-tall scowly Russian with the cheekbones—*he's coming in!*" she jumped back as the door crashed open.

Radimir's face was an icy mask...then he focused on me and that mask just *shattered*. He gawped at my hair, the tail, the seashells and then his eyes flared with raw lust. His gaze licked up and down my body. Suddenly, my exposed skin wasn't cold anymore.

"I..." I looked down at myself. "I'm about to go read those children a story," I said apologetically, waving towards the front of the store.

"I'll stall them," said Jen immediately and backed out of the door, giving me frantic *go for it* gestures behind Radimir's back. She'd been trying to get me dating again since Nathan dumped me. She'd seen Radimir when he came into the store to buy the second book, but she had no idea who he was, and I didn't dare tell her. I knew she'd warn me to stay away.

The door closed and I looked at Radimir, confused.

He stepped forward, pulled a sheet of paper from his jacket and unfolded it. "This is your new lease," he told me, handing it over. "The rent is back to the normal rate. And it's locked in for five years."

I stared at the lease. I was struggling to read the words because my mind was short-circuiting as it tried to process what he was saying. *The rent's back to normal? I can stay open?*

I CAN STAY OPEN?!

I drew in a breath and felt it shudder. Oh God, was I about to happy cry for the first time ever? "I don't—I don't understand, how did you—Did you talk to him or—"

That's when I finally managed to take in the logo at the top of the lease. *Aristov Incorporated.* My eyes flicked to Radimir's face.

"I am your landlord, now," he confirmed.

I could feel my mouth hanging open. *What...the fuck?* He was staring right back at me and there was a war going on in those frozen sky eyes, a ferocious warmth struggling to get out from behind bars of ice.

He bought the building?! "W—Why are you doing this?"

His jaw twitched and he dodged my gaze. Then he tugged his waistcoat straight. "I'm a property developer and I want to encourage small businesses in the area."

I stared at him. I knew that wasn't the truth. But the other explanation, that he'd done it for me...that was even crazier. I put my hand on the wall to steady myself, overcome. *I can stay open. I can stay open!* And then I remembered something. "The coffee shop next door: will you give her the same deal?"

Radimir blinked at me. From his face, he'd forgotten there even *was* a coffee shop. He frowned, like he couldn't understand why I'd care. Then his face softened, and he looked at me like I was a freakin' baby bunny. "Of course," he said levelly.

My lungs filled. I'd have to call Cassie, the woman who ran the coffee shop, and tell her the good news. *Everything's going to be okay*. I mean, the bookstore was still losing money and things were going to be even tougher, now that I'd sold off half my stock in my going-out-of-business sale. But I wasn't closing down tomorrow and that made all the other problems feel manageable. "*Thank you!*" I told him and, instinctively, I put my arms out to hug him.

He hesitated for just a fraction of a second, his eyes sweeping down my body, and that's when I remembered I was wearing two cardboard seashells held on by elastic. But now it was too late because he was stepping forward and his arms were coming up and Oh God his eyes were *blazing*—

Our bodies met and my mostly naked breasts pillowed against his chest. His arms wrapped around me and his big hands took possession of my bare back, one just above my waist and one between my shoulder blades. Everywhere he touched was naked skin and I could feel the warmth of him soaking into me, rolling inward in waves and turning into liquid heat as it reached my groin. I inhaled and felt my chest swell against him, the flimsy cardboard seashells shifting and moving, and he growled low in his throat, just as he had in my fantasy. I was pressed up against him tight, all the way down to our ankles, and I could feel his cock thickening and lengthening against my thigh.

I looked up. Oh God, he really was *big:* I was barefoot, under the mermaid tail, and my mouth was only just at the tops of his pecs. And now I was looking up at *his* mouth, at that hard upper lip and that soft, full, lower one.

He stared down at me, his eyes molten, and his hands tightened on my back, tugging me a little harder against him. This wasn't a hug, anymore. I could feel the huge, hard muscles of his back under my palms, feel the sheer brute strength of him...

That's when something sank in. He'd stormed out of the store and, just a few hours later, he'd come back having bought the building. That was impossible. These things take weeks, months, with teams of lawyers and stacks of paperwork. Unless...

Unless he'd *scared* my former landlord into selling.

For a moment, I'd forgotten who he was. Now sick fear unfurled in my chest, sending out cold tendrils. All the stories I'd heard about him: the bodies buried under his buildings. *A monster.* And I was in his arms.

I tensed and he felt it. His eyes narrowed for a second, possessive, and for a moment I thought he was going to trap me against him. But then his hands loosened on my back, and he gave me a tiny nod. *What does that mean? 'Yes, I'm a monster?' 'Yes, you should stay clear?'*

I lifted one foot, ready to step back from the hug. But then I remembered the way he'd looked at me, when I'd been crying in the bookstore. He'd stared down at me, his face thunderous, and I'd felt so.... protected.

I looked left and right, along his broad chest and huge shoulders, and I realized I didn't feel threatened. I felt safe, like I was behind a wall that could stop anything.

Radimir Aristov *was* a monster. But I knew, right then, that he'd never hurt me.

I looked up at his face. He was scowling again, *willing* me to step back. Trying to protect me from *him.* But I could see something behind the anger. I could feel it as a tension in his arms, like he was a half-second from pulling me in again.

He was as lonely as I was.

I stayed stubbornly where I was. I saw his eyes narrow, then flick to my lips. Time seemed to go syrupy and slow—

"I— "said Jen, throwing open the door. "Ohhh..."

I jumped back out of Radimir's arms, forgetting the mermaid tail, and nearly fell on my ass.

"Um. I'm running out of children's songs out there," said Jen.

I nodded. "On my way." I shuffled as quickly as I could towards the door, feeling hazy and muddled, still drunk on the scent of him, the feel of him.

Radimir followed and, in the hallway that led to the main store, he overtook us. "Goodbye, Miss Hanford," he threw over his shoulder. It sounded so...final. Like I might never see him again.

I swallowed. "We should celebrate. Drink a toast to our new... partnership." The wrong word. Or was it?

He stopped.

"Can you stick around until after the story?" I asked.

He looked back over his shoulder, his expression unreadable. Then he gave me one of his curt little nods and walked towards the main store.

"What the actual *fuck* is going on?" hissed Jen. "Who is he? What's with all the *Miss Hanford* stuff? Were you about to kiss him?"

"The store's not closing," I told her, rushing through the answers. "He's a..." —I didn't want her to worry—"Russian property developer who just saved my ass. I like the Miss Hanford stuff, he's old fashioned. And..." —I flushed—"maybe. Now I have to go read a story."

Jen nodded, stunned. "Go." Then she held up a hand to stop me. "But, um...maybe fix the seashell malfunction first."

I looked down. One breast was fully on show, nipple and all. *How long has it been like that?* I flushed deeper and tugged the seashell back into place. Then I shuffled into the main store for story time...and whatever came next.

6

RADIMIR

BRONWYN'S FRIEND had turned down the lights in the main store and the place was lit with strings of fairy lights. About twenty children were sitting cross-legged on the floor, facing a chair decorated with aluminum foil fish. As my eyes adjusted, I realized that there were parents there, too, sitting in a ring around the edge. I found a corner to stand in.

Bronwyn walked in, mermaid tail swishing. The children whooped and cheered. There were a few men in the audience, and they all suddenly sat up straight, craning for a better look at Bronwyn's barely-covered breasts. I instantly wanted to kill every one of them.

The image of her in the hallway, with one creamy-white breast and its pink, pencil-eraser nipple peeking out over a seashell, was burned into my mind forever. As was the feel of her bare back under my hands and the warm press of her breasts against my chest. The way she'd looked up at me with those big green eyes. Scared of me, as she should be. But at the same time warm. Caring.

I didn't need anyone to care about me. I certainly didn't want anyone feeling sorry for me. But the way she looked at me went straight to my soul. It wrapped around the icy cogs that were *me* and snarled and tangled them.

Bronwyn looked right at me and grinned, and I felt that lift in my chest that was becoming addictive. I'd made her happy, with something as simple as money.

This is dangerous, a little voice inside me warned. But I couldn't bring myself to walk out.

Bronwyn gave me an expectant little smile. I glanced around the room and found everyone looking up at me.

They wanted me to sit on the floor, like a child. *Me!*

Very slowly, I sank down, awkwardly crossing my legs until I was sitting on the floor for the first time since school. I scowled. But then Bronwyn smiled at me and it was worth it.

I'd presumed that I was going to spend the time just staring at that gorgeous, curvy body. I wanted to trail kisses down her neck to her bare shoulders. I wanted to fill my hands with those gloriously full, soft breasts, the cardboard seashells sliding over my knuckles as I pinched her nipples and made her arch and beg in my lap.

But as soon as the story began, I was transfixed. She had such a passion for it, bringing the characters to life with different voices. In the dramatic scenes she amped up the tension until the kids were hanging on her every word. In the comedy scenes, she flung her arms around, not afraid to act goofy, and the whole room cracked up. She made sure all the kids got involved, even the nervous ones who needed coaxing. *She'd make a good mother.*

I frowned. I'd never thought that about a woman before. It just wasn't something I considered, when I was having a one-night stand with one of the Russian women who hung around the Bratva.

Like the children, I didn't want the story to end. When it finally did, I applauded along with them and then waited while they slowly filed out. Bronwyn's friend was the last person to go, and the two of them had a muttered conversation as they hugged goodbye, presumably along the lines of *are you sure you're okay with him?*

Bronwyn looked at me and nodded.

Her friend gave me a warning look, then left. And then it was just the two of us.

7

BRONWYN

I SHUFFLED over to the door, my heartbeat quickening. The swish of the mermaid tail was the only sound in the room.

I flipped the sign on the door to *Closed* and shot the bolt.

I could see his reflection in the glass, a wide-shouldered, shadowy form behind me. *What are you doing, Bronny? He's a freakin' criminal!* It took me three tries to get the key in the lock, my hands were shaking so hard.

I turned around and led the way to the back room. He followed behind and his presence, so close, made me skittish and giddy, each heavy footfall behind me notching my heart rate higher.

In the back room, I rooted in a drawer. "I'm pretty sure I've got..." I tried another drawer. "Got it." I pulled out a bottle of Scotch with only two fingers gone. "I drank a toast with my grandmother when I opened this place. Seems appropriate to get it out again, now that you've saved it." I couldn't find any glasses, so I grabbed my *Throne of Night* mug and one slightly chipped one that said *I'll Deal With It After This Chapter.* As I put everything on the table, a cold draft from the front of the store hit me. It was late, the heating had been off for a while, and I was still only wearing a couple of cardboard seashells on my top half. I shivered.

He slipped off his jacket and pulled it around my shoulders. It was deliciously warm from his body, with a silky lining that felt amazing next to my bare skin, and it smelled of his cologne, that magical, dark citrus scent. He fussed with it, pulling the lapels so it covered my front. "Better?"

I nodded mutely, warmth blooming in my chest. It was such a small gesture, compared to buying the building but it was so...*caring.* And sort of old-fashioned, too. Maybe it was because he was Russian, maybe it was because he was a little older than me, but there was something gentlemanly about Radimir. He made the guys that Jen had tried to set me up with feel like boys. And they always wanted to be non-exclusive. I couldn't imagine Radimir sharing me with anyone.

I pulled out one of the chairs at the tiny table where I ate my lunch. He glanced towards the door as if having second thoughts. Then he looked at me, his eyes burning...and sat.

I poured what I estimated was a shot into each mug: I'm more of a cocktail girl. I raised my mug. "To...the future."

He clinked mugs with me. "To the future." In his accent, *fu* was like *fuck* made into a soft kiss and *ture* was like the rasp of his stubble against your cheek. I crushed my thighs together inside my mermaid tail.

We sipped and the burn of the whiskey didn't do anything to steady my nerves. It just wrapped golden, scorching threads around all my dark fantasies and pulled them tightly into shape. *He could just throw me down across this table. Or up against the wall. And then there's the money. He bought the building: does he think that buys me, too?* Was it wrong that the idea of being indebted to a Bratva boss made some secret part of me go weak?

His chair creaked as he leaned forward, and I held my breath. Then, very slowly and deliberately, he put his elbows on the table, his muscles flexing under his shirt, and put his hands together, fingers curling tightly around his bunched fist.

It was like he was holding himself back, so he didn't...pounce.

And the thought that I was making him almost lose control made a weird kind of pride bloom in my chest.

He frowned at me over the top of his hands, saying nothing, just...*studying* me. I flushed and squirmed, dipping my head.

"What's wrong?" he asked immediately.

"I'm not that interesting."

"You most certainly are." His voice was still cold, almost angry, as if I was something he didn't understand but needed to. His hand squeezed his fist, the knuckles white, and he glanced away for a second. "Tell me about your plans for the bookstore," he ordered. "I want to know that my tenant is going to stay in business."

And so I told him. Slowly at first, my fingers nervously tracing the rim of my mug. But for someone so scary, he was surprisingly easy to talk to: he actually listened, taking in every word instead of just going through the motions like a lot of men. I told him about how I'd first started up the store, and why, about being raised by Baba and being held back because I didn't have a degree. His face darkened at that, as if he didn't like anyone getting in my way. I told him about hosting book groups and the story evenings and the social media promotion I was doing. "But it might not be enough," I told him. "I'm still losing money each month."

He nodded, still watching me over the top of his hands. "You'll find a way."

I blinked. He sounded so certain.

"You don't let anything beat you," he said. "I can tell."

It might just have been the nicest thing anyone had ever said to me. "Thank you, for what you did," I said earnestly. "I'd be out of business if it wasn't for you."

He looked away and adjusted his tie. "It was a sensible investment," he muttered.

I stared at him. Was he...*embarrassed?* "It was kind," I said firmly.

It was like I'd woken a sleepwalker from a dream. He glared at me, his eyes suddenly so cold that I jumped. *What did I say?* He knocked back the rest of his Scotch and put the glass down with a barely perceptible clink: even furious, he was so *controlled.* "Thank you for the drink, Miss Hanford."

He stood and I scrambled to my feet, panicked. If he left now, like this, I might never see him again. "I told you all about me," I said. "I don't know anything about *you.*"

"You know who I am." His voice was ice-hard, like he wanted to push me away. "You know what I do."

"Is that all there is to you?" I asked quickly, "What they say in the news?"

He tugged his waistcoat straight. "What else would there be?"

"Your family," I tried. "What are your parents like?"

He drew in his breath and, just for a second, his icy mask fractured. I saw what it hid: deep, soul-scarring pain.

Then the mask refroze. "My parents are dead."

He took the keys from the table and stalked out. A moment later, I heard the bell on the door jangle as it closed behind him.

8

BRONWYN

"OOF." I set down a carton of books, stretched my aching legs, and looked around for my box cutter. "How's the sign coming?"

"Great," mumbled Jen. I'd asked her to put together a display table of her favorite detective novels and she was biting her lip in concentration as she drew on a blackboard.

I found my box cutter and sliced open the top of the carton, then sighed as I looked at the stacks of books inside. I was restocking all the books I'd sold off cheap when I thought I was shutting down and shelving them all would take forever. It was already nearly eight in the evening and there was a lot more to do. At least work stopped me thinking about *him.*

It had been a week since I'd had the drink with Radimir. The next day, Jen had showered me with questions. I'd told her, truthfully, that nothing had happened, but I hadn't told her who Radimir was.

I kept rerunning our last conversation and wishing I could undo it. I'd been getting somewhere. I'd glimpsed something more than a cold-hearted monster. And then I'd said the wrong thing, and he went right back to icy and distant. I wasn't sure if I'd ever even see him again.

Maybe it's for the best. Me, and a mafia boss? I was a nerdy bookworm, not a gangster's moll. He was wrong for me in every single way...

Except the one way that mattered. When I thought of him, when I guiltily buried my nose in the jacket he'd left behind and inhaled his scent, it triggered a dark, forbidden ache right at the core of me that twisted down to my groin.

I sighed, made a stack of books and headed towards the shelves. On my way past Jen, I stopped and looked at the sign. "What are those?"

"Handcuffs," she said proudly.

"Nice. But can you add some red and blue lights or something? Otherwise, people are going to think this is the BDSM Romance table."

Jen smirked. Then she saw something over my shoulder and her eyes widened. "Um. Someone's here."

I drew in my breath. It could only be one person. I put the books down and spun towards the door—

It wasn't Radimir.

The guy was leaning against the window looking in at us, his face lit up by the pink neon *All You Need is Books* sign. When the wind caught his brown leather coat, you could see he was lean in that stripped-down, dangerous way, like he survived on alcohol and cigarettes. Something in the way he smiled sent alarm bells ringing in my chest.

I glanced at the street outside. The other stores were all closed for the night. The bookstore suddenly felt horribly isolated.

The door was unlocked but *he* didn't know that. I'd just walk over there, nice and calm, and shoot the bolt before he had a chance to come in. I started walking, trying to look casual. The man watched me the whole way, but he didn't move from the window. *It's going to be fine. Just some creep.* It was only three steps to the door, now. *Nice and calm, Bronny.* Two steps. One.

I lifted my hand to shoot the bolt and that's when the second man stepped out of the shadows. *Fuck.* I grabbed for the bolt, but I'd hesitated just long enough. The first man rammed his hand against the door, and I had to dodge back before I was hit in the face.

"We're closed!" I managed, hating how panicked my voice sounded.

"Door's open," he said with a shrug. He had a British accent. He sauntered past me, deliberately slamming his shoulder into me and sending me staggering.

I caught my balance just as the second guy breezed in. He had tightly curled, bleached-blond hair and skin even paler than mine. I glanced at Jen in fear. Neither of the guys were especially big, but they were still bigger than us.

"Books!" The British guy's voice was mock-playful and loud enough to make me flinch. "Fount of all knowledge." He tapped a drum riff on the tables of books he passed. Then he put his hands on two tables and swung there, kicking his legs in the air. "You read, Yoz?"

The blond one, Yoz, shook his head.

"You *should.* Educate yourself." The British one grabbed a book at random from a table. "This one's about...people in Bosnia." He tossed it over his shoulder, and I winced. He picked up another. "Some cowboy thing." He threw it like a frisbee, and it smacked against the wall. Another. "Sci-fi: well, that's all bollocks." He folded the book back on itself, cracking the spine, and it started shedding pages.

"Can you stop, please!" I snapped.

The British guy looked at Yoz, grinning. "*Can you stop, please,*" he mimicked.

"You're damaging the books!"

"*Damaging?* Yoz, she thinks I'm damaging things." He raised his hands in innocence. "I'm just mucking about." Then he suddenly marched towards me, and I had to force myself to stand my ground. He stopped when he was only a few feet away. "Let me show you what damage looks like," he said quietly.

He pulled out a lighter, grabbed a book and lit one corner of it.

"No!" I yelled, trying to grab the book. "Stop it!"

He shoved me back. The book's glossy cover bubbled and peeled.

Then the flames caught the pages and the whole thing became a mass of fire. He dropped it on a table of paperbacks and the fire spread outward, eating away at the thick stack of books.

I started forward again, and he pushed me back again, this time with his hands on my breasts. I was so panicked, I only registered the touch afterwards. It wasn't just the money he was costing me: there was something deeply wrong about seeing books destroyed. "Please!" I begged.

British guy nodded to Yoz, who grabbed a fire extinguisher. Water blasted the burning stack of books, sending some of them flying off the table. Steam billowed up towards the smoke alarm, which had started wailing. When the extinguisher ran dry, Yoz hurled it at the smoke alarm, smashing it off the ceiling and silencing it.

I stared at the wreckage. I remembered carefully arranging the books, a multi-colored patchwork of beautiful covers. Now the top few layers were a charred, pitted mess and the books that weren't burned were soaked with water. My business brain ran the math: twelve books wide by ten books long times five books deep equals about $3000 dollars of stock I'd just lost.

"That's the problem with books," said British guy. "They're flammable." He looked around at the store. "Imagine if someone threw a petrol bomb through the window."

"What do you *want?*" sobbed Jen, her voice cracked.

But I already knew. I'd heard about this happening in this part of town. "Protection money," I said dully.

"I prefer *specialist insurance,*" said British guy with a flourish. He advanced, forcing me to back up towards the counter. "We'll work out a nice monthly sum that protects against fire, burglary...intruders in your store..."

"You two, working here late at night, all alone," said Yoz, strolling towards Jen. "Anything could happen." He looked at British guy. "I'll take the blonde."

My stomach flipped. I grabbed Jen's arm and pulled her with me towards the back of the store. "I'll pay you."

British guy grinned. "I know you will."

My ass hit the counter. "I'll pay you, *stop!*"

He kept coming. "I think it's good if we develop a *close personal* working relationship."

I was so scared, I thought I was going to throw up. It was the slow, creeping inevitability of it, the way they were so smugly confident. They'd done this before. They'd do it again. And there was nothing we could do to stop them.

I checked over my shoulder. The back room had a door with a lock, but they were too close, they'd grab us before we could get in there.

I looked at Jen, at the tears streaming down her cheeks. Maybe it didn't have to be both of us.

I pulled out my box cutter, flicked out the blade and launched myself at the two men, slashing wildly. "*Run!*" I screamed at Jen. She stared at me in horror, then ran for the back room.

British guy dodged back, then got under one of my swings and punched me in the stomach. I doubled over, all the air knocked out of me, and he ripped the box cutter from my hand. Yoz stalked past us and tried the door to the back room, then kicked it, furious. "She's locked herself in there!"

I wheezed for air, holding my stomach. At least Jen was safe.

British guy grabbed me by the throat and now I couldn't breathe *at all.* "Looks like it's both of us on you," he told me.

I closed my eyes as he reached for the button of my jeans.

9

RADIMIR

I SAT low in the big Mercedes, scowling at the world as I swept through the darkened streets.

In the week since I'd walked out of her store, I'd taken to driving myself home from work. It meant I didn't have to explain to Valentin why I was taking a diversion to drive down one particular street.

I'd never go back in. Never contact her again. I'd come too close to something dangerous. But I allowed myself this one indulgence, speeding past the little glowing storefront every night so I could glimpse her. I knew it wasn't healthy, but I couldn't stop.

The line of stores before hers had grown familiar. A closed-down jewelers, a grocery store, the coffee shop and then—

Control yourself, you idiot. I inhaled and gripped the steering wheel as I approached. I wouldn't look. I'd keep my eyes on the road and that would be the end of it.

But as we passed, that *pull* I felt to her was too much. My eyes flicked to the side, just for an instant.

That glimpse of long red hair, as expected. But there were two people who shouldn't be there. I recognized the brown leather coat and the bleached blond hair instantly. Doyle and Yoz.

And Doyle had his hand around Bronwyn's throat.

I buried the brake pedal in the carpet. The wheels locked up and painted thick black lines of rubber along the street and I came to a screeching stop. A taxi that had been behind me had to slam on its brakes too and stopped an inch from my rear bumper.

I threw open the door and stalked toward the bookstore. The taxi driver leapt out to yell at me, then got a look at my face and backed away.

Something had taken hold of me. It had me in its grip and it was squeezing tighter and tighter. I reached the bookstore and kicked the door so hard it flew back on its hinges and cracked its glass.

Doyle looked over his shoulder, annoyed. Then he recognized me, and all the blood drained from his face.

I marched towards the counter. Books were scattered everywhere, some of them burned and ruined, and the floor was soaked. This place that had felt so alien and strange a month ago had become special to me because it was hers. And they'd destroyed it.

The anger was part of me, now, heating my skin, pouring through my veins, making my muscles swell. I was dimly aware of Yoz running towards me, but my eyes were on Doyle. He still had Bronwyn by the throat.

Yoz punched me hard in the face and my head snapped to the side, but I didn't feel any pain. I looked at him dumbly and he got in two hits on my ribs before I finally focused on him.

When he punched me again, I grabbed his wrist and twisted, pulling his arm up behind him until I heard a bone snap. Then I grabbed a handful of his hair and rammed his head into the edge of a table.

As he fell, I started moving towards Bronwyn again. Now I could see that the front of her jeans were open, and the anger changed, becoming a crimson drumbeat that shook my entire body.

He was dead now. They both were.

Doyle must have seen the possessive fury in my eyes because his gaze suddenly went to Bronwyn, and he released her throat like it had burned him. I saw his legs go rubbery as he realized the scale of his mistake. "I didn't—"

I punched him in the jaw with the full force of my anger, sending him flying backwards. He crashed to the floor and I was on him before he could move, driving my fists into his face, left then right. Again. And again. And again. I only stopped because I didn't want him to die. I needed him to suffer.

I wiped my hands on his shirt and stood up, then walked back to Bronwyn. She'd fastened her jeans and was leaning against the counter for support. Her chest was heaving, her body trying to cry but her mind still too panicked to allow it. "Jen. Jen is in the back room," she told me between breaths. "They wouldn't leave. I said I'd pay. They didn't stop—"

I knew what to do because I'd seen American men do it in movies. I held out my arms and beckoned her in. She collapsed against me; I folded my arms around her and for the second time in a week I was hugging a woman. And after a few seconds, the tears started, big heaving sobs against my chest.

It was nothing like when she'd thrown her arms around me in the back room. That had been *thank you* and relief and happiness, and she'd been carefully made up and half naked. This was her clutching at me for support, teary and red-eyed and trusting me to take care of her when she was at her most vulnerable. It made me clutch her so tight that it felt like we were one: each sob hurt *my* chest. And the pain seeped inward and made something shift and open, deep inside me, something I'd managed to keep locked up for years. I'd never had anyone trust me like that.

Behind me, I could hear Yoz grabbing his friend and dragging him to the door. It didn't matter. This was my city and there was no place they could hide where I wouldn't find them. However much I wanted to kill them right now, holding her was more important.

I waited while Bronwyn comforted Jen and called her a cab. "Shouldn't we call the cops?" asked Jen.

Bronwyn looked at me, then turned to her friend. "They'll never come here again," she said firmly.

When the cab arrived and they were saying their goodbyes outside, I called Gennadiy. As his phone rang, fear and guilt twisted like snakes in my guts: *I nearly didn't look.* I'd been trying so hard to stay in control, to not feel, that I almost drove right past.

Gennadiy finally answered. "Doyle and Yoz," I said. "They do protection shake-downs on the west side."

"I know of them." Gennadiy sounded confused. "They're strictly small time."

"Find them. Do whatever you have to, but I want them found by dawn."

I could hear Gennadiy sitting up, the tone of my voice sending him into attack mode. "It'll be done. What do you want doing with them?"

I looked at Bronwyn through the glass as she walked back towards the store. "Take them to the warehouse. Break their arms and legs. Then leave them for me. And Gennadiy? Bring pruning shears."

I ended the call as Bronwyn pushed the door open. "I think she'll be okay," she said, looking back over her shoulder at Jen's cab. "I'll call her tomorrow." Then she looked up at me and—

Something happened.

The rage that had sent me marching in here was dying away. But it had melted the chains that had kept things in check. I looked down into those big green eyes and I was just...*overcome* by her. She'd been through hell, and she was still worried about other people. She was honest and good, and *I nearly lost her*—

She blinked up at me. "Radimir?"

I took her cheeks in my hands, leaned down and kissed her.

10

BRONWYN

I HAD time for one little mewl of shock as his lips came down on mine. Then the mewl turned to a groan as my brain caught up and heady pink pleasure rolled through me.

He broke the kiss for a second, looked at me and breathed something in Russian, a word so delicate and pretty it sounded like it was made of tinkling, fragile glass. "*Krasavitsa.*" I didn't know if it was a nickname or a compliment or both but it made a warm rush of pride flood my body.

Then he was kissing me again. His kiss was warm and surprisingly gentle: it lifted me, comforted me, and his hands on my cheeks anchored me in place and stopped me drifting back to the two men. But there was something else, a trembling undercurrent like the rumble of a massive machine that's being held at an idle. I could *feel* how much he wanted me, even if he was only letting one percent of it out, right now. It throbbed down from my lips and raced through my body, turning to raw, liquid heat as it hit my groin.

My lips parted. And everything changed.

His lips spread mine, his tongue tracing them before plunging inside. He twisted our bodies around, the kiss growing and rising. I grabbed for him, my hands climbing his back. I needed handholds because it felt like the bookstore was dissolving around me, leaving me in a hot, dark world where I couldn't think at all and there was nothing solid except him. His lips pressed and moved, tasting me, while his tongue sought me out. And the instant the tip of my tongue brushed his, I heard him growl, deep in his throat...

He broke the kiss, panting. I opened my eyes, confused. He dropped his hands from my face and grabbed my hands instead, lacing his fingers with mine. He was on the very brink, wrestling for control.

I was still kiss-drunk and I had to swallow and work my lips before I could speak. "You don't...want to?"

His hands tightened on mine. "I've wanted to since the first second I saw you." His accent carved the words into silky-smooth ice that seared my mind. He took a deep, shuddering breath. "But..." He glanced at the ruined bookstore. The counter where the British guy had tried to—

He was saying it was okay. He was saying he understood. He was saying he'd wait. "Do you want to stop?" he asked quietly.

I took a deep breath, thinking. What I wanted was to chase the memories away. "Fuck no," I panted.

His hands squeezed mine and I saw his whole body tense, an animal ready to pounce. His white shirt pulled tight over his pecs, and I saw the shadows of his tattoos. *What the fuck did I just do?*

Then he tugged me against him and his lips were on mine again. This time, he wasn't gentle. This time, it was about releasing the pent-up need, kissing me before he burst with it. And I understood because I needed him that much too. I kissed him like he was giving me breath, like I'd die if we disconnected again. He was pressed against me, a wall of warm granite that I crushed my softness to. The brutal energy of him throbbed down into me with every hard press of his lips, crackling streamers of pleasure arcing down inside me and filling me up. The heat of him soaked into me, washing away the memories until all that existed was *now.*

However hard we kissed, it wasn't enough. Panting and breathless, we started to move, shuffling away from the door, pinwheeling blindly as we bumped into tables. My hands broke free of his: I had to feel him. My hands grabbed his forearms and slid up the deliciously solid contours, up to his biceps, his shoulders, feeling the broad swells of muscle through his suit and shirt. *Too many layers.*

He must have thought the same because I suddenly felt his fingers working the top button of my blouse. I could still feel the bright burn of the store's lights on my closed eyelids: anyone walking past would see whatever happened next.

I didn't want to open my eyes, but I had to check where we were. I opened them and found our whirling dance had taken us to the middle of the store. Radimir was *on* me: oh, *God,* he was so on me, hulking over me, and the size of him, so close up, made me go weak. I didn't want to break the kiss, but I had to, just for a second. I wasn't strong enough to drag him where I needed us to go unless he cooperated. I dragged my lips from him. "*One sec,*" I panted.

His eyes half opened, his lids heavy with lust. I grabbed hold of his shirt and pulled him with me, backing us up to the door. Then I turned the key to lock it and wiped my hand across the panel of light switches, plunging the store into darkness. I went to kiss him again, but I didn't get time to: the instant I turned back to him, he was kissing me again and I moaned, the kiss lifting me like a wave.

He started moving us again, pushing me back as he popped the buttons on my blouse, stopping only when my ass pressed up against one of the book tables. My blouse came open and he pulled the sides wide. His hands skimmed around my back and my bra suddenly went loose. Then I groaned as he palmed my breasts, filling his hands with them and squeezing in time with his kisses, my nipples stiffening as they stroked his palms.

He whirled me around, then pulled my back against his chest. He kissed down the line of my jaw, down my neck, down to my collar bone, while his strong hands squeezed my breasts with just the right amount of urgent roughness. He circled my nipples with his thumbs, coaxing them to sweet, agonizing hardness and I trembled against him. I could feel his cock, hot and hard and powerful, grinding against my ass, and it made the pleasure twist into a needy ache. I said his name, except it didn't come out as *Radimir.* "Mr... Aristov," my fuddled brain managed.

He growled and his hands slid down my body to the fly of my jeans. The buttons popped open in a machine-gun rattle that made me catch my breath, and then his hands slid inside. He smoothed his hands over my ass, squeezing my cheeks through my panties. Then one hand swept around to the front, and I groaned and folded forwards as he stroked my pussy with two fingers. I could feel how wet I was, the filmy fabric soaked through.

He returned one hand to my breasts and used it to press my upper body back against him. His lips moved against my ear as he began to rub me. "Your breasts are beautiful." He squeezed one breast, then rubbed his thumb over the nipple and I gasped. His voice tightened with lust. "My innocent little librarian, tending her bookstore..."

Is that how he thinks of me? Then his fingers stroked up the length of my wet lips and I moaned.

His accent carved his words into heavy blocks of ice that slid straight down to my groin. "But no one knows she's soaking wet for a gangster." He pressed inward through the gauzy, slick material and I felt myself flower open. I moaned again, louder, feeling my cheeks go hot in the darkness.

His teeth nipped at the side of my neck and my legs went shaky: I would have melted right down to the floor if he hadn't been holding me. "She wants the bad guy to fuck her. Doesn't she?" I swallowed and nodded helplessly.

But that wasn't enough. His fingers circled my clit through the sopping fabric, and I groaned. "*Doesn't she?*" he demanded.

"*Yes!*"

He pushed my jeans down with both hands and suddenly I was helping him, twisted my hips to shimmy them down, using one sneaker to pry the other off and then scrape at the cuffs of my jeans to help them along. There were flashes of pain in my joints as I flexed and wriggled but they were distant, muffled explosions, drowned out by the roar in my ears. The bundle of jeans, socks and sneakers collected around my ankles. I pulled one foot free, then the other, and then I was bare-legged and barefoot. I felt his thumbs hook into the waistband of my panties and then they were being stripped down, too. I swallowed as the cool air of the store kissed my soaking, sensitive pussy. *This is real. This is actually happening.* It wasn't a fantasy, this time. He was actually about to fuck me.

My panties fell around my feet, and I stepped out of them, the blood thundering through my veins.

He spun me around to face him, then grabbed my waist. I yelped as I was lifted into the air and carried over to the counter. My eyes came open as he set me down sitting on the edge. The store was dark, the only light coming from the passing headlights of cars on the street. I was almost naked, my bra up around my neck and my blouse open, my pale body gleamed in the darkness.

He stepped closer, looming out of the shadows. I drank him in: that gorgeous face, his gray eyes burning with need. The huge, heavy slabs of his pecs, his chest filling my vision as he came closer still, towering over me. I could see the dark shapes of his tattoos better now through his shirt, as if the dark revealed what he really was.

I understood his aura, now. I'd realized as soon as I saw him destroy those two men. It wasn't just power. There were other men who had more money and controlled more territory. Some men controlled whole countries. But Radimir didn't just have the power to have you killed. He had the strength to end you *himself* and that gave him an unshakeable authority like I'd never known. It was what made him a monster. It was what made me feel so protected by him.

Movement drew my eyes down: he was unbuckling his belt. My gaze locked there, hypnotized, as his pants opened and his cock sprang out. It strained upward, naked and primal against his respectable business suit, and I swallowed. God, he was big. Thick *and* long, the shaft rock hard, the satiny head gleaming with a jewel of pre-cum. Nerves fluttered in my stomach.

He put his hands on my ass and tugged me to the very edge of the counter. I opened my knees, and he stepped forward between them. I heard my breathing notch higher, my eyes flicking between his face and his cock.

He pulled a condom packet from his pocket, tore it open and rolled the condom on. Then he put one hand on the small of my back to hold me in place and brought his cock to my sopping pussy. I swallowed as the arrow-shaped head parted my lips. “Go—Go slow,” I begged.

His cock twitched, as if the sound of me begging excited him, and I caught my breath as he slipped up and down between my slickened lips. His eyes blazed but he gave me one of those curt little nods. Then he angled his cock and—

I felt my mouth open into a wide, red ‘O’ as he pushed into me. Just an inch, just enough for the head of him to open me. He shifted back, pushed forward again, gliding between my soaking lips, and the pleasure trembled outward, feathery-light and delicate. He stopped, letting me get used to his size, and the pleasure became an ache: I could feel him, hard and hot and primed, could feel where he’d be, and I began to shift and rock, wanting him.

He growled low in his throat, feeling my neediness, and moved both hands to my ass. Then, as he held me in place, he slowly pushed into me, inch by thick inch. The pleasure tightened, becoming heavier, darker, and I grabbed his biceps as he stretched me. More. My toes danced as he slid deeper, the pleasure turning silver edged as he filled me. More. My legs came up, hooking around him, my back arching. *More.*

I felt the root of him press up against my lips. He was completely buried inside me and I could feel every twitch, every pulse of him. My hands slid up his arms and stroked his chest, desperate to pass on some of the sensation. My hands worked at his tie but it took me three attempts to loosen the silk. Every tiny shift of my body moved me on his cock, sending tight waves of pleasure outward through my body like ripples on a pond. I panted: thinking became slow and difficult, and I had to focus on each shirt button as I undid them. Then I was smoothing my hands across his chest, pushing his shirt aside. My fingers traced blue-black tattoos: stars and words in Cyrillic and a rose wrapped in barbed wire. There was a whole story there, written in symbols I didn't understand about a world I didn't know. It was starkly, coldly terrifying. *They kill people.* But his muscles were deliciously warm and ruggedly hard. I ran my fingers over his nipples, pink and big as silver dollars...

He changed his grip to better pin me in place, his thumbs in the creases of my hips and his fingers spread across my ass. Then he slowly drew his cock from me and I gasped at the long, silken *pull.* He moved back until the head almost slipped from me and then drove back in *deep* and I bit my lip at how good it felt. He pulled back again and now he wasn't *going slow* anymore...but by now I wanted—*needed* it hard.

He began to pump at me, harder and harder, and I hooked my chin over his shoulder, my mouth opening wide again as the sensations overwhelmed me. Every time he pulled back, silvery pleasure earthquaked out from every millimeter he'd touched. Every time he thrust deep, that pleasure heated, glowing brighter and brighter.

My legs tightened around him, shamelessly pulling him inward. His hips pounded between mine, making my breasts sway and bounce, my nipples skimming his chest and making me gasp. I grabbed for his shoulders, his muscles like rock under my fingers, and just hung on as he fucked me, the pleasure getting tighter and hotter, my orgasm close. I was going to come right there on the counter. How was I going to stand there serving customers, after *this?*

He leaned in and kissed me, urgent and hard, our teeth clacking together before our tongues met and danced. My ankles locked around the small of his back. His thrusts sped up, his cock plunging into me again and again, the root of him stroking against my clit on each stroke. I dug my fingers into his shoulders as the tight ball of heat inside me trembled, shook...and exploded. I cried out against his lips as the orgasm ripped through me, wave after wave of pleasure that shook me like a doll. I felt myself spasming around him and he groaned and pushed deep one last time. Then he was erupting inside me in long, hot spurts and we kissed as we rode the wave on and on into oblivion.

11

RADIMIR

I WOKE UP, disoriented and groggy. I was lying on a hard wooden floor: had I fallen out of bed?

Something else was different. I always sleep alone, but I was pressed up against a soft, warm *someone,* my arm protectively around her. I inhaled and smelled strawberries and violets. My memory finally kicked in. *Bronwyn.*

I looked around. We were lying on the floor of the bookstore, behind the counter. The sky was just starting to lighten, and I guessed it was about six in the morning. The temperature had dropped, which was probably what had woken me: both of us were naked and our only blanket was my suit jacket, which only covered about half of us. I was cold, aching, and I had a crick in my neck from using a beanbag chair for a pillow.

And yet somehow, I was the most comfortable I'd ever been. I'd forgotten what it was like to sleep with someone. I hadn't meant to fall asleep. I'd just meant to cuddle her for a moment, in the afterglow, and somehow... She was just so relaxing to be with, a balm to my soul. And the sex. God, the little moans and gasps she made when I drove deep into her. The urgency, as she'd torn at my shirt. She was so good, the light to my dark, but that goodness hid a sex drive as powerful as mine. Even now, my cock was hardening against her ass. I'd happily fuck her every night for the rest of my life.

The first bar of Stravinsky's *The Rake's Progress* split the silence, and I cursed under my breath: *chyort*! I scrambled to find my pants, pulled out my phone, and breathlessly answered it before she woke. "Yes?" I whispered, furious.

"Where are you?" asked Gennadiy. "You told me to find Doyle and Yoz and then I didn't hear from you again."

I smoothed Bronwyn's hair back from her face. *Still asleep.* I started to gently inch my body away from hers. "Sorry," I whispered. "I got held up."

"Why are you whispering?" Gennadiy paused and I could hear him thinking. "Are you with a *woman?*"

"Of course not," I whispered. I managed to roll away from Bronwyn and climbed to my feet. Naked, I stalked into the back room. "Did you find them?" I asked in my normal voice.

"Of course I found them. They're at the warehouse waiting for you. And I brought...pruning shears."

The pause was deliberate. He wanted me to know that *he* knew something was going on. Pruning shears have a very particular purpose, in our world, and that purpose made no sense at all for someone like me without a wife, girlfriend or sister.

But one of the good things about being the boss was that I didn't have to explain myself. "Good work," I told him. "I'll be along later."

"That wasn't what I was calling about," said Gennadiy. "We just heard: Borislav Nazarov is leaving for a week's trip to Vegas tomorrow."

Chyort! That meant I'd have to kill him that evening. I glanced through the open doorway to where Bronwyn slept, and a knot formed in my stomach. *Guilt?!* Over killing a rapist bastard like Borislav?

I closed my eyes and sighed. In those few hours with her, I'd forgotten what I was. Now I'd been reminded, and it was like being violently slapped awake. "I'll get it done," I told Gennadiy, and ended the call.

I found a pen, pulled a piece of paper from her printer and wrote her a note. There was a throw blanket in the back room and I laid that over her so she'd be warm. Then I dressed, taking the suit jacket I'd left the last time, as well. I didn't want to leave myself any excuse to come back. Fucking her had been a mistake. Getting close to her, a worse one.

I bent down to kiss her and felt that *pull* again. I just wanted to climb under that blanket with her and stay there...

I forced those feelings down inside. This had to end *now,* for her sake. I kissed her sleeping cheek. "Goodbye, *Krasavitsa,*" I whispered.

And I walked out of her life forever.

12

BRONWYN

SUNLIGHT WAS TRYING to force its way under my eyelids and there were voices. I cracked my eyes open a slit and saw a mom pushing a kid in a stroller up a vertical cliff.

My brain reoriented itself. I was lying on the floor, looking at everything sideways. People were walking past outside, because it was morning. And I was naked.

I looked down at myself in disbelief. *Yep.* I was stretched out naked under a blanket. Luckily, only my head was poking out from behind the counter. Unluckily, my clothes were strewn all over the floor.

Cursing, I waited for a lull in the people walking past, then wrapped the blanket around me and ran around the store grabbing my clothes. I made it to the back room and closed the door just as the next person walked past. Then I dressed, put some coffee on and walked back into the store. I looked around at the burned, soaked books Doyle and Yoz had left. The crack in the door glass from when Radimir had hurled it open. The place on the counter where we'd...

I ran a hand through my tangled hair. My joints ached but I felt deeply, completely, *well-fucked* in a way I'd never felt before.

That's when I saw the note on the floor. I'd missed it, in my panic to get some clothes on.

Krasavitsa,
I will never forget you.
R.

Only five words but I read them over and over, trying to squeeze more meaning out of them. He'd never forget me...but he left in the middle of the night? He'd never forget me...and that was it, forever? I had so many questions and I knew I wasn't going to get any answers.

And all at once, I felt it. Like a hairline fracture in the surface of my skin that no matter how hard I tried, I couldn't close. Ice water poured in, soaking right to the center of my soul and filling it up. I sagged against the counter, wrapping my arms protectively around me. I'd felt this before. When my parents died. When Nathan bailed on me. When Baba got sick.

He was gone, and I was on my own again. And I was a fucking idiot to think that he ever wanted me, to think there was some feeling there beyond just sex. I was an idiot to think that I was *enough.*

Hot tears pricked at my eyes but I furiously blinked them away and threw myself into tidying the store. I'd get everything cleaned up, order new stock to replace what was destroyed, get a new fire extinguisher, check Jen was doing okay, figure out some nice, safe explanation for why Radimir wouldn't be back, and that night, I'd go to see Baba.

I'd cram the day full and that way, there'd be no time to think about him.

~

A little before ten that night, I was trudging home from the care center. It had warmed up enough for the snow to turn to a heavy gray rain that pummeled my shoulders and hissed off the sidewalk. My coat was waterproof, but my jeans were soaked and my teeth were chattering.

I suddenly stopped and stared. Wasn't that...*Radimir?*

He was crossing the street ahead of me and hadn't seen me yet. He had his head down against the rain, but I'd have recognized his angry, impatient walk anywhere. And he was heading for my apartment building. He must have gotten my address from my old landlord. *He's coming to see me!* My heart lifted. *He's going to apologize. Explain.* Only he was going to find I wasn't home. I hurried across the street to catch up to him, but my joints were burning and stiff, and I couldn't move fast.

Then Radimir walked straight past my apartment block. *Where's he going?*

I followed him to the end of the street and across the intersection to the next. The buildings here were a little flashier, and he hurried up the steps of one of them and started fiddling with the door lock.

I hung back in the shadows. *Who is he going to see, this late at night?* But the answer was obvious. *A woman. Is that what he does, come down to our part of town and find women to fuck? Is she just like me?* I blinked rain out of my eyes. I had no idea why I was so upset. We weren't even *dating,* we'd just met a handful of times. But...

But I'd thought it felt...special. *God, I'm so stupid.*

Radimir pulled the door wide and disappeared inside. I started forward and then caught myself. *What the hell am I doing?* Was I a crazy stalker ex, now? I'd already followed him for almost a block. I couldn't go in there!

The door was slowly swinging closed. *Go home,* I told myself. *Don't be stupid.*

It was just so unfair: he had all the power. He could stop by the bookstore anytime, but I couldn't just show up at the front desk of Aristov Incorporated. And I needed answers.

I cursed, ran up the steps and grabbed the door just before it shut.

The lobby was much nicer than the one in my building, with a desk for a security guy—who wasn't there—and thick red carpet. I could hear Radimir climbing the stairs, already a floor ahead of me. I guiltily wiped my feet and started after him.

On the third floor, he turned left and went to a door at the end of the hallway. I hunkered down on the stairs, watching him through the railing as he quietly inserted first one, then another metal thing into the door lock and fiddled with them. *Wait. Is he...is he PICKING THE LOCK?*

The door swung open and Radimir crept inside, leaving it open. I stared at the doorway. *Okay, enough.* Whatever was happening here, I wanted no part of it. I turned to walk back down the stairs. He'd never know I followed him and tomorrow, I'd go back to my normal, boring life.

Then I heard a grunt of surprise and a muffled yell from inside the apartment. The shuffle of feet, more grunting. A fight! What if Radimir was being attacked?

I crept over to the open door. I was looking across the apartment's hallway and straight into a bathroom. Radimir was wrestling with a huge, bald man who was soaking wet and wrapped in a towel. He had his hand over the bald man's mouth, muffling his cries. As I watched, Radimir forced the man to the ground. Then he took hold of the man's head, lifted it—

Radimir brought the man's head down on the tiled edge of the shower stall. There was a sickening noise I'll never forget, like a boiled egg cracking. The man's body went utterly still. I looked at his chest. It wasn't moving.

And that's when Radimir looked up and saw me.

13

RADIMIR

I FROZE. My brain just locked up with the impossibility of it. She couldn't be there. She had to be a hallucination. I blinked, honestly expecting her to vanish.

She didn't. She just stared at me, her eyes wide and her chest shaking. Then she was gone, sprinting out of the apartment.

Fuck. I launched myself out of the bathroom and out of the apartment, pulling the door closed behind me. I could see her on the floor below, already starting down the next flight of stairs, and I forced my legs to go faster.

It had all been going so well. The hacker I'd paid had disabled the security cameras in Borislav's building and would delete the footage from cameras in other, nearby buildings. The guard was on his break, as planned. The lockpicks had worked like a charm. When they found the body, everyone would think Borislav had slipped in the shower.

Except she'd seen me do it.

By the time I reached the lobby, she was already running down the street. I raced out into the rain and chased after her. I had no idea what I was going to do. I just knew I needed to fix it, somehow.

I thought of that morning, at the warehouse, I'd sat straddling a chair, looking down at the naked and bloody Doyle and Yoz. "There's something I've been struggling with," I'd said slowly. "But I haven't been able to tell anyone. I haven't been able to..." —I'd looked at Doyle—"what do you British say? *Get it off my chest.* People would think I was weak. But I can tell you two." I'd leaned closer. "I can tell you because I know you won't leave this room alive."

And I'd told them. I'd told them that I liked her. It felt good, to say it out loud, just that once. It made me sure that I'd done the right thing, walking away from her. And it made Doyle and Yoz understand what I was going to do to them, and why.

I'd picked up the pruning shears and made two quick snips. And then I'd waited until the screaming stopped and the blood slowed to a trickle, and they were dead.

I'd thought I'd never see her again. Now, somehow, she was here. I kept rerunning the look of raw horror she'd given me, my stomach twisting into a cold, hard knot. I couldn't leave it like this. *I have to catch her.*

She was running with everything she had and even with my longer legs, it took me a full block to close the gap. Finally, I managed to grab her shoulder and tug her to a stop.

She spun around. "*Get away from me!*"

I staggered back. It felt like she'd emptied a shotgun into my chest.

"Get away from me," she repeated, her voice shaky.

I'd always been proud that I scared people. Until now.

"Get away from me." This time, it was a plea. When her eyes filled with tears, I felt that protective urge take hold of me, and I reached for her, but she flinched back.

I wanted to kill the thing that was scaring her. But the thing that was scaring her was me.

I couldn't fix it.

I stepped back, my hands raised in submission.

And for the second time in a day, I walked away from her.

14

BRONWYN

He killed him. I kept seeing it in my head, the bald man's head hitting the shower stall. *He killed him.*

I'd always known he was a criminal. But all those little moments in the bookstore had made me convince myself, stupidly, that there was warmth in him, hidden away under all that ice.

But no. He really *was* a monster.

I watched him go, silent tears flooding down my cheeks. I'd hurt before, when he'd walked out on me. But this was much, much worse. I'd been completely wrong about him, I was scared and shaken and there was no one I could go to, no one I could tell. Baba was too ill. Jen and my other friends I couldn't face: I felt too stupid. *Yeah, I knew he was a gangster, but I thought he wasn't like the others.*

You fucking idiot, Bronwyn.

Should I go to the police? That would have consequences. This was the *Russian mafia,* they could hurt me or hurt Baba to get to me. I knew now what he was capable of.

But the hardest part was...even now, I still couldn't shake the feeling that he wouldn't hurt me. A traitorous little part of me wondered, *is this why he walked out on me? To keep me away from all this?*

Even now, I still wanted to believe in him.

15

RADIMIR

For the next three days, I stomped around in an even fouler mood than normal. I couldn't stop seeing Bronwyn's horrified face, or hearing her tell me to get away from her. I should never have given in to that first moment of weakness, when I'd seen her in the bookstore. I'd fucked up badly.

But it was much worse than I thought.

I was standing on the top floor of a half-built tower block when it happened. The block was one of my pet projects, paid for by the tens of millions we'd made from our gambling operations, and I was grilling the foreman on why construction was behind.

Then Gennadiy stepped out of the elevator, followed by Valentin and Mikhail. The look in Gennadiy's eyes was murderous. Valentin didn't look much happier and even the always-upbeat Mikhail looked grim.

"Tell your crew to take a break," I told the foreman, and he quickly cleared his people from the building. When I was sure we were alone, I turned to Gennadiy. "What's up?"

Gennadiy pushed his phone under my nose. "This. This is what's up."

He played a video. Security camera footage, the outside of

Borislav's apartment building seen from across the street. There was me, head down, hurrying up to the front door and punching in the access code...

...my stomach lurched as Bronwyn raced up the steps, caught the door and followed me in.

I stayed silent and sweated it out. Maybe I could pretend she was a random civilian, some tenant who'd happened to walk in just after me. But the security footage kept playing. Bronwyn came charging out of the door and I chased after her.

"Our hacker deleted the footage from the buildings across the street like he was supposed to, but he was so worried by what he saw, he sent me a copy. *What the fuck is this?*" snarled Gennadiy.

I faced off against him, glaring. I was still his *Pakhan,* his boss. But Valentin got between us. "Please, brother. Tell us what this is so we can fix it."

I sighed and the fight went out of me. They were only trying to protect me from myself. I ran a hand through my hair and told them about Bronwyn.

Gennadiy stared at me. "All this because you shoved your dick in some woman?"

"It's not like that!" I snapped.

Gennadiy and Valentin looked at each other, worried. "What *is* it like?" asked Gennadiy.

I said nothing, fuming.

"Why was she following you?" Mikhail wanted to know.

"I think she was mad at me." I rubbed the back of my neck. "After we fucked, I... left her there."

"You just *left?*" Mikhail raised his eyes to heaven. "Did I teach you boys *nothing* about women?"

Valentin stepped forward. "Radimir, you say she saw you kill Borislav. She's a witness."

"She won't go to the police," I said firmly.

Gennadiy shook his head. "You don't know that."

"I do," I told him. "I can control her."

Mikhail sighed. "Radimir, she's a woman. God himself couldn't control her!"

Gennadiy waved his phone at me. "*This* video is gone, but what if there are other cameras we don't know about? What if a passer-by saw the two of you? Even if she doesn't go to the police, the police might come to *her!*" He paced, too angry to stay still. "She didn't just witness a murder, she knows the biggest secret there is: that it was us who killed Borislav! Have you thought about what happens if one of the other families gets to her? How many people have seen you going into this bookstore of hers? How many have guessed that there's something between you? What if they get hold of her to use as leverage against you? Will she hold her tongue when they're pulling her fingernails out?"

I glared at him even though I knew he was right. I'd put her in danger the moment I let myself get close to her.

Gennadiy sighed and stared off into the distance. The view from up here, looking out across Chicago, was incredible, but I could tell he wasn't seeing it. He was trying to control that ferocious temper of his so he could speak calmly. And when he spoke, I found out why.

"Brother," he said gently, "she's a witness. You know what you have to do."

It took me a second because, despite all the lives I'd taken, my mind just hadn't gone there. Not with Bronwyn. I drew in my breath. "*No.*"

"You don't have a choice," said Gennadiy, his voice still gentle.

"I'm not killing her," I told him.

"You have to," said Valentin quietly.

"I'm *not. Killing her.*" I spat.

Gennadiy raised his hands in submission. "Okay. Okay, it's alright." His gentleness was driving me crazy. He started walking away.

Fear grabbed my heart in a cold fist and I ran after him and grabbed his shoulder. "*You're* not doing it either!"

He looked at me in pity. "I'll make it so she doesn't suffer."

I grabbed his shirt in both hands. "If you touch one hair on her head, I will *end* you!" I roared.

Gennadiy finally lost his cool. "Then end me!" he yelled. "I'll still have protected you!"

We glared at each other, our faces only a foot apart. I felt myself fracture inside: I knew he loved me, I knew he was only trying to protect me. And I knew that however much we yelled at each other; he really would die to save me. But I couldn't let him touch Bronwyn.

"Maybe you could marry her," said Valentin.

All of us turned to stare at him. "*What?*" I demanded.

"If she's your wife," Valentin explained, "the cops can't make her testify against you. And if you're together, none of the other families would dare touch her."

Everyone went quiet. I glanced around: they all looked thoughtful. "*No!*" I said quickly. "No. Unacceptable."

"It's a good solution, Radimir," said Mikhail.

"Except *she hates me!* She'll never agree to it."

"She was happy enough to fuck you," said Gennadiy mildly.

"That's different! And now she..." *Now she's seen what a monster I am.* "She's *scared* of me! And we barely know each other! She doesn't want to marry me; she doesn't even want to *see* me!" I shook my head. "I'm not ruining her life just because I made a mistake."

"She'll be compensated," said Gennadiy. "A nice apartment. Fancy clothes."

"She's not a whore!" I didn't mean to yell it, but I did. Gennadiy cocked his head at me, curious, and I looked away. "You don't understand. She's not like us. She's not part of this." I waved my hand at the four of us. "I'm not bringing her into it!"

Gennadiy put his hand on my shoulder. "You know the alternative, brother."

I shook off his hand and marched to the edge of the roof, thinking furiously. *Marry* her?! She had her whole future ahead of her, she deserved to meet someone *good* and go off and have children and vacations and all that civilian crap. And it would ruin *my* life, too. Sharing an apartment with her while constantly lusting after her.

Knowing I could never give her what she deserved: I could never love her. It would be hell. And it would be *forever:* it wasn't like we could ever divorce.

No. I couldn't do it.

But...—I felt myself tearing apart inside—I couldn't kill her, either.

I scowled and cursed but at last I sighed and turned to my family. "Okay," I said.

"We're coming with you," said Gennadiy immediately.

I felt the anger build in my chest again: *don't you trust me?* But no, they didn't. And they were right not to. If I was on my own, it would be too easy to give in to temptation, give her a hundred thousand dollars and put her on a plane. But wherever she went, she'd still be in danger. My brothers were just trying to protect me.

"Fine," I told him. "But we're making a stop on the way. If I'm going to do this, I'm doing it right."

16

BRONWYN

We were having a busy morning, for once. The line of customers stretched almost to the door and I was working non-stop to serve them while Jen restocked shelves and dealt with queries.

"Enjoy!" I told a woman who was buying an enemies-to-lovers shifter romance called *I Can't Bear You*. "We just got the sequel in, *I Can Bearly Bear You Either*, so come back when you're ready."

For the last three days, I'd thrown myself into my work, reaching out to local book clubs to offer them discounts, creating a new window display and redoing all the book tables...anything to stop me thinking of him. I wasn't getting much sleep, but the extra effort was paying off.

There'd been a few other pieces of good news. The day after I'd followed Radimir into that building, a man had appeared and started fixing the cracked glass in the door. When I argued with him, saying I couldn't afford it, he said that Aristov Incorporated had already paid him. And later the same day, a package arrived in the mail. Three thousand dollars in cash. *To cover the books that were destroyed,* said the note. I wasn't comfortable taking criminal money, but the alternative was going out of business: I had to replace those books.

"Is this okay for a thirteen-year-old?" asked a mom, holding up a dark romance.

"*Definitely not.*" I whipped it out of her hand and passed her a teen romance book from under the counter: I keep a stack for exactly these moments. "But this is excellent." I rang the book through for her and smiled at the next customer, a guy in his twenties clutching a graphic novel. "Be right with you." I looked down at the computer for a second, checking if the delivery I was expecting was still on track: it was. I smiled and looked up. "Okay, will there be anythi—"

Radimir was standing in front of me.

My mouth moved for a second, but nothing came out. I was scared and angry and... *God,* he looked good. His gray eyes were icy with brutal efficiency, but I could see the cracks there, the raw emotion underneath.

He tugged his waistcoat straight. "We need to talk."

I swallowed. "I don't want to see you." I hated how shaky my voice sounded.

"I'm aware. But we still need to talk."

We stared at each other. I wanted to run, to lock myself away somewhere until he'd gone. I was scared because of what I'd seen: he really was the monster everyone said he was. But I was just as scared by how much he'd managed to hurt me when he walked out after the sex. I hadn't realized how deeply Nathan and losing my parents had scarred me. I shook my head. "Please leave."

"Bronwyn, please."

Jen inserted herself between us, hands on hips, and glared up at Radimir. "You heard her," she growled.

Radimir looked at me over the top of her head. I saw the ice in his eyes fracture and break. He was pleading.

"Five minutes," I mumbled. I asked Jen to jump on the register and led Radimir to the back room, away from the gawping customers. I shut the door, leaned against it and crossed my arms, trying to look strong. But inside, I was a mess. Part of it was fear: I'd seen him *kill*, just snuff out a man's life like it was nothing. I shouldn't be alone with him, shouldn't even be in the same *building* as him... But there was something else going on, too. That deep attraction that had been there ever since I first laid eyes on him...it hadn't died when I saw him kill, like it should have. I was scared of him, but I still wanted him.

Radimir sighed and ran a hand through his hair. "You witnessed something."

"I won't tell anyone," I said quickly.

"I know that. But others don't. And there are people who could force you to talk." He was always so confident, but suddenly he was as awkward as a teenager asking someone to prom. "I have to keep you safe. And there's only one way to do that."

He took something out of his pocket, flipped open the top and—OH MY GOD—

"I need you to marry me," said Radimir.

I stared at the diamond ring as the room seemed to tilt under my feet. There was a brief second of shock and then a joyful, indescribable rush that made it impossible to speak. It was the fairy tale I'd been waiting for my whole life, ever since I was a little girl dreaming of princes. I'd had it once before, with Nathan, but that hadn't felt like *this*...

Then cold reality shattered the dream. It all came lurching back: what I'd seen. Who he was. I shook my head, sick with fear.

"You have to," he said. "So you can't be made to testify. So that no one will touch you."

I shook my head again. I could feel myself going pale. *Marry him?!* My whole life...*gone.*

"Bronwyn, my brothers will *kill you* if you don't. They will kill you to protect me!"

I clapped my hand to my mouth, tears filling my eyes. "But I didn't—I don't want any of this. I don't even *know* you!"

"I know." I could hear the pain in his voice.

"I'll go to the police!"

"We have people in the police."

"I could run away! Change my name!"

"We'd find you," he said tiredly, and lifted the box towards me. "Bronwyn, I'm sorry. But this is the only way to keep you safe." He grabbed my wrist, took the ring and pushed it onto my finger.

I pulled my hand away and stared at the ring in horror.

Then I threw open the door and ran out of the store.

17

RADIMIR

Fuck. "Bronwyn, wait!"

I dashed through the main store, where Jen and the customers were all standing in slack-jawed shock, and out onto the street. Ahead of me, Bronwyn stumbled to a stop. She'd just seen the three big guys in suits lounging against the black Mercedes.

Gennadiy, Valentin and Mikhail all started towards her. Bronwyn's eyes widened in panic and she bolted off down the street. *Fuck!*

"Wait there!" I snapped at my brothers. "I'm handling it!" And I took off after her.

18

BRONWYN

I RAN. I ran until my joints filled with lava and then filled up again with concrete and glass shards. When I finally staggered to a stop, I was down by the river, on a desolate scrap of snow-covered wasteland. My dad used to bring me there, to feed the ducks. Maybe I'd run there on instinct, to feel safe.

I paced, panting for air. *How is this happening? When did it go wrong?* When I followed him into that building? When I let him kiss me? When I called after him, that first time in the store?

I looked down at the ring and gave a big, shuddering sob. What really hurt was that I'd always wanted this: to have some prince swoop in and carry me off for a fairytale wedding. Except now, this fake version would mean I'd never have the real thing. I'd never meet someone who loved me. I'd be fake married...and alone forever.

I pulled the ring off and hurled it on the ground. Then the world dissolved behind a curtain of tears.

I stumbled down to the river's edge and stood there, tears raining down into the water, for a long time. With the wind blowing in across the river it was bitterly cold. I let the freezing air blast me, hoping it would strip away the pain, but it didn't. I shivered and sobbed until I was all cried out and at last I looked around...and saw a blurry, dark-suited figure.

I blinked away the last of my tears. Radimir was standing silently watching, and he looked like he'd been there for a while. I sniffed and lifted my head, looking him in the eye.

His icy confidence was gone for a moment. I'd seen him mad. I'd seen him burning up with lust. This was the first time I'd seen him humble.

His accent was still beautiful, but the edges of the words were extra rough with emotion. "Bronwyn, I'm sorry. I know this isn't what you wanted. I know *I'm* not what you wanted." He bent and picked up the ring. "But I promise I'll always take care of you." His eyes blazed. "And I'll never let anyone hurt you."

He held out the ring. Offering, this time, not demanding.

There was no choice.

I stepped forward and gave him my hand. He took it, his own hand gloriously warm, and slid the ring into place. It was different, this time. The ring felt heavier. My stomach flipped. I was *his*...forever.

He took my hand and pulled me close. "You're freezing," he told me. And he pulled me against his chest, wrapping his overcoat around us both. I let my face press against the warm curve of his pec, too shell-shocked to argue. An arm settled around my back, hugging me close. With his other hand, he brought out his phone and made a call. "Come pick us up," he told someone. "I've got her."

Moments later, a black Mercedes pulled up, its shiny paintwork out of place in the litter and muddy snow. As the men got out, Radimir introduced his brothers, both of whom looked at me suspiciously. Valentin, young and gorgeous in a romantic, intense kind of way. And Gennadiy, stubbled and broodingly handsome. Both of them were terrifying. And soon they were going to be family. *How am I supposed to bond with them? They wanted to kill me.* Only Radimir's uncle, Mikhail, seemed warm and friendly. He was older, smiled a lot, and told me to call him *Misha.*

Gennadiy looked at me and muttered something in Russian to Radimir.

Radimir glared at him. "Be polite," he said tightly. "Speak English."

Gennadiy gave a gracious nod, but I noticed Radimir didn't translate what he'd said for me.

"So what happens now?" I asked nervously. "We find a courthouse?"

"It has to look real," Radimir told me. "We don't want anyone asking questions." He was back to cold, clinical efficiency and my heart sank. *This is how it will be? Forever?* "The wedding will be in three weeks," he said.

Gennadiy nodded. "You should bring her this afternoon. It's important that she's seen."

What's this afternoon?

Radimir told the others that we'd need the car, and they obediently headed off to get a cab. He opened the passenger door for me, but I hung back, watching Gennadiy walk away. "What did your brother say when he spoke Russian?"

Radimir's jaw tightened. "It's not important." He gestured towards the car.

But I stayed where I was. "Please."

He scowled at me. Then, when he saw I wasn't going to give in, he sighed. "He said...that you wouldn't survive in our world."

That hurt, even if Gennadiy was probably right. But Radimir looked pissed, and that warmed me a little. I climbed into the car and Radimir slammed my door and climbed in beside me.

"What's this afternoon?" I asked. "This event I'm going to be seen at?"

Radimir started the engine. "A funeral."

19

BRONWYN

RADIMIR DROVE me back to my apartment to change. On the way, I called Jen and reassured her that I was okay and that everything was fine, and she said she'd watch the store for the rest of the day. Then I sat there staring out of the window. I was waiting for it to sink in, to become real, but it just wouldn't. *Engaged? To him?!* It was too big, too much.

We pulled up outside my apartment building. I saw Radimir's jaw tighten when he saw the graffiti-covered exterior. Inside, the elevator was out again so we had to walk up four floors and after all the running, my joints hurt so much my legs shook. "What's the matter?" Radimir asked from behind me.

"Nothing," I told him. "Just tired."

Upstairs, he scowled at the hallway with its peeling wallpaper, and I felt stubbornly defensive. Okay, so my building sucked, but it was all I could afford. There was no need to be snobby about it.

Inside, I searched around for something black to wear. Radimir stood there just *looming,* his gaze coldly analysing everything. "A monkey?" he asked.

I turned and saw he was looking at the tattered photo on my wall. It was of a baby monkey, with just a few wisps of dark hair on its head and huge, black eyes. "Spider Monkey," I told him. I stared hard at the clothes in my closet and forced my voice to stay level. "My dad took it when he was working in Cancún when I was a kid. My folks said they'd take me to see them when I was older." I couldn't stop my voice tightening. "They died before they could."

Radimir was silent for a moment. Then, "I'm sorry."

There was a surprising amount of softness in his voice, and it threw me. I nodded quickly, not trusting myself to look at him, and went back to searching.

By the time I finally found my one black dress, I'd got myself back under control. "I'll put this on," I said.

He just stood there, watching me.

"That was your cue to leave the room so I can change." I knew I sounded a little testy, but I was exhausted, in pain and emotionally wrung-out.

He lifted his chin. "I've already seen you naked."

I felt myself flush, remembering that night at the bookstore. And... *shit,* that was something I hadn't even had time to think about, yet. How was the sex going to work? We were engaged, now, was he expecting...*am I basically his sex slave?*

Deep inside, a traitorous flare of heat rippled down to my groin and made me crush my thighs together. "At least turn around," I said stubbornly.

For a second, I thought I saw a hint of a smile on his lips, like he liked me standing up to him. Then he nodded and turned his back.

I quickly stripped off my jeans and sweater, then realized I needed to swap my bra for a black one, so the straps didn't show. Then I couldn't *find* a black one. "Finished?" he asked, half-turning.

"*No!*" I squeaked, in just my panties.

He turned his back again. I was flustered and I told myself *that* was why it took three attempts to hook my bra clasp. Not because being so close to him, when I was nearly naked, was making me heady and giddy. Not because I knew he was toying with me, and it turned me on. Not because I could hear in his voice how much he wanted to just spin around and grab me.

Oh God. I still wanted him, despite what I'd seen him do. That power he had over me was stronger than ever.

I pulled the dress over my head. "Done," I announced.

He turned around, watching as I pulled my hair into an updo and put on a little make-up. "Is this okay?" I asked, turning from the mirror.

His lungs slowly filled and his gray eyes gleamed. "Yes, *Krasavitsa.* It's perfect."

The musical, delicate name threw me. He hadn't called me that since his goodbye note. "What does that mean?" I asked, turning away and trying to sound uninterested.

He was silent for a moment, as if the name had slipped out by accident. "Beauty," he said at last.

I gave a quick, stiff nod of acknowledgment. Inside, my stomach was doing somersaults. *That's* what he'd been calling me? *Me,* curvy, copper-haired *me?* When Nathan had broken up with me, he'd snuffed something out, right at the core of me, and there'd been nothing but cold dark there ever since. *Krasavitsa* made a tiny, warm light flicker into life, fragile as a firefly.

Without words, I stomped out of my apartment and led the way back to the car, my jaw set determinedly.

It didn't matter that I still wanted him. It didn't matter how he made me feel. *He's a monster.*

Radimir drove me to the edge of the city, to a street with high hedges that blocked any view of the houses. A black iron gate slid silently aside as our car approached and we drove down a long, sweeping driveway. A three-story mansion built from beautiful, smooth gray stone crept into view. "Gennadiy's house," Radimir explained.

I stared. As I understood it from the media, Radimir was the boss. If this was Gennadiy's house, what was Radimir's place going to be like?

Radimir's brothers were waiting for us inside, both of them in black suits. Radimir left me with them while he went to change into *his* funeral suit. Silence descended and it was beyond awkward. Valentin looked worried. Gennadiy looked full-on hostile.

Then there was a patter of paws from behind me. I turned just in time to see what looked like a wolf pack racing towards me. As they surrounded me, I realized they were Malamutes, big ones, with bright blue eyes and huge, fluffy tails. All four of them pushed close, sniffing curiously, pushing their furry heads at me for ear scratches and licking at my hands. I crouched, delighted, and started handing out strokes and ruffles, having to use both hands to deal with all of them.

Mikhail, looking dashing in his funeral suit, came over, grinning. He let the dogs have their cuddles but gave quick little commands in Russian whenever one of them was in danger of actually knocking me over. "They're normally suspicious of strangers," he told me. "But they like you."

I smiled back at him. I've always loved dogs. But then I straightened up and smiled at Gennadiy and he just stared back at me coldly. My heart slumped. He and Valentin were going to be my brothers-in-law. *I just want them to like me!*

But this was the Bratva. I should have realized: wanting to be liked was seen as a weakness.

20

RADIMIR

I WALKED BACK DOWNSTAIRS STILL TYING my tie...and stopped on the landing as I saw her again. She looked stunning, her black outfit setting off her milky skin and that shining, copper hair. Pinned up, it exposed whole new areas of soft, sensitive skin behind her ears and down the sides of her neck that I immediately wanted to kiss. And it made me want to run my hands through her hair, knocking out the pins and freeing it so it tumbled down onto her shoulders, then strip that dress off her until she was completely...*undone.*

I wanted her. Cared for her, in some way I was trying hard not to think about too much. But I was destroying her life, trapping her in a relationship with a man she hated. I had to find some way to make this work, for her sake.

And there was something else, the thing that maybe unsettled me the most. Whenever I thought about the fake marriage, there was this tiny, secret part of me, way down deep...that almost wanted it to be real. That wanted to have someone I could share my life with, tell anything to, have a future with...

I tore my gaze away and stomped down the rest of the stairs. As I reached the bottom, Valentin intercepted me. "Are you sure this is going to work?" he asked, glancing at Bronwyn over his shoulder.

"This was your idea!" I reminded him.

He sighed, worried. "I didn't know she'd be so...innocent. Fragile."

I glowered. First Gennadiy, now him. I knew they only wanted to protect me, but they were wrong about her. I'd seen how she protected her friend when Doyle and Yoz came into her store. She was tougher than they knew. But they were right: she wasn't like us.

The limos arrived to pick us up. While Mikhail argued with the limo driver that *yes,* the dogs were coming, Bronwyn took my hand and pulled me behind a pillar. I struggled to focus on what she was saying: all I could think about was how good holding her hand felt.

"This funeral," she asked. "You haven't told me who died. Were they...family?"

I shook my head, mad at myself. I'd forgotten that she didn't know. "His name was Borislav Nazarov." And then, watching her carefully. "You met him."

She blinked, confused. Then realization hit and she clapped her hands over her mouth. "No! Oh God, why would you—Why are we going to the *funeral* if you—"

"We have to pay our respects to his brother, Spartak."

Her eyes went huge. "I can't stand there and talk to his *brother* when you—"

I nodded quickly. "Yes. Yes, you can. You have to."

"*Why?* Why are we going?"

"Because it would look suspicious if we didn't." I took hold of her shoulders. "You can do this."

And I led her to the limo.

As we pulled up, I cursed under my breath. I'd known that Spartak Nazarov would put on a big event to remember his brother, but I hadn't counted on *how* big. There were at least twenty limos pulling up: every mafia family in the city plus some from Milwaukee and Detroit. Everyone was gathering behind a funeral carriage pulled by white horses. Right at the front of the procession, I spied Spartak, followed by thirty of his men, all no doubt armed.

It was a mile to the cemetery and Spartak had picked a route that went right through all the neighborhoods that he controlled. Shopkeepers, bartenders, construction workers...they all stopped work to line the streets, too scared not to. It was a testament to how much the Nazarovs were feared...and how much trouble we were in if Spartak ever found out I killed his brother.

I glanced to my left. Bronwyn was walking next to me, hand in hand. She bit her lip as if in pain and I gave her a questioning look.

She shook her head. "It's nothing. My feet hurt. I shouldn't have worn heels."

The ceremony was short, and in Russian. As I watched Spartak toss soil on his brother's coffin, I felt an unexpected tightness in my chest. I didn't like Spartak, and I certainly hadn't liked his brother but the man just looked *broken,* and I actually felt sorry for him. I couldn't imagine losing Valentin or Gennadiy.

The wake was held in a dark, wood-paneled bar that I guessed was one of Spartak's places. As we walked in, Bronwyn gazed around at the fifty or so people around us. "All of these people, they're...they do what you do?" she whispered.

I nodded.

She shook her head in wonder. Like most civilians, she'd had no idea how big the Bratva is: and this was just the leadership. "Different families...so they're all your enemies?"

"Some are enemies. Some are rivals. Some allies." I frowned. "But I wouldn't trust any of them not to put a bullet in my back."

She blinked at me. "How do you live like that?"

I cocked my head to one side, thinking. This world was normal to me. "Family," I said at last, nodding towards Valentin, Gennadiy and Mikhail. "You trust your family, because they'll never betray you."

I could see how scared she was, the lone civilian in a room full of criminals. She seemed to get smaller with each step, closing down and turning inward. "Don't worry," I told her. "None of them would dare lay a finger on you. Not when we're engaged."

Her head snapped up and she stared at me in shock: she'd forgotten, for a moment. I kept my face cold and impassive. But inside, a sudden, stupid rush of emotion had filled my chest. *She's mine!*

As I led her deeper into the room, I could see her nervously glancing at the other wives. "Do they grow them all in a lab in Moscow?" she mumbled.

"What do you mean?"

"I don't exactly fit in," she said out of the side of her mouth. "They're all..."

I looked around. The other wives were the usual type: very thin, blonde, and Russian, sporting handbags that cost as much as cars, dresses straight from the catwalks and artful make-up that must take them hours. I frowned and drew Bronwyn closer. "They're all *what?*"

"Perfect." She flushed and looked away. And suddenly, I was mad. Not at her, at whatever man had made her doubt herself.

"Bronwyn." She looked at the floor, so I put a finger under her chin and gently lifted it until she *had* to look at me. "You are the most beautiful woman here," I told her firmly. "Do you understand?"

I saw her eyes flick away as if she didn't believe me. But then she timidly looked at me again and this time she must have seen something in my eyes because her gaze locked on mine in shock. She swallowed...and nodded. And then she flushed again, but in a good way.

And now the problem was, I couldn't look away. I'd meant what I'd said and the sight of her, those lush green eyes looking up at me, that copper hair all piled up tight and just waiting to be freed, those soft lips quirked in a shy little smile...

I knew it wasn't appropriate at a funeral. But I just wanted to lean down and kiss my fiancée.

At that moment, someone tapped me on the shoulder. I looked round, scowling, the spell broken.

And looked right into the face of Spartak Nazarov. I'd been so focused on Bronwyn, I hadn't noticed him walk up.

"Well," said Spartak, looking right at Bronwyn. "Who have we here?"

21

BRONWYN

THE GUY WAS *BIG*. Not quite as tall as Radimir but *wide,* with a heavy build and enormous shoulders and arms. He sauntered forward, invading my personal space and my stomach flipped: I felt...*fragile,* next to this man, like he might just pick me up and snap me for fun. I wanted to shuffle backwards but it felt like everyone was watching me: these people didn't show fear, and I couldn't, either. I lifted my chin and looked up into his eyes.

And froze.

With some men, you just *know.* It was the same sort of powerful, instinctive reaction I'd had with Radimir. But Radimir's gaze made me feel protected and appreciated. He'd lusted after me but in a way that made me feel lifted up.

This man's cool blue eyes *took.* They sliced away my black dress until it felt ruined. They measured and probed my body until I wanted to squirm, embarrassed by the parts he liked and humiliated by the parts he didn't. I felt like a bug he'd pinned under one thick thumb so that he could play with me. And as I twisted inside, I suddenly realized I recognized his face. He had thick, mousy hair where his brother had been bald, but there was no mistaking the family resemblance.

We killed his brother. My stomach plunged.

Radimir stepped forward, inserting himself between the man and me, forcing him to take a step back. "I was very sorry to hear of your loss, Spartak," he said solemnly. How could these people lie so easily? "This is Bronwyn. *My fiancée.*"

All my fear was forgotten for a second because, out of nowhere, I was floating up, up, *up,* bobbing towards the ceiling. The growly, possessive way he said it. The way his accent carved the word *fiancée* out of ice, making it sparkle with pride and letting Spartak know I was off limits. I knew it was all fake, but it didn't matter. Hearing him call me his fiancée tapped straight into those stupid, childish fantasies and made me feel like I was flying.

A hush descended. Radimir had said the last two words loud enough that they carried, and then whispers spread them to every corner of the room. Women glared. Men looked at me with new caution. I suddenly realized that the engagement wasn't just about stopping me testifying. It was Radimir's way of protecting me. *Don't even think about touching her. She's mine.*

Spartak raised an eyebrow. "Well, you certainly kept *that* quiet. Congratulations." He glanced around and then snapped an order in Russian, so quick it was more of a noise than a word. I expected a dog to come trotting up, but a woman slunk to his side, instead. "This is Liliya," he said proudly. "My wife."

Liliya pressed up against him, her hip to his hip, as if it was something she'd been trained to do. She was leggy and graceful, with beautiful blonde hair plaited into a single braid that fell down her back and soft, tan skin. She gave us a nervous smile, her eyes flicking fearfully to Spartak.

"It was a beautiful service," said Radimir calmly. Then he laid a hand on Spartak's shoulder. "Your brother would have liked it."

Spartak stared into Radimir's eyes, and my chest went tight. But Radimir just gazed back at him, cool and sincere. *How the hell does he do that?* How could he lie so brazenly, right to Spartak's face? My stomach twisted. How was I ever meant to trust him, now I knew he could do that? What if he lied to *me?*

What if he already has?

Then Spartak looked right at me. “My brother would have liked you. It’s a pity you never got to meet him.”

My throat locked. *Does he know?* My lips mouthed soundlessly. *No. of course he doesn’t.* But if I didn’t say something, he might guess. “I’m —I’m sorry too,” I managed.

Spartak nodded slowly, then turned away. His wife didn’t follow quickly enough, and he grabbed her wrist and pulled her. For the first time, I noticed that her black dress had long sleeves.

My chest went tight with worry for her. But I was marrying a gangster, too. Was I just kidding myself, was Radimir really any different from Spartak? I stared at Liliya as her husband dragged her along. *Is that what I’ve got to look forward to?*

I’m going to marry him. It hadn’t been real. Suddenly, it was, and I couldn’t breathe.

“I need some air,” I croaked, and ran for the door.

22

BRONWYN

I STUMBLED on shaky legs to the back of the bar and found an exit. As I burst out into the parking lot, there was a rumble of thunder from overhead. The sky looked bruised, a deep mass of black fading to purple-blue at the edges, and it had turned ferociously cold.

I heard a sound behind me and turned, expecting Radimir. But it was Gennadiy who stepped casually out of the bar.

"You were right," I told him, still breathless. "I can't survive in... *this.*"

He pursed his lips and leaned against the wall. He did *arrogant lounging* very well. Then his face softened, just for a second. "You did okay in there."

I blinked at him. He looked away, like even that tiny shred of warmth had been an embarrassing slip.

Radimir burst out of the door and marched straight over to me. "Are you alright?"

I wanted to nod because, whether I liked it or not, just having him close immediately made me feel better. But it wasn't that simple. I took his arm and towed him between the parked cars, out of earshot of Gennadiy. "How can you do that?" I demanded.

"Do what?"

"Lie. Lie right to someone's face!"

"I've had a great deal of practice."

I shook my head. "I could never do that. You put your hand on his shoulder, you sounded so *sorry!*"

He studied me for a moment. "You can do anything, if it's to protect the people you care about."

I stared back at him. *His family,* I told myself firmly. *He means his family.* The first drop of rain fell, so big and heavy it made a *thunk* when it hit the trunk of a car. "What about me?" I asked in a small voice.

He looked blank. "What about you?"

More raindrops fell around us, but I ignored them and crossed my arms for courage. "Have you lied to me?"

And I saw something in his eyes I'd never seen before, something that jolted me right to the core. He was *shocked* by the idea. Then his stony face cracked, and he gave a little laugh and shook his head. "No, Bronwyn." He cupped my face in his hands. "I would never lie to you."

It started to rain full-on, but I just stood there staring up at him. That laugh reassured me in a way no amount of words could have. He really meant it. The rain pelted us, soaking straight through my dress and stripping all the warmth from my body. But my face was gloriously warm where he touched me and, for a second, that was all that mattered.

Gennadiy hurried over, hunched over and scowling up at the rain. "The rest of us will hang around here for appearances," he told Radimir. "Go be with your fiancée."

Radimir nodded, took my hand and led me towards where the limos were parked. I wasn't going to argue: I wanted to get as far away from Spartak as possible. And as we walked, I looked down at our joined hands. He held mine securely, protectively...but like we were equals, not like I was a piece of luggage or a disobedient pet.

He wasn't the same as Spartak.

He held the door for me and motioned me in first so I could get out of the rain, then climbed in himself. "Let's get you home,"

Radimir told me. And he gave the chauffeur an address. One I didn't recognize.

I turned to him. "When you say *home*..."

He cocked his head to the side. "To my apartment." As if it was obvious.

I felt my eyes widen. "Wait, we..." I glanced at the chauffeur. There was a glass privacy screen between us and him, but I lowered my voice anyway. "We're living together?"

"You're my fiancée. Of course we're living together."

I tried to ignore the warm little bomb that detonated inside me each time he said that word. Everything had happened so fast: I hadn't had time to think about how my life was going to change. The idea of losing my independence was terrifying. "No. I like where I live."

He frowned and shook his head. "You're not spending another night there."

I bristled, remembering how judgey he'd been at my place. "There's nothing wrong with my place! Turn this thing around, I'm living there!"

He stared at me. I glared back at him. His glare changed, heating rapidly, and I felt myself flush. *What?* I wasn't doing anything. Maybe my lower lip had crept into a pout but...

He turned and stared out of the window at the rain hammering the sidewalks...and then he turned back to me, the lust locked under control...*just.* He sighed, and seemed to soften slightly. "I'm sorry, Bronwyn. I should have talked to you about this. But you're in danger, now, and I can't have you living in a place with broken security cameras and doors with shitty locks. You can make whatever rules you want, but you're coming to live with me so I know you're safe." His voice left no room for argument: he *would* protect me.

I just...melted. He hadn't been turning his nose up at my apartment. He'd been casing the joint like a criminal, thinking about how easy it was to break into. I gave a quick little nod and then, when I trusted my voice, I said, "Can we at least stop there on the way, so I can pick up a few things?"

He nodded solemnly and the look he gave me, like he was proud of me and wanted to tear my dress off and he cared about me, all at the same time...

I quickly looked out of the window. *He's just a monster,* I reminded myself.

Right?

23

BRONWYN

At my apartment building, I hit the button for the elevator out of forlorn hope but...*nope,* the button didn't light up. So for the second time that day, I had to walk up four flights. All the running I'd done when he proposed, plus the funeral parade, had left my joints so swollen that each step sent sharp, hot pain knifing through my legs. I pushed on, grimly determined. But I couldn't stop the pain from showing on my face.

"What's the matter?" he asked as we reached the first landing.

"Nothing. I'm just tired."

I started forward but he blocked me with his arm. "No," he said, patient but firm. "You were in pain this morning. You're in pain now. What's going on?"

I did my best to out-glare him, but he was a *lot* better at it than I was. Eventually, I huffed and crossed my arms. I couldn't hide it from him forever, not if we were living together. In fact, why was I so reluctant to tell him? If he reacted like Nathan had...well, he couldn't break up with me, could he?

But he might want to, a little voice whispered, and I hated how vulnerable I suddenly felt.

I took a deep breath. "I have a problem with my joints," I muttered.

He nodded. "What sort of problem?"

I looked at the graffiti on the stairwell wall. "Rheumatoid arthritis." And I waited for him to say what everybody says: *but you're young!*

Except he didn't say that. He said, "You should have told me." And he said it with a tenderness I hadn't thought he was capable of. Slowly, tentatively, my gaze crept back to him. I could see that warmth in his eyes again, like sunlight breaking through ice, and it was so beautiful I had to force myself to remember who he was. *What* he was.

I swallowed and turned away. "Would it have changed things?" I asked, my voice hollow. "Would you have let them kill me instead if you'd known I was...flawed?"

His hands went straight to my shoulders, and he turned me to look at him. When I looked away, he took my chin between thumb and forefinger and made me meet his eyes. He softly shook his head. "You are not flawed. Don't ever say that."

I glared: *of course I am.* But he just gazed steadily back at me.

And as he soaked up all my defensive anger, that tiny, fragile light he'd sparked in me grew and spread. I gave a quick, embarrassed nod and looked away.

Then I yelped because he slid his arms under my knees and back and lifted me into the air. "What are you doing?!"

"Carrying you." He cradled me against his chest.

I tried to ignore the feeling of his pec pressing against my boob. "You can't carry me up three more flights of—"

He started climbing and I discovered that yes, he could quite easily carry me up three flights without even slowing down. And when we passed an old lady coming the other way and she gave me an approving nod, I felt ridiculous and... lucky.

~

I changed out of my dress, packed a small bag, and he drove me downtown. We rode an elevator up to the penthouse of one of his buildings. As we stepped out into the hallway, I gazed around at the thick scarlet carpet and pristine white walls. *His hallway is nicer than my apartment.*

He held out a silver key and I blinked stupidly at it, then stared at him. "You're giving me a key?"

"You're my fiancée, Bronwyn, not a prisoner. Or did you think I was going to keep you chained to the bed?"

That rare ghost of a smile again. But I didn't miss how his eyes flared. And I was very aware of the treacherous ribbon of heat that lashed straight down to my groin. I focused very intently on sliding the key into the lock, turning it and—

Wow.

There was an echoey rush of *space.* Polished wood floor seemed to stretch on to infinity and there was so much light and air. As soon as I stepped inside, I saw why: the place was double height, the ceiling at least twenty feet high. And one whole wall was glass, with sliding doors that opened onto a balcony. Even with the storm clouds overhead and rain sluicing down the windows, it was beautifully light and open. When the sun came out... I could imagine lounging on one of the soft leather couches, reading a book: it'd be like being outdoors.

Most of the penthouse was one huge room. There was a fancy kitchen at one end with a granite countertop and island and lots of stainless-steel appliances. A big TV hung on the opposite wall and there was enough floor space for a seriously lavish party.

But something about the place felt...off. It wasn't just that everything was expensive, or achingly cool. It wasn't that it was all hard surfaces and clean lines: that was very Radimir, cold and efficient. Something else...

I finally figured it out. There was no *stuff,* no personal clutter. No books, no photos, no ugly porcelain figurine given to you by an aunt that you feel too guilty to throw away, no piece of driftwood that you found on a beach on your first date with your partner. Nothing that was *him.* I glanced sideways at him, my stomach knotting. *He must think anything sentimental is...weak.*

I turned on the spot, taking it all in. I felt like I was on the set of a movie, or in a show home but *this is my home now.* I glanced at Radimir. *And he's going to be my husband.*

I stumbled over to the wall of glass and pressed my forehead against it. The rain was coming down so heavily it looked like we were underwater, and I was looking down on a blurry, undersea city. My head went light and my stomach flipped, but it wasn't vertigo. This was the first time since he'd proposed that I'd had a chance to just stop and process things.

I was going to be a mafia wife, like Liliya. Maybe Radimir would treat me a little better than Spartak treated her, but he was still a criminal. People were terrified of him. He *killed* people. It didn't matter how much I was attracted to him, I couldn't *love* him.

I heard him walk over and caught his reflection in the glass. He stopped behind me, watching me. "You must have questions. Ask them." His voice was tight, like he was bracing himself. "They won't be able to make you testify, once we're married."

I didn't turn around. I wasn't sure I could ask this stuff if I looked into his eyes. "How many people have you killed?"

"More than twenty, over the years. I didn't always do it myself, but I gave the order."

"They were all bad people, though, right?"

"They were all part of my world, yes. We don't kill civilians."

Civilians. There was a shock as I realized that's what I was. And then a second shock when I realized that I wasn't, anymore. I didn't have that protection now. If someone murdered me, it would be *Bronwyn Hanford, a known associate of the Aristov mafia family.*

"What do you...*do?* I mean, drugs, or prostitution or...?"

"Mainly what you'd call...white collar crime. Bribes and sometimes blackmail so I know which pieces of land will become valuable. Backroom deals so my property company gets the contract. We run a lot of gambling in the city, move stolen goods, sell guns. We take a piece of other people's activities and we run protection for a lot of neighborhoods and businesses...but no, we aren't involved with prostitution, or trafficking. And we don't sell drugs."

"The man I saw you kill, Borislav. He was...*bad?*"

"He was a rapist piece of shit," said Radimir coldly. He told me about all the women Borislav had attacked, and I felt a tiny bit of the tension in my chest unwind.

"And that's why you killed him?" I asked hopefully.

"No," said Radimir bitterly. He explained about The Eight and their order to kill Borislav, even though he was Spartak's brother, and the two families had a truce. My head started to spin again. *How can he just kill someone, on an order?* I didn't understand his world and I wondered if I ever would. "And if the guy at the funeral..." I asked nervously. "Spartak...if he finds out you killed his brother..."

"He'll come for me," said Radimir. "And everyone close to me." He looked at me and I saw a flicker of fear in his eyes.

My stomach lurched and I must have gone pale because Radimir marched over to me and put his hands on my shoulders protectively. "That'll never happen. He'll never find out."

I nodded weakly but the fear barely receded. *How do they do this? How do they live their lives knowing there are people who want to kill them?* I had to focus on something concrete or I was going to lose it. I pushed off from the window and looked around the rest of the apartment. There was a wet room with a rainfall shower, another bathroom with a beautiful copper, freestanding tub, a gym with a weights bench, floor mats and a punch bag and an office. That only left...

I pushed open the final door and found a bedroom with a king-size bed. I stood there staring at the plump white pillows and crisp sheets as Radimir walked in behind me.

"There's only one bedroom," I said, my voice slow with shock. I whirled to face him. "How is there only one bedroom, it's a freakin' billionaire penthouse!"

"There were three bedrooms," said Radimir, tugging his waistcoat straight. "But I had one converted into a gym, and one into an office. Why would I need more than one bedroom?"

"But there's only one...bed."

We stared at each other. I saw the heat rise and flare in his eyes and felt the traitorous depth-charge of heat bloom in my groin. I quickly looked away and started pacing, running my fingers through my hair. I'd had this thought as soon as he proposed but I'd been pushing it out of my mind. I couldn't put it off any longer. "We need to talk about how this is going to work."

He crossed his arms. "Very well."

"I presume that part of this arrangement is that you get sex. That's the deal, right? I get to stay alive, and you get to do whatever you want to me." My heart was hammering, and my breathing was tight. *From fear. It's completely from fear.* I turned to him. "Right?"

He moved closer and I swallowed. Those frozen-sky eyes had gone molten, and I saw his lips form the shape of *yes.* But he said nothing for a heartbeat, just stared into my eyes. And then—

"If something happens," he said, his voice ragged with lust, "it'll be because you ask for it. I wouldn't touch a woman against her will."

I swallowed. *And now I want him even more.* It was suddenly very quiet. I licked my lips to speak, and his gaze instantly flicked to them. What would it take, right now? Saying his name? Just parting my lips a little? I could feel that *pull* towards him, like I was sliding over a cliff...

I broke his gaze, staring at the floor as I silently counted to three. I had to resist. I had to stay cold and clinical, like him. Negotiate this stuff the way one of the mafia women would.

I lifted my gaze and banished all emotion from my voice. "I guess if this isn't a real marriage, I can't expect you to be faithful."

He hesitated. Then, in a voice as cold as mine, "That's right. There'll be other women."

I tried not to let that affect me. *Why should I care?* I pulled away from him and walked over to the window. *Cold and clinical.* "Fine."

"Fine," he agreed. Then his voice changed. "Wait, are you saying the same applies to you?"

"Well...yeah. If I meet some man and I want to fuck him then—"

I heard him march across the room in three big strides. He

grabbed my arm and spun me around to face him. Suddenly, all pretense was gone. He scowled down at me and the possessive fury in his eyes made me go weak. "You are *not* fucking anyone else!"

"Well...then I guess you aren't, either," I muttered.

He nodded, glowering. But I didn't miss the flicker in his eyes: *relief.*

While Radimir worked in his office, as ruthlessly efficient as a machine, I wandered the penthouse, getting a feel for my new home. I couldn't get over what a long walk it was, from one end to the other. In the bedroom, there was a walk-in closet that was bigger than my entire bedroom. It was full of Radimir's suits, shirts and ties, all meticulously arranged, and it smelled of him.

"I will clear some space for you."

I jerked and looked up. Radimir was gazing at me from his office. How long had he been watching me?

"No need," I told him, and pointed. "My entire wardrobe will fit between your blue shirts and your white shirts."

"I'll buy you more," he said solemnly.

So, I look the part, like Lilliya. The perfect mafia wife. I couldn't imagine power-dressing like the women at the funeral. I spent my life in jeans and sneakers. *He's marrying the wrong woman.*

I dropped onto one of the big leather couches and brooded. I couldn't love him, and I wasn't going to give in to temptation and let him fuck me again, however much I craved that. But if we were going to be trapped in this marriage, I wanted us to get along. *What if I learned Russian?* That would help, right?

I downloaded a language learning app for my phone, put in some earbuds and stretched out on the couch for a few hours, repeating—and mangling—things like *What time is the train* and *I'd like to buy a hat.* When my stomach started rumbling, I went into the kitchen and dug through the refrigerator. There was some weird stuff with Russian labels I wasn't brave enough to try but there was enough regular food that I managed to whip up one of my triple-decker comfort sandwiches with turkey, cheese, tomatoes, mustard, pickles and chips. I made one for Radimir, too. He was on some sort of conference call, so I just set it down on the corner of his desk and quickly retreated. He looked up, surprised, and nodded in thanks.

I hit the Russian app for another hour and then, when my brain was fried, I pulled out a book and lay on one of the couches to read. It was long enough that I could lie on my stomach, my favorite position for reading ever since I was a kid. My mind slipped into the story: I was in sun-drenched Texas and my horse was sick and the only guy who could help her was the one I'd sworn I'd stay away from—

"You'll strain your eyes."

I jerked, rolled onto my side to look up and nearly fell off the couch. I must have been reading for hours because the penthouse was dark. Radimir was standing beside the couch, gazing down at me, his expression unreadable in the shadows. "It's time for bed," he told me, and his accent carved so much into those four words. A touch of humor, like he thought it was cute that I'd gotten caught up in reading. A little protectiveness, as if he really didn't want me to strain my eyes. And an undercurrent of heat that soaked right to my core and rippled down between my thighs.

I put my book down and followed him through to the bedroom. He started to undress, and I watched his body slowly appear. It was the first time I'd seen him with his shirt off in good light and suddenly I couldn't drag my eyes from the hulking, caramel swells of his shoulders and the thick slabs of his pecs. He was so...*hard,* everything deliciously sculpted. Nathan, my ex, had had muscles, too, but they'd looked pumped up, somehow, built over time with gym sessions and protein shakes. Radimir looked like he'd started out big and then his brutal life had stripped away anything unnecessary until there was only muscle left. And there were so many scars: thin, raised lines that had to be from knives and a couple of circular, glossy scars that must be from bullets. I could see his tattoos more clearly now, too, the stars and rose on his chest that I knew must be to do with the

Bratva, and a long string of Russian words that wound around his torso like a rope.

He got into bed and—*wait what the hell?* I'd caught a glimpse of his feet as he slid them under the covers and for a second, it had looked like... *Nah.* It must have been a trick of the light.

He looked at me and I realized I was still standing there fully dressed. *Shit.* I should have quickly shed my clothes while he was occupied. I lifted my hands to the hem of my sweater. *He's already seen me naked. It's no big deal.* But I just couldn't, not with him lying there, watching me. I panicked and darted into the en suite, then stood there gripping the edge of the sink, staring at myself in the mirror. *Are we really going to share the bed, just lie there next to each other all night and not...* I trusted him to stick to the rules. I wasn't sure I trusted myself.

I looked at the bag of clothes I'd brought. *What do mafia wives wear in bed?* Lipstick, stockings and a willing smile, probably. I needed to send a message. I needed to make sure he knew sex was absolutely off the table.

I took off my make-up. Then I dug through my bag and found a dark green nightshirt with a curled-up cartoon raccoon and the words *Sleepy time, now.* I took a deep breath, walked back out into the bedroom and stood there looking at him, head held high. *There. That's as sexy as you're getting.*

Except...it didn't go how I'd hoped.

He turned to look at me and his eyes instantly narrowed in lust. The muscles of his chest and arms tensed, like he was about to pounce, and he actually leaned forward an inch or two before he managed to stop himself. I gulped. But I also felt a deep rush of something like pride. He made me feel more wanted, like this, than Nathan ever had even when I'd been dressed up in silk and lace.

I slipped under the covers and lay on my side, turned away from him. And then, because it felt awkward not to, "Goodnight."

I could feel his gaze sweeping up and down the outline of my body under the sheets. Then, "Sleep well, *Krasavitsa.*" And he turned off the light.

I lay there, my heart hammering, waiting for the first touch of those big hands on my ass, my legs, my breasts. *Any second now.* He'd grab my arm and tug me flat on my back, then kick my legs apart and—

Seconds passed and I fought to make my breathing slow and easy. I didn't want him to know I was lying there expectantly. Ready. *Aching. What's happening to me?*

I was trapped with a monster. One I couldn't resist.

24

RADIMIR

I LAY there staring at her. At that mass of copper hair that spilled across the pillow. At the tiny scrap of pale, bare skin visible between her hair and the collar of her nightshirt. At the hills and valleys her body made under the sheets. *Fuck.* That nightshirt was the sexiest thing I'd ever seen. The way her breasts swayed and bobbed under the soft cotton, making it obvious she wasn't wearing a bra? The way it emphasized her long, bare legs, reminding me that I could just sweep my hands up her thighs and tug down her panties and she'd be ready to go? The way it looked so fucking innocent, but her curves made it so *not...*

I knew I wasn't being rational and that was the problem with Bronwyn: I was never rational, around her. *Why is she so different?* I'd never been so close to losing control with any of the Russian women I'd fucked. What made it worse was that I knew she wanted me, too. I'd seen it in her eyes and now I could hear it in her breathing.

I sighed and stared at the ceiling. if something was going to happen, it had to come from her. I was a monster. But I wasn't going to act like one.

This is going to be hell.

25

BRONWYN

I CAME AWAKE SLOWLY from lovely, tangled dreams. I was a mermaid, wearing my seashell bra, and I was basking in the sun at the edge of a beach in Texas, my tail in the water and my top half cuddled up to the roguish cowboy outlaw who'd helped me save my father's ranch. I wasn't *completely* sure how I'd ridden horses and worked the ranch with a tail, but it'd made sense in the dream. And it had been so *real...*I could still feel the warm press of the outlaw's chest under my cheek and the muscles of his torso under my fingers.

Alarm bells started to ring at the back of my mind. The outlaw felt *too* real. I reluctantly clawed myself the rest of the way awake—

Oh *shit.*

I was lying on my side with my head on Radimir's bare chest. One arm was hugging his waist, tight as a teddy bear, and one leg was wantonly across him, my knee kissing up against the hard bulge in his jockey shorts. I shut my eyes for a second and cursed. Then I began to extricate myself, inch by tentative inch. I drew my knee back from his cock. I unwound my arm from around his waist. Then I slowly lifted my head. *Don't wake up, don't wake up, don't wake up—*

I started to turn my back to him. But at that moment, he gave a sleepy grunt, threw his arm around me and came with me, rolling over on his side so that he was spooning me from behind. I swallowed. I knew he was still asleep because he was snoring softly, his nose buried in my hair like a big, snuffling bear. But his hand had landed right on my breast and his cock was now snugged between the cheeks of my ass.

And it felt freakin' fantastic. I could feel my nipple hardening against his palm and the press of his cock reminded my body exactly how good it had felt inside me, that night at the bookstore. I could feel myself getting wet. God, I almost wanted to...

No. I was *not* going to rub myself off while I was in his arms.

I bit my lip. *But I could just slip a hand down, he'd never notice...*

No! Definitely not! But my hand started to move—

Electronic beeping shattered the silence: Radimir's phone alarm.

A lot happened very quickly.

Radimir came instantly awake, felt my breast under his hand and jerked his hand back. I snatched my hand back from my groin. Both of us sat up in bed, staring at each other.

"I'm sorry—" he started.

"It's okay!"

"I must have...*Chyort!*" I was guessing that was some sort of Russian curse. He ran a hand through his hair, guilt stricken. "I was *asleep!*"

"It's alright." I knew I should come clean and say I'd grabbed him first, but I wasn't that brave. "I'll, um...go jump in the shower."

The shower in the wet room was fantastic, like standing under a waterfall. As the water beat on my shoulders, I tried to figure out what the hell we were going to do. The three weeks until the wedding were just the beginning: we were going to be trapped together *forever.* This sleeping-in-the-same-bed-but-no-sex thing couldn't last, not when we wanted each other this much. But I kept reliving the moment I'd seen him kill Borislav. He really *was* a monster, and I couldn't love a man like that. *So how does this end?*

When I reluctantly dragged myself out of the shower and got dressed, I found him whisking eggs in the kitchen. He gestured to a stool at the kitchen island and I sat, staring as he crushed garlic with the side of a knife. "You can *cook?*" I asked, amazed.

He didn't answer, just carried on cooking, chopping herbs and adding them to the mix. But then, his eyes still on the food, he said, "My brothers were young when I brought them to America. I had to feed them on a budget."

He brought them here? Were his parents already dead, by then? What happened to them? I had so many questions but I was getting big, heavy *don't ask* vibes, so I stayed quiet.

He hadn't put his waistcoat and jacket on, yet. As he cooked the omelets, his white shirt kept pulling tight around the hard globes of his biceps and the slabs of his pecs, and that reminded me of how good that warm muscle had felt when I'd been cuddled up to him...

I tore my eyes away, flushing, and glanced around the apartment. Last night's storm clouds had disappeared and the sky was a fierce pale blue. The whole penthouse was drenched in sunlight and the view across the city was amazing: I could see most of Chicago.

Radimir slid an omelet onto my plate, and I dug in. It was amazing, light and fluffy and dotted with little pieces of salty goat's cheese and juicy ham. He'd made coffee, too. "Thank you," I said, sincerely. "This is...amazing."

He glanced up from his food and caught my eye, then gave me one of those curt little nods. My chest went tight: he was *trying*. And God, he looked good, sitting there in his shirt sleeves. But I couldn't ignore what he was.

Something else I couldn't ignore: my joints. My hands were stiff, and the pain in my knees had been getting steadily worse over the last week. I could tell I was heading into a major flare-up, which might last a month or two. By the time the wedding came, I wouldn't be able to walk down the aisle. And even though the whole thing was fake, some stubborn part of me refused to let my illness spoil the big day. Fortunately, there was something I could do, even if it had consequences. I messaged my Rheumatologist and got lucky: she had a cancellation and could see me that afternoon.

Just as we were finishing breakfast, a delivery driver arrived with two packages. They were addressed to Radimir, but he passed them both to me.

I opened the first one, mystified. Inside was a shallow black box and when I opened the top, I was staring at a glossy black rectangle with raised silver letters: *B. Hanford.* "What is this?" I asked.

"A credit card."

"I know it's a credit card. I didn't sign up for one."

"It's on my account. The bills will come to me." He gestured at the penthouse, himself, everything. "You didn't choose this. I can at least make sure you're comfortable."

I gawped at the card. "What do you think I'm going to spend it on?"

He opened and closed his mouth a few times. "...shoes?"

I showed him my battered sneakers. "You really don't know me at all, do you? Look, thank you, but...I'll earn my own money." I pushed the card across the breakfast bar to him.

He frowned, then sighed and his eyes softened, like I'd impressed him. "Then don't use it," he said, pushing the card back to me. "But at least keep it in your purse, in case you change your mind?"

I nodded reluctantly, took the card back and signed it. Then I opened the second package. A beautiful, slender watch, silver with a white leather strap. "Radimir, this is very generous, but I don't need gifts..."

"It's not for showing off," he told me. "It's for safety." He grabbed my arm, placed the watch on my wrist and buckled it on. I sat there staring: partly because I was shocked into silence but mostly...the brush of those big fingers against my sensitive skin felt incredible. And there was something about the way he cinched the leather strap tight that was very...*possessive.*

He pointed to the watch face. "If you're ever in trouble, turn the bezel a full turn clockwise."

I blinked. "What happens then?"

"I will come for you."

My stomach flipped. *In trouble.* I was a target, now, because I was with him. I looked at the credit card and the watch. *My new life.* Luxury and danger.

Radimir told me he'd drop me at the bookstore on his way to work, even though I was pretty sure it wasn't *on* his way. It was still really early but that was fine: I could get an early start. As we were riding the elevator down, I got a message from Jen. *Want to get lunch? Sadie and Luna are in.*

And that's when I realized that Jen and my other friends had no idea I was getting married.

For a moment, I thought about not telling them until it was all done. I could keep a secret for three weeks. But I already felt isolated enough, with Baba in hospital. I was going to have to do this without a family. I couldn't do it without friends, too. I needed to tell them, even if I had to be economical with the truth. So I typed back *Absolutely.*

All morning, as I worked in the bookstore, I rehearsed different ways of telling them. But by lunchtime I was no closer to figuring it out. I hung the Closed sign on the door and locked up. I felt guilty closing even for an hour, but it was quiet and I had to close to go to my hospital appointment anyway.

The restaurant was just down the street, a little Italian place we'd been going to for years. It was tucked away in a basement, with tiny tables and low ceilings, but the *tagliatelle misto* was amazing and it was loud and chaotic enough that my big news wouldn't draw much attention...I hoped.

The others were already there. Jen was playing a breadstick drum solo on the edge of the table. Luna was almost hidden behind her menu, looking like a baby owl as her big, round glasses peeked over the top. She's a hospital lab technician and the quietest of us. Sadie, the only one of us in a suit, was hunched forward over the table, trying to hear the phone she had pressed to her ear. She's an account manager for an advertising firm and her bosses push her harder than can possibly be healthy.

I've known all three of them since I was eight. When my parents died and Baba took me in, I had to move schools, right in the middle of elementary school, and the kids weren't exactly welcoming. But Jen, Luna and Sadie had already formed their own little group of outcasts and invited me in, and we've been friends ever since.

I slid into a seat, and we ordered. As soon as the waiter had gone, Jen put down her breadsticks and leaned forward. "What is it?"

"What do you mean?"

"You've got that look," said Jen. "Is it the Russian guy again?" She leaned in even more. "Yesterday, you said it was okay. Is it *not* okay? Do I need to break his kneecaps?"

"Who's the Russian guy?" Luna wanted to know.

I tried to get a word in but didn't make it. "Growly suited hottie," Jen told her. "But he chased her out of the store in tears yesterday."

"Why was he in *tears?*" Luna asked.

Jen rolled her eyes. "Not *him, her!*"

I finally got to speak. "Yes, it's him and yes it's okay—" I looked around at them helplessly. *Oh God, how do I do this?* And then I sighed and just *womped* my left hand down in the middle of the table.

All three of them froze and stared at the ring. "I'm gonna have to call you back," Sadie mumbled into her phone, and ended the call.

"What. The. Fuck?" asked Jen, her eyes bugging out. She flagged down a passing waiter. "We need a bottle of Chardonnay and four glasses, *stat!*"

"His name's Radimir. I've been seeing him for about five weeks." I conveniently left out the part where in all that time, we'd spent a few hours and two nights together. Oh, and the part about him being a frickin' Russian mafia boss.

"Five *weeks?!*" asked Sadie, mouth wide.

"I know it's sudden—" I began.

"*Sudden?* Five *months* would be sudden," said Sadie.

"It must have been really...intense," said Jen slowly. "You must have been seeing each other, like, every night, those five weeks." She looked at her plate. "You always say you're too busy at the bookstore to hang out. Why didn't you just tell me you were seeing someone?"

She looked hurt. They *all* looked hurt. I looked around at them helplessly. I really *had* been busy working late at the bookstore. But now I had to pretend I'd been seeing Radimir all those weeks, or they'd get suspicious. "Sorry. I was just worried it might not work out, so I wanted to keep it private."

The wine arrived and everyone went silent as Jen poured four big glasses. *Shit.* They all thought I'd been keeping things from them. I knew Jen would take it especially hard: we've always told each other everything. But I couldn't tell them the truth. If they tried to stop the wedding, or went to the police, they'd be in danger. *Maybe I should have just disappeared,* I thought miserably. *Cut off all contact with them.*

But I'd underestimated them. "So," said Jen, rallying. "A whirlwind romance. But it's probably a long engagement, right?" She gave me a brave smile, determined to be happy for me, and I just melted inside. Even hurt, they were great friends. "What are we talking about, a year?"

I took a big gulp of wine for strength. "Three weeks."

Jen's jaw dropped. "You're *pregnant!*"

"Should you be drinking?" asked Luna gently.

"I'm not pregnant!" Saying it sent my mind spinning in a whole new direction. *Would I have kids with Radimir?* I wanted a family, someday. But I couldn't raise kids in a loveless marriage. And I couldn't love a man like him...right?

"Then why *three weeks?*" Sadie asked. "Don't you think you're rushing into this?"

I took a deep breath. "I know. I know it seems crazy but..." *Crap.* I really wasn't good at lying. I stared at my plate as my mind groped around for an explanation. Then suddenly, it locked onto something. "He makes me feel protected," I told them. "Like no one else ever has. He takes me just as I am. When he found out about my disability, he was fine with it." I thought of how he'd bought the building to save the bookstore. "And he'd move mountains just to make me happy."

Silence. I tentatively looked up and found all three of them wearing big, goofy grins. "You love him," said Jen softly.

I nodded. My stomach unexpectedly flipped, even though it was just a lie. *I could never love someone like him. I could never even have feelings for him.*

Jen looked at Sadie and Luna and all three of them nodded. "Well, okay, then," she said, her voice shaky with emotion. And she stood and pulled all of us into a hug. "If you love him, that's all that matters."

I felt tears prickling my eyes. "Can you all please be bridesmaids?" I croaked. The hug got tighter. They thought I was crying with happiness.

~

I went straight from lunch to my hospital appointment. My Rheumatologist was running late, so I sat in the waiting room trying and failing to lose myself in a book. I hate hospitals. The disinfectant smell takes me back to all the times I've been painfully poked and prodded and that first, scary diagnosis. They're huge and echoey and I always feel small and alone.

Someone sat down next to me. I kept my eyes on my book.

Then I caught that citrus-and-vanilla scent. My head snapped around and I looked right into Radimir's frozen-sky eyes.

"What are you doing here?" I squeaked.

He frowned. "My fiancée is at the hospital. Where else would I be? Now: what's the matter?"

I stared at him. "How did you know I was here?"

"Valentin has been following you." He nodded across the room, and I saw Valentin step out of the shadows.

"*What?!* You had someone follow me?"

"Not *someone.* It's Valentin. He's family. And very good at staying out of sight: you didn't even notice him, did you?"

I glared at Valentin, who at least had the decency to look embarrassed. "No," I admitted.

"And *yes,"* said Radimir. "I had him follow you. I needed to make sure no harm came to you. Now: what's the matter with you?"

I stared at him. It was controlling and arrogant and a violation of my privacy...but it was also protective, in a clumsy way. "The arthritis is getting worse," I told him. "It happens, sometimes: a flare up. When that happens, my Rheumatologist usually changes up my medications and puts me on steroids for a while to damp things down."

He frowned. "Won't that damp down your whole immune system, as well?"

I shrugged. "Yeah. If I catch a bug, it'll be worse. But it's better than the pain. And flare ups could damage my joints permanently if the inflammation isn't kept under control."

His brows lowered and he looked *pissed,* like he wanted to reach inside me, tear the arthritis out and beat it to death on the tiled floor. "I don't want you getting ill. But I don't want you to be in pain, either. There are no other options?"

I shook my head.

Those gorgeous lips pouted, and he nodded. Then he lifted one arm and stretched it out. He did it so hesitantly and awkwardly, I didn't know what he was doing, at first. Then the arm settled around my shoulders, and he pulled me into his side. And however awkward it was, it worked. The arm felt like a protective barrier, shielding me from the scariness of the hospital. I still felt small but for the first time, I didn't feel alone.

When my name was called, I hurried in. My Rheumatologist is fantastic, and she agreed that I needed to change my maintenance medications. As I expected, she prescribed a short course of steroids to calm things down while the new medication was kicking in. But she reminded me I'd need to work hard to avoid catching anything because even a mild bug could make me really sick.

When I came out, Radimir was pacing, restless as always. He didn't see me and I took a moment to just admire him. The elegant lines of his cheekbones. The brutal power of his muscles, even under his suit. He really was gorgeous.

Then I saw a nurse nod towards him and whisper to her friend, and they both blushed and giggled, but went pale when he glanced towards them. A family on their way to visit a sick child, clutching a teddy bear and balloons, saw Radimir and veered off, giving him a wide berth. Two doctors, discussing an x-ray as they walked, broke off to stare at him. "Fuck," muttered one in fear. "That's Radimir Aristov."

My stomach flipped. I'd been seeing these little glimpses of warmth and somehow, between them and the attraction, I'd forgotten what he was. What he was capable of. But everyone else knew, that's why they were scared of him. Radimir Aristov was a cold-hearted killer.

And in less than three weeks, I'd be his wife...forever.

Radimir drove me back to the bookstore and for the rest of the day I beavered away updating displays and refilling tables. But it felt hopeless because there just weren't enough customers. If I didn't figure out some way to get more people through the doors, or cut some costs, or both, I'd be out of business in a couple of months.

I rode the subway to Radimir's neighborhood. When I got above ground, the air was so cold it hurt my cheeks, and I figured it was going to start snowing again any minute. I started walking fast, arms hugging myself for warmth. But then I passed a hotel with golden light spilling out of an open doorway and a sign: *Wedding Expo.*

I slowed to a stop. I'd never been to a wedding show. Nathan and I had never gotten as far as planning things. I felt a guilty little surge of excitement, like the one I'd gotten at age six, pretending to be a princess on her way to marry her prince in one of Baba's old nightgowns.

I knew that my wedding to Radimir was fake. But it couldn't hurt to take a look...right?

I edged nervously inside, down a hallway...and emerged into a huge, warm ballroom lit with fairy lights.

I looked around, stunned. It was a wedding *paradise!*

There were caterers offering free canapes. There were entire stalls devoted to stationery and others to tableware. One big area was given over to wedding cars, everything from a vintage Rolls Royce and a 1950s Cadillac to modern limos and supercars. A string quartet was playing in the corner and wedding bands were offering up headphones so you could audition them. There was a guy who'd carve you an ice sculpture of the two of you for your wedding table and a woman with a guitar who'd write you a song about how you met.

Someone offered me a glass of Prosecco and I wandered deeper. There were photographers and videographers. There were wedding dresses—so many wedding dresses! —and bridesmaid's dresses and groom and usher's suits and even mini-suits in case you wanted your dog to be the ring bearer. There were at least twenty different wedding cakes to try, and cupcakes and chocolate fountains and travel companies selling honeymoon packages...

At first, I just wandered around, stunned. But then someone gave me a free tote bag and once I had a place to put things, I thought I might as well take a pamphlet for this gorgeous country mansion that was offering itself as a wedding venue. And that kind of broke the seal and suddenly I was trying cake samples and wedding bands and having in-depth conversations about stationery. That wedding fantasy I'd had ever since I was a kid started to come alive as I painted in every detail.

Then the lead guitarist of the band I was talking to asked, "Do you know what you'd like for the first dance? Most people pick the first song they ever danced to, or the song that was playing when they met."

I'd been buzzing and glowing, somewhere up near the ceiling. It felt like he'd grabbed my ankle and slammed me down to the floor, leaving my stomach behind. *We don't have a song,* I screamed at myself. *Because it's just a fake wedding you fucking, fucking idiot. It's just to get a marriage certificate, it'll be in a courthouse with Radimir's brothers there to make sure I don't escape—*

"I'm sorry, I made a mistake," I mumbled to the guitarist, and turned and tried to run out of there. But the aisles were blocked by happy, excited brides and now I could feel the tears prickling at my eyes, my vision swimming with them, and I tried desperately not to blink. As I threaded my way through the crowd, my chest started to tremble and now people could *see,* and they were all looking at me in sympathy and that made it a thousand times worse—

As I plunged into the freezing night, a big, heaving sob broke through and I doubled over and just howled, grabbing onto a railing for support. How could I be so utterly, pathetically stupid? How could I forget what this really was? It was snowing again but the cold wasn't enough to cool my face: my tears burned my eyes and made scorching rivers down my cheeks. I cried for all the years to come, trapped in a loveless marriage to a monster. And I cried because now I'd never have it for real: I'd never know what it was to be loved by someone so much that they want to spend their life with you.

People were looking. I used the cotton tote bag to wipe my eyes and then I marched off through the snow, trying and failing to make my face an impassive mask, like one of the Russian wives.

When I got back to the penthouse, I stuffed the tote bag and all the pamphlets I'd collected into a drawer and slammed it shut.

26

BRONWYN

I HADN'T HAD the nightmare for three nights. I'd been hoping that meant I'd finally shaken it off and left it to die in Baba's apartment. But that night, as I lay sleeping in the penthouse, it caught up with me.

It was a beautiful Fall day and the trees outside our house had formed a rustling, gold-and-scarlet canopy overhead. Already, the sidewalk was ankle deep and just the *whump* of me slamming the door of Baba's Volvo made another few leaves drift down.

The drapes were still closed, even though it was past nine. "We're a little early," muttered Baba. "They may still be asleep." It *was* Sunday and dad *did* like his Sunday morning lie-ins, sprawled on his back, shaking the house with his snores. She ruffled my hair. "Want to go to the park for a little while?"

I grimaced. "I need the bathroom." Then I thought of something and grinned. "Give me your key, I'll sneak up and surprise them."

Baba considered. "Okay," she said at last. "But if their bedroom door's closed, you *knock* before you go in there, you hear?"

I nodded and she passed me the key. I bounded up the steps with an eight year-old's enthusiasm and slotted it into the lock, then quietly turned it. Hopefully I could make it all the way to their room without waking them.

I inched open the door and started up the stairs, quiet as a cat burglar. I couldn't hear my dad snoring...were they already up? But the kitchen was quiet, and the lounge was dark. I crept higher and peeked around the landing. Their door was ajar.

I was on the last stair when a floorboard creaked. I froze, wincing...but the bedroom stayed silent. I opened the door a little wider and slipped inside, and now I could see the mountain of my dad's body under the covers and the smaller, slimmer hill of my mum, nestled alongside him. I grinned and slunk sideways, planning my attack. This had to be *perfect.* A jump onto the bed, then a second jump right on top of my dad, and as he came awake, I'd ride him like a whale.

One. Two. *Three!*

I jumped up onto the bed and then launched myself forward, starfishing myself atop my dad. *"It's morning!"* I yelled and then clung on tight, waiting for the grumpy earthquake.

But he didn't move. At all. Neither of them did. *They knew,* I realized. They'd heard me creeping up the stairs and they were pretending to still be asleep.

There was only one thing for it: *tickles!* I snaked my hands under the covers and found the backs of their necks, tickling madly—

But they didn't move. And they were cold. There was a lurch in my chest as it clicked that something was very wrong.

"Wake up." I took a shuddering breath. "Wake up!" My voice went brittle as I shook them. "Wake up! Wake up! *Wake up!*"

I surfaced in a blind panic, soaked in sweat. I scrambled out of bed and crawled across the room, trying to get as far away from the memory as possible. I made it to a corner and pressed myself against the wall, hyperventilating. And then, as I came fully awake and remembered for the millionth time that *it wasn't just a dream, they're dead,* I started to cry.

The bed creaked as Radimir got up. He moved cautiously around the bed, trying to find me in the dark, then slowly padded over to me.

"Bronwyn?" He switched on a lamp and stared at the tears flooding down my cheeks. "What is it?"

I wanted to say *nothing, a nightmare.* But I was still eight, still feeling their cold skin under my chubby little hands. And at the same time, I was twenty-seven and they were gone and never coming back and Baba had left too, and Nathan had left, and I was all alone and now I was locked in this marriage forever and—I looked up at him through a haze of tears and shook my head helplessly.

He slipped his arms around me and hugged me to his chest. And I threw my arms around him and clung on *hard,* like he was a six-foot teddy bear. He smoothed my hair. "Shh *Krasavitsa,*" he breathed. "I'm with you."

It made no sense: he was a monster, he'd killed a man right in front of me, and he was the reason I was never going to be able to fall in love and marry someone for real... But I clutched him and sobbed into his shoulder, my tears rolling down his back, and gradually, my sobs started to slow. I unwound myself, sniffing and embarrassed.

"What was it?" he asked, his voice surprisingly gentle.

I shook my head.

He turned around and awkwardly sat down next to me so that we were side-by-side against the wall. His shoulder snugged up against mine, huge and warm. "Tell me," he said, his voice gentle but firm.

I gaped at him. Tell *him?* I barely told anyone. *I'm an adult, I should be over it by now.* But he stared back at me, those frozen-sky eyes infinitely patient.

And, haltingly, I told him the whole thing. "It was carbon monoxide poisoning," I said when I'd finished. "A seal had gone. A two-dollar piece of rubber." I closed my eyes and rested my chin on my knees, all talked out. After a few seconds, I felt his arm wrap around me and his hand gently squeeze my shoulder, and we stayed like that until his phone alarm went off, telling us it was morning.

"Thank you," I said awkwardly, as he strode across the room and silenced his phone. I felt better for telling someone, even if he was the last person I ever thought I'd tell.

"You needed someone," he said simply.

I looked at my toes, embarrassed. "It was just a nightmare."

He shook his head. "They're not *just* nightmares." He looked away...and then his jaw set, and he seemed to make a decision. "I know," he admitted. And then he turned and walked out, headed for the bathroom.

He has them too. I stared at his retreating back, stunned. What could give a man like *him* nightmares?

The next day, I borrowed Jen's car so that I could move my stuff into Radimir's penthouse. I was hoping that having my things there would make it feel a little more like home. Jen's car is a twenty-year-old station wagon that droops on its suspension like it's permanently depressed, and it still has butterfly stickers along its sides from when it was a rolling advertisement for Jen's failed home-visit nail salon business a few years ago. But it's still six thousand times better than my car because I don't *have* a car.

The elevator at my place still wasn't working so packing my stuff into boxes and getting them all down the stairs took ten journeys up and down four flights and by the end of it my knees and ankles were so tight with pain that I could barely push the car's pedals. With hindsight, I probably should have waited a few more days to let the immunosuppressants kick in. But I was here now, and I wasn't giving up.

I grimly drove to Radimir's penthouse, parked in the underground parking lot and started taking boxes up in the elevator, then carrying them along the short hallway to his place. By my third trip, my legs were *shot.* I kept staggering sideways like I was on the deck of a rolling ship. I was slumped against the wall, trying to gather up the strength to carry on, when I heard a stern Russian voice behind me. "What are you doing?"

"Moving," I grunted, not looking around. I tottered another few steps. I wouldn't let him see me being weak.

"I can see that." Radimir sounded testy. "But do you have to kill yourself to do it?" He stalked over and plucked the box from my arms like it weighed nothing. I glared. "There are people who do this sort of thing," he told me.

"I can't afford a moving company," I kept my eyes on the door of his penthouse and stumbled another step.

"I would have paid for one," he snapped. Why was *he* in a bad mood? Was he worried I'd drip sweat on the carpets? Which, to be fair, I was. He marched off into the penthouse and put the box down. I tried to hobble after him, but the first step made my left ankle light up cherry red with pain and I had to grab the wall to keep from falling.

Radimir marched back to me, his face furious. I avoided his eyes. He ducked and—

"Stop!" I yelped as he scooped me up. "You don't need to—Jesus, you can't just *pick me up* whenever you—"

"I *can* and I *will*." He straightened his legs, boosting me into the air and cradling me against his broad chest, and I went a little heady. *Just head rush,* I told myself angrily. He stalked into the penthouse and laid me gently on the couch. "*You* will stay there. I will be your moving company."

"But—"

"No *buts*." He glared at me and—

It was the first time I'd met his eyes. I could see something flickering, behind all that frozen gray. A deep, protective need.

He *was* mad. But not at me, at himself. He thought he'd caused me pain, by making me move in with him. I swallowed and went quiet.

Radimir marched out into the hallway, and I finally listened to my body and let myself just flop on the couch. I was pretty sure that if someone poured cold water over my knees and ankles, steam would billow off them.

He carried the boxes in two at a time, arranging them in precisely straight rows. By the time he was done, I was capable of helping again, even if I wasn't capable of standing. I crawled over to the boxes, opened one and started figuring out where things were going to go.

Radimir paced around as if he didn't want to interfere but wasn't going to leave me alone to over-exert myself, either. "What's this?" he asked, touching a four foot long *something* wrapped in towels that was leaning up against the wall.

"Nothing!" I grabbed the bundle and put it protectively behind me. I'd hide it somewhere later.

"What's in this one?" he asked, nudging a box with his toe.

"Books."

"And this one?"

"Also, books."

He nodded politely but he looked bemused. As if reading, relaxing, doing anything fun was alien to him. *Does he do anything aside from work?*

I dug through the box and pulled out a blanket. It was hand-knitted, a mix of pink, pale green and yellow.

"What's *that?*" He sounded annoyed but curious. Maybe annoyed *because* he was curious.

"Baba—that's my grandmother—knitted it for me. It's been on my bed ever since I was a kid." Just running my fingers over the soft wool made me feel better. Then I looked around at the penthouse, sighed and stuffed it back in the box.

"What are you doing?" he asked.

I gave him a look. "It doesn't fit in here." I waved at all the stainless steel and granite, at the designer light fittings that probably cost more than my rent. "This place is too...cool."

He pulled the blanket from the box and stalked into the bedroom. Through the open door, I saw him spread the blanket out on the bed. I felt myself bite my lip, and a warm ache started to spread through my chest. *Don't,* I warned myself.

He walked back to me, scowly and gorgeous. "This..." he blurted, gesturing at the penthouse. "Not having personal things...it's not...*cool.*"

And suddenly, everything flipped around in my head. When I'd first seen the bare, soulless penthouse, I'd assumed he'd ruthlessly shed all his personal belongings because he saw them as a weakness.

But what if...what if he never had any? What if he lost *everything,* every photo of a loved one, every heirloom, every beloved childhood toy.

I saw the ice in his eyes fracture and melt and he quickly looked away. I was right.

"Tell me where you want things," he told me. "So, you don't have to move."

I nodded quickly and started unpacking. But inside, my mind was whirling. *What the hell happened to his family?*

27

BRONWYN

THAT EVENING, Radimir came with me to see Baba. I tried to tell him that he didn't have to come but...

"She raised you after your parents died?" he'd said.

I'd nodded.

"Then she is like your mother. And she will want to meet the man who's marrying her daughter." And he'd given me a look I was getting to know, the one that said his mind wasn't going to be changed, and I'd sighed and nodded. But I was worried. I had no clue how Baba was going to react to him...or to the news I was getting married.

As we walked in from the parking lot, a guy was coming out. He screwed his eyes closed and inhaled and suddenly Radimir pushed me behind him...just in time to get the guy's sneeze in his face. "Cover your mouth next time!" he snapped at the guy. The guy scuttled off, terrified. And I stood there blinking in shock. *He's trying to stop me from getting ill.*

Outside Baba's room, I put my hands on his chest to stop him. "Let me go in first," I insisted. "And let me do the talking." I took a deep breath...and went in.

Baba was sitting in her chair, like always, looking as if she hadn't moved since the last time. It broke my heart when I knew what a ball of energy she normally was. "Heyyy," I said lamely, pulling up a chair. "Um. Listen. Announcement. There's someone I'd like you to meet."

I looked towards the door. Radimir took my cue and walked in but...something was different. He was still as big and intimidating as always but he looked sort of...humble. He dipped his head in deference to Baba, as if she was the most important person in the room. "Mrs. Hanford," he said in that carved-ice accent.

Baba's head lifted and I saw her focus on his face. She was fighting the brain fog, and it made my chest go tight.

Radimir sat down beside me. "Radimir is, um." I swallowed and then swallowed again. "We're, uh...he's going to..."

"Mrs. Hanford, I'm going to marry your daughter," said Radimir. He took my hand and squeezed it, and something swelled in my chest, a bubble that threatened to lift me right out of my seat. I tore the bubble open and crushed the shreds back down. *He's just pretending,* I told myself viciously.

Baba gave me a look I hadn't seen since she caught me and Jen with a bottle of beer, aged seventeen. She managed to raise one eyebrow. *What's going on?!*

"It's okay," I promised. "Honestly." The last thing I wanted to do was worry her. I told her the same story I'd told my friends: that he was a Russian property developer, that we'd been seeing each other for a while, but had kept it quiet. But Baba wasn't stupid. She knew something was wrong.

To my surprise, it was Radimir who managed to reassure her. He was polite, respectful and engaging: he even managed to make her laugh a few times. We stayed for over an hour and by the end, it seemed like Baba at least wasn't going to call the police, even if she was still suspicious.

As we prepared to leave, I saw him looking around at the cramped, windowless room with its peeling paint and dirty plates. When we closed the door, he tugged his waistcoat straight. "This is *unacceptable,*" he told me. He looked up and down the empty, echoey hallway. It really was like a prison. "Do the staff even go into her room?"

I shook my head, my stomach twisting. "I know it's horrible. But she needs constant care and this is the best I can afford."

He took my hand. "Come. We're going to look for another facility."

"But—"

"The best one *I* can afford."

I felt my eyes go wide. "*What?* I can't let you do that!"

He turned to me. "She is your family. I will look after her like I would *my* family."

I stared at him, tears filling my eyes. I felt like this huge, warm wave was lifting me up: I'd been out on my own, worrying about Baba, for so long, and suddenly it felt like there was someone with me. But there was another feeling, too: as my feet lifted off the ground, I knew I was losing control. If I let him do this, Baba and I would be dependent on him. What if he used it against us?

I stared into those frozen-sky eyes. Then I took a deep breath...and nodded. I couldn't explain it but, despite what he was, I trusted him.

After a few internet searches, we found a facility that specializes in stroke rehabilitation. I figured that because it was already late, we'd have to visit it tomorrow. I hadn't realized the lengths places will go to for ultra-rich clients.

We were given a guided tour and shown the spa pools and physiotherapy center, the art, sculpting and games rooms, the gardens... I met the nurses who'd be on Baba's team and saw the kitchens packed with nutritious, hand-prepared food. "We'll build a program especially for your grandmother," the manager told me. "There are also some drug therapies we can try to see if she responds. They do come with some additional costs, though."

"The cost is not an issue," Radimir told him. I squeezed his hand in thanks...and that's when I realized I'd been holding his hand throughout the tour. We'd just sort of done it naturally, and it felt so comforting and right. *What does that mean?*

Back at the penthouse, I took his hands in mine. "Thank you," I said with feeling. "Thank you."

He looked embarrassed. "Your family," he said simply. "My family."

It made me think of how he'd reacted to the blanket Baba knitted. Was he being kind to my family because he didn't have one of his own? "Radimir?" I asked gently. "What happened to your parents? Why did you have to bring your brothers to America on your own?"

He sighed and hung his head. His hands squeezed mine. "*Krasavitsa...*" he said at last, "please, don't ever ask me that again."

I felt my chest contract. I could hear the ragged pain in his voice, and I wanted to help. But—

Three loud bangs on the door, shaking it on its hinges. "*Chicago PD! Open up!*"

28

RADIMIR

I CHECKED the door viewer and then swung the door wide. Two people, both in suits. Not uniformed officers but detectives. Alarm bells started ringing in my head.

"Detective Winwick," said the woman. She gestured at the man standing next to her. "Detective Bickel. Can we come in?"

It's always a tricky dance, when I'm dealing with the police. I didn't have to let them in, but objecting would be suspicious. I keep the penthouse clean: there was nothing there that could incriminate me. A week ago, I wouldn't have cared if they entered. But now, with Bronwyn there and her possessions everywhere, it didn't feel like a sterile, throwaway place. It felt like a home. *Our* home. And I resented them invading it.

I stepped back and wordlessly held the door open. The two detectives trooped in. Bickel was big and powerfully built, with a slick, midnight-blue suit. Winwick was tall, blonde, and very pretty: I got a hint of her perfume as she passed, like sweet spice and exotic berries. But there was only one woman I cared about. Bronwyn had retreated into the main room and was standing behind an armchair, looking terrified.

"And who are you?" Detective Winwick asked. Her smile was

sweet, but I could see her eyes assessing, measuring, trying to get a read on Bronwyn.

"My fiancée," I said, scowling. I sat down on one of the couches and motioned the detectives to another. I was hoping Bronwyn would take the hint and escape to another room. She didn't need to suffer this. "What's this about?"

Winwick looked me right in the eye. "We're investigating the murder of Borislav Nazarov."

I didn't so much as blink, despite the snakes twisting in my stomach. I've had a lot of practice being questioned. "I heard it was an accident."

"New evidence has come to light," said Winwick. "So, I'm curious, where were you, about 10pm on the sixth?"

Bronwyn hadn't left. She was still standing there, shifting from foot to foot. She'd probably never had any contact with the police and that thought unleashed a fresh wave of protective need. She didn't deserve to get in trouble. *Get out of here,* I silently willed her. "*I'm* curious why you'd come to me," I told Winwick. "I'm a well-respected businessman."

"One with past ties to the Nazarov brothers," said Winwick. "I've done my homework. And you haven't answered my question. Where were you?"

I swallowed. I didn't have an alibi. I hadn't thought I'd need one because I'd staged the murder to look like an accident. But apparently I'd missed some detail, probably when I ran to go after Bronwyn. "This is ridiculous," I told her, standing up.

"We can talk about this here, now," said Winwick, her voice rising in excitement, "or we can talk about it downtown. One more time, Mr. Aristov: *where were you?*"

Bronwyn suddenly stepped forward. "He was with me."

29

BRONWYN

Every head turned to me. My stomach dropped forty floors to the basement. *What the fuck did I just do?*

Detective Winwick looked at Radimir. Then she glanced back and forth between the two of us, maybe trying to figure out our real connection. "Are you sure you have the right night?" she asked. "Think carefully, now."

She was giving me an out. All I had to do was shake my head and walk away. And Radimir was glaring at me, furious. *He* wanted me to walk away, too, and let him take the heat.

But I couldn't do that. Not just because the guy he killed had been a rapist. Because I didn't want Radimir to go to jail. "I'm sure," I said.

Detective Winwick pressed her lips together. "Alright," she said. "Why don't you sit down and tell me about that night?"

Oh shit. Naively, I'd been hoping that *he was with me* would be all she needed. On legs that were suddenly shaky, I walked around the couch and sat down next to Radimir, directly across from Winwick.

"What's your name?" asked Detective Winwick.

"B—Bronwyn. Bronwyn Hanford."

She smiled encouragingly at me.

Oh my God, I'm about to lie to the police. I'd never even spoken to a cop before. I knitted my fingers together. *Wait, that looks guilty.* I gripped my knees instead, my palms sweaty. "Um..."

Detective Winwick leaned forward, a slinky cobra ready to strike. I was way out of my depth and she knew it.

I fumbled for a story, my heart crashing against my ribs. *We stayed in and watched a movie. No, then she'll ask which movie. He was working late at the office. He's a workaholic, that fits.* I opened my mouth. *No, idiot, I said he was with me and why would I be at his office?* I clamped my mouth shut again.

"In your own time," said Detective Winwick sweetly.

Oh shit, I can't do this. Nothing I came up with sounded remotely convincing. "Uh..." I saw Winwick's lips twitch in victory—

"We were in his car," I blurted.

Everyone stared at me. "In his car?" asked Winwick.

"Yeah. I'd been to visit my grandmother at the care facility she's in. A little before ten, I was walking home and... Radimir drove up beside me and offered me a ride home. Except he didn't take me home. He parked in a side street and fucked me in the back seat."

Winwick stared at me, not even trying to hide her disbelief. "You and Mr. Aristov were...making love at the time of the murder?"

"I mean..." I swallowed. "I wouldn't call it *making love.*" I knew my face was red, but I just went for it, letting the memories spill out. "He ripped my bra off. Licked my breasts. Shoved my jeans and panties down and started fucking me. Hard and deep. But we didn't stay like that. After a while he turned me over onto my hands and knees—well, just my knees, really, because he was holding my wrists behind my back. By the time we got our clothes back on, it must have been more than an hour." I stared right into her eyes. "Is that okay, or do you need a blow-by-blow?"

Now *she* was blushing. "No, that's...um..." Her eyes searched my face, confused, as if she was convinced by my lie but knew something was off. At last, she sighed. "I'll be in touch if I need anything else."

The two detectives filed out. When the door closed, I shut my eyes and flopped back on the couch, a limp jellyfish. The couch creaked as

Radimir twisted around and I felt him glaring down at me. I grudgingly opened one eye.

"You shouldn't have done that," he told me.

"If I hadn't, you'd be in handcuffs right now."

He cocked his head to one side. "How did you lie like that?"

"I wasn't lying, exactly..." I avoided his eyes. "It was a fantasy. I had a fantasy about you, the night we met."

His voice roughened with lust. "A fantasy with all those details? Me ripping your bra off?"

I got up and stomped over to the kitchen area. "Yes."

I heard him get up and follow me. "You on your hands and knees and—"

"*Yes,* okay?"

The room went very quiet. I didn't look at him, but I could feel the glow of pride and lust coming from him. Then: "I had fantasies about you, too."

My feet turned me around without me willing them to. I looked up at him and his gray eyes were scalding, melting me...

And then suddenly, I *shook,* a whole-body shiver that left my stomach churning. My whole life, with my folks and then with Baba, I'd always been raised to stay out of trouble. The police only chased the bad people, the criminals, and now suddenly I was one of them, an accessory to fucking *murder,* I could go to *jail,* for *years* and—

Radimir rushed forward and grabbed me, and I slumped against him. My heart was going faster and faster, out of control, and the shaking wouldn't stop. "*What's—Why am I...?*"

Radimir crushed me against him. "It's the adrenaline," he told me. I could hear the pain in his voice, the guilt that he'd put me through this. "It'll pass." And he began to stroke his palms up and down my back. It wasn't sexual, it was calming. Caring. He pressed his chin against the top of my head and cursed in Russian. Then, "I'm sorry I got you into all this," he muttered.

He held me like that for a long time and I gradually felt my heart slow. I moved back from him, looking up in wonder. There was another side to him, one nobody saw. I thought back to what we'd been talking about, just before the police arrived. What happened to him and his parents...and was that why he was so cold? I wanted to help him, but he'd made it clear the subject was off limits. I'd have to wait until he chose to go there.

"How did they know?" I asked in a small voice. "The police. How did they know it wasn't an accident?"

He squeezed my shoulders. "I don't know. But I'm going to find out."

30

RADIMIR

An hour later, Valentin, Gennadiy, Mikhail and I sat down at the big table in Gennadiy's dining room. "What's going on?" I asked.

Gennadiy sighed and leaned forward, steepling his fingers. "According to our guy in the police, they know it was foul play. They found a partial footprint in the bathroom: someone wearing shoes, and Borislav was naked."

"How have they found it *now?!*" I demanded. "It's been almost a week! Borislav is in the ground! I thought they'd closed down the crime scene and gone home!"

"They had," said Valentin sympathetically. "Spartak has cops in his pocket just like we do. Word is, he suspected it was murder and pushed them to go back and take a second look."

I put my head in my hands and unleashed a long string of curses. It had been raining that night, my shoes had probably been wet and dirty. Why hadn't I checked the floor before I left? But I knew the reason: I'd been racing after Bronwyn. I lifted my head and looked around the table. "I'm sorry," I said solemnly. "I fucked up."

Gennadiy reached across and patted my hand. "You're human, brother, much as you like to pretend it's not true." The others nodded sympathetically. But Valentin looked drawn and tense. He was probably thinking that it should have been *him* in that bathroom, doing our family's dirty work. *If I'd let him, we wouldn't be in this situation. He* wouldn't have been running after his lover. But I'd been too determined to protect him... I cursed again.

"The good news is, the police don't know it was you," said Gennadiy. "All of the families have had visits from the police."

"The bad news is that Spartak has heard," said Mikhail grimly. "He knows now that his brother was murdered. He's called a meeting of all the families. He wants us there *now.*"

"Your woman—" Gennadiy began.

"She has a *name,*" I cut in.

He nodded apologetically. "Bronwyn. Is she going to be able to handle this?"

I glared at him. He'd wanted to kill her. That had always been his preferred solution, cleaner and simpler than marrying her. And what really bothered me was...if the situation was reversed, if he or Valentin or Mikhail had gotten themselves involved with a woman, I knew that I would have been pushing *them* to kill *their* lover, to protect them, just as he was trying to protect me. "She's already lied to the police for us," I said. I thought of how hard she worked, how she refused to quit despite being in constant pain. "She's tougher than you think!" It came out sharper than I meant it to, and I felt my face heat.

We both dropped our gazes. I stood up. "Let's go and see Spartak," I muttered.

Spartak could have held the meet at his house, or at a club. But he demanded that we all go to an abandoned theme park on the edge of town. The wind whipped snow sideways, rocking the Ferris wheel back and forth a few degrees. Above us, an old-fashioned roller coaster sagged sideways, looking like it might collapse on us at any second. And the haunted house, once comically unscary, had been turned into something genuinely unsettling by mold and rot, the roof sagging and the broken windows gaping like jagged maws. At one in the morning, in the middle of a snowstorm, there was no one but us for miles and Spartak's message was clear: he could kill us all and no one would know.

We formed a circle: about twenty of us, the same mafia families who'd been at Borislav's funeral, but everyone had left their partners at home. Spartak was in the center and the instant I saw him, my chest contracted in fear. He was stalking around like a riled-up bull, his fury so great that he couldn't stand still.

The last person arrived, and Spartak's men formed a wider circle outside ours. "For security," Spartak told us. But they faced inward, not outward, their guns at the ready. My stomach started to churn.

"My brother," spat Spartak, "has been murdered. And everyone with a motive is standing in front of me." He paced around the circle, glaring into faces. People gulped and tried to meet his gaze.

Spartak reached our side of the circle and stared at Valentin, then Mikhail, then Gennadiy...and then me. "I'm going to find out who it was," he told us. "And when I do, I'm going to take whoever you care about most and make you watch while I take them apart, piece by piece."

I imagined Bronwyn, screaming and bloodied, and wanted to throw up. But as Spartak stared at me, I forced my expression to be stony and cold. A flicker, and I was dead.

Spartak finally nodded that we could go. I climbed into the car, shaken. I'm used to being threatened but Spartak's threat was suddenly real in a way it wouldn't have been a month ago.

For the first time, I had a weakness.

31

BRONWYN

One evening, a few days after I moved my stuff into the penthouse, I was pushing the vacuum cleaner around while a Russian language lesson played on my ear buds. Suddenly, out of nowhere, I sneezed.

Radimir marched out of his office and gave me a worried look.

I shook my head. “It’s just the dust.” Although...my head did feel a bit weird.

“Why are you cleaning?” he asked. “The maid comes tomorrow.”

“I know, I’m just...” I sighed. I wasn’t used to this lifestyle, yet. I felt guilty about having someone pick up after me. And I felt guilty about spending money: the credit card he’d given me still hadn’t left my purse. I hadn’t taken him up on the offer of new clothes, either: the idea of me in designer dresses and heels just felt ridiculous.

Then I sneezed again, and now Radimir looked *really* concerned. “Dust!” I insisted. But my head was spinning, so I gave in and went to bed. He stayed up late, working in his office: he had a big meeting with a state senator the next day. I was half asleep when I heard him creep into the bedroom, trying not to wake me.

Ever since that first night, we’d slept back-to-back. I’d taken to cuddling a pillow to stop me throwing my arms around him while I slept, and it worked, and he stayed on his side of the bed, too. But...

one side effect of the steroids is insomnia, and there were two or three nights when Radimir thought I was asleep, but I'd seen him in the mirror, lying propped up on one arm, watching me.

The bed creaked and shifted as Radimir lay down. Immediately, the scent of him and the warmth of his body, so close, made the ache start between my legs, growing stronger and stronger until it blocked out everything else. *I could just reach out a hand. Run it over his cock and he'd have me on my back, legs spread, in three seconds...*

But *he killed people.* I couldn't un-know that, couldn't close my eyes to it. So I hugged my pillow tight and tried to sleep.

The next morning, I went to roll out of bed and the movement sent my stomach and brain spinning in opposite directions. I grabbed the mattress and lay very, very still. *Everything* ached and when I tried to reach for my water glass, my arms felt like blocks of lead. The sheets were damp, and my hair was clinging to my face with sweat.

I was sick. *Really* sick, thanks to the immunosuppressants putting my body's defenses on vacation. *Fuck.*

"What's the matter?" asked Radimir. He stalked over and stood over me in just a towel, a rugged, shower-damp colossus.

"Nothing," I lied. "I'm fine." I tried to prove it by getting up but wound up flopping on my back like a sweaty, belly-up turtle.

Radimir frowned and he laid a palm on my forehead. "Call Jen," he ordered. "You're not going to the store today. I'll look after you."

"But you have work."

"I'll take the day off."

Had he ever taken a day off in his *life?* "But you've got your meeting with the *senator!*"

"The senator can wait." And as if to make a point, he pulled on some gray sweatpants and a black t-shirt. I'd never see him in anything but a suit. I hadn't been sure he even owned casual clothes. But he looked amazing in them, the t-shirt showing off his biceps and the sweatpants giving occasional hints of the bulge between his thighs.

I grudgingly messaged Jen, who was happy to watch the store for the day. I knew she needed the money, but I hated asking so much of her when I couldn't take her on full time. *One day,* I silently promised.

Radimir helped me sit up a little and brought me painkillers. Then he brewed me a cup of fragrant, clear tea. "Ginger," he told me. "To settle your stomach."

It worked. By lunchtime, I was less nauseous. Radimir banged around in the kitchen and I heard him chopping and frying. A strange smell filled the penthouse. Then he returned carrying a bowl, which looked absurdly small in his big hands. He perched on the edge of the bed, hulking over me.

"What is it?" I asked weakly. It was steaming and violently red.

"Borscht."

"What is *borscht?*"

"Beetroot soup." He spooned some of it up.

"You don't have to *feed me!* I can—" I tried to grab the spoon but couldn't focus on it, and my hands were shaky. "Fuck."

Radimir lifted the spoon. "Open your mouth," he ordered. Which shouldn't have sounded as sexy as it did. I reluctantly opened and he started to feed me. The soup was actually really good, tasty but light enough not to upset my stomach, and I finished the whole bowl.

After lunch, Radimir tidied the kitchen and then prowled around like a big, sulky bear. There was nothing more he could do to heal me, and I was learning that he wasn't a man who could sit on his hands. When I threw my book down and groaned, he was there in a second, eyebrows raised. "What's wrong?"

"Nothing." I shook my head, which made it spin, and I groaned again and lay down. "I was going to read to take my mind off things, but I can't focus on the words."

Radimir stared at the book. Then he marched over and sat down on the bed. He grabbed the book and turned to the bookmark.

"What are you doing?" I asked cautiously.

He cleared his throat. "*After the dazzling sunshine, the barn is dark, with only laser beam shafts of sunlight lancing down from the cracks between the planks. My eyes adjust and I glimpse him, plaid shirt half off, water droplets sliding down his bare chest as he—*"

I sit up. "*Stop!*"

He stopped and looked at me over the top of the book.

"You can't read that," I mumbled.

"Why?"

"It's romance."

"That much was clear. Lie down."

I lay back down, squirming a little. But he didn't read it mockingly. He sounded a little bewildered, if anything, but he did his best. "*—as he glugs from a water bottle. Then he sees me and lifts the brim of his Stetson. 'I checked in on Shana just now. Don't worry, she's doing better.'*" Radimir looked at me. "Shana is...her sister?"

"Her horse. She's sick. The hero—he's a cowboy called Kurt—is helping heal her. He's in love with the heroine but he won't make a move on her because she's the widow of his best buddy."

"Thank you," said Radimir, and carried on. As the pages turned and he picked up the story, his tone started to relax and lose some of its stiffness. At times, it almost seemed like he was enjoying it. And once I got over my embarrassment, being read to was freakin' wonderful, especially with his Russian accent caressing the words and leaving them silky smooth in places and deliciously rough in others. He read for hours, and I finally drifted off to sleep, soothed by the sound of his voice.

When I woke again, it was dark outside. At first, I thought I was alone but then I heard him breathing. I cracked one eye open and saw him sitting in a chair across the room just...watching me. He'd missed a whole day of work for me, he probably had a million things to catch up on, but he was just sitting there, hunched forward, chin resting on his fist.

His phone rang in the next room. He got up and I closed my eyes, pretending to be asleep.

I heard him take a step towards the door...then he changed direction and came towards me. *What is he doing?* I tried to breathe slowly and steadily.

I could feel him standing over me. He pushed my hair back from my face, staring at me from just a few inches away...

His lips brushed my forehead in a tender kiss. "*Popravlyaysya, Krasavitsa,*" he whispered. *Get well, Beauty.* Then he walked off to answer his phone.

I stayed still and silent, but inside, the warmth of his kiss was spreading through my shocked body. He really did care...and that scared me. I had to burn it into my brain that he was a monster because if I didn't, I was going to do something stupid.

Like fall for him.

32

BRONWYN

WITH EVERY DAY we spent together, the sexual tension wound tighter, until it became a straining guitar string, sending out vibrations that made *everything* sexual.

It turned out that the massive penthouse was actually *tiny*. Somehow, we were always running into each other. I'd have to squeeze between the kitchen island and the breakfast bar while he was standing there, which meant either I faced him and my nipples dragged across the hard curves of his chest, or I faced away from him and felt his cock harden as I stroked it with the cheeks of my ass. Either way, I was twitchy and horny for the rest of the day.

Or he'd come into the bedroom just as I was coming out of the shower in a cloud of steam, naked except for a towel. He'd always do the gentlemanly thing and walk back out so I could change...but not before his eyes raked hungrily up and down my body...and then flicked to the bed. I knew he was imagining all the things he wanted to do to me. I knew because I was imagining them, too.

The lust, I'd expected. What I hadn't expected was how good living with him started to feel. He'd be sitting in his office working and I'd lie on the couch reading, or sometimes watching a movie in Russian to help me learn his language, and I'd look up and see him, and sometimes catch him looking at me, and... I felt *warm,* in a way I couldn't describe. We fitted: he was a good cook and always made breakfast, which suited me fine because I needed help to get going in the morning. But he hated doing the laundry, so I gradually took it over. It was heartbreaking because I was getting a glimpse into how good things could be if we actually loved each other. He even cleaned, running the vacuum cleaner around the place between maid visits because he knew it made me happy.

It was when he was cleaning, one night, that there was a metal clang from the bedroom. I sat up, startled, dropping my book. Then it dawned on me what had made the noise, and I cursed and ran through to the bedroom. But it was too late.

The things wrapped in towels I'd stashed behind the dresser had fallen out. Radimir was staring at two long, shiny tubes of metal with big, hospital-gray handles. My crutches. "I don't need them often," I said quickly. "Hardly ever. Only if things get really bad."

Radimir looked up. "They're fine." His forehead creased. "Why did you hide them?"

I avoided his eyes and said nothing, but he was infuriatingly patient. "They're...*ugly,"* I said at last. "They make *me* ugly." *God, that sounds shallow.* I sighed. "Everyone can see. Okay? Everyone can see I'm..." I waved at my legs. "When I use them, I can't hide it. Everyone *knows."* I looked at the floor, humiliated. I wanted to stuff the crutches *and* myself behind the dresser and hide there forever.

Radimir stepped over the crutches and put his hands on my shoulders. I stubbornly stared at the floor, but he just stood there, his hands warm and calming, until I finally looked up.

"Nothing in the world could make you ugly," he told me. His voice was absolutely level. But I could hear how hard he was working to keep it level, and that made me melt.

I looked at the crutches. "I don't want them to see me struggling," I mumbled.

"They won't see you struggling," he told me. "They'll see you fighting."

That cracked something, deep in my chest, and something

poisonous I'd been carrying around for years started to drain away. My throat bobbed and I nodded, staring up at him...and then I quickly turned and walked away before I did something stupid.

Everyone else, even his brothers, knew him as the cold-hearted *Pakhan,* the Bratva boss. But I kept seeing flashes of another man, maybe the man he used to be, or the man he could have been. What if he could be *again?*

But then there were the times when I realized I didn't know him at all. Early one morning, he was coming out of the bathroom just as I was going in. I was trying not to stare at the way the little jewels of water chased each other down the curving slabs of his pecs and the shampoo bottle slipped out of my hand. I crouched down to grab it and—

I froze, staring at his feet. That first night, it *hadn't* been a trick of the light. He was missing two toes on his left foot and one on his right. *Oh Jesus.* An image flashed through my head: Radimir tied to a chair, trying not to scream, as bolt cutters— God, someone tortured him and it took three toes before he talked?

I realized I was still staring. I grabbed the shampoo and stood, but he knew I'd seen. I looked up into his eyes and I could see the raw pain there. The thing he'd told me never to ask about. *What the fuck happened to him? What happened to his parents?*

33

RADIMIR

It was hell.

Ever since I arrived in America, I'd kept my life pared-back and simple. Suddenly, everything was messy and complicated.

The penthouse used to be ruthlessly bare and efficient. Now it was full of books and blankets and candles—why did women need so many candles? —and there were jars of chocolate hazelnut spread in the cupboards and throw cushions on the couches *even though couches are already soft* and—

And I liked it. I didn't want to admit it, but I liked it. For the first time, it felt like a home. Things that I'd never used, like the leather couches and the enormous copper bathtub, now got used all the time. She'd lie on a couch when she was on the phone to her friends, unaware of how fucking hot she looked, with her denim-clad legs languidly stretched out and her copper hair waterfalling over the arm. And she'd soak in the tub for hours while I went quietly crazy, listening to the sound of the water sloshing in the bathroom and imagining her bare, wet breasts bobbing.

I couldn't take my eyes off her. I used to be able to just robotically grind away at work for hours. Now I kept glancing up, looking through the open door of my office to watch her lying on her stomach reading. I'd fantasize about grabbing her wrist and flipping her onto her back. Bringing my mouth down on her startled lips and filling my hands with those full, soft breasts. Or unbuttoning her jeans and tugging them down to reveal her creamy-white ass, then pulling her up to her knees and burying my face in her pussy, thrusting my tongue deep into her while she gripped the arm of the couch and moaned. I'd lose myself in all the ways I wanted to fuck her, staring at her until she finally looked up and caught me.

But however much I wanted to fuck her again, I wasn't going to touch her...not unless she asked me to. And I knew that wouldn't happen.

She'd never fall for me. She was horrified by the Bratva, and it was part of who I was. Just yesterday, I'd caught two of the Armenian gang dealing on our territory and taken them to the warehouse to teach them a lesson. When I was done, my knuckles were raw, and they were barely alive. *Fall for me? Who'd fall for a monster?* She deserved better.

And it wasn't like I felt anything for her. *Right?* The thought triggered a sudden flutter of...*something* in my chest. She had no idea, but sometimes, while she was still sleeping, I'd just lie there drinking in her beauty: the silky pout of her lips, the way her copper hair spilled across the pillow like fire...

I crushed the feelings down inside. I was fond of the woman. That was all it was.

Work was no escape. It didn't matter if I was in meetings, visiting a construction site or thrashing out the details of something less than legal with my brothers, I was thinking of her.

Like right now. I'd driven past the store even though it was way out of my way, just so I could check on her. But that wasn't enough. I got out of my car and crossed the street, then crept closer until I could watch her through the window. As usual, the place was almost empty, just Bronwyn and one customer. The store wouldn't last much longer if she didn't get more people through the doors, and seeing the stress on her face every day... I scowled, and had to force the feelings back down again. Seeing her stressed...*displeased* me.

I heard breaking glass behind me and turned around, then stared in disbelief. Two guys had just smashed the side window of my Mercedes and were opening the door. Maybe I'd been stupid to leave a car like that unattended in this neighborhood, but it was broad daylight. They must be desperate.

I marched across the street towards them. They'd both gotten into the car and were so busy trying to start it, they didn't see me until I was almost next to them. Then one of them glanced up and his jaw went slack in horror as he recognized me. "Oh holy *fuck,*" he whispered.

He looked about fifteen. The other one wasn't any older and neither of them looked like they'd eaten in a week. "We didn't know!" babbled the one in the passenger seat. He looked around at the broken glass, the wires they'd pulled out of the steering column. "Fuck. Fuck fuck fuck." I saw him glance at his door, wondering if he could run for it before I could get around the car. But then he looked at his friend: he didn't want to leave him.

I grabbed the first one, hauled him out by his shirt and slammed him up against the side of the car. I reached for my gun: I'd put a bullet in each of them and leave them on the street. Word would spread: *those idiots tried to steal Radimir Aristov's car.*

And then I thought of *her.* What she'd think of me. How she'd look at me.

I scowled at the kid. He stared up at me, panting and terrified...

I nodded across the street. "Do you see that bookstore?"

He nodded frantically. "Yes sir."

I reached into my pocket and pulled out twenty dollars. "Go and buy a book."

He blinked up at me, incredulous. "What book?"

"Any book."

He nodded, snatched the money and ran. He disappeared into Bronwyn's bookstore and a few minutes later came back clutching a thick paperback. "Now you," I told the other one, handing him a twenty.

He ran across the street and bought a book, then came back. The two of them stood there clutching their books. "Now what?" one asked.

"Go! Go home," I snapped.

"What do we do with these?" he asked, looking at the books.

"Read," I growled. They ran.

"Hey, I'll do it," said a voice behind me.

I turned around. A kid of about twelve on a bike had ridden up and must have been listening. I put a twenty in his hand and he rode over to the bookstore and went in. He was back a few minutes later with a book. "Want me to do it again?" he asked hopefully.

I frowned, thinking. She'd recognize him if he went in again. "Got any friends?" I asked.

The kid pulled out a phone. He kept his voice low, but I still heard him. "*Crazy Russian dude's giving people cash to buy books!*"

Soon, I had a crowd around me and a steady stream of kids running over to Bronwyn's store. I kept it going until I ran out of cash, then swept the broken glass off my seat and drove to a garage.

That night, I was working in my home office when Bronwyn came and leaned against the door frame. "I had a really good day in the store today."

I glanced up, my face carefully neutral. "Good."

"*Really* good." She came closer and I tried not to watch the sway of her hips. "*Suspiciously* good. Kids kept coming in and buying books."

"Children do love to read."

"One bought a book on Keynesian economics."

I looked down at my work. "Precocious child."

She planted her hands on my desk and leaned forward. I caught her scent, that strawberries and violets smell, and had to look up. She was so close that a few strands of copper hair tickled my nose. Her breasts were swaying forward under her sweater and all I could think about was burying my face between them. But I forced my face to be impassive and just raised one eyebrow.

"Thank you," she said gently.

There was no point denying it. With hindsight, maybe I should have stopped after twenty kids. But the idea of making her happy had been addictive. "You're welcome."

"You can't do that again," she told me.

I pouted and frowned. "Yes I can." I could do it every day and it would barely put a dent in my finances.

She sighed. "I mean...I want to make the store work. But I've got to do it on my own."

I scowled stubbornly. But I had to admire her strength. I hadn't realized it before, but she reminded me of me, when I first came to America, building things up from nothing. "Very well," I allowed.

She nodded gratefully and left me to my work. My eyes followed her as she went into the kitchen area, probably to make one of her enormous sandwiches. I suddenly didn't want to be shut away in here, working. I wanted to be out there, with her...as a couple.

Ridiculous. I had no time for a relationship. I had a corporation to run, an Armenian gang to keep out of our territory and a police investigation to worry about. At any moment, they might find something that linked me to Borislav's murder, and if that happened I wouldn't even make it to jail because Spartak would wipe me and my whole family out in revenge.

And yet... I looked down at my paperwork, but I couldn't concentrate. Even without seeing her, I knew exactly what she was doing, her little ritual burned into my mind. The way she peered into the refrigerator so seriously, figuring out exactly which toppings to use...the way she hummed to herself as she buttered the bread. It was *milyy*. *Sweet.*

My fingers stiffened on my pen. *Since when did I find things sweet?*

Something else was bothering me, too: what had happened with the two car thieves. A few months ago, I'd never have spared them.

It was just a moment of weakness. That had to be the reason, because there was only one other possibility: she was changing me.

~

That evening, we visited Baba at her new care facility. We'd been going every few days and every time, we could see a small but real improvement: she was able to take a few steps, now, with the help of a couple of walking sticks, and she was talking. Her color was better and there was a light in her eyes that hadn't been there before. She was doing so much better that we borrowed a wheelchair and took her to a shopping mall so she could get an outfit for the wedding.

I waited patiently while Baba and Bronwyn debated between six different outfits that all looked identical to me. It should have been infuriating but it wasn't. Every time I glanced at Bronwyn, I felt this *lift* in my chest.

Then Baba sent Bronwyn off to look for a matching hat. As soon as Bronwyn was gone, Baba turned to me. "What's the real story with you and her?" she demanded, her voice slurred but iron hard.

I tried to play dumb. She poked me in the chest with one of her walking sticks, pressing my white shirt so my tattoos showed through. "Don't bullshit me, *Mr. Aristov.* I'm old but I still know who's who in this town. I know what you are. I know there's something going on."

I looked her right in the eye. "And yet you haven't tried to stop the wedding."

"Because I see the way she looks at you," said Baba.

Deep in my chest, childish, giddy hope flickered into life. I looked away and straightened my tie, trying to crush the feeling.

"Be careful, Mr. Aristov." Baba poked me in the chest with her stick again and glared up at me: I knew now where Bronwyn got her fighting spirit. "If you break her heart, I'll beat you to death with this thing."

I looked her in the eye, saying nothing. Then I nodded solemnly.

34

BRONWYN

A FEW NIGHTS LATER, I was stretched out on my favorite couch, reading. It was past midnight and I'd been promising myself I'd go to bed in a minute for the last four chapters. Then I heard the door to the penthouse unlock. *Radimir's home!*

I tried to ignore the lift in my chest. I shouldn't feel *anything.* But I did, and it was more than just the animal attraction of that scowly, gorgeous face and big, chiseled body. It was more than just the way he made me feel safe. There was a tension, when he wasn't there, an ache...

I kept my eyes on my book as Radimir walked into the main room. *No.* I was not, I was *absolutely not* falling for him. "Late night," I said, without looking around. "Want me to fix you a sandwich?"

He grunted. That wasn't like him: he was cold, but always polite. He moved across the room but that sounded different, too. I'd come to know his heavy, impatient footsteps, like he was crushing his enemies under his expensive shoes. Now his steps were slow and faltering. I finally glanced over my shoulder...and went rigid.

Radimir was stumbling across the room, one hand pressed tight against his upper arm. He slumped against the wall for a second, then pushed off, leaving a bloody handprint.

I moaned in panic, jumped off the couch and ran to him. I hooked an arm around his waist and made him lean on me, even though it made my knees burn. "Come sit down! Come on!" He mumbled protests but I ignored him and hauled him along, groaning under his weight. I finally got him to an armchair and eased him down into it. "*There!* Hold on, I'll call an ambulance."

He shook his head. "*Nyet.* No doctors."

"You're *bleeding!*" The arm of his suit was soaked through, and blood was dripping from the cuff. "How much blood have you lost?!"

"I can deal with it," he panted. "I need the bag...bottom drawer, in my office."

I ran to his office, pulled open the bottom drawer and found a red bag. I brought it back to him and opened the zipper. It was a full medical kit, with bandages, syringes and bottles of drugs.

"Thank you," he breathed. He began to take off his jacket but had to stop, wincing in pain. "Go," he grunted. "I can do this."

"No you can't!" I shook my head, staring at the blood in horror. "Jesus. Let me help." I quickly eased his jacket, waistcoat and shirt off him. There was a four-inch gash down the side of his arm, and I felt my stomach lurch, not at the blood but at the thought of someone hurting him. "Who did this?"

"An Armenian." He closed his eyes. "He's dead."

I shook my head in silent horror. How could mafia wives *do* this? How could they wait patiently at home every night, knowing their husbands were out there getting knifed and shot and killed? I pressed a pad of gauze against the wound. It instantly soaked through.

"Pressure," he rasped.

I pressed down on the gauze. He grimaced in pain, and I almost stopped, but he laid his hand on mine. First reassuringly...and then he squeezed my hand a little as if touching me helped.

The bleeding slowed. Radimir opened his eyes. "It's too big to close on its own," he told me. "It will need stitches." He nodded at the first aid bag. "The suture kit, please."

I picked it up and stared at the needle and thread. "You're going to sew your—*No,* you're about to pass out! I'll do it."

He shook his head.

"You looked after *me,*" I told him firmly. "I'm going to look after you." I tried to think calmly. "What can I give you for the pain?"

"A drink."

I ran over to the kitchen and brought a bottle of vodka. He spun the cap off one-handed and took a big slug. I threaded a needle and then, wincing, I slid the needle in and began my first stitch. *"Why?!"* I wanted to know. "Why did this guy stab you?"

"The Armenians are new in town. Young, flush with money, trying to make a name for themselves. They think being a gangster is all about looking cool, like in a video game. They even bought a fancy bar as a base, a place called *Worship.* They've been trying to take over our territory and that led to...a *disagreement.*"

My stomach flipped. A disagreement that ended with a guy dead. But at least it was him and not Radimir. I fell silent and began the next stitch.

Radimir winced in pain. "Talk to me," he grunted. "It helps."

I pulled the thread slowly through. "Talk about what?"

"How is the wedding planning going?"

My stomach went heavy. I focused on suturing, not meeting his eyes. "There's nothing to plan."

"What about the dress?" I could hear the frown in his voice. "And the band? And the cake?"

I slid the needle through again. "There is no dress. There is no band. There is no cake. It's just to get a marriage certificate. We don't need all that stuff."

"Look at me," he said quietly. Then, when I carried on suturing, "Bronwyn, look at me."

I grudgingly looked at him.

"This is the only wedding you'll ever have." He managed to make his voice gentle, despite the pain. "I want it to be special for you. You can have anything you want."

I did another stitch. "What makes you think I even *want* a big wedding?" I asked sullenly.

Without warning, he stood up, thread and needle still dangling from his arm. I yelped at him to sit down but he ignored me, stumbled over to a drawer and pulled it open. Inside was the bag of wedding expo stuff.

He dropped back into the armchair, panting. "Listen to me, *Krasavitsa*." Between the blood loss and the vodka, he was slurring. "I've already ruined your life. I'm not going to spoil your wedding dreams too. Let me do this one thing for you. Have whatever you want. The cost doesn't matter."

Something swelled in my chest, and suddenly I couldn't speak. He *did* care. And he wanted me to be happy. I mechanically did the last few stitches, then bandaged the whole thing up. "There," I told him. "You're done."

He thanked me and talked me through giving him a shot of antibiotics. Then I got him up, through to the bedroom and onto the bed. He passed out almost immediately. But I sat there watching him for a long time.

The next morning, I changed the dressing for him. Despite the wound, he insisted that he had to go meet with his brothers, so I helped him put on a shirt. As I stood in front of him doing up the buttons, my knuckles brushing his abs, he said, "I meant what I said last night. About the wedding."

I looked up at him, then away. "It's irrelevant anyway. People book weddings a year in advance. Ours is a week away. Everything will be booked up."

He shook his head. "You forget who you're marrying."

Later that day, when things were quiet at the bookstore, I tried to sort through my feelings about the wedding. Ever since I was a little kid, I'd dreamed of this magical day, with a big dress and my friends there and me feeling like a princess. It felt wrong to do it with Radimir, when the whole thing was fake. But...he was right, this was the only chance I'd ever have, and throwing away all those childhood dreams felt wrong, too.

And there was something else, something I didn't want to admit to. A fragile silvery butterfly in my chest that made a functional, courthouse wedding feel...wrong.

I decided to make a few phone calls. At least then I could tell Radimir I'd tried. I started with my dream venue, the mansion I'd seen at the wedding expo. "Hi! I was wondering if you had any availability for, um...one week from today?" I asked.

There was a stunned pause. Then the woman burst out laughing. "Oh, darling," she said, syrupy-sweet and just a little patronizing. "Our first free date is two years from now."

I sighed, feeling dumb. "Yeah, I figured."

"Can I ask your names, for our records?" she asked. "And how you heard about us?"

I closed my eyes and rubbed at my forehead. "I picked up one of your brochures at a wedding expo. And the names are Bronwyn Hanford and Radimir Aristov."

She went dead silent. Then, "Just a minute." I heard frantic whispering: all I could make out was the name *Aristov.* Then she came back on the line. "We'd be *honored* to accommodate you next week, Miss Hanford."

I opened my eyes and blinked in disbelief. *What? That's fantastic!* Then I had a sudden, horrible thought. "I don't want you to cancel someone else's wedding for me!"

"We don't have a booking that day," she reassured me. "We're closed for staff training. I mean, we *were* closed. We'll reschedule it."

I could hear the fear in her voice. And when I called caterers, florists and bands, the same thing happened. Radimir had been right: these people's customer base were Chicago's rich and famous, of course they'd heard the name *Aristov* and they were all ready to bend over backwards to avoid offending him...and by extension, me. *Is this what life's going to be like?* I knew some people would relish being feared, but I'd always just wanted to be *liked,* however pathetic that made me.

I'd absently doodled *Bronwyn Hanford* and *Radimir Aristov* on a sheet of paper while I'd been giving our names for the bookings. Now, for the first time, I tried combining them. *Bronwyn Aristov.*

My stomach dropped. It suddenly felt so *permanent.* In a week's time, I'd be married to a man I didn't love.

That silvery butterfly in my chest, again. I didn't love him. Couldn't love him. Right?

35

BRONWYN

THE NEXT DAY, I went dress shopping with my friends. We found the bridesmaid's dresses after only four stores: deep green halter-neck gowns with matching heels. They looked amazing on everyone, but I saw Luna nervously playing with the price tag and Jen looked worried, too. "Relax," I told them. "Radimir has said I can have what I want. And what I want is for you to not have to worry, so it's on me. Your dresses, the bachelorette party...everything."

"I gotta meet this guy," said Sadie.

My wedding gown was harder. There were plenty of dresses that looked great on the store window mannequins, but when I tried them on I felt like an elephant in a tutu. I was giving up hope when Jen led us down a back alley to a tiny place she'd found online. They specialized in designs for curvier brides and as soon as I saw the dress, I *knew*. I listened politely to all the store clerk's patter but as soon as she'd finished, I pointed to it. "Can I try that one, please?"

It was a long, cream dress with delicate silver details, and when I tried it on it was *perfect*. It hugged me just right and the long, slender skirt seemed to add about three inches to my height. There was a train that flowed down my back like a silky waterfall and trailed behind me for a full eight feet. I looked at myself in the mirror and suddenly, it all welled up inside me. *I'm getting married.* I didn't normally get emotional, especially over a *dress,* but—

I burst out of the changing room and looked at my friends. Luna, Sadie and Jen clapped their hands to their mouths.

"It's—" I managed

Luna nodded wildly. Sadie flapped her hand in front of her face to cool her eyes. Jen grinned. "It *is!* It totally is!"

For the first time, I thought about checking the price. My stomach suddenly dropped. Okay, it was beautiful, but I could literally buy a car for that.

Jen saw my face. "He did say anything you wanted," she said gently.

I thought of how serious Radimir had been, the morning after I'd patched him up. He really did want to make me happy. "Okay," I managed. "Okay, *yes.*" I dug out the credit card he'd given me, took a deep breath...and handed it over.

"Now," said Sadie, "I *really* have to meet this guy."

I smiled sadly and looked away. Radimir never willingly interacted with civilians and if they did meet him, they'd be shocked at how cold he was. But on a whim, I called him.

He picked up immediately. "What's the matter?"

"Nothing's the matter. Um. Are you free right now? For coffee?"

There was a stunned silence, and I imagined him staring at the phone, bemused. He never took breaks, even though he worked twelve-hour days. "I have a lot of work to do," he said at last.

I nodded. "I guessed you would. It's fine, I'll see you later."

"Bronwyn, wait. Why was it you wanted to meet?"

I glanced over my shoulder at Luna, Sadie and Jen. "I wanted you to meet my friends." It sounded dumb, now. "I'm marrying you and they've never even met you."

I heard him stand up. Then there was a rustle of fabric, and I knew he'd just tugged his waistcoat straight. "Where are you?"

I told him the address.

"I'll be there in ten minutes."

"But you have work!"

"I also have a fiancée, and this is important to you."

He ended the call. I stared at my phone, biting my lip as a warm bomb went off in my chest.

Ten minutes later, Radimir pulled up in his Mercedes and whisked us all off to a nearby coffee shop. Luna, Sadie and Jen bombarded him with questions and...he was *nice.* Pleasant and patient and as close to warm as I'd seen him. He even managed to not wince too much when Jen patted his arm right where the knife wound was. He was trying. Or...maybe even changing?

My friends loved him. As they were getting ready to go, Jen pulled me aside. "This is still super-fast," she said doubtfully. "But...he *is* kinda great."

I could hear the hurt in her voice: she still thought I'd been having a secret romance with Radimir for weeks and keeping it from her. And I couldn't tell her the truth, or she'd try to save me. "He is," I agreed.

"And he's obviously crazy about you," said Jen.

My heart started racing. I tried to sound casual. "Crazy about me?"

She smirked. "He can barely drag his eyes from you. And when he talks about you, his voice changes. It's adorable."

He's acting. That's what it was. It had to be. I looked over at Radimir. He wasn't *capable* of falling for someone. Right?

Radimir insisted on driving my friends back home, so they didn't have to get cabs. "It's good that you have friends," he said as the last one of them waved goodbye.

"What about you?" I asked.

His jaw tightened. "People like me don't have friends. Civilians don't understand my world. And the people *in* my world all want to stab me in the back. All that's left is family." He put the car into gear, and we accelerated away.

"Isn't there *anybody?*" I asked.

He shook his head. Then, half a block later, he stuck out his lower lip and reluctantly shrugged. "There was one man, once..." He glanced across at me and sighed. "I wasn't always a *Pakhan:* a boss.

When I first came to America, I..." He looked around the car, scowling. "I did what Valentin does now."

He used to be a hitman! That explained how he'd killed Borislav so easily, how he'd dealt with the two men who attacked me in the bookstore. But he hadn't wanted to say it out loud. I realized I was going to have to get used to that: watching what I said in case the car was bugged. "Go on."

"My brothers and I were in New York, back then. I worked for a man called Luka Malakov. This man was Luka's best...*problem solver.* The best in the whole city. He taught me and we became...close." He scowled at the rear-view mirror, not meeting my eyes. "We lost touch when I moved to Chicago."

"You could get *back* in touch," I said gently.

He shook his head. "It was a long time ago.

There was clearly more to it than he was saying, but with Radimir I always knew when a subject was closed. A lot of his past seemed to be off limits. I still didn't know what happened to his parents, or why he and his brothers had come to America. Was he ever going to let me in?

We fell into silence, and I watched him as he drove, the setting sun painting gold highlights along the hard lines of his jaw and cheekbones. God, he was gorgeous. And my gut instinct had been right, back when I first met him. Under all that coldness, he was completely alone...

The feelings had been building for weeks but I'd been fighting, denying, pushing them back behind a dam. Suddenly, as I stared at his profile, that dam began to creak and buckle.

He's alone and he shouldn't be. There's a side to him no one else sees, a side that's good.

The dam started to spring leaks, faster than I could patch it. The feelings began to blast their way through, a firehose that threatened to knock me right off my feet.

He doesn't deserve *to be alone. And he doesn't have to be because... Because...*

The feelings surged and the dam disintegrated.

Because I've fallen for him.

I sat there motionless, barely breathing, my mind spinning. Then I slumped back in my seat, turning it over in my mind.

I'd fallen for him. But that didn't change what he was. I still hated the world he lived in, the senseless violence of the gangs. I couldn't just ignore that. So, for there to be any chance of us working, I had to understand it. Accept it.

"Radimir," I said, my voice a little shaky. "Could you tell me about...what you do?"

He glanced at me and his jaw hardened. "You don't need to know." Protecting me, as always.

I shook my head and put my hand on his. "I *do* need to know," I told him. "I need to understand. I need you to tell me why you do what you do."

He stopped the car at a stoplight and turned to me, frowning. He must have seen something in my eyes because he suddenly inhaled, and his face lit up with hope before he managed to control it.

The light changed and he threw the car into a U-turn. "I can't tell you," He said, his voice tight with emotion. "But I can show you."

I thought he'd take me to see the buildings he'd constructed, or the flashy casinos he ran. But he drove me to one of Chicago's poorest neighborhoods, instead. He offered me his hand, and we started walking down the street, our shoes crunching in the snow.

The first few people to see him shied away and I felt my heart sink. *Everyone's scared of him.* But then the owner of a convenience store hurried out to speak to him. "Mr. Aristov! I wanted to thank you. I would have lost my whole business." As I listened, I pieced together that the city had wanted to close him down over a planning dispute, and Radimir had smoothed things over. Then an old Korean lady stopped to shake his hand. Her son had been beaten up by a couple of cops, and the police department had looked the other way. Radimir had made sure the cops knew never, ever, to do something like that again. It went on and on, as we wandered down the street. Requests for him to use his contacts with the city to get the potholes fixed. Pleas for loans to start businesses, from people who'd been turned down by the banks.

I started to notice something. The neighborhood was poor, but it looked different to others I'd seen. It took me a while to figure out why, because I had to realize what there *wasn't*. There wasn't any graffiti. There wasn't anyone selling drugs. It felt weirdly...*safe*.

I realized not everyone was scared of Radimir. To the poor people, he was a lifeline. He actually listened to their problems and made sure things happened. And he understood what was going on here far better than the people in City Hall who never left their air-conditioned offices.

Radimir pointed at two of his skyscrapers downtown. "All of *that* starts here. This is where my brothers and I started, in this neighborhood. And we're still here. We still run it."

Then Radimir led me down a side street. We walked for a block, crossed an intersection, and suddenly the neighborhood changed. It was still the same kind of housing, but I could feel an edgy desperation in the air. People didn't make eye contact. Stores were boarded up, there were snow-covered mounds of trash between the houses and there was what looked like a crack house on the corner.

"This is what happens," Radimir told me, "when no one is in charge."

And for the first time, I understood. He wasn't claiming the Bratva were good. But they were better than the alternative, because the alternative was chaos.

"It isn't just on the street," he explained. And he told me about corruption in City Hall, fraud in the big construction companies and the police and judges who'd take bribes from anyone. "Someone has to guide things, to make sure the little people don't get crushed."

A freezing wind gusted down the street, whipping up snow and trash into a dirty blizzard. I shivered and Radimir opened his overcoat, pulled me against him and wrapped me up. I could feel his heartbeat against my back, smell the dark citrus scent of him. He whispered, his words hot in my ear. "You wanted to know why I kill. I kill to stay in charge, so that things don't fall apart. I kill last of all, after deals and bribes and blackmail and favors have all failed. But I *do* kill. And I will keep killing, when I have to. To stop it all spinning out of control. To protect my family. And to protect you."

I could feel something shifting inside me, a sort of rebalancing. It wasn't that Radimir was better than I'd thought. It was that the world was much, much worse. I'd been sheltered from it, growing up as a civilian but now, seeing what Radimir did in context, I was starting to understand.

I looked up at him, torn. Understanding wasn't the same as accepting. And even if I could accept it...then what? My stomach lurched. In less than a week, we'd be getting married. And even though I'd finally admitted to myself that I'd fallen for him...I still had no idea if he had real feelings for me.

36

BRONWYN

FOUR DAYS LATER, it was my bachelorette party. Jen organized it like a military operation, with all of us in sparkly dresses of different colors and a long list of cool bars to go to. By midnight, we were in a neighborhood I'd never been to, climbing stone steps that led to a set of enormous wooden doors. I was glad I'd brought my crutches because it was turning out to be a long night. I still didn't like them but since that talk with Radimir, I was a little less self-conscious about them.

As we approached, doormen pushed open the wooden doors and—

Wow. The place was one huge room with a beautiful, vaulted wooden roof that reflected the thumping dance music back down until it seemed to be coming from everywhere at once. The bar was a long slab of glass, lit up from within so it glowed with an ethereal light, and in front of it was a sea of Chicago's young and beautiful: chisel-jawed guys in suits and women who must be models in shining, colorful outfits: suddenly, the cyan, sparkly dress Jen had persuaded me into made sense. The whole place was misted with smoke and lit up cobalt blue by lasers. I looked down at the floor: huge slabs of stone, worn smooth by time. That's when I realized the place used to be a church: there were marks where they'd ripped the pews out.

Something scratched at the back of my brain, a ghost of a memory, but I'd had at least two Porn Star Martinis too many to figure it out.

"Isn't this place *great?*" asked Jen, grinning. And it was, classy and cool without being intimidating.

There were big, round tables made of burnished copper and as soon as we sat down at one, a waiter came over and took our drinks order.

Jen and I looked at each other and our eyes locked. It still felt like our friendship was cracked...but she'd put the tension aside for tonight to give me a great time and I loved her for that. She grabbed my hand, interlacing her fingers with mine, and the diamond on my engagement ring flashed blue and silver in the laser light. "I still can't believe it," she said slowly. "He must be quite a guy, for you to fall this fast."

I swallowed. "Yeah," I managed. "He really is." The last time we'd had this conversation, in the Italian restaurant, I'd had to lie about how I felt about Radimir. Now I wasn't lying...and in some ways that scared me even more because I had no idea if he loved me back.

The waiter returned. *That was fast!* But his tray was empty. "Ladies," he announced, "my boss has told me to upgrade you to our VIP area. If you'll follow me?"

We all gaped at each other and then fell into line behind him. I was last and as I got my crutches under my arms and set off; I saw a guy watching us from the podium where a preacher once stood. He was in his late twenties, lean, with his hair shaved down to stubble, and he was wearing a sleek, white suit. *He must be the boss who upgraded us.* I gave him a nod of thanks, still not understanding *why.*

The waiter showed us to a flight of wooden stairs at the back of the room and down a dark hallway to the organ loft. The organ was still there, a huge thing with silver pipes that stretched up to the ceiling. The rest of the space was filled with black velvet couches and armchairs, and thick glass had been installed so that we could look down onto the main room, but the sound was damped down enough that we could talk. There were even velvet drapes that could be pulled if you wanted privacy. Another waiter arrived with our drinks.

"See, *this* is how we should roll," said Jen, falling into one of the couches.

"Do they think we're someone else?" asked Luna, sounding worried.

"It's fine," said Sadie. "If someone asks you for an autograph, just smile and do a squiggle."

The door opened and the guy in the white suit strutted in. "Ladies! Having a good time?" He spoke with some accent I'd never heard before, metered and precise, with a hard edge. That memory scratched again, but I still couldn't recall it.

"Yes!" Jen told him. "Thank you!"

Two more men filed in behind the boss. Their suits were black, and they had the heavy build of bouncers, but they weren't the guys we'd seen on the door.

The boss gave us a big, mocking grin as he looked around at the four of us. "We didn't know we were being visited by someone so important..."

Alarm bells began to ring in my head.

He looked right at me. "...Miss Hanford. Or, soon, *Mrs. Aristov.*"

Too late, the memory clicked into my brain, sharp and clear. *The Armenians. They bought a fancy bar as a base. A place called Worship.*

Worship. A bar made out of a deconsecrated church. Jen had unknowingly brought us into the home of one of Radimir's enemies.

I fumbled for my watch. My hands were suddenly sweaty but I managed to twist the bezel a full turn. Nothing happened. *Did it work?* "We're leaving," I said, getting to my feet.

The boss reached into his jacket and brought out a switchblade. The blade popped out with a nasty little *snkt.*

Fuck. My heart was hammering. My friends were staring at me, bewildered and terrified. "Bronwyn?" asked Luna.

"The man your fiancé killed," said the boss, drawing lazy figure eights in the air with the tip of the knife, "was important to me."

"You've got the wrong woman," croaked Jen. "Her fiancé's a property developer." She looked at me. "Right?" I didn't reply. "*Right?*"

I looked back at her helplessly. *Fuck. Why did she have to pick this bar?* But it wasn't her fault. I should have told her the truth.

The boss moved closer. I tried to move but I was awkward on my crutches and he was right in my face before I could get away. "Where I come from," he told me, "when someone is killed, there must be *p'vokhhatuts'um. Compensation.*" He looked thoughtfully down at my dress, then slipped the tip of the switchblade under one of the shoulder straps. I caught my breath as the point nicked my skin. "We're going to extract that compensation from you." He jerked the switchblade, and the strap parted. My dress sagged.

As if a signal had been given, his men shut the drapes that covered the glass wall. No one downstairs would see what was about to happen. Over the thumping music, they wouldn't even hear the screams.

The boss moved the switchblade to my dress's other strap. Fear had made my mouth dry and I had to struggle to speak. "Not them," I managed, glancing at Jen, Sadie and Luna. "Just me. They don't even know who Radimir *is.*"

The boss smirked at his men. "She wants us all to herself." He leered at me. "Fine. They can watch." The switchblade severed the other strap, and my dress started to slide down. I grabbed it and jumped back, staggering on my crutches, but the boss just laughed. My back hit the wall: there was nowhere to run. The boss pocketed his switchblade and advanced.

I closed my eyes. Maybe I could block it out, shut down all my senses while it happened. But then I heard Luna moan in fear, and something snapped inside me. The unfairness of it, the swaggering male arrogance of it.

If they were going to have me, they weren't getting me without a fight.

I opened my eyes and as the boss stepped forward, I leaned on my left crutch and swung the other one up and around. The crutch was heavy, and it made a very satisfying thump as it hit the side of his head. He staggered, clutching at his scalp, and I drove the tip of the other crutch into the middle of his belly, doubling him over. But now I was off balance and when he came for me again, I couldn't get a crutch up in time—

Jen, Sadie and Luna all swarmed him, grabbing arms and legs. "*Get away from her!*" panted Jen. I managed to get a hit in with the crutch and stepped forward for another.

But then the boss's men grabbed Luna and Sadie, plucking them off and hurling them aside, and the boss shook off Jen and turned to me, red-faced and furious. He stepped forward and, before I could react, he punched me in the face. My head snapped to the side, and it felt like a bomb went off in the center of my brain. Everything throbbed red and black, and I fell sideways, crashing down onto one of the couches, ragdoll-floppy.

The boss was on top of me in a second. "Just for that," he spat, "I'm going to make it hurt."

The door flew open.

A figure stood in the doorway. The flickering blue lasers turned him into a silhouette, but I would have recognized those wide shoulders and the ramrod-straight posture anywhere.

The boss scrambled off me and fumbled for his switchblade, but Radimir was already stalking towards him, a slender dagger in his hand.

"W—Wait," the boss stammered. He'd gone as white as his suit and he suddenly looked like a kid, playing at being a gangster. "You can't kill me; you'll never get out of here al—"

Radimir stabbed him in the heart. It was so fast and so vicious that the boss was lifted almost off his feet. All of us jerked in shock.

Radimir pulled the boss into an embrace. His voice was ice cold and rough with emotion. "You were dead the second you touched her." He let go and the boss crumpled to the floor, dead, a sticky red flower blossoming on his white suit.

The boss's men ran at Radimir, but they were shaken and Radimir was ruthlessly efficient. He stabbed one in the stomach and slashed the other's throat and they both fell.

Radimir held out his arms and I ran to him, abandoning the crutches. I crushed myself to his chest and he wrapped his arms around me like he wanted to protect me from the entire world. The adrenaline started to sluice out of me and I went shaky, squeezing my eyes shut as I thought about how close I'd come. "I'm sorry," I babbled. "I had no idea this was their place, I'd been drinking..."

Radimir put his hands on my shoulders and gently pushed me back. "Why are you apologizing?" He glared down at the boss. "This was only one person's fault, and it isn't you." The words were iron-certain, and I felt the tension in my chest unwind a notch. He hugged me again, furiously tight, so tight I could barely breathe, but I didn't want it to end because it felt so good.

Shouts from outside. Running footsteps. Radimir cursed in Russian and reluctantly released me. "We need to go."

I beckoned to my friends, but they hung back, staring at Radimir in horror. "It's okay," I promised. "Please." They looked at each other, and then Jen walked over and Sadie and Luna nervously followed.

We peeked out into the hallway. There must have been security cameras in the VIP room because four men in suits were running up the stairs and even in the dim light, I could see some of them had guns. They took up position in the hallway, waiting for us to come out. *Shit.* We were trapped.

"Stay behind me," Radimir warned, and moved towards the door.

I grabbed his arm. "There's four of them! There's only one of you! You're not getting killed saving me!"

He looked right into my eyes. "If I need to, I *will* give my life to protect you. But not tonight...because there isn't just one of me."

The man furthest from us suddenly disappeared, snatched away into the shadows. Then a figure in a long black coat emerged from the darkness. *Valentin!* He started creeping towards the next man, who was still oblivious. Valentin slipped an arm around his neck, gentle as a lover, and then there was a sudden, violent motion, and *that* man was dead, too. My stomach flipped. But he was doing it to save us, and when I thought about what the Armenians had been going to do to me...

As Valentin dealt with the third man, the last man suddenly realized what was happening behind him and spun around...only to get Radimir's knife in his back. Radimir and Valentin embraced, then led us down the stairs. But as we stepped into the main bar, there were loud *crack*s from the far end of the room, like fireworks going off, and the glass bar shattered. People started screaming and running and Radimir pushed me to the floor. *Oh fuck: that was gunfire!*

All I could see were feet as everyone ran for the exits. Then, as the crowd thinned, I glimpsed men with guns, moving towards us. And we were right out in the open...

There was a grunt and a crash. I looked around to see Gennadiy: he'd upended one of the big metal tables and he waved us all behind it. We scrambled into its shelter and my heart jumped into my throat when I heard a bullet ricochet off the metal surface, only a few inches from my head.

"Stay with them," Radimir ordered. "We'll clear an exit."

Gennadiy nodded grimly. Radimir and Valentin hurried away and Gennadiy pulled out a gun and started firing over the top of the table, holding the Armenians back. The shots were deafening, so close, and I threw my arms around Jen, Sadie and Luna as hot bullet casings fell around us. I was shaking. *Jesus Christ, people are shooting at us!* All I wanted was to go back to my safe little bookstore.

Then I saw blood running down Gennadiy's calf. He'd taken a hit, either from a bullet or flying glass, running in here to save us, and he was bleeding a *lot.* I let go of my friends, ripped one of the dangling straps from my dress and tied it tight around the wound. "Weren't you ready to kill me, just a few weeks ago?" I muttered.

He glanced down at me and I thought I saw a flash of guilt. "I do what I have to, to protect my family. You're part of it, now."

I felt an unfamiliar warmth spread through my chest.

Radimir waved to us from a fire exit across the room. We ran, scuttling across the open space while Gennadiy fired again and again. As we burst into the cold night air, we saw a big, black Mercedes holding up traffic in the middle of the street with Mikhail at the wheel. We all piled in and the car roared off before we'd even got the doors closed.

I'd wound up sitting on Radimir's knee, in the passenger seat. I craned around. "Everyone okay?"

With five people in the back, it was a cramped tangle of limbs, but they all nodded. I let out a long breath. *We're okay.*

"Bronwyn?" Jen's voice was so small and shaky, I barely recognized it. "What's going on?"

37

BRONWYN

BACK AT THE PENTHOUSE, the men went into Radimir's office and dressed Gennadiy's wound while passing around a bottle of vodka. And I sat down with my friends and laid it all out for them. I told them about being a witness, without saying who Radimir had killed. I explained why I had to marry him and why it was the least worst option. Straightaway, they wanted to call the FBI and I had to talk them out of it, explaining just how powerful the Bratva were.

"Look, it's okay," I said. "They're not what you think."

My friends stared at me in amazement.

"They do a lot of good, too," I said. "They protect people."

More stares. Jen put her hand on mine, shaking her head slowly. They thought I'd been brainwashed, and I understood why. If you'd told *me* a few weeks ago that I'd be defending a mafia boss, I'd have thought I was crazy, too.

"It's okay," I said again, more softly. I looked around at each of them. "I swear it is. Okay?"

Jen stared at me. "Oh God. You're in love with him. *Really* in love with him."

I glanced towards Radimir's office. The door was closed: the men couldn't hear. "Yes," I said quietly.

Everyone leaned in. "Does he love you?" whispered Jen.

That was exactly what I'd been asking myself. I knew he cared for me. He felt responsible for me, protective of me. But did he *love* me? "I don't know," I whispered helplessly. I sighed and closed my eyes. "Look...you don't have to come to the wedding."

"Are you kidding?" asked Jen. I opened my eyes and she was staring at me, horrified. "We're not going to let you go through this on your own!" The other girls were nodding.

I felt tears burning my eyes and I leaned forward, pressing our foreheads together and then pulling them all into a hug. *I should have told them from the start.*

Radimir and I drove them all home. Jen was the last one to be dropped off and as I moved in to hug her goodbye, she poked me hard in the ribs.

"*Ow!* Jesus!" I yelped.

"That's for making me think you'd been secretly seeing him for months and not telling me." She poked me on the other side. "That's for not telling me the truth."

"Ow, *okay!*"

She threw her arms around me and hugged me tight. "And this is me telling you to be careful."

The tension between us evaporated and I felt the crack in our friendship heal. I nodded against her shoulder and squeezed her back hard.

By the time Radimir and I got back to the penthouse, it was almost four in the morning. I stumbled through the door, exhausted and shaky. Before that night, I'd never even seen a gun in real life. Now I was a target, because of who I was marrying.

"I'm not ready for this life," I thought. Only I was so tired, I mumbled it out loud.

Radimir turned to me. He'd been quiet ever since we left the bar, scowling and brooding, and now that we were alone, I could see the anger he'd been bottling up. "I know," he whispered, putting his hands on my shoulders. "I know you're not. I'm sorry."

Sorry?! "You saved me!"

A curt little shake of his head. "I'm the reason you were in danger."

I studied his face. This wasn't the cold rage that had been in his eyes when he killed the Armenians. This was dark and poisonous...and turned inward. *No! It wasn't your fault!* I put a hand on that big, broad chest but he looked away.

"What do you need?" he asked stiffly. "How can I make you feel better? Do you need sleep? A drink?"

I was too tired and freaked out to think straight, but my mind was spinning too fast for sleep. "Could you just...hold me?" I asked, my voice quavering.

He closed his eyes for a second and he seemed to crumple, as if I'd slipped a knife through a crack in his armor. He nodded and scooped me up. For once, I didn't complain.

He carried me over to the couch and sat down, cradling me to his chest. I closed my eyes and he stroked my hair, whispering softly in Russian until I fell asleep.

38

RADIMIR

It's alright. Everything is going to be okay. I'll take care of you. I whispered the words over and over until her breathing slowed and she fell asleep. And then I kept whispering them into the silent room, as if trying to convince myself. But it was a lie.

Everything was not alright. It was not going to be okay. And I wasn't sure I could take care of her.

I sat there glaring into the darkness. The anger had returned, boiling up inside me, burning through all the ice that keeps everything locked down. I was furious, not just at myself but at—I looked around the penthouse—at all of it, at the Bratva, at my whole world. It had nearly killed her and for that, I wanted to rip it all down.

But the anger was just the emotion that escaped, like lava that bubbles up to the surface. It was coming from somewhere down deep, a hot, burning core that had been growing for weeks, that got denser and hotter every time I tried to crush it down. The horror of nearly losing her made me finally face up to it...

I was in love with her.

The hand stroking her hair stiffened into a claw. *Chyort! How did this happen?*

But I knew how. Because she was funny and *voskhititel'nyy—*

adorable—and a shy librarian but a moaning, thrashing minx when I got between her thighs and because she was *good,* and she reminded me that the world could be good. She made me…

Happy. A few months ago, I hadn't thought it was possible to be happy.

I stared down at her sleeping face. *Now what?* I'd admitted it to myself. But could I tell her? *Should* I tell her? I thought back to the night I killed Borislav, the way she'd recoiled from me. *Don't touch me!* She'd hated me. What if she still felt the same way?

Feeling these things for my supposed-fake fiancée was hard enough. If she rejected me…I wasn't sure I could take that.

I scowled down at her. *Damn you, woman.* She made me happy. But she also made me vulnerable.

39

BRONWYN

THE NEXT MORNING—THE day before the wedding—I woke with the world's worst hangover, a blue and purple bruise on my cheek and a swollen lip. Radimir insisted I wasn't going to work. I immediately dug in because being closed for the day was going to make my already tiny profits even smaller, and we eventually compromised and said I'd open the store after lunch, but only if he drove me there and back. While I was working, he and his brothers would run the rest of the Armenians out of town.

Then he demanded I change into exercise gear and dragged me into the penthouse's small gym. "This is for you," he said, handing me a small, silver switchblade. I tentatively pressed the button and almost took my thumb off when the blade shot out. "*Jesus!* I'm not carrying a *knife!*"

"Yes you are." His jaw set stubbornly. "It's small enough to fit in your purse."

"That's not the—"

"It has carvings on the handle," he said, pointing. "Vines. Feminine."

I looked. There *were* carvings and they *were* pretty, and part of me wondered what strings he'd pulled, to have someone find an antique switchblade like this and have it delivered here, all before I'd even woken up. There were dark circles under his eyes. *Did he even sleep?* "Thank you, it's lovely, but I'm not carrying a—"

He took hold of my shoulders. "*I need you to!*"

For the first time, I saw the fear in his eyes. I shut up.

"We will practice with this," he said, handing me a rubber knife. "Now. I will try to grab you."

He spun me around by the shoulders and grabbed me from behind. One arm wrapped around my waist, the other brushing the underside of my boobs, and immediately, a rush of heat went through me. He pulled me back against him, his warm pecs pressing into my back. I felt his cock swell between the cheeks of my ass and my groin throbbed and tightened.

"Fight back," he ordered. "Go for my neck."

Right. Yes. That's what we were doing. I reached up and drew the rubber knife along the side of his neck.

"Not like you're giving me a shave," he said coldly. "Like you're *cutting my throat*. Again!"

I reached back and *slashed* across his throat, my stomach flipping, and he grunted as if that was *acceptable* and released me. "Now I will grab you from the front," he told me.

For the next hour, he came at me from every angle: grabbing my wrist, my throat, knocking me off my feet. Three weeks of being close to him with no relief had left me horny as hell. After just a few minutes of his hard body rubbing against mine, I was a red-faced, panting mess and my panties were damp. But aside from his hard cock, he seemed completely under control. When he wrestled me to the floor and pinned me there, his hips between my thighs and my breasts pillowed against his chest, I stared up at him in disbelief. *How is this not affecting him?*

Then I saw it in his eyes, just for a second. The lust was there, but it was trapped behind an even stronger need. He'd always wanted to protect me, but now he *needed* to. Last night had changed things.

Next, he showed me how to stab. "Twist it as it goes in," he told me, guiding my hand. His Russian accent made the words even colder. "The more damage you can do, the faster they'll bleed out."

I stared at him, appalled. "Who taught you this stuff?"

His eyes went distant for a moment. "My...friend, in New York. Alexei." Then he seemed to remember himself. "Let's continue." He stepped forward to come at me again.

I stepped back. "Why *did* you lose contact with him?"

He gave me one of those curt little shakes of his head and circled to box me in. "It's not important."

I sidestepped. "It *is* important." I put the knife stubbornly down at my side.

He sighed and scowled. "Bronwyn..."

"No stabby-stabby 'till you tell me."

He glowered, but his eyes gleamed, as if part of him liked the way I stood up to him. He looked at the ceiling, cursing in Russian, and I got the impression he was counting to ten. God, he looked magnificent, with that big chest rising and falling under his tight black tank top and his jaw set angrily. I had to stop myself just melting and giving in. But this *was* important, this Alexei guy was the closest thing to a human connection he seemed to have, outside of his family, and I needed to know what went wrong.

He lowered his eyes to me and gave a long-suffering sigh. "Alexei...met a woman called Gabriella. He was sent to kill her, but he fell in love with her. He betrayed his employer for her and turned his back on the Bratva. They live together in Queens, now."

"That's *amazing!*" I said. I couldn't help grinning, it was so *romantic!*

Radimir scowled at the floor. "I thought it was...weak."

I stared at him. "Is that still what you think?"

He turned his head and looked at me, his eyes blazing. His lips moved, as if he was about to say something. His hands closed into fists—

Then he stormed out of the gym. "I will make us lunch. Then I will drive you to the store."

40

BRONWYN

As we drove to the store, I gazed out at the city...and realized I was seeing it with new eyes. Thanks to Radimir's explanations of the Bratva and the other gangs, I knew why *that* skyscraper got planning permission, but *that* site had lain derelict for over a year. I knew why the mayor would be re-elected and why the unions would get the pay deal they were pushing for. I knew why certain neighborhoods were dangerous after dark and others weren't, despite being within a few blocks of each other. I'd grown up in this city but I'd never known the shadow world that existed beneath the normal one, a place of backroom deals, money and violence. It still scared the crap out of me, but...I felt sort of privileged, to be one of the insiders. And I couldn't imagine going back to being oblivious.

Last night had been terrifying. But it had also shown me that Radimir and his brothers weren't the same as the other gangsters. They only killed when they had to and when I thought about how Gennadiy, Valentin, and Mikhail had risked their lives to rescue us, it gave me an unexpected warm glow. I'd never had brothers or sisters and ever since I'd lost my parents and Baba got ill, I'd felt like I was on my own. Now I'd gotten a tantalizing glimpse of what it was like to be part of a family.

Tomorrow, I'd actually join that family. I'd become *Mrs. Aristov. I should be happy.*

But as I worked away at the store, a cold dread started to creep through me. I thought back to when I'd stood on that freezing riverbank, sobbing my heart out because I had to marry him. Now everything had flipped around. I loved him. But the more I thought about it, the more I was sure he didn't feel the same way. Why should he? He'd been forced into this marriage, too. *And he'd have said something by now, right?*

The dread built all day. Then, at closing time, Radimir arrived to pick me up. I locked the door and my eyes fell to the sign Jen had made to cover us for the next day: *Closed due to Wedding,* with little wedding bells...and suddenly, realization hit and I wanted to be sick.

The wedding had started out as fake, just a way to get a marriage certificate. But while I'd been busy falling for him, it had become real, even if I hadn't admitted it to myself. That's why I'd done as he asked and planned a big wedding. Somewhere, deep down, I'd known I loved him and I'd thought it was going to turn into some fairytale happy-ever-after where he loved me, too.

I let out a little moan, staring at the sign in horror. *I'm a fucking idiot.* And now, while Radimir and everyone else just went through the motions, I was going to be there in my wedding gown trying to smile while inside, my heart was breaking because *of course he doesn't love you.* It wasn't a fairytale, it was a nightmare.

That night in the penthouse, I watched sadly as Radimir prepared to leave. He picked up his bag and the suit carrier that held his wedding suit, then stopped when he saw my face. "You *do* want me to go?" he said. "It was your idea: you said I'm not meant to see you, the night before the wedding."

I nodded quickly. It *had* been my idea that he go to Gennadiy's house tonight: I'd mentioned it a week before, when I was in a golden haze of wedding planning and traditions...and before I knew I was in love with him. "Yep," I said, forcing my voice to be light. "Go."

He frowned, looking concerned, but left. I went over to the window and a moment later, I saw his car drive away through the snow. And then I spotted another car I recognized, parked across the street. *Valentin!* Radimir hadn't been willing to leave me unguarded, even for one night, and even through the pain, it made a smile tug at my lips.

I tried to distract myself. I double-checked everything was ready for the wedding: it was. I made a sandwich but couldn't face eating it. I tried reading but couldn't concentrate.

I finally decided to turn in, even though I knew I wouldn't sleep. But there was one thing I had to do first. I knew I wouldn't be able to persuade Valentin to go home but I wasn't going to leave him sitting in his car all night when it was below freezing. I went out into the street and told him that he could guard me just as well from the couch in the penthouse, and after he'd gotten over his embarrassment at being spotted, he agreed and came upstairs.

I stretched out on the bed, staring up at the ceiling. *How did this happen?!* Tomorrow should be the happiest day of my life but it had been twisted into a cruel joke. I was going to have to pretend all day and Radimir would think I was fine because *it's all just fake* but really... And God, I'd have to keep it together in front of Jen, Sadie and Luna, why had I invited my *friends?!*

I wished I hadn't fallen for him. A fake wedding I could have handled but *this,* being the only one, meant something to...

I didn't want to make a noise because the door was ajar, and Valentin was right there in the next room. I closed my eyes and let the tears spill silently down my cheeks.

What's worse than being forced to marry a monster?

Falling in love with him. And thinking he'll love you back.

41

RADIMIR

GENNADIY GREETED me at the door of his mansion, whisked away my bags and put a glass in my hand. "To marriage," he said, and clinked glasses with me. I knocked back the vodka and while we drank another, he updated me. The news was good: all of the Armenians had been run out of Chicago and the police investigation into Borislav's murder had hit a dead end. I should have been happy, but something was bothering me, leaving me sullen and brooding.

Bronwyn. She'd seemed...sad. Weren't women meant to enjoy weddings?

After the third vodka, I went outside into the snow and called Valentin. "How is she?" I asked immediately.

"Um...I think she's crying."

"*Crying?!*" I felt my chest go tight and fought to keep my voice level. "How can you tell, from down there?"

"I'm in the penthouse," he said guiltily. "She invited me upstairs."

Of course she did. "And she's *crying?*"

"Not noisy crying," he said. "Quiet crying."

I ended the call and stood there scowling, the fury boiling up in my chest until it felt like the snowflakes were sizzling as they hit my skin. I wanted to annihilate whoever had hurt her...but just like the night she'd seen me kill Borislav, the person who'd hurt her was me. And I had no idea what to do about it. "*Chyort!*" I cursed. *Why did I ever get involved with a woman?*

Because she's amazing. That's why.

I stomped back inside. Gennadiy had gone to bed, so I poured myself another vodka and knocked it back, but it didn't help. *What the fuck am I going to do?*

Then I heard the pad of feet behind me, too soft to be human. I turned to see one of Mikhail's Malamutes standing watching me. And suddenly, I knew exactly what I had to do. I walked over and stroked his furry head and he circled me, fluffy tail wagging.

I grabbed the bottle of vodka and another glass. "Go on," I told the dog. "Take me to him."

The dog trotted off along a hallway and led me to a book-lined study. Mikhail was sprawled in a leather armchair, a book open on his lap, softly snoring. The other three dogs were curled up in front of a roaring fire, pressed so close it was difficult to tell where one dog ended and another began. The dog who'd found me pushed his way into the pack, turned around three times and snuggled down.

I gently shook Mikhail's shoulder. "I need your help." I poured two glasses of vodka and put one in his hand. Mikhail rubbed his eyes, sipped, and nodded.

I fell into an armchair, then took a deep breath. "Bronwyn." Just saying her name made me *lift* inside. "She's sad. Crying. The night before our wedding."

Mikhail leaned closer. "She didn't ask for this marriage," he said gently.

I nodded and tousled a sleeping dog's head for comfort. "But...while we've been living together, I thought..." I could feel my face going red. "I thought she'd started to...feel something for me."

Mikhail frowned thoughtfully. "And do *you* love *her?*"

I looked away. "What does that matter?"

Mikhail sat back in his chair. "Answer the question!"

I bristled and glared, my face heating even more. "Yes," I muttered. "I love her." It felt like I'd carved the words out of shining silver, two feet high, and laid them on the rug for anyone to walk in and see. I'd never felt so horribly vulnerable. If this was the *being open with your feelings* that American women were so obsessed with, I didn't like it at all. And yet, at the same time, there was a tiny part of me that *jumped* when I said the words, like my heart had somersaulted right over a beat. "But I haven't told her," I said.

Mikhail stared at me for a moment. "You really are an idiot."

I sat up, scowling, and Mikhail waved me back. "It's not your fault," he sighed. "You didn't have your mother to teach you about women. And by the time I got there, it was too late. Vladivostok had left you...*cold.* Just as it left Gennadiy hard and Valentin..."—he sighed—"I'm not sure Valentin will ever be okay." He shook his head and put his hand on my shoulder. "A wedding is the fairy tale women get to star in. They spend their entire lives building up to that one moment. Bronwyn is sad because she thinks she's going to marry a man who doesn't love her. You must tell her."

I frowned. "What if she doesn't love me? What if that's why she's sad?"

"Then telling her you love her can't make it any worse."

My stomach turned over. "But..."

"But you could be hurt," Mikhail said gently. "Yes. That's part of love. If you love her, you have to tell her anyway."

He knocked back the last of his vodka, patted my shoulder and got up. His dogs came sleepily awake and followed him out of the room, their fur warm from the fire as they brushed past my legs. I sat there staring into the fire, furious, trying to find some solution where I didn't have to put myself at risk...but there wasn't one.

Chyort! For years, I'd forced myself to feel nothing, to never get close to anyone. The idea of being vulnerable was more terrifying than a room full of thugs with knives, or a lifetime in prison.

I hurled my half-finished glass into the fire. The vodka flared and roared. *If she rejects me, it will destroy me,* I thought bitterly.

The flames died away. The room went still. *But if I don't do this, she'll be in pain.*

And that, I realized, was *unacceptable.*

I tugged my waistcoat straight. I knew what I had to do.

42

BRONWYN

THE WHITE VINTAGE Rolls-Royce stopped with a soft crunch of gravel and the chauffeur jumped out and opened my door. But I just sat there, focusing on the back of the seat in front of me, trying not to cry.

Jen leaned in close. "We can just get out of here," she whispered urgently. "Please don't do this if it's not what you want." Baba looked worried, too.

I shook my head. However I felt, I still had to marry him: Radimir and his family *would* find me if I ran. But the irony was, I *did* want this. I just wanted it to be real. I wanted him to love me, too.

I climbed out of the car, tasting the cold, crisp air. The snow had stopped, and everything was silent and perfect. The mansion looked amazing, with fresh snow dusting its roof and clinging to the window ledges. Golden light spilled from the windows and lit up the arrangements of deep red roses that led up the path to the door. A string quartet in ball gowns started playing.

"Let's do this," I said shakily.

Jen adjusted my veil. Luna and Sadie joined us, the three of them looking amazing in their long green dresses. Baba moved in next to me: she still needed a stick to walk, but she was getting stronger every day. A photographer started snapping pictures. I was pretty sure he couldn't see the tears in my eyes through the veil.

We walked slowly up the path to the house. For once, my legs barely hurt at all. My plan of going on the immunosuppressants had worked: if things were different, I'd be able to enjoy my big day.

We passed through the entrance hall, my heels echoing on the tiled floor, the scent of fresh flowers surrounding us. Ahead of us, two ushers pulled open a set of double doors and I caught my breath as we stepped into the huge room. Hundreds of people all turned to look at me. But my eyes were on the aisle, following it to...

Radimir, resplendent in his dove gray suit, had been saying something to Gennadiy, his best man. As he heard the doors open, he turned to face me. My world seemed to narrow down to just him. As his eyes met mine, his chest lifted and filled and his eyes, normally so cold, gleamed with...*joy?*

I swallowed and nearly stumbled, my heart suddenly hammering. *No. Don't let yourself hope.* But I couldn't help it.

I tried to remember how to put one foot in front of the other. In the cream and silver gown, with my hair tamed into shining copper waves and a silver tiara sparkling, I *did* feel like a princess, just like how I'd imagined it as a kid. But now I wasn't sure what I was walking towards.

I arrived beside him. I could feel that powerful, magnetic presence pulsing into me: it was impossible to not look up at him. But I was terrified of what I'd see. What if I'd imagined it?

As the officiant greeted us and started to speak, I slowly turned my head and looked up at Radimir, barely daring to breathe...and saw him gazing down at me, his jaw set, raw determination in his eyes. *What does that mean?!* The officiant's words faded out as we stared at each other. And then we reached the vows.

Gennadiy passed Radimir a neatly printed card to read. Jen stepped forward and gave me mine.

Radimir glanced down at the card in his hand...then crushed it in his fist and let it fall. I jerked like someone had touched me with a live wire. *What the fuck is this?*

Radimir looked out across the sea of faces. The rich and the powerful. The other mafia families.

And then he turned away from them and focused only on me. He took my hands, his fingers gloriously warm. "Bronwyn," he began. I'd never get tired of how his accent carved my name. "Some things...aren't easy to say, at least not for me. But I never meant you to suffer because I wasn't brave enough to say the words. And I'm sorry." The crowd murmured but he ignored them. I stood there staring up at him, beyond shocked. Was this *him,* was this really *Radimir* saying these things?

His voice was warm and even though he spoke haltingly, his tone was certain. This was from the heart. "So now I want—I *need* you to know..." —he drew my hands towards him and squeezed my fingers. "I love you. I'll never stop loving you."

I drew in a huge, trembling breath, my whole body filling up with silvery excitement. Tears sprang to my eyes, but they were happy tears. I wasn't capable of speech, and just gave a kind of sob, squeezing his hands. And then I saw the fear in his eyes, and *oh God he doesn't know, "I love you too!"* I blurted, grabbing his hands and pressing them into a ball. Radimir's face, always so controlled, broke into a huge, dumb grin. Off to my left, I heard Baba sob in delight and Jen gave an adoring *Oh!*

We turned to the officiant, who was grinning at us. "Do you have the rings?" he asked Gennadiy.

Gennadiy handed the rings to Radimir. Radimir went to put the ring on my finger, but my hand was shaking so much, he had to hold it firm. "Hold still," he told me, mock-gruffly, and people laughed, *I* laughed, even *he* was smiling and he *never* smiled. I was drunk on happiness, bursting with it, and then *oh God,* the ring was sliding up my finger and nestling against my engagement ring and I was *his,* forever.

Then it was my turn to take the much bigger ring and slide it onto his finger. *And he's mine. Forever.* Without words, we touched our rings together and then knitted our fingers.

"By the power vested in me by the state of Illinois, I now pronounce you man and wife. You may kiss the bride," said the officiant.

Radimir flipped my veil back over my head, leaned down and kissed me. Everyone was cheering and applauding, and it felt like I was flying. All the excitement and happiness I'd always thought would be there on my wedding day, everything that had been missing, was suddenly filling me up, from toes to the top of my head, and I wanted to whoop. I settled for tangling my hands in Radimir's hair and pulling him down into the kiss, and it felt like we were spinning together, right up to the ceiling.

When we finally broke the kiss, I stared up at him, panting in disbelief. *He loves me.* And then I felt the weight of the ring on my hand. *He's my husband.*

The photographer took us outside for photographs, working quickly because it was freezing. But cuddled up to Radimir's side, I didn't feel the cold at all. There were speeches: first one from Gennadiy, short but heartfelt, about his brother. Then a much longer, meandering but very funny speech from Mikhail, who seemed to be made for moments like this, with his easy-going nature and his infectious laugh. I couldn't help noticing, though, that his stories were all drawn from Radimir's childhood, with nothing past his teenage years. *What happened to him? To Gennadiy and Valentin, to all of them?*

The dinner passed in a blur. I just remember glancing at Radimir sitting next to me again and again, thinking *is this real?* He was smiling and slapping people on the back: he was *happy!*

Everyone seemed to be having a good time: Mikhail had brought his dogs and was feeding them scraps under the table, Luna, Sadie and Jen were getting a lot of interest from the single men and there were even a couple of kids running around between the tables, presumably the children of some of the Russian guests Radimir had invited because none of my friends had kids yet. That got me thinking: did I want a family with Radimir, someday? Three weeks ago, I would have been horrified by the idea, but now... I shook my head. *Later.* I just wanted to enjoy today.

We cut the cake, a five-tier creation cloaked in white icing and decorated with winter berries and sugar roses, their petals dusted with icing sugar snow. Then more drinks and a lot of Russian people shaking our hands and wishing us well. I was glad I'd started learning Russian: I could only understand maybe one word in three, but...baby steps.

Before I knew what was happening, the tables had been cleared and the band was starting up. *God, it's going so fast!* The lights dimmed and everyone formed a circle with Radimir and me in the center.

"What is this?" asked Radimir, confused.

"The first dance!" I told him excitedly. "It's traditional."

He looked around suspiciously. "I don't dance."

I grabbed his hand and towed him into the middle of the dance floor. "Just one dance, I promise."

He put his hands on my waist and tugged me close. My breasts pushed against his chest and I felt his cock harden against my thigh. He growled, pinned me firmly in position and whispered in my ear. "One dance. Because any more than that, feeling you against me like this, and I'm going to be dragging you into the nearest storeroom."

I felt my face light up red but the words, said in *that* accent, spiraled straight down to my groin and made me crush my thighs together. He'd been holding back, all these weeks, until he knew I wanted him. I could feel the need in him: in his hand, gripping my waist, in the way his eyes kept going to my lips, and in the press of that thick, hot cock. It felt like he was one second away from just ripping my wedding gown off in front of everyone and throwing me over one of the tables. I went weak inside and pressed myself closer to him, reveling in the feel of his body as we slowly spun around the dance floor. I was giggly and heady: I glimpsed Jen smiling at us as we whirled past and I felt my own big, stupid grin on my face. I couldn't remember the last time I was so happy.

There was a scream, down at the end of the room. Radimir and I stumbled to a stop and looked in that direction but for a moment we couldn't see anything through the crowd of people. Then another scream, the crowd split apart and—

Spartak Nazarov, his lips twisting in hatred as he saw us. And standing in front of him, three men with machine guns.

I gave a strangled cry of terror as they opened fire.

43

RADIMIR

I'D DONE EXACTLY what I swore I'd never do: I'd let my guard down. Spinning around and around the dance floor, with Bronwyn's breasts soft against my chest and her white gown billowing out behind her, I was *happy.* I knew I was grinning and that people from the other mafia families could see it, and I didn't care at all.

Then Spartak and his gunmen burst in, and it took me a few seconds to come out of that warm, pink fog. The first spray of bullets would have killed us both if a man from one of the East side families hadn't run in front of us in his bid to escape. He was cut down, and as he fell screaming, I finally woke up, picked up Bronwyn and *ran.* I dived behind the waist-high wall of amplifiers the band was using and pressed Bronwyn to the floor, covering her body with mine. Bullets tore into the amps, sending out showers of sparks and deafening screeches of feedback. The band fled the stage, sending their mic stands tumbling. The guests were all trying to get out but there were too many people and not enough doors.

More bullets slammed into the amps. They hummed and crackled, belching white smoke that stung my nostrils. *I don't have a gun!* When I'd been getting dressed that morning, I'd been too focused on trying to figure out what to say to Bronwyn. Plus, who takes a gun to a *wedding?*

Answer: my brothers. I peeked out and saw Valentin and then Gennadiy returning fire. *Where are my security guys?* I'd had three men stationed outside but there'd been no warning: they must have been slaughtered before they even got a shot off.

The amps started to spit blue arcs of electricity and I flinched as one of them singed my jacket. "We've got to move," I told Bronwyn. When the gunfire stopped for a second, I pulled her to her feet and ran for one of the doors.

Time seemed to slow down. For the first time, I could really see the devastation. People lay bleeding, perhaps dead. Tables around the edge of the room had been overturned as people fled and the exits were still clogged by the crowds. Spartak had disappeared as soon as my brothers fired back but his gunmen were still there, reloading their weapons to fire again.

Suddenly, Bronwyn tore herself out of my grasp and veered off to the side. I grabbed for her but missed. *Where the hell is she going?*

Then I saw him. In the middle of the room, stumbling through the glittering snow of glass shards. *Shit!* A kid, no more than six, forced by his parents into a little three-piece wedding suit. He was red-faced and bawling, blind with tears.

Bronwyn was running straight towards him, sprinting. I raced after her, skidding a little in my dress shoes. The floor was polished wood, slick with spilled champagne, and she was in heels: it must have been hell on her joints, just staying upright. *Chyort*, my little librarian was brave. But the gunmen were going to fire again long before she could get the kid to safety. She scooped him up and looked desperately around for cover but there wasn't any: we were right out in the open. I picked her up and spun around, clutching her and the kid to my chest and putting my back to the gunmen. Then I closed my eyes tight and waited for the bullets to tear into me.

There were three heavy thumps behind us and then screaming. A machine gun fired but it hit the ceiling, not us. I tentatively uncoiled from around Bronwyn and the kid and looked behind me.

The three gunmen were on the floor, rolling and sobbing. Two had a dog's jaws locked into their arms and had dropped their guns. The third had been foolish enough to keep hold of his gun. He had a dog on his chest, its jaws on his throat, and he wasn't moving anymore.

That's the thing about Mikhail's dogs. They're adorable bundles of floof...right up until the moment they see one of the family in danger.

Mikhail, unflappable as ever, collected up the guns and then recalled the dogs. They trotted over obediently, wagging their tails, one of them with its jaws dripping red.

"Baba!" said Bronwyn suddenly. "Where's Baba?"

"She's fine," said Gennadiy, reloading his gun as he walked over. "I got her out of the room as soon as the shooting started."

Bronwyn put the kid down, ran over and wrapped Gennadiy up in a hug. Gennadiy grimaced and pouted, unused to affection.

We reunited the kid with his parents and checked the guests. One man was dead. Three more people had been hit by bullets but would survive, several more had cuts from flying glass and two had been hurt in the crush at the doors. The three security guys I'd had stationed outside were all dead and that hit me hard: they were all good men who'd always been loyal to me. But I knew it could have been much, much worse.

The police arrived and started asking a million questions, but between Mikhail's smooth diplomacy and a phone call to the police commissioner, who we had an understanding with, we managed to smooth things out. *No, officer, we have no idea who these men were, or why they shot the place up.*

But in reality, I knew exactly what had happened. Spartak had somehow found out I killed his brother. *How?*

The guests started to leave. Bronwyn was just hugging her friends goodbye when Gennadiy took me aside, saying there was something he needed to show me. He rounded up Valentin and Mikhail, too, and we slipped away from the police and out into the house's gardens. It was very still and very quiet, and so cold that the snow that covered the tops of the hedges had frozen into a thick, sparkling crust.

"Spartak just sent me this," Gennadiy told me, pulling out his phone.

At that second, Bronwyn ran out of the house and over to our group, still in her wedding gown. "What is it?" she asked, seeing our faces. "What's happened?"

Gennadiy looked shifty.

"She's family, now!" I snapped.

He sighed and showed us a video on his phone. It was shot from a low perspective, maybe waist height. I recognized Borislav's apartment immediately. The camera showed the living room but in the background, I could see the open door to the bathroom. And I could see *me,* slamming Borislav's head against the tiled step of the shower, and Bronwyn standing in the hallway watching.

Bronwyn slapped a hand over her mouth. "If he shows this to the cops, you're going to jail."

I gazed down at her, overcome. Anyone else would have been worrying about themselves: the video showed that she'd lied to the police and might even make her an accessory, but she was only worried about me. *I don't deserve this woman.*

"Spartak won't show it to the police," said Valentin sadly. "He wants revenge. He sent us this, so we know why."

"I'm sorry," I told my brothers tightly.

"You couldn't have known there was a hidden camera," said Gennadiy. "From the angle, it's probably in a bookshelf or something."

"I wouldn't have spotted it either," said Valentin quietly.

I nodded gratefully. I was glad now that I'd insisted on being the one to do the killing. At least I would be Spartak's prime target and not my baby brother. But if I was in danger, that meant Bronwyn was in danger, just being close to me... I pulled her against my chest and wrapped my arms around her protectively.

"Why would Borislav have a hidden camera in his apartment?" asked Bronwyn.

I thought about it, then grimaced, nauseous. "The bastard had a reputation for...doing things to women. My guess is, he had cameras set up to film it."

Bronwyn twisted in disgust. "*Eww,* Jesus!"

I sighed. "We're lucky the police didn't find the camera when they searched the place. Spartak must have found it just today..." I rubbed my face. "Shit. He was probably clearing his dead brother's apartment." I felt a stab of guilt. I didn't like Spartak, but the poor guy didn't deserve to come across a video of his brother being murdered. No wonder he'd tried to kill me. And he'd *keep* trying: he wouldn't stop now until I was dead. That's why he wasn't showing the video to the police, he wanted me free so he could get to me.

Gennadiy put his hand on my shoulder. "I'll talk to The Eight. They told us to do this. They have to back us up, now that Spartak knows."

I nodded. I just hoped he was right. We'd broken the truce by killing Spartak's brother. The Eight were the only thing standing between us and all-out war. "What can I do?" I asked.

Gennadiy's eyes flicked to Bronwyn and his face softened. "It's your wedding day," he told me. "Go be with your wife."

I looked around at all of them. Valentin was nodding and Mikhail, too. It sunk in that they'd all heard my speech. They knew how I felt about her. And they weren't looking at me with pity, or like they thought I was weak. They looked...happy for me. I put a hand on Valentin's shoulder, and one on Mikhail's, so that we were all joined, and nodded back gratefully.

Then I took Bronwyn's hand and led her to my car. By now, almost all of the guests had left and there were more police walking around than civilians. Not the way I'd imagined our wedding ending. But we were alive, unharmed and—I squeezed Bronwyn's hand—the night was just beginning.

Yes, Spartak wanted me dead. Yes, the violence could turn into a full-blown war between our families. But there'd be time for that tomorrow. Tonight, I needed to fuck my brand-new wife.

44

BRONWYN

We were met at Radimir's apartment building by four serious-looking Russian men in suits toting automatic weapons. Two more were waiting for us upstairs outside the penthouse: after what happened at the wedding, Radimir clearly wasn't taking any chances.

He opened the door but stopped me before I could go through it. "I believe there's a tradition," he told me firmly.

"What tra—"

I yelped as he scooped me up into his arms and carried me over the threshold. Behind us, the bodyguards took up their positions outside and quietly closed the door.

Radimir marched straight through to the bedroom and then gently set me down. I looked up at him: even in the heels I'd braved for the wedding, he was taller than me. He gazed down at me with something like wonder. "My bride," he breathed, tracing his hands along my shoulders.

I slid my hands under the sides of his jacket and held his waist. "My husband," I said. My stomach dropped at the words, and I took in all of him: the Bratva tattoos that showed through his white shirt, the muscled, rugged bulk of him, the sheer malevolent presence of him. I was married to a gangster. But as I thought about him carrying me when I was in pain, about him buying the building to save the bookstore, about him risking his life for me, the fear faded, and a warm glow replaced it. Yes, he was Bratva. But deep down, he was *good.* And yes, we were in danger now from Spartak. But I knew Radimir would keep me safe. I was married to a gangster...and it was the happiest I'd ever been.

Radimir slid his hands up to my cheeks, then tilted my head back, sinking his fingertips into my hair. My eyes fluttered closed as his lips came down on mine. The gentleness of the kiss took me by surprise: it was soft and slow, tasting me, as if he was just discovering me. Each brush of his lips infused me with a pink glow of pleasure, filling me up and making me heady. But then the kiss started to change. His lips wandered, laying kisses like hot little bombs along my cheek, down my throat, on my collar bone... My body arched against him, and I heard myself start to pant. He kissed my lips again, his tongue teasing at them, and I opened, welcoming him in. The kiss turned hungry, his tongue darting in to explore me while my hands roamed over his back. The pink pleasure was moving inward, now, coalescing into a glowing ache that needed more than kissing.

Radimir broke the kiss and pushed me back. He was panting, too, and his eyes were hooded with lust. He reached around behind me, searching for the zipper of my gown and then tugged it down. The gown loosened around me and, as he started kissing me again, I shimmied while he pushed it down off my shoulders, and eventually it fell around me. There was so much skirt that I was still knee-deep in material, so, still kissing me, he put one arm around my waist, one hand under my ass and lifted me up out of the dress, then turned around and set me down again. His hands traced my back, my ass, my thighs, and I felt his surprise. He broke the kiss again and stepped back to look, and I giggled.

Jen had helped me choose the bridal lingerie. It was cream, to match the dress, and finished with gleaming gold thread: we'd agreed it was *princess on her wedding night.* The bra gave me a pretty amazing cleavage, the panties were cut high at the sides and back to make the most of my ass and the stockings made my legs look endless, especially because I was still wearing my heels. But the *piece de resistance* was the matching corset which was beautifully embroidered with swirls of gold. It had straps that went down to my stockings and the boning gave me a silhouette that was kind of *wow*.

Radimir's eyes flared with lust. He took my hands in his and spread my arms wide while he gazed at me. Then he whirled me around and pulled me back to him, so that my arms were imprisoned, crossed in an X across my chest, and my ass was grinding against his cock. "Had I known what you were wearing underneath, the wedding would have been a *lot* shorter." He kissed the sensitive spot on the side of my neck, and I squirmed in delight.

Radimir reached between us and unhooked the clasp of my bra. Then he spun me again, pulling the bra down and off my arms, and pushed me up against the wall, capturing my wrists and holding them above my head. It happened so fast I gasped, my boobs bobbing and swaying as my bare back was pressed to the cool plaster. I could feel my nipples crinkling and hardening both from the sudden shock of the cool air and the deep throb of heat that soaked through me whenever he was rough like that with me. It was because it came from urgency, not cruelty, as if I turned him on so much, he couldn't wait to fuck me. That and the safety of knowing that he'd never hurt me.

He gazed down at my breasts, his eyes burning. "I've waited three weeks to see these again." He leaned forward and licked a nipple, and I gasped. He began to stroke my breasts with one hand, squeezing softly as he lashed my nipples with his tongue. I drew in my breath and arched my back, wanting more, that ache inside becoming needy. But he held me pinned by my wrists and slowly teased me, covering his teeth with his lips and softly biting the sensitive buds until I thrashed and moaned.

He finally moved back a little, still holding my wrists, and looked down towards my groin. "There's another part of you I've been looking forward to seeing, *Krasavitsa*," The ache became heavy, sinking right down between my thighs.

He looked right into my eyes. Then, with his free hand, he

gripped the waistband of my panties and tugged the right side down an inch. "It was dark, in the bookstore," he explained, his voice thick with lust. He tugged the left side down, still holding my gaze. "I couldn't see you properly." He tugged the right side again, and my breath caught as I felt the cool air of the room on my sensitive folds. "Ever since then, I've been imagining what you look like. And now..." He tugged the left side again, pulling my panties down around my thighs. He held my gaze a moment longer...and then at last, he allowed himself to look down. I flushed and twisted as I felt his eyes devouring me: the delicate pink lips, the small strip of red-brown hair.

Radimir's eyes flared with lust. He gave me a wolfish smile, then grabbed me by the waist, twisted and threw me onto the bed. I squeaked in delight, landing on my back with my legs kicking in the air.

He was on me instantly, his knees between my thighs, his hands cupping my cheeks, pressing me down onto the bed with his kiss. His hands went to my spit-wet breasts, his thumbs strumming the nipples as he rolled and squeezed. Ribbons of deep pink pleasure rippled down from my breasts to my groin and my ass started to circle on the bed.

He kept kissing me as he skimmed one hand down my body and then up the inside of my thigh. Two fingers brushed my pussy lips, and I moaned into his mouth. I felt him grin, and the fingers began to rub. He broke the kiss and pulled back a little so that he could watch me. Then he slid two thick fingers into me. I groaned as they stretched me, that needy ache inside me becoming heavier and denser, making me roll my hips and demand more.

Radimir kissed me again, then took my lower lip between his teeth and bit it gently. "You're soaking wet, Mrs. Aristov."

My face and neck flushed, the ache got denser, and my chest went fluttery, all at the same time.

"I think," he mused, his accent turning the words to dark poetry, "I'm going to have to give my new wife plenty of *Long. Hard. Fucks..."*—he pushed his fingers a little deeper with each word and I gasped—

"...to keep her satisfied." He curled his fingers inside me, and I panted and humped my hips against his hand, unable to help it.

I reached up and grabbed his shoulders: I was practically naked, and he was still fully dressed. "Please," I panted.

He buried his hand deep in my hair and used it to hold my head in place while he bent down and kissed me deep. "Please what?"

"Please fuck me."

"Say it in Russian. *Pozhaluysta trakhni menya.*"

That was unexpected. But I could hear the lust in his voice, feel it in the way his hand tensed in my hair. And I wanted to please him. All that time learning Russian helped my pronunciation a little but I knew I was probably going to mangle it. "*Pozhaluysta trakhni menya,*" I tried.

Radimir went *wild.* He kissed me as if my lips were his only source of oxygen, pressing my head down into the bed while his tongue darted deep. His whole body seemed to go hard, every muscle tense, and he drew his fingers from me and started to tear at his clothes, shucking off his jacket and waistcoat and then loosening his tie. I'd never known him to be so out of control but the knowledge that it was *me* that had done this to him, with those three little words, sent a warm blush of pride through me. I had my eyes closed, riding the waves of pleasure from the kiss, but I reached up and started blindly popping the buttons of his shirt, working my way down his body as far as I could reach. I heard him strip his shirt off and hurl it away and the next time his chest brushed my breasts, it was naked. Then there was the leather creak of his belt and a rustle of fabric. A couple of heavy thumps that had to be shoes hitting the floor. He was getting naked, *fast,* and all the time he was still kissing me, kissing me....

He finally broke the kiss and pulled back a little. I opened my eyes to see him naked, positioning himself between my thighs, his cock in his hand. *God,* I'd forgotten how big he was. And he was rock hard, the head bulbous and thick, the shaft so firm...

He stroked his cock. A clear bead of pre-cum glistened at the tip. "Ready to be made my wife?" he growled, rolling on a condom.

I nodded. I could hear my heartbeat pounding. "Yes."

"Say it."

"I want to be made your wife." And then...I'd never been good at talking dirty, but looking down at my body, seeing the corset and the stockings and the heels...it almost felt like a costume that let me be as filthy as I wanted. And the Russian made it easier, too. "*Pozhaluysta trakhni menya...moy muzh,*" I said in a rush. *Please fuck me...my husband.*

His eyes gleamed. He planted one hand next to my head and positioned himself, the head of him just parting my lips. Then he surged forward with his hips.

I grabbed at the sheets with both hands as he spread me, *stretched* me. That glorious silken slide as he plunged deep inside me, the heat of him filling me, then the nervous flutter of my walls as they adjusted to his size. He pulled back and thrust again, his ass clenching, and pushed deeper. I arched my back: each new millimeter of me he touched set off a fresh burst of silvery, shimmering pleasure. He drew back again, and this time when he thrust, he kept the movement going, flexing his hips to press himself deeper, deeper...

Deeper. I felt the base of his cock kiss my entrance and knew that he was hilted in me.

He put his forearms either side of my head and settled lower on me and *God,* the feeling of his muscled body on me, his hips spreading my thighs, his pecs pressing against my breasts. I looked down at the tattoos that covered his chest: I'd never seen them so close before. A dark tapestry of stars, symbols and writing in Cyrillic that left no doubt as to what he was. Naked, with all his powerful muscles on show and without the suit to give him a veneer of respectability, he looked even more dangerous. Tattooed, naked and between my thighs, with me in my bridal lingerie, he really did look like a villain, claiming an innocent princess as his prize. A dark pulse of heat rippled down my body and my pussy tightened around him.

He began to move and God, the silken friction of him as he slid from me, the rush of heat and silvery pleasure as he filled me again. Taking his weight on his forearms, he cupped my face in his hands and stroked my cheekbones with his thumbs. He looked deep into my eyes, and I could see the concentration on his face as he fucked me in gentle waves. It was glorious. *Loving.* But each stroke *out* made the aching need more intense. And each stroke *in* fed the heat that was building inside me...but not quite enough for it to ignite.

I looked up at him. It was because we were married, now. He was holding himself back, being gentle with his new wife. But *gentle* wasn't what I needed. Three weeks ago, I couldn't have said the words out loud, but now...

"H—Harder," I said.

He stared at me in astonishment. Then his eyes narrowed in lust. But he still hesitated.

"Harder...*please.*" I felt my face heat, but it felt freeing, too.

It was like my words unleashed him. He put his hands under my knees and raised them, bending my legs and opening me more to him. Then he planted his hands on my shoulders, pinning me in place...and began to fuck me *hard*.

Before, my body had been moving a little with his thrusts. Now, pinned in place by his weight, I felt every ounce of his power as his cock pistoned in and out of me. *Oh God,* it was incredible! Now that more of his weight was on me, his pecs were stroking my nipples on every thrust, sending out circular ripples of pleasure that combined with the ones coming from my groin and became a hot wave. It was carrying me inexorably upwards towards a climax, and every thrust accelerated me.

His gray eyes took in my flushed face, my desperate moans. "So, *Krasavitsa*, you like it rough." His accent made *rough* into something so deliciously, darkly sexual, I wanted to bathe in it.

I panted up at him. I wasn't capable of denying it, even if I'd wanted to.

He leaned down to speak in my ear. "I'll make sure I treat you right, darling wife." And he started to really pound me, his hips rising and falling effortlessly, burying his cock in me each time. The base of his cock was grinding against my clit and with his weight on me, all I could do was lie there and be fucked, be his *plaything,* and *God...* I could feel myself racing upwards towards my orgasm, each deep plunge of that perfect cock into me, each brush of my hardened nipples taking me higher. I could feel him getting closer, too, his breathing quickening, his cock seeming to swell even more inside me.

I reached up, wanting to stroke his muscled back, but he immediately grabbed my wrists and pressed them down to the bed above my head. I stared up at him, shocked, and instinctively tried to pull free. But his grip was like iron. And something about feeling so helpless made me soar upward even faster. I rocketed through the clouds and exploded, my breasts and hips grinding against him as wave after wave of the climax shook me. As I spasmed around him, he growled, gave one final, hard thrust and then shot in long, shuddering streams inside me.

The climax finally died away and I lay still beneath him, limp and utterly sated. He released my wrists and gently rolled us over so that he was on his back, and I was on top.

I laid my head on his chest and closed my eyes. He wrapped an arm protectively around me. And we lay like that, with me listening to the sound of his heartbeat and him lovingly stroking my hair, until we fell asleep.

45

BRONWYN

I WAS LYING on the most comfortable bed in the world. The mattress was heated to keep me toasty even though I was naked, and the pillows had been molded to perfectly fit my head. But one shoulder was cold, so I groped for the covers and tugged them higher. *Perfection!*

Then the mattress moved and mumbled in Russian. And I remembered and opened my eyes.

It was dawn and I was stretched out, naked, on top of Radimir. On top of...*my husband.* The whole world seemed to shift around me, everything suddenly different.

I lifted my head, careful not to wake him, and looked down at him. He looked so peaceful in sleep, as if whatever it was that drove him to do what he did was forgotten for a few hours. *What is it?* What happened to his brothers and their family that put him on this path?

And could I ever pull him away from it? My stomach tightened. I'd never thought of that before: I'd never needed to. A mafia boss would never give up his empire for his fake wife. But what about his real one?

Yes, I'd accepted that the Bratva was part of him. Yes, I'd fallen in love with him. But what happened *now,* now he was in love with me?

What about the long term? What about *kids?* When he'd first told me I was marrying him, I'd been focused on the life I was losing. I'd never thought about what a life together would look like. My stomach shrunk down to a cold, hard knot. *Can this really work?*

But then I gazed down at him. At those gorgeous cheekbones and that imperious scowl. At the hard globes of his biceps that made me feel so protected when he wrapped his arms around me. I thought about him paying for Baba's care, reading to me when I was ill and paying kids to buy books in the bookstore.

And then I nodded firmly to myself.

I was going to *make* it work.

I lay back down and, as soon as my cheek pressed against the warm slab of his pec, I felt my heartbeat slow, and my stomach unknot. Despite all the danger, I felt safer with him than I ever had with any man.

These doubts? I'd address them. Every one of them. I'd figure out a way. Because I loved him. And I wasn't giving him up.

I was only just climbing out of the shower when there was a knock at the door. I threw on a bathrobe and padded over there, wet-haired and barefoot, because Radimir was in the middle of cooking breakfast. Through the door viewer, I saw Gennadiy...and the same two security guys who'd been there when we came home. *They've been standing there all night?!*

I let Gennadiy in and fixed him a mug of coffee and insisted on taking coffee out to the poor security guys in the hall, as well. Gennadiy, Radimir and I pulled up stools at the breakfast bar. "I've told The Eight what Spartak did yesterday," Gennadiy told us. "They're discussing it. In the meantime, they've called a ceasefire so we should be safe." He studied the two of us thoughtfully. "Even so, it's best if you avoid Spartak until this whole thing's resolved. It's probably a good thing you won't be around."

Radimir nodded but I cocked my head to the side, confused. "Why won't we be around?"

Radimir turned to me. "We'll be on our honeymoon." I stared at him, and he looked mock-shocked. "Did you think I wouldn't give you one?"

I gaped at him. "But...*what?" Is he joking?* "A honeymoon's for...*real* marriages."

Radimir stood, took my hands in his and looked right into my eyes. "This *is* a real marriage, now."

I bit my lip and just melted. "Where are we—"

"Cancún." He was grinning, enjoying my surprise.

He'd remembered, even though I'd just mentioned it once. Emotion swelled in my chest, until I could barely speak. "When?"

Radimir made a show of checking his watch. "We're leaving for the airport in... thirty-seven minutes."

"What?! I'm not packed!" I wasn't even *dressed.*

"What do you need for Cancún? Passport. Sunscreen. Sunglasses." His eyes gleamed. "A swimsuit."

Books, I added mentally. "But I don't have summery clothes..."

"There are shops at the airport. I will buy you whatever you want."

"But the store—"

"I've already spoken to your friend Jen. She's happy to watch the store. She said to say, "don't *worry and have a good time."*

Oh my God. I flung my arms around him. *"Thank you!"* Then I shook my head in amazement. "How did you book all this? *When?!"*

"Yesterday. Remember just before the wedding dinner, when I went to the bathroom? I made a few phone calls."

He'd organized a honeymoon as soon as the wedding turned real. I hugged him even tighter. And then I ran off to get dressed.

Less than an hour later, we were climbing out of a limo at O'Hare International Airport. I started making my way towards the end of the long, snaking check-in line. But Radimir slipped his arm around my waist and led me to a small desk at the end of the room marked *Platinum Club Check In.* "Radimir Aristov," he told them. Then he glanced at me proudly. "And my wife."

I wasn't ready for the way my heart lifted when he said it like that. I found his hand and squeezed it hard.

In less than sixty seconds, we were checked in and shown through to a private lounge. A waiter passed me a glass of champagne. There were plates of pastries and fancy coffee machines, five different gateaux, canapes and *you could just take whatever you wanted.* Or I could get my nails done, or a facial.

"Would you like a massage?" asked Radimir. "Very soothing."

"Maybe later." I was looking at the other women in the lounge. They were all effortlessly elegant, lounging in white armchairs in flawless white travel outfits, their matching white leather carry-on bags with their gold Gucci logos artfully displayed beside them. I was in jeans, sneakers and I'd thrown my books and other essentials into a blue nylon backpack with a broken strap. "Were you serious about buying me clothes?" I mumbled.

"Of course." He tugged his waistcoat straight. "And a swimsuit," he said firmly.

That was the second time he'd mentioned swimsuits. No one had ever gotten excited about seeing me in one before, but there was no mistaking the lust in his eyes, and it lit a warm glow inside me. I nodded and he took my hand and led me towards the airport's stores.

A few hours later, I was sitting in a huge, gray leather seat that turned into a bed, thirty-thousand feet in the air. Another glass of champagne was in my hand, and I was browsing the lunch menu in amazement. Did I want the pan-seared salmon with a lemon-garlic butter sauce served on a bed of lime cilantro rice? Or the honey-glazed pork chop served with mango salsa and roasted green beans?

And barely four hours after *that,* I was walking out of the air-conditioned airport in Cancún and into scorching tropical heat. After months of freezing winds and damp slush, it felt like heaven.

As the limo whisked us off to the resort, I stared out of the window at the ocean. I'd always figured the photos were Photoshopped but...no, it really *was* that beautiful cyan shade you see in the ads.

The hotel was an ultramodern block of smooth white wrapped in bands of smoked glass windows, as if someone had parked a spaceship next to the beach. But after check-in, we were taken down a winding path to a quiet glade where a handful of traditional villas looked out over their own private beach. "Will we get our own *villa?*" I squeaked.

Outside, the villa had white stucco walls and traditional, heavy wooden shutters. But inside it was sleekly modern, with crisp white bed linen and a wet room. I looked out of the window at the ocean, then back at the hotel where there were four restaurants, six pools and a spa. "What do you want to do first?" I asked, overwhelmed.

He stepped closer and his eyes glazed with lust. For a moment, I thought he was going to just toss me on the bed. But then his eyes went to the collection of paper bags I'd picked up in the airport stores. One bag in particular.

"*Oh,*" I said. "I get it."

"You could wear it to the pool," he told me. "Or to the beach. Or just...in here."

I felt a smile tug at my lips. He was always so sophisticated, so in control...but when something turned him on, he transformed into a big, horny beast, and I loved him for it. "*Okay,*" I said, defeated. "Give me a minute."

In the bathroom, I adjusted straps and tweaked fabric until it was sitting right. Then I put my hair into a braid, so it didn't turn into a damp cloud if I swam and opened the door.

He'd helped me pick out the swimsuit—he'd *insisted* on it—but he'd only seen it on the hanger. Now he saw it on me and—

His jaw dropped. Literally dropped, like in a cartoon, and he let out a long string of Russian curses. I felt an odd swell of pride: I'd never done that to a man before.

The swimsuit was deep, emerald green but with a metallic gleam, almost like a superhero costume. It was cut just right for my curves and was fairly demure on the bottom half. But at the top, a scoop neck showed a valley of milky cleavage. Radimir's eyes locked on the scoop neck and when I side-stepped, they followed, like they were magnetized. I burst out laughing. "You really do like it."

He finally tore his eyes away and smiled. "Yes, *Krasavitsa*. I really do." He stepped closer. "What is *this?*"

"What is what?"

He poked my braid. "I didn't know you could do that."

"You didn't know women could change their hair?"

"I didn't know you could make yourself look even more like a librarian."

"I could probably do a *bun,* if I thought about it..." I coiled the braid into a bun shape to show him...and then stopped as I saw the look in his eyes. If I turned him on anymore, we weren't going to make it out of the villa. I quickly let the braid fall back down. "Maybe another time." Wow, I was learning all sorts of things about him, this trip.

He got changed and we headed to the beach. As we walked, I basked in the heat, letting it chase the last of the winter chill from my bones. We passed a line of sun loungers and the men lifted their heads to look at me. But then I saw them turn pale and quickly look away.

I glanced across at Radimir. He was wearing a pair of red swim trunks and nothing else, his muscles and Bratva tattoos on full display, and he was giving each man who looked at me a glare of pure ice. "What are you doing?" I asked gently.

"Letting them know I'll cut their balls off if they keep looking at you," he said. One of my admirers was close enough to hear and he suddenly took great interest in his newspaper.

I squeezed Radimir's bicep. "We're on vacation, let's try not to cut anything off anyone," I told him, secretly delighted. Radimir was attracting a lot of attention from the women, too: I could see them eyeing his tattoos and scars and whispering to each other. I remembered how I'd stared, the first time I'd seen him without his shirt. There was a new scar, now: the one on his arm where I'd stitched him up. I'd become part of his story.

When we walked hand-in-hand into the surf I let out a little moan of amazement. Even though it was now early evening, it was so *warm!* We paddled, then waded and then started lazily swimming. It was a revelation: even after a half hour swimming up and down, my joints barely felt it at all. I hadn't swum in years, I'd never had time, and I'd forgotten how much I enjoyed it. *Okay, I need to start doing this when we get back.*

We swam and kissed and splashed water at each other like kids until the sun sank into the waves and we stumbled up the beach, giggly and pleasantly tired. It was *idyllic,* everything I'd dreamed of. He'd changed so much in the last three weeks. I remembered the days when he never even smiled.

But...

I could feel something hanging over us like a gathering storm. When the honeymoon was over, we had to go back to Chicago...and he'd want to go back to his life.

Radimir wrapped his arms around me from behind and we stood there in the surf, watching the sun turn from melting copper to cherry red as it set. I wrapped my arms over his and squeezed them even tighter around me,

I was terrified I was going to lose him.

The wedding had shown me how easily one of his rivals could snuff out his life. Every time I closed my eyes, I saw the gunmen at our wedding, spraying bullets across the room. And it wasn't just Spartak: a week ago it was the Armenians, another time it would be the Italians...he had enemies everywhere, not to mention the police and FBI.

It felt like the Bratva was this huge, dark part of his life that every day threatened to snatch him away from me. Eventually, one day, something would happen. And there was nothing I could do about it.

I was an outsider. *Just the wife.* My job was to wait at home every night for the phone call that told me he was dead or in jail. And that drove me crazy. It was like watching the person you love sit in a car that was slowly rolling towards a cliff edge, and not being allowed to stop it.

I frowned and shaped the fear into flinty determination. *I'm not losing him.*

There was only one solution I could see. I didn't know if he'd even consider it but I had to try and I had to do it in Mexico, while I had him away from his brothers.

I pressed my back even more firmly to Radimir's chest.

Today was paradise. Tomorrow...I had to ask him if he'd leave the Bratva for me.

46

BRONWYN

THE NEXT DAY, we had breakfast on the private terrace outside our villa, overlooking the sea. Then Radimir took me into the jungle to see the spider monkeys and they were freakin' adorable, with huge, dark eyes and little furry heads. We took about a million photos, including one of Radimir with a monkey on his head.

In the afternoon, we rented a thirty-foot sailboat. I thought it looked enormous, but Radimir had done this before and assured me the two of us could handle it together. And after I'd figured out my mainsail from my jib, and he'd patiently agreed that *port* and *starboard* were just stupid and I could use *left* and *right,* we got the thing skimming through the water so fast I felt like we were going to take off. Eventually, it came time to turn back towards shore and head in. But I kept the boat stubbornly pointing out to sea. "Part of me wants to just keep going," I mumbled.

Radimir must have heard the worry in my voice because he sat down beside me and slipped his arm around my back. He nodded, watching me intently. *Go on.*

"But we have to go back," I said. I looked at the tattoos on his chest. "Don't we?"

He followed my gaze and nodded. "Even if I wanted to, I couldn't leave."

"They don't let anyone leave?" I asked. "Ever?"

He shook his head. Then he winced and gave me a half-hearted nod. "There *was* a man, once. He got out."

"Your friend in New York. The hitman who fell in love with his target."

"*Former* friend. Yes. His boss let him out because...well, he did something huge for him."

"But you *are* the boss," I said gently. He said nothing. "But you still can't leave, can you? You don't want to."

He sighed. "It's not about not wanting to. It's...this is in my blood, Bronwyn."

My heart sank.

He took my hand. "It's who I am," he said. "It's who I'll always be." He looked down at his chest and pointed to one of his scars, on the side of his pec. "Here. Look."

I looked. It was small and circular, so I'd taken it for a bullet wound. But it wasn't the same as the others. The edge was too perfectly circular and there were ridged lines in the center that almost seemed to form a symbol.

"After my father died..." He stopped suddenly and looked away, unable to continue. "Before we went to Vladivostok...." He broke off again. I kept quiet, giving him space, my chest aching. *What happened to his father? What happened in Vladivostok?* I wanted to help but I couldn't, until he told me. And I wasn't sure he ever would.

He took a deep breath and started again. "My father had this metal seal, passed down through the family, for sealing letters with wax. He never used it: no one writes letters anymore. But it was *his,* and it had our family's symbol on it. And—"

I put my hand over my mouth as I realized what the scar was. "Someone *branded* you with it?!"

He shook his head. "No. *I* did." He met my eyes and held them. "And then I did it to Gennadiy. And Valentin. Before we went away. To remind us that we were Aristovs, and that we needed to stick together. And that one day, we'd build something together, something no one could ever take away from us." He shook his head. "I can't leave them, Bronwyn. And I can't leave the Bratva. I'm sorry."

I nodded and rested my head on his shoulder. I could feel things shifting inside me, realigning. I wasn't mad at him, I understood. And I couldn't ask him to change. But what he'd said confirmed everything I'd been afraid of: there'd always be this big, dark presence in his life, pulling him away from me.

"Having regrets?" he asked after a while.

"No," I said immediately. I twisted and looked up at him. "Not for a minute." And I meant it. Him walking into my bookstore was the best thing that ever happened to me. Him leaving the Bratva had always been a long shot, but I'd had to try. I'd just have to find another way to make this work.

We ate dinner in one of the hotel restaurants and then, when we got back to our villa, Radimir told me to put my swimsuit back on. At first, I thought he just wanted to fuck me wearing it. But then he gestured me out onto the terrace and up a flight of stone steps on the side. I slowly climbed them, mystified.

It was a rooftop terrace, with a wall at the back to give us privacy, a spectacular view out over the ocean...and our own private hot tub.

Radimir appeared behind me with an armful of towels. "I know how much you like baths. So..."

Delighted, I climbed down the steps and into the tub. Underwater lights made it glow, and the water was bathtub warm and gently bubbling. I sat down—the seats were *padded!*—and felt all my troubles melt away as I immersed myself right up to my chin.

Radimir climbed in after me, his red swim shorts billowing in the bubbles. He got comfortable, then adjusted the controls and I squeaked as bubbles erupted under the soles of my feet...then groaned as the jets started to massage my soles. I lay back against the padded headrest. "This may be the most comfortable I've ever been," I murmured.

A wicked grin crept across Radimir's face. "I think I know a way to make it better."

He waded across to me, put his arm around my waist and lifted me. Then he sat and put me down in his lap, leaning us both back so that we were almost lying, with my head resting on his shoulder. Now I had the gloriously hot water, the bubbles...and his rugged, near-naked body underneath me.

He began stroking up and down the outside of my thighs and hips, easing the tension from them. I closed my eyes and sighed. With my legs bouncing gently in the stream of bubbles, I felt like I was floating in space. I could hear the surf crashing on the beach, Radimir's slow breathing beneath me, and nothing else. *Bliss.*

Radimir's hands moved to the fronts of my thighs, working out the knots there. Then, slowly, they moved inwards. I caught my breath as his fingertips skimmed up the sensitive skin of my inner thighs, just a few inches from my groin. I could feel his cock hardening beneath me. His fingers gradually circled inwards...*upwards.* I stiffened as they reached the edge of the narrow band of fabric that covered my groin. "Shall we go inside?" I asked.

"Why would we go inside?" His fingers moved to my pussy, rubbing in slow circles through the swimsuit.

My eyes flew open. The roof was private but not *that* private. There were other villas on either side of ours, and if they were up on their roofs, all they had to do was glance to the side. Not to mention the high-rise hotel behind us which overlooked everything. "People could see!" I whispered.

"Then they'll be jealous of me," he told me. And his fingers began to stroke up and down through the thin fabric. I bit my lip, still conflicted. Public sex was something I'd never been brave enough to try, even though the idea was kind of hot. But as he rubbed and circled, the pleasure started to override the fear. He knew exactly how much pressure to use, exactly what speed to go at...my hips began to helplessly circle. I glanced down at the water. The surface was foaming with bubbles...*maybe they won't be able to see what he's doing.*

He used the pad of his thumb to grind my clit, just rocking it back and forth through my suit while his fingers stroked. I started to breathe hard. God, I could feel my lips parting under his pressure, could feel how wet I was getting. Had he planned this? When we'd stood at the airport, choosing the swimsuit, had he looked at that narrow band of fabric that would cover my groin and imagined rubbing *exactly there,* and what it would do to me?

Now he brought his other hand into play, reaching up and massaging my breast through the suit. A fresh wave of pleasure rolled through my body, making me arch my back. It wasn't like wearing clothes, or even wearing just a bra. The swimsuit was thin and with it being wet, too, the heat of his hand went straight through the material: it felt like I was naked. My nipple rolled across his palm and started to harden into a peak, and I ground my ass against him. It only made his cock harden more.

Radimir kissed me on the side of my neck, my weak spot, and I moaned. Then he slipped one of my shoulder straps down, and my breast popped out into the steam-filled night air.

I sucked in my breath. It felt scary but thrilling. *Are we really doing this?*

He smoothed his hand across my breast, his palm stroking my nipple, and I gasped. *Yes. Yes, we're doing this.*

He dipped his head, leaning over my shoulder to take my nipple into his mouth and I squirmed, ribbons of pleasure whip-cracking down to connect with the heat that was building in my groin. He tugged the other strap of my suit down and now I was topless, my breasts throbbing and sensitive as the breeze wafted against them.

I bit my lip. The idea of people watching us made every sensation, every touch of his hands on me, feel more intense. It was past midnight, so we didn't have to worry about kids seeing and it was our own private villa: we weren't doing anything wrong. But something was making me hesitate. I'm curvy, not a willowy model, and my insecurities were whispering.

He put his lips to my ear and, as he used both hands to squeeze and rub my breasts, he whispered, "Your body is incredible. Since I first saw you, I dreamed about doing *this.*" He squeezed my breasts, just the right kind of roughly, and kissed the side of my neck.

I whinnied and looked out at the darkness. "People might see me."

"I hope so," he told me. "They can see what an incredible wife I've got and be jealous."

I went warm inside and the fear dropped away. The only opinion that mattered was his.

I leaned back against his chest and let the sensations take over. His lips worked up and down my neck and a slow drumbeat of pleasure began in my core, vibrating out through my whole body. I reached back and ran my hands down his sides, fingers trailing over the hard ridges of his abs and the muscled hardness of his thighs.

He tugged my swimsuit down over my stomach, down to my groin. Then he lifted me for a second and suddenly the swimsuit was sliding down my legs and off. It floated to the surface, and I settled back down onto his lap, panting in shock and excitement. There were suddenly so many sensations: warm currents in the water caressed the delicate lips of my pussy, jets of bubbles were rushing over the inside of my thighs, and I felt suddenly so...*free*. His cock was rock hard, now, and I was basically straddling it, the shaft between the cheeks of my ass and the head just nudging my pussy. The wet fabric of his swim shorts was so thin that it might as well not have been there. I swallowed, that drumbeat inside me pounding faster and faster.

He took one breast in his hand and squeezed it while pulling me back against his chest. The other hand went down between my legs and began to rub my now-naked pussy: steady, expert strokes that made me tremble and thrash, my toes breaking the surface. He leaned down and kissed me, his tongue darting into my mouth as fingers pushed slowly into me, finding me soaking and ready. I could feel his chest moving against my back: he was panting and when he broke the kiss for a second, I could hear the raw lust in his voice. "*God!*" I moaned.

He suddenly lifted me off his lap, helping me stand so that I was hip-deep in the water. He slid out from behind me and then gently pushed me down into the padded seat. Looming over me, he adjusted my position, pulling me forward until I was right on the edge of the seat. Then he sank to his knees, ducked his head beneath the surface and—

I threw my head back and gasped, my mouth open wide as he buried his tongue in my pussy. He wasn't building up slowly or teasing me, this was full-on and hungry, his strong hands holding my legs wide, thumbs circling on the sensitive skin of my inner thighs, as his tongue dived deep and his upper lip rubbed at my clit. It was incredible: the warm, bubbling water was stroking every part of me, like I was being kissed everywhere at once, and his tongue was fucking me in a rhythm that made me his helpless puppet, my hands grabbing at the rim of the tub while my legs kicked, and my ass twisted in the seat. I reached down and tangled my fingers in his dark hair, out of control.

I began to buck against his face. The drumbeat that was crashing through me was going so fast, now, that it was an endless vibration, making my body tremble. "Fuck," I said, even though he couldn't hear me. "Fuck. Fuck, Radimir..."

The orgasm roared towards me, and I closed my eyes. The fact we were in public was forgotten; *everything* was forgotten. He put his lips over my clit, flicking it with his tongue and sucking, and I lost it. My thighs clamped closed against his cheeks and I trapped him there as the climax thundered through me, wave after wave. Only when it finally let go of me did *I* let go, opening my thighs, and he stood up, panting but laughing, water streaming down his shoulders and flanks. "Trying to drown your husband for the insurance?" he asked.

I was barely capable of speech. "Sorry," I croaked.

He grinned at me, his eyes gleaming. "It would have been a good way to go." He waded over to the edge of the hot tub and pulled a foil packet from the bundle of towels he'd brought up to the roof with him. Then he turned to me, pushed down his swim shorts and stepped out of them. He stared into my eyes as he rolled the condom onto his cock, then sat down in one of the other seats, his cock standing straight up underwater. "Come here."

My legs were still shaking, and it took me a moment to stand. Steam rose from my body as I waded over to him. Little aftershocks were still trembling through me from the orgasm, and I could hear myself panting.

I stepped forward so that my legs were either side of his and he scooched forward to the very edge of the seat. I slowly squatted down, my hands on his shoulders, and he guided his cock to me. God, the water made everything so much more intense! I could feel the currents stroking at my sensitive, engorged lips as they flowered open...and then the shocking heat of the head of his cock, pushing at my entrance. I gasped, adjusted my angle and sank onto him. The buoyancy made it easy; I could go *really...slow...* I closed my eyes and bit my lip as the head of him stretched me...and then he was gliding up into me, eased by my wetness, and it was the best thing in the world.

I sank down and it was tight, silken perfection, every inch he touched sending out shimmering, silver stars of pleasure. I stopped, panting, then pressed on his shoulders and pushed myself up again, drawing him from me until just the head held me open, then sinking back down again. This time, I kept going, a long, satiny rush, and he cursed and clutched me tight as I took him right down to the root.

We stayed like that for a moment, breathing hard. I was sitting in his lap, with his arms wrapped around me and my breasts gently brushing his chest as the currents moved them. With him hilted inside me and my groin pressed tight up against his, I could feel every tiny movement he made, every breath he took, and I felt so incredibly close to him.

I tentatively pushed myself up again, not used to being in control, and he growled deep in his chest as I moved on him. Up, up, up...and then down, unleashing another starburst of pleasure, one I had to have again, *now*. I started to rise and fall on him, using my legs to power me and wrapping my arms around his neck for support. I stared right into those eyes that once had been so frozen: now, they were meltingly hot and completely locked on mine. Each time I lifted myself it was a long, slow loss that only made my downward rush sweeter. I kept it slow at first, wanting to savor the feeling, and he cursed under his breath...but controlled himself and let me set the pace. But I couldn't go slow for long: the silvery explosion of pleasure as he rushed into me was too addictive and I started moving faster and faster, bouncing in his lap, turning the surface of the hot tub into rolling waves.

He ran his hands up my body and cupped my breasts, rubbing my nipples as they bounced in his hands. I moved faster, and the silvery bursts of pleasure started to merge together, crackling through my whole body. I went even faster, my ass slapping against his thighs underwater, and the starbursts began to melt...but I couldn't move fast enough to heat them to full, molten silver. The water was hard to move through quickly and my joints were beginning to ache.

He understood. He gripped my hips and used his strength to move me, hauling me up and ramming me down on his cock. My mouth opened but I couldn't speak: each deep, hard stroke sent out another silvery rush and now they were melting together, becoming a dense, molten ball that was compressing and compressing. He slid his hands under my ass and squeezed my cheeks, slamming me down on him, now, the water churning and splashing over the edges. He began to squeeze my ass cheeks in rhythm with the fucking and the slight roughness made it even better. He moved me faster and I sucked in my breath, *faster* and I trembled. I closed my eyes and pressed my forehead to his, feeling my walls beginning to flutter around him...

He braced his feet against the bottom of the hot tub and strained upwards with his hips, grinding against my clit, and that was enough to send me over the edge. I moaned into his ear, feeling myself beginning to come, and he clutched me tight to him as I writhed against him and he shot and shot inside me.

When we'd recovered, he gently lifted me out of the hot tub and lovingly dried me with a towel, then carried me downstairs, a limp, happy mess.

I woke, but didn't know why.

The bedroom was quiet and still but I had a vague half-memory of hearing something. *Several* somethings. Soft thumps on the floor. Had Radimir gotten up and was walking around?

Eyes still closed, I felt for him...then relaxed when I felt the reassuring warm slab of his pec under my cheek. God, I was so *happy!* Happy like I'd never been. When I felt the first twinge of worry in my stomach, I blocked it out. *Nope. Not spoiling this.*

But as I lay there in the darkness, the worries multiplied, creeping in from different angles until I had to acknowledge them. This was *literally* the honeymoon period. Was this really going to work, long term, when there was this huge part of his life that I wasn't part of, and that might wind up killing him?

Part of me was disappointed about our conversation on the sailboat: I guess on some stupid, secret level, I'd hoped he'd say *Of course I'll leave the Bratva for you, my love,* and become a hedge fund manager or something, and that would be that. And another part of me was almost jealous, as if he was choosing it over me.

But most of me understood. If he *had* left the Bratva for me, I'd have felt guilty forever. And he hadn't chosen the Bratva over me, a gangster was just what he was. I'd fallen in love with all of him, including that part. He'd already changed for me, more than I'd thought possible. I couldn't expect him to throw away his whole life. And maybe things would calm down now. Gennadiy had said there was a ceasefire, right? Maybe the worst was over.

I squeezed the sleeping Radimir a little tighter: *Mine!* Then I stretched out my legs, getting comfortable, so I could get back to sleep.

My foot brushed something cold and leathery, and I frowned. *Aw, crap.* I must have put my purse on the bed at some point, and it had somehow wound up under the covers. It would keep catching on my toes and annoying me if I didn't move it.

Very carefully, so as not to wake my husband (my *husband!),* I unwound myself from him and burrowed down under the covers to grab it. *Where's the strap?* I strained for it but couldn't quite reach. I burrowed a little deeper, strained again, and managed to touch it.

And the leathery thing moved towards me, slithering over my hand.

47

RADIMIR

NORMALLY, I come awake slowly, shaking loose the monsters that try to drag me back into my dreams. But there are some sounds that have me instantly awake: a gunshot, a siren, the sound of a door being broken down.

That night, I discovered a new one: Bronwyn's scream.

It was loud enough that they must have heard it in the other villas, loud enough that it hurt. I sat bolt upright, but she'd already shot from the bed, moving faster than I'd ever seen her go. She flattened herself against the wall next to the bed, panting in fear.

"What is it?!" I jumped out of bed and padded over to her. "What's wrong?"

She couldn't speak. She pointed to the end of the bed, still heaving for breath.

I frowned and took a few steps. Was someone there? An intruder? I squinted through the darkness, but I couldn't see anyone. All I could see was a black electrical cable hanging out from under the covers. Had Bronwyn left a hairdryer in the bed?

Then the cable slithered onto the floor and into the shadows.

I jumped backwards. *Chyort*! A snake! "Did it bite you?" I demanded.

She shook her head, white-faced.

How the fuck did a snake get in here? I shook my head. Hotel security could deal with it, or they could call Animal Control or something. "We're getting out of here," I told Bronwyn. Keeping one eye on the patch of shadow where I last saw the snake, I grabbed one of Bronwyn's dresses and tossed it to her, then her shoes. I scrambled into my pants and a polo shirt. *Where are my shoes? Fuck, right where the snake is.*

I grabbed our passports and my wallet, too, because no way was I coming back here. *Why is it so dark?* Shouldn't there be some moonlight coming in through the windows? I wished I could turn the lights on, but I was too far from the bed to reach the light switch, and the other one was over by the door. "Come on," I told Bronwyn, taking her hand. Barefoot, I took a careful step towards the door...

And saw movement in the shadows, right in front of us. *Fuck. How did it get all the way over there?* We couldn't get to the door. "Back up," I murmured, trying to keep my voice calm. "We'll go out through a window."

We backed away, then turned and headed for the far side of the room, where the windows were. I went fast, knowing the thing was safely behind us.

A noise made me freeze. A noise I'd only ever heard in cowboy movies, a dry, fast rattle. And it came from in *front* of me.

There's more than one snake.

48

RADIMIR

I PICKED up Bronwyn and climbed up onto the bed, the only place I was pretty sure was safe. Two big, bouncy steps took me to the head of the bed, and I finally managed to turn on the light.

Bronwyn gave a whimper of terror. There were three snakes on the floor under the windows. Two near the door, another under the desk and one climbing the leg of the coffee table. Panic clawed at my chest. Then I glanced at the windows, and everything suddenly got much, much worse.

The shutters were closed. On every window. That's why it had been so dark. We'd definitely left the windows ajar when we went to bed to let a breeze in, and the shutters had been latched open.

I suddenly knew how the snakes had gotten into our room.

I put Bronwyn down, walked over to the edge of the bed and leaned out over the floor towards the nearest window. There was a snake coiled right below me and I tried not to think about what would happen if I slipped and stepped down onto the floor.

I managed to *just* reach the window. I pushed against the shutters...and they creaked but didn't move. Something was holding them shut: a chain, or a zip tie, something on the outside. Someone had emptied a bag full of snakes through our window, and then they'd trapped us in here. They'd probably done something to the door lock, too, even if we could reach the door, which we couldn't. *Fuck.*

I joined Bronwyn in the middle of the bed, and we looked at each other, panting in fear. Then I saw something behind her and pulled her behind me.

A snake had slithered up the foot of the bed and was poking its head over the top, watching us.

"Where's your gun?" asked Bronwyn breathlessly.

"In Chicago. We had to go through airport security."

The snake shot towards us, moving across the covers in big, winding 'S's, moving inhumanly fast. I backed up as much as I could, until Bronwyn was sandwiched between me and the wall, but the snake kept coming, heading straight for my ankles. I frantically scrambled onto the pillows, then grabbed the covers and hurled them off the bed, taking the snake with them. I could feel sweat running down between my shoulder blades. Someone had done this deliberately, which meant they'd have picked the most lethal snakes. One bite might not kill us, but it would leave us semi-conscious and writhing in pain, and then the rest would bite and...*fuck, fuck, fuck!*

Another snake climbed the nightstand on my side of the bed. Thin and black, with bright yellow bands. It coiled, ready to strike at my legs...

Bronwyn sidestepped around me and slammed one of her thick hardback books down on its head. The snake's tail stopped moving. I nodded my thanks, but the rest of the snakes were exploring the room: it was only a matter of time before more climbed up here. I looked around, desperate, but I couldn't see any other ways out. *Call for help?* By the time someone got here and forced open the windows, we'd already be dead. I looked around again and felt my hair brush the ceiling: the room wasn't designed for someone my height to stand on the bed.

The ceiling! I looked up. Above us was the flat concrete roof with the hot tub. But below that was a suspended ceiling, to hide all the air conditioning and plumbing. I pushed one of the ceiling tiles up and to the side, making a hole a few feet square.

I heard a strangled gasp from Bronwyn. Two more snakes had crawled up onto the bed.

I looked at the hole in the ceiling. I had no idea what was up there, but it had to be better than here. Grabbing Bronwyn by the waist, I lifted her up through the hole. "Can you climb up?"

Her waist twisted in my hands as she looked for a handhold. The two snakes began moving lazily towards me. *Fuck.*

Bronwyn swarmed up into the hole. I jumped and grabbed the edge—

The ceiling tile snapped and fell, unable to take my weight. The hole in the ceiling ripped open, tiles and support struts dangling. Bronwyn screamed. I fell back down to the bed and nearly went full length, right onto the snakes. *Chyort! Chyort! Chyort!* I stood there wobbling for a second, then glanced up. The hole was too big, now. There was nothing for me to grab onto, even if I jumped.

Bronwyn lay down full length in the ceiling space and reached down through the hole, offering me her hand. "Come on!"

I'm too heavy. What if I pull the whole ceiling down? One of the snakes struck at me, close enough that I could see its fangs. I dodged and its head brushed my leg.

"*Come on!*" Bronwyn yelled and offered her hand again. "I'm not leaving you!"

Chyort. I didn't deserve her. As the other snake coiled to strike, I jumped and grabbed her wrist. She grunted at my weight. I heaved myself up until I could grab a support strut, then used it to haul myself up into the ceiling space. The ceiling creaked...but it held.

We lay there panting for a second, watching as more snakes climbed onto the bed. Then I looked around and found the big, silver air conditioning duct that funneled hot air to the outside through a vent. I pulled the duct away from the vent and then kicked at the vent's plastic slats until they broke, and we had a hole big enough to crawl through. I went first, dropping down to the ground and then helping Bronwyn down. We were out, and we hugged each other in the cool night air, shaking and soaked with sweat.

I looked around. It was still dark and there were a million places to hide in the shadows between the villas. Whoever did this could still be around. "Come on," I told Bronwyn, taking her hand. And I pulled her into a run, even though I knew it would put a strain on her legs. I didn't dare carry her in case someone stepped out of the shadows, and I had to fight.

We ran all the way to the main hotel: I wanted to be somewhere public, with cameras, somewhere no one would dare touch us. In any other hotel, the bar would have been long closed but there was a group of women still knocking back cocktails and tearfully hugging each other, even at 5 am. *Thank God for bachelorette parties.*

I walked right up to the bar, where everyone could see us, and only then did I let myself stop and think. *Who tried to kill us?* Someone who'd wanted us to die scared, and in agony. Not just a rival, then. This was personal.

My stomach dropped. *Spartak.* He had connections with one of the Mexican cartels.

I reached for my phone, then remembered it was back in the room. I waved over the bartender and asked to use the landline and then, since we were in a bar and my hands were still shaking, I asked for a vodka.

"Make it two, please," Bronwyn added, surprising me. She was still shaking too, and I pulled her close and stroked her hair while the bartender fixed our drinks. Then we both knocked them back...and I called Gennadiy.

He answered on the third ring, despite it being the middle of the night. "I'm pretty sure Spartak just tried to kill us," I told him.

I heard him rubbing at his face. "He'd never break the ceasefire. The Eight would order him cut off." Being cut off is the thing every Bratva family fears. If The Eight decide a family can't be trusted, they can make them pariahs: no one is allowed to help them or even talk to them. No family can stand on its own, so being cut off is a death sentence: your enemies wipe you out within days.

"Well, something's happened," I said. "Find out what." And I gave him the hotel number to call us back on. Then I slipped my arm around Bronwyn's waist and pulled her close. She'd been amazing, back there. Calm, strong, and she'd saved my life twice. I hated that she was in danger because of me. "I never meant for you to be part of this," I muttered.

She pressed herself to my side. She'd stopped shaking but she was still pale and drawn. Considering what she'd just been through, she was holding together amazingly well.

Just a few minutes later, the hotel phone rang, and I snatched it up. I could hear Gennadiy breathing at the other end, but he didn't speak. "What is it?" I growled, and held the phone so that Bronwyn could listen, too.

He took a deep breath. "The Eight have thrown us under the bus, brother. They're denying they told us to kill Spartak's brother. They're saying we broke the truce, all on our own. They told Spartak last night that the ceasefire is over and that it's open season on us." Gennadiy swallowed. "They've cut us off, Radimir. We're *dead!*"

49

BRONWYN

I'D ALWAYS THOUGHT of Radimir as unbreakable. But he just slumped, all his power and confidence gone. It was terrifying. He was the one who protected me from people like Spartak. If he was beaten...

But then I forced the fear down inside. The *Pakhan* needed his wife.

I gently put a hand on his back. He turned, but his eyes were distant, and it took him a few seconds to focus on me.

"It'll be okay," I told him. "You'll figure it out. You'll find a way. You always do."

He took a deep, shuddering breath...and then he straightened up a little and nodded gratefully. His eyes locked with mine and a little of his strength seemed to creep back. His hands reached for his waistcoat and then he realized he wasn't wearing one. But he tugged his polo shirt straight instead. "Let's get back to Chicago," he said.

A few hours later, we were on a plane. I had a blanket wrapped around me, but I couldn't get warm: a cold fear was sinking into my bones. We'd escaped...but we weren't flying to safety. We were heading back to Chicago, right into the lion's den. I looked across at Radimir. I'd almost lost him tonight.

And that's when I realized something. If I couldn't drag him away from the Bratva, there was only one option left. It scared the hell out of me, but it was the only way I could at least have some input, and maybe help keep him alive.

I had to become one of them. Part of the Bratva. A mafia wife.

50

BRONWYN

We were met at the airport by two of Radimir's men, who escorted us back to the penthouse so that we could freshen up and change. Radimir looked much more like himself, back in his normal three-piece suit. But he still looked grimly serious. I remembered the early days, when I'd wondered if I'd ever see him smile. Now I wondered if I'd ever see him smile again. He told me he had to meet with his brothers, and I nodded. "I'd like to come too," I said nervously. "If that's okay."

First, he blinked at me. Then he cocked his head to one side and gazed at me for a long time, and he must have seen the change in me because his eyes suddenly became warm, as if I'd just made him very, very happy...and a little sad, at the same time. "Yes," he told me, his voice ragged with emotion. "Yes, *Krasavitsa*, of course."

When we arrived at Gennadiy's house, a steady, ice-cold rain was hammering the roof and windows. We got soaked just running from the car to the door. Gennadiy showed us in, but seemed a little surprised to see me.

Radimir fixed him with a glare. "I told you: she's family now."

Gennadiy sighed and nodded and took us through to a wood-paneled room with a huge oak table. We all sat down and it was only when Gennadiy reached for the vodka bottle to pour himself a shot that I saw his hand and gasped. He was wrapped in bandages up to the wrist.

"Burns," he muttered. "Spartak torched one of our casinos last night. I went in to make sure all the staff got out okay. Everyone's alive but it was close."

Valentin was hurt, too: someone had side-swiped his car and he'd rammed into a lamppost. The airbags had saved him, but his head was wrapped in bandages. And Mikhail was glowering, his hands shaking as he petted his dogs. He had two nestled on either side of him and was hugging them protectively. "We were walking downtown, and someone threw a piece of meat right in front of them. I managed to get it out of their mouths, and it was full of fucking rat poison. What sort of bastard tries to poison *dogs?!*" It was the only time I'd ever seen him angry.

Gennadiy got up and started to pace. "Spartak has put a price on all our heads." He looked at me sadly. "Even yours. He has a lot more men than we do and they're well trained. This place is fortified but you're not safe outside these walls. Don't go anywhere, not even down the street to get a cup of coffee."

I nodded, feeling sick. Someone wanted me dead. Someone was willing to pay money to *end my life*: I couldn't wrap my head around that.

Gennadiy sighed and leaned forward over the table. "I've called The Eight over and over. They're still denying they told us to kill Spartak's brother. They say this is all our fault and they won't rein Spartak in. In the last twenty-four hours, he's hit seventeen of our places. Bars smashed up, warehouses torched." He dropped into a chair, defeated. "I'd say we've lost about a quarter of what we have."

A quarter! A quarter of the Aristov empire just *gone,* in a day. Three more days and they'd have nothing left. Then I corrected myself and sat straighter in my chair. *We. We* would have nothing left. I was a part of this, now.

"Why would The Eight *do* this?" asked Valentin. "Call us, give us the order and then deny it? We've always obeyed them. And they want peace: that's the whole reason all the families obey them, to keep the peace. They must have known this would start a war."

We all looked at him hopelessly. No one had an answer. But then I frowned. A half-idea was slowly forming, a reflection of something Valentin had said. It felt like looking at the moon in a rippling puddle: there was something there, but I couldn't see it clearly, yet.

"Our legal businesses aren't doing much better," said Radimir. He'd spent most of the flight making phone calls. "Three construction projects have just stopped because politicians have withdrawn their approval at the last minute. They're people I have no hold over, I was relying on the other families to pressure them, because we all benefited. But no one's playing ball anymore. We're losing about two and a half million a day."

Even the Aristovs would be bankrupt soon, at that rate. I kept frowning, still trying to make my idea come into focus.

"No one will even return my calls," said Mikhail sourly. "They know that if they help us, The Eight will cut them off, too."

Gennadiy knocked back a shot of vodka and poured another. "I wish I'd never answered that fucking call."

And in a rush, the idea stabilized and snapped into focus. I drew in my breath...but I couldn't speak. The four men had started arguing about what to do. And despite how much I'd gotten to like Gennadiy, Valentin and Mikhail, they were still intimidating as hell. They were *Bratva.* I was an outsider. But I couldn't just stay silent. The words swelled up inside me as the argument got louder and louder. And finally, I closed my eyes and blurted. "What if they didn't call you?"

The room went silent. I opened my eyes just in time to see Gennadiy shove his chair back from the table and stand. "You think I'm making it up? You think you can come in here and call me a liar, just because you spread your legs for my brother?"

Radimir's chair screeched as he stood, too. "That's my *wife* you're talking to. Speak like that to her again and I'll smash your teeth out on the edge of this table."

I stood up, my heart thumping, and put my hands up to try to keep the two of them from leaping at each other. "I'm not saying you're lying, Gennadiy. But what if the call wasn't from The Eight?"

Gennadiy scowled at me. "It was! It was *Domaslav!* I've spoken to him a hundred times; he deals with all the families in Chicago!"

I put up both hands to try to calm him. "Deep Fakes."

Everyone stared at me. Then Radimir said, "What?!"

"Before I started my bookstore," I said, "I did a business course at night school. One of the modules was on banking and avoiding fraud. One of the growing threats is deep fakes. Someone calls you, pretending to be someone you know. They sound *just like them* because they're using a computer to mimic the voice. They tell you to pay someone or move money to a different account. People have lost millions, *tens* of millions. Now what if...someone used the same trick on you? On this family? Only instead of defrauding you for money...they tricked you into killing Spartak's brother?"

There was a moment of stunned silence. Then, "That's ridiculous," said Gennadiy. But he sounded shaken.

I leaned in. "When Domaslav called you, did he know anything?" I asked gently. "Anything that only one of The Eight would know? A password, a code, anything that *proves* it was actually him?"

"We don't *use* passwords!" snapped Gennadiy. "We're—" He unleashed a long stream of curses in Russian, but I knew the anger wasn't directed at me, and I knew what he meant. *We're Bratva.* They were deeply traditional, they had honor. They did things based on trust, on promises. But that was exactly what had made them vulnerable and the fear in his eyes meant he'd realized it, too.

"Gennadiy?" asked Radimir quietly.

Gennadiy cursed again. Valentin put a hand on his back, but he shook it off angrily. "No," he said at last. "No, they didn't say anything that proves it was them." He looked around at our horrified faces and shook his head wildly. "But that doesn't mean..."

Mikhail nodded sadly. "Bronwyn is right. It's the only thing that makes sense. Ever since you got that phone call, we've been asking why The Eight would want us to break the truce. Now we know: they didn't. Someone fooled us."

We all looked at each other in slack-jawed horror as the scale of it sank in. We'd been fooled into starting a war, and at the same time cutting ourselves off from all help. One fake phone call was going to destroy the whole Aristov empire.

I saw Gennadiy's legs shake. He sat down heavily and put his head in his hands. "This is..." he swallowed. "It's all my fault."

We all came around the table and put hands on his shoulders. "Any one of us could have taken that phone call," Radimir told him firmly. "We wouldn't have questioned it, either."

But Gennadiy just stared at the table, inconsolable. When he finally lifted his head to look at me, all the hostility was gone. "Thank you," he said quietly. "Without you, we'd never have known."

The others nodded. Radimir looked at me with such a look of love and pride that I melted. But it was the looks the other three gave me that made my throat close up. For the first time in a long time, I felt like part of a family.

"So, who did this?" asked Valentin.

I thought about it. "It would have to be someone who'd spoken to The Eight, so they could sample Domaslav's voice."

Gennadiy ran his hands through his hair. "That's a long list. Domaslav deals with all the families in Chicago. Any of our rivals could have done it. There are plenty who want us gone." He shook his head as he finally accepted the reality of it. "It's the perfect fucking crime. One phone call, and they make us start a war with a rival *and* cut us off from all aid. They'll wipe us out without ever firing a shot."

"Can we go to Spartak and explain what happened?" I asked.

Radimir shook his head sadly. "We killed his brother. He's not going to forgive that just because we were tricked into it. Besides, we've got no way of proving it."

"All we can do," said Gennadiy, "is get ready for war."

51

RADIMIR

As the meeting broke up, Gennadiy reiterated that none of us should leave the mansion until this was over. "All of you are staying here," he told us firmly. "I have plenty of room."

I took Bronwyn up to the room I always used when I stayed over at Gennadiy's, a first-floor bedroom with a huge, arched window overlooking the gardens. I sank down on the bed, suddenly exhausted.

"Level with me," said Bronwyn, sitting down next to me. "How bad is this?"

I sighed. "*Bad.*" I was silent for a moment. I'd always believed that a king had to stand alone, locked down tight, and never show weakness. And of course I'd never had anyone to share my troubles *with.* But that had changed, and so had I. I started to explain, the words coming slowly at first. "Since the truce began, years ago, my family—" I looked at her and corrected myself—"*Our* family has focused on our legitimate businesses. But Spartak, he's old school. He's built a drug empire and an army. He's prepared for war...and we're not." I closed my eyes, rubbed at them and groaned. I'd barely slept, I'd been traveling most of the morning, I'd had too much coffee to wake me up and too much vodka to try to calm me down. *Chyort*. I was a mess.

"I know what you need," said Bronwyn softly. "Take off your clothes."

I opened my eyes and looked at her, feeling my cock instantly rise and harden.

"Not *that!*" She swatted my arm. "I mean...maybe later. But no. You need a bath."

For a second, I thought I'd misheard. But then she disappeared into the bathroom, and I heard water running. "*A bath?* No!" I shook my head as she returned. I never took baths even in normal circumstances: I didn't have time. "*Krasavitsa*, that's very sweet but it's the middle of the day, we're at *war*, I can't—"

She put a hand on each of my knees and leaned forward over me. "Is there anything you can practically do *right now?*"

I opened my mouth. Closed it again. Partially because she was right, partially because I recognized that tone and knew she wouldn't budge and partially because it was very hard to think when her breasts swayed like that. "No..."

"Then you can have a bath. It'll relax you and help you think." She straightened up and crossed her arms. "You're my husband now and I'm going to take care of you."

Those icy, efficient cogs inside me that I was so proud of...they softened. *Melted. God, I don't deserve her.* She was being the perfect wife...and I still couldn't tell her about Vladivostok. I knew that keeping such a huge part of my past off limits was wrong, that it meant she could never fully understand me. But I just couldn't face re-opening those wounds. I loosened my tie. "What are *you* going to be doing?"

She reached around to the zip on the back of her dress. "It's a big bath..."

I stood and started shedding my clothes, suddenly much more enthusiastic.

By the time I was naked, the bath was ready. It *was* big, and antique, like most of the things in Gennadiy's house, with clawed feet and softly curving edges that were comfortable to lean on. Bronwyn must have added something to the water because there were bubbles, and I could smell grapefruit and lavender. I'd been planning to climb in first, looking forward to having her ass pressed against my cock and her breasts in easy reach of my hands. But she insisted on getting in first and told me to lie back against her. I climbed in and....

Ohhh. The hot water rose around me, and I felt the tension start to ease from my body. I frowned. It was just possible that women, with their bath obsessions, were onto something. And then I lay gently back against Bronwyn and her soft, wet breasts pillowed against my back and... *ahh.* She gently touched my forehead and guided my head. I lay back against her shoulder and... *wow.* I felt relaxed and secure. *This is what it feels like to be cared for.*

I closed my eyes and inhaled the sweet scent of the bubbles. *I'm going to smell like a woman.* But I was already too comfortable to care. For a few moments, the only sounds were the lapping of water and the soft crackle of bubbles popping. Then Bronwyn said, "The other families in Chicago won't help us, because they're scared of The Eight. But what about in other cities?"

"The Eight scare *everyone,*" I said sleepily. "Every Bratva family, everywhere, obeys them."

She went quiet for a moment, thinking. "What about the man you used to work for, in New York?"

"Luka Malakov. Yes, even him." She'd been right about the bath: the warm water was relaxing me and that made my thoughts spin more easily. "About the only person in the Bratva who *doesn't* listen to them is Konstantin."

"Who?"

I felt my lips tug into a half smile. "Konstantin Gulyev runs most of New York. No one knows exactly how much money he has, but it's billions. Some say he once bought up an entire TV network just so he could force them to keep making his girlfriend's favorite show. And that he has a BDSM dungeon in his basement. And that when he kills his enemies, he has them encased in stone and made into statues, and there are statues like that all over his mansion.

I felt Bronwyn stiffen in horror. Then she said, "If he doesn't listen to The Eight, that makes him the one person who might help us."

I opened my eyes. *She's right.* "In theory," I said slowly. Then I sighed. "But he'd want something in return, and we don't have anything he wants."

"Tell me about his business," she insisted. "Every detail."

I looked round at her in surprise. And then I closed my eyes again and lay back against her breasts while I told her everything I knew about Konstantin, his empire and his network of allies. When I'd finished, she said nothing. She was silent for so long, I eventually twisted around to see if she'd fallen asleep. I found her staring into the corner of the room with furious determination, her red-brown eyebrows tilted sharply down. I could *feel* her brain working. She was trying to find a solution and she was doing it for me. For *us.* I felt my chest swell. *God, I love this woman.* It was useless, of course, there was nothing we could offer Konstantin. But just a few weeks ago, she'd hated my world, my empire. The fact she was fighting, even futilely, to save it was—

"I think I know what we can offer him," said Bronwyn. And she laid it out for me. Now *I* frowned. It sounded crazy, it was too...*big.* But as she talked me through it, quiet and persuasive, my perspective started to shift. Bronwyn had broken down Konstantin's operations using her analytical business brain. I'd always thought of Konstantin's and my empires as opposing cities, towering blocks of black and white facing off against each other. But now the blocks seemed to flip on their sides, the opposing blocks sliding together like a key into a lock.

"*Chyort,*" I muttered. "That's clever. But he'll never agree. People like us don't make those sorts of deals."

"If I persuaded you," she said gently, "maybe we can persuade him."

I thought about it. It was a desperate play. But a desperate play was better than no play. "I have no way of contacting him," I thought aloud. "We'd have to go to New York. Ambush him and hope we can get him to talk to us." I felt a cold, hard knot form in my stomach. "It's risky. Spartak's looking for us." The thought of putting her in danger to save our empire made me want to throw up. But *not* trying her plan wasn't an option, either: Spartak wasn't going to stop until my whole family was dead and that included her. I twisted around to look at her. "I don't suppose there's any point trying to convince you to stay here while I go alone?"

She gave me an *as if* look and I felt the emotion well up in my chest. I loved that she was the one person who always stood up to me.

"Gennadiy won't go for this," warned Bronwyn. "He doesn't want us to even leave the house."

"Then we'd better not tell him we're going." I stood up, water sluicing off me. I felt energized. There was hope, however small, and it was thanks to her. I took her hand and hauled her up. The smile she gave me hit me right in the chest. It was nervous and hopeful and *proud,* and...

It felt like we were a team. I squeezed her hand, and she squeezed back.

"Pack a bag," I told her. "We're going to New York."

52

BRONWYN

RADIMIR LEFT to make some phone calls, trying to figure out where we could ambush Konstantin. I got dressed and sat on the bed, thinking. *Are we really going to do this?* Gennadiy was going to be pissed. Radimir might be the boss, but Gennadiy did most of the day-to-day running of things, sort of like a Chief of Staff to a President. And he'd be rightfully mad when the President ran off with his new wife on a secret mission in the middle of a freakin' war to try to strike a deal he knew nothing about. He might blame me for leading his brother astray. I sighed. *I'll worry about that when we get back.*

If *we get back.* My shoulders slumped. That was the other reason this was a bad idea. Spartak's men were hunting us and even if we made it out of Chicago alive, we'd be in a strange city with no backup.

But my crazy plan was our only hope. We *had* to do this. I straightened up...and caught a glimpse of my reflection in the mirror.

We had to do this...but I couldn't do it like *this,* in jeans and a t-shirt. I was going to be negotiating with one of the most powerful mafia bosses in the world. If I was a mafia wife, I had to start looking like it.

Gennadiy had handed us new phones to replace the ones we'd had to leave in Mexico. It only took me a few minutes searching on social media to find the person I wanted: the top personal stylist in the city. I sat staring at the message box for a while, trying to figure out what to type. Then I decided to just be honest. *Hi. I'm Radimir Aristov's new wife. And I need to look like it. NOW, this afternoon. Can you help me?* I hit the Send button and prayed, but without much hope.

No more than ten seconds later, a reply came back. *Send me your address, your measurements and a photo. I'll be with you in an hour.*

Fifty-seven minutes later, a van screeched to a stop in front of Gennadiy's mansion. The security guards pulled their guns, thinking we were under attack. But instead of gunmen, a woman in an immaculate white trouser suit and scarlet blouse leapt out and shooed them away, completely unfazed by the weapons. "Clear the way!" she yelled in a British accent.

The guards sheepishly put their guns down and the woman banged twice on the side of the van. A sliding door opened, a ramp slid down, and two racks of clothes were wheeled down, pushed by a guy with chin-length black hair and Mediterranean-sea eyes.

"Rachel Waltham-Kutz," she told me as she approached. "Behind me is Alfredo. You must be Mrs. Aristov?"

I nodded, awestruck.

"Good." She strutted past me and clapped her hands twice. "*Come come!* We have work to do."

I scurried after her into the living room, which she'd apparently decided was where we were doing this. She chased away a bewildered Valentin, closed the doors and turned to me. "So. You want to look like *them*. The..." —she glanced around and then said, diplomatically—"*Russian* women."

I nodded, then looked down at myself hopelessly. "But I'm not..." I indicated my curves. "They're all..."

"It's not about being skinny, darling, or having blonde hair. It's about projecting strength. Using the weapons you have. You need to stop thinking you're in their territory and start making them feel they're in yours. You married the king; they should be bowing down to you as their queen. Alfredo, number seven!"

Alfredo whipped a dress from the rack with a flourish and

passed it to me. I ran off into the next room to change and... *what?!* How did this fit me so perfectly? It was a black, figure-hugging dress that finished just above the knee with a complicated crisscross webbing across my boobs and short, angled sleeves that somehow balanced out my hips. It was sexy, giving a little hint of cleavage, but the webbing also looked kick-ass, like something a futuristic alien queen would wear. I turned around, gawping at myself in the mirror. It was even *comfortable!* I ran back to Rachel. "I love it!"

"Of course you do. Alfredo, shoes!"

While I'd been away, Alfredo had brought in a huge, wheeled trunk. He opened the top and the whole thing folded outwards, becoming a three-tier display of shining, towering heels. Rachel passed me a pair of black, three-inch heels. "For normal occasions." Then she passed me a pair of five-inch ones. "For emergencies."

I tried the three-inch ones. My knees and ankles complained but *wow,* they did wonderful things to my legs, and the height boost gave me confidence.

Rachel unfolded a folding chair with a flick of her wrist. "Sit."

I sat. Rachel opened a make-up case that probably cost a month's rent. Then, to my surprise, Alfredo picked up scissors and a comb. He saw my startled expression and raised an eyebrow. "You thought I was only here to fetch and carry?" he asked in a melty Italian accent.

"No," I lied, flushing.

He gave me a long-suffering sigh, then smiled to let me know he was kidding. He went to work on my hair while Rachel went to work on my make-up. She talked me through what products she was using and how she was applying them, recording the whole thing as a video on her phone so I could use it as a training aid. Even working at their expert speed, it took nearly an hour for them to finish. But when they did, and they handed me a mirror...

I sat there entranced, turning my face this way and that. I was having some sort of out-of-body experience: that wasn't *me,* my eyes weren't that big and my nose was bigger than that and my lips *definitely* weren't that perfectly, softly pink and... holy shit, *I* wanted to kiss me. And it felt so light and natural, even though I knew I was wearing a lot.

And my hair! Alfredo had somehow tamed it, and it looked almost liquid, falling in a sleek copper waterfall down my back. The black dress made it pop and then Rachel slipped a white jacket over the top and gave me a sleek silver-and-black purse to hold and... *wow.* I felt invincible. Untouchable.

I suddenly understood why mafia wives dressed like this. This stuff was armor.

Rachel ran through more dresses with me, as well as skirts, blouses and tops. Everything fitted perfectly: it was like being in a store stocked only for me. I was in a slate-gray suit and white blouse when Radimir walked in behind me. "What is all this?" he asked, his accent leaving the words wonderfully rough.

I turned around and marched over to him, managing to only totter a little in my heels. "New wardrobe," I said proudly.

"I've found out where we can meet our friend," he told me in a low voice. He ran his eyes over me slowly, as if he was savoring every tiny part of me. "You look..."

"...good?" I asked hopefully.

He moved closer. "You looked good *before*," he chided. "I was going to say you look ready for battle."

He put his hand on my back and pulled me to him, then brought his lips down on mine, teasing me open and then devouring me, probably ruining all the carefully applied lipstick but I didn't care. As soon as he let me up for air, Rachel shooed him away. "Make sure you get some lingerie," he told me as he backed out of the door. "Something really sexy."

Rachel shut the door, and we turned to each other. "Um. *Do* you have any lingerie?" I asked, feeling my cheeks go hot.

"*Darling!*" She sounded almost hurt. She nodded to Alfredo, and he wheeled in a whole rack of lingerie, from simple bras and briefs to things that weren't much more than a collection of leather straps.

When Rachel and Alfredo left, I had six full outfits, a selection of shoes and purses, an entire make-up kit and an armful of lingerie. I also had a bill for...my stomach dropped as I saw the figure. I knew Radimir wouldn't even raise an eyebrow but...*am I ever going to get used to this?*

I packed a bag with a selection of clothes and went to look for Radimir. The mansion was huge, but I finally found him in the kitchen. "I've booked us flights," he told me. "If we leave now, we can—"

We both turned, startled, as Gennadiy stalked in. He looked back and forth between us, suspicious. "What's going on?"

53

BRONWYN

Radimir and I were silent, caught utterly off guard. All I could think about was my bag, packed for the trip. It was right behind me on the floor. Did my legs hide it enough for Gennadiy to miss it? "I was just about to make a sandwich." I said, shocked at how easily I lied, now.

Gennadiy blinked at me. Then his face cracked into a rare smile. "He's told me about your sandwiches."

I glanced at Radimir, amazed. *He talks about me?*

Gennadiy's smile faded. "I came to tell you that Spartak's men shot at two of our guys as they were walking through the old neighborhood. Both of them are going to be okay, but..." He went silent for a moment, running a hand through his hair. "Spartak's men weren't too careful where they sprayed bullets," he said bitterly. "Some of them went through the wall of a house. A four-year-old was killed."

I looked across at Radimir and saw him grip the edge of the kitchen island, his knuckles white. He didn't rage, didn't shout. I knew all of the anger was being directed inward, that he'd blame himself for this. *It isn't your fault!*

"I'll make sure the family is taken care of," said Gennadiy. "Whatever they need."

Radimir nodded stiffly. Then he glanced across at me and I could see the pain and desperation in his eyes. We had to stop this war. *Now.*

"I'll leave you to your sandwich making," Gennadiy told us. I saw him glance between us and for just a second, I thought I saw something like longing in his eyes. Then he turned away and marched towards the door. "There's turkey, ham and cheese in the refrigerator, bread in the bread bin," he called over his shoulder. "I'm not sure where the chef keeps the mustard but it's in here somewhere."

Radimir suddenly ran after Gennadiy, spun him around and pulled him into a fierce hug. "Thank you for everything you do, brother," he told Gennadiy. "I always know our family is in safe hands."

He's saying goodbye, I realized, and my chest went tight. *He thinks he might never see him again.*

Gennadiy seemed surprised, but then he returned the hug just as fiercely. He stepped back, his eyes full of emotion, then nodded to Radimir and headed off down the hallway.

Radimir and I let out a long sigh of relief, but it was tempered: Gennadiy had reminded us just how bad things were, out there. And we were going out there without backup.

"We can't take my car to the airport," Radimir told me. "Spartak will have people watching for it."

"Don't worry," I told him. "I thought of that."

We crept out of the mansion through the scullery. Gennadiy had men patrolling the grounds but they were looking outward, not inward, and we stuck to the shadows and managed to make it to the perimeter wall. Radimir lifted me up and I clambered over it, none too gracefully, and dropped down on the other side. Radimir dropped down next to me. "Now what?" he asked.

I pointed at Jen's ancient station wagon, parked across the street.

Even from here, we could see how it drooped despondently on its wheels.

Radimir stared at the butterfly stickers and peeling paintwork. "*That?!*"

"No one's going to think you're a Bratva boss," I pointed out, and we hurried across the street. My legs were starting to throb already. I'd thought about bringing my crutches, but they'd make me stand out a mile, plus they aren't made for sneaking. For as long as this crazy plan took, I'd just have to manage.

Jen had left the car keys under the wheel arch—it wasn't like we had to worry about anyone trying to steal it. We climbed in and I got the engine started on the third try.

Radimir squeezed my hand. "Alright. Let's go and find Konstantin."

A little over an hour later, we were cruising at 30,000 feet, heading east towards New York. With the setting sun behind us, the clouds glowed red and amber and everyone was snapping pictures through the windows. But I barely glanced up: I was on my phone, reading every scrap of information I could find on Konstantin, determined to know everything I could about him. Two things were obvious: firstly, the man was freakin' gorgeous. He had the face of a king, like he should be sculpted in bronze in some art gallery somewhere, with elegant cheekbones and a strong jaw, and eyes that were just barely blue, as if he'd *allowed* the color to creep in. My heart belonged to Radimir but if I'd been anyone else...

Secondly, he wasn't shy. He was all over the press and social media, shaking hands with politicians, opening children's hospitals and sipping champagne at society parties. A pretty brunette was always by his side, his arm around her waist as if they were inseparable. "His girlfriend?" I whispered to Radimir.

Radimir nodded and then, despite all the stress, the corners of his mouth tweaked into a half smile. He leaned closer, brushed my hair back from my ear and whispered. "I heard a story. A good one. I don't know if it's true."

I did my best pleading face. It worked maybe *too* well because his gray eyes flared and melted, and he grabbed my hand as if he was about to march me off to the bathroom. Then he managed to get himself under control and he whispered, "I heard Konstantin had a girlfriend. A woman as evil as he was. When the two were apart for a few months, the FBI caught her and gave one of their female agents plastic surgery to make her look just like the girlfriend. The agent learned to walk like her, talk like her, *everything.* Then they sent this agent back to Konstantin...and he believed she was his girlfriend and welcomed her in. Except instead of spying on him like she was supposed to..."—he paused for effect—"she fell in love with him. And he fell in love with her."

I sat there staring. "Is that *true?*"

Radimir shrugged. "It's Konstantin. Who knows what's true?"

My mind was spinning. "Do you think you'd know if *I* was an imposter?"

Radimir leaned close again. "Bronwyn," he whispered, his rough-smooth accent caressing my brain, "I know the feel of every...single... *inch* of you." His lips almost brushed my ear. "Inside and out." I flushed down to my roots. "And besides, no imposter would hum like you do, when you make your sandwiches."

I stared at him. "I don't *hum!*"

"Yes, you do. When you're buttering the bread. Always the same tune." He smiled. "I call it your sandwich song."

All those weeks in the penthouse, he was watching, listening...

I threw myself at him and kissed him hard, and he wrapped me up in his arms and kissed me back even harder. For a moment, I forgot everything else.

But then the tannoy bonged and we were told we were starting our descent into New York. We reluctantly unwound and exchanged worried looks. *This is it.* Either my crazy plan would work...or the whole Aristov empire was about to fall.

A few hours later, Radimir pulled our rental car over to the curb and turned off the engine. "That's it," he told me, nodding at a house across the street. "Konstantin's in there."

We were on a quiet residential street full of beautiful old townhouses that probably cost ten million each. Something was going on at the house Radimir had pointed at: two couples were climbing the stairs and, as I watched, a limo dropped off another three people. "A party?"

Radimir looked strangely furtive. "Not...exactly."

I frowned, confused.

He sighed. "It's a sex club."

"*What?!*"

"A very exclusive sex club, for the rich."

I stared at him. Now I knew why he'd told me to buy lingerie. Why he'd told me to change into it, when we checked into our hotel. I was wearing it right now, under a swishy, satiny black cocktail dress I'd got from Rachel. *Oh God, am I going to have to strip off?* "You couldn't have mentioned this before?!" I squeaked.

"I didn't want to make you nervous."

I stared at him. Half of me was furious, the other half was too busy being terrified.

"I'm sorry, *Krasavitsa*," he said softly. "But it's the only place he's not surrounded by bodyguards."

I sat there staring at the house. My leg had started jiggling with nerves. It wasn't just that I'd have to take my clothes off in front of a bunch of strangers, it was not knowing what to expect. I'd never even thought about going to a sex club. Sex in the hot tub, sort-of-kind-of-maybe in public, was daring enough for me. I felt like the high school geek, accidentally invited to the cool kids' party full of drugs and booze. "Fuck," I muttered.

I took three quick breaths...and then I got out of the car.

Radimir scrambled out after me. "What are you doing?"

"*Going.*" I adjusted my dress. "This is our only chance and if I don't go now, I'm going to chicken out." I held out my hand.

He looked stunned and then proud and then just utterly besotted. He grabbed my hand, squeezed it tight and we walked across the street towards the house.

What the hell am I doing, I asked myself. Then the doorman nodded to us, pulled open the door...

And we went inside.

54

BRONWYN

For the first thirty seconds, everything was weirdly normal.

The owner of the townhouse had knocked a few rooms together to create a huge, high-ceilinged reception area. A beautiful wooden staircase curved up to the next floor and a chandelier hung overhead. By the door, a man in a suit and tie was standing behind a desk, checking names and IDs, and Radimir paid him what looked to be a hefty entrance fee in cash. Three couples were standing around, talking and laughing, and other than everyone looking seriously rich —I was suddenly very glad I'd gone to Rachel and got a makeover—it could have been any classy party. A waiter in a crisp white shirt offered us flutes of champagne and I grabbed one and knocked most of it back in one gulp. *Okay. Okay, see this is okay? I can do this, it's not so—*

A gorgeous woman about my age emerged from a doorway at the back of the room. She was in stockings, heels, and nothing else. I froze, a bunny in the headlights, as she strolled towards me. I crushed Radimir's hand so hard in mine that it must have hurt. *Do I look? Do I not look?* I somehow wound up staring right at her bouncing boobs, watching them come closer and closer. Then, at the last minute, she turned and strolled up the stairs. I locked on to her naked ass for a few seconds and then managed to drag my eyes away and looked around. Everyone else seemed to be completely unphased.

I looked up at Radimir for help. He was glancing around the room. "Konstantin's not here," he said quietly. "Let's try upstairs."

We walked hand-in-hand over to the stairs, trying to look nonchalant. But a pretty, blonde-haired woman in a smart blouse and skirt stepped smoothly in front of us. "I'm afraid you'll have to dress down to go upstairs."

My stomach sank because I was fairly sure *dress down* didn't mean *jeans and a hoodie.*

The woman pointed to the doorway at the back of the room. "You'll find changing rooms through there."

Oh crap.

We turned around and headed through the doorway. There were discreet silver symbols pointing men one way and women the other, like something out of a high-end spa. My heart was booming in my chest. The thought of walking around in my underwear was waking up every demon that had ever sat on my shoulder telling me I was too curvy, too pale, that there was too much of me. I stopped in front of the sign and looked down at our joined hands, not ready to let go.

Radimir brought our hands up and kissed my knuckles. "We can turn around and walk out of here," he said firmly. "We can find another way."

I loved him for that. But there *was* no other way. I squeezed his hand...and let it go, marching off into the changing room before I could change my mind.

Inside, it was just like a changing room at a gym, but with lower lighting and a scented candle burning. A few other women followed me in and started undressing, which made it a little easier. I found a locker, unzipped my dress and slid it off. But that was the easy part.

I caught sight of myself in a mirror. The lingerie set I'd got from Rachel was absolutely gorgeous, the dark blue of the sky just as the first stars come out, with detail embroidered in delicate silver thread. The material was silky and felt amazing against my skin, with pretty lace edging. There was a bra, a pair of panties and a suspender belt.

With stockings and my black heels, I had to admit it looked vampish and amazing...but I'd never planned on wearing it in public. I swallowed, staring at myself. It wasn't just being nearly nude. It wasn't just feeling huge and pale next to all the slender, tanned women getting changed around me. It was that, even fully dressed, I didn't have the confidence to strut around with everyone looking at me. On the rare occasion I did go to parties, I stood in the corner. I felt the panic rise in my chest. *This isn't me! I don't go to sex parties, I run a freakin' bookstore!* I glanced towards the door and just the thought of going upstairs dressed like this made my legs go shaky. I was *this* close to putting my dress back on, yelling for Radimir and running.

Then a flash of metal in the mirror caught my eye. I looked down at my hand and saw my wedding band.

I was a geeky bookworm who ran a bookstore. But I was also *Mrs. Aristov.* And *she* wouldn't be scared.

I felt something harden inside me. My spine straightened. The panic didn't disappear, but it was sucked down deep.

I dug out a lipstick and touched up my lips. Then I locked my dress and purse in the locker and turned towards the door. *Okay. I can do this.* I took a step and then just kept going and *God* it felt weird, wearing this stuff outside the bedroom, but then the doorway was coming up in front of me and—

I emerged into the hallway and Radimir was right there waiting for me, in a pair of black jockey shorts and nothing else. He looked me up and down and his eyes became molten. He put his hands on my shoulders, and I could feel the tremble of raw lust: he was just barely controlling himself. He slid his hands up to cup my face and said, "You look like a goddess." He leaned down and kissed me softly, then led me by the hand towards the main room.

I tried to focus on him to keep my panic in check. If I was a goddess he was most definitely a god: the slow sway of his wide shoulders as he walked, the broad, caramel swells of his pecs and that tight, hard midsection. I felt like nothing could hurt me, with him by my side.

We stepped out into the main room. There were three couples in their underwear, now, and only one newly arrived couple who were still dressed, which made it a little easier. But I still nearly stumbled as I felt the cool air of the big space brush over my near nakedness. And then everyone turned to look at us and for a second, I just wanted to disappear…

But it was like jumping into a swimming pool. There was a quick shock of cold and then, after a few seconds, it started to feel okay. People looked...but then carried on with their conversations. I felt the tension in my chest start to ease.

Radimir led me to the staircase again and, this time, the woman smiled at us and stepped aside to let us pass. As we climbed, we could hear voices and laughter from upstairs. And then another sound: rhythmic cries, rising steadily. I swallowed. *Yep. That is the sound of someone being fucked.*

"*Sooo*...people come here to, um...have sex with other people?" I mumbled. "I mean...with people not their partner?"

"Some just come to watch, or to *be* watched. But mostly, yes."

Anxiety suddenly clawed at my chest. "But *we* won't have to...I mean, if someone asks us to—"

He stopped and turned to face me. "Do you really think I'd let someone else touch what's mine?"

I relaxed a little. We climbed up the last few stairs and—

This floor was laid out in an elongated C, wrapping around the staircase. It was darker, up here, with just a few wall sconces throwing out warm pools of light, and flickering candles casting moving shadows everywhere. The walls were a classy dark blue and the low light meant that they dropped off into blackness long before the ceiling, so it felt almost like we were outside. Four doorways led to bedrooms, all with their doors wide open, and inside…

I stopped, transfixed. I was vaguely aware I was blocking the stairs, but I couldn't make my feet work.

I'd never actually seen other people having sex: not *live,* not right in front of me. The woman I'd seen downstairs, in opera gloves and stockings, was riding one man while another knelt behind her and cupped her breasts and a third stood beside the bed, kissing her. A noise from the next bedroom along made me turn and suddenly I was looking right into the eyes of a black-haired man as he fucked a petite, dark-haired woman with a nose stud who was on all fours. He gave me a proud grin, running an adoring hand over his girlfriend's rump, and I quickly looked away.

The sex wasn't confined to the bedrooms. Two couples were going for it up against the walls. And dotted around the wide hallway, I could see every stage of the process: people meeting, chatting, flirting, finding a bedroom together. And I could feel the sexual energy throbbing through the air: I'd never realized before that lust was infectious. My skin was hot, and time felt slow, as if we were all in a dream. But at the same time, I was starting to feel urgent and needy: I could hear myself breathing fast and there was a pulse of arousal rolling down my body and becoming wetness when it hit my groin. I glanced at Radimir and saw his gray eyes narrowed and hungry: it was affecting him the same way.

And yet for all the lust, it felt...*safe.* It didn't feel like a nightclub or bar where men stalked and hunted and women were prey. And there wasn't that same suspicion from the women that can so easily turn vicious and sharp. I made the mistake of looking too long at a gorgeous, blond-haired guy with a beard and then an arm slid around him from behind and his partner's face appeared over his shoulder. I jumped guiltily, bracing myself for the outraged *are you looking at my man?* But she just smiled and stroked his pec. *Are you looking at my man? Yeah, he's hot, isn't he?*

I blinked and looked away, stunned. *Am I supposed to feel like that, too?* I saw a few women staring at Radimir and I felt...not exactly *poke their eyes out with my heels* but there was definitely jealousy stirring in my stomach. I felt like the geek at the cool kid's party all over again.

Then I looked round and froze. Radimir had locked eyes with a man and was scowling, absolutely furious, his hands balling into fists. I tensed. Was the guy an enemy? One of Spartak's guys?

Radimir grabbed my hand and very firmly and publicly wrapped his fingers around mine. And it clicked that the guy's crime had been *looking at me.*

And as I turned a slow circle, I realized other men were looking at me. A lot of them. I'd been so self-conscious, I hadn't even realized. When Radimir saw them, he pulled me against him, then rubbed his hand up and down my side, caveman style. *She's mine.* And the guys, seeing his Bratva tattoos, went deathly pale and instantly dropped their eyes. My paranoia about being uncool exploded into a deep, warm glow that lit me up from the inside out.

"Let's find Konstantin." Radimir's voice was a low growl, throaty with lust and possessive anger. I nodded mutely and he marched down the hallway keeping me close against him.

But it was impossible to move fast. We had to check every room we passed and there were just too many people standing in the way. And every second we stayed there, surrounded by the soft moans of women and the hard cries of men, I could feel the tension building in Radimir.

We made it to the end of the floor and started up the stairs to the next floor. But progress was getting slower and slower: there were people fucking up against the wall and others watching, and we had to skirt around them. Radimir glared at two more men, scaring them off. Then he looked at me and—

I saw the look in his eyes and gulped. Ever since we got there, he'd been carefully controlling himself. But the atmosphere, the possessive jealousy the other men were stoking, the sight of me in lingerie, it had all finally pushed him past his breaking point.

"They need to know you're mine," he hissed. "And *mine only!*"

He hauled me up the last few steps, spun me around to face him and then his lips were on mine, hard and hungry and brutal, and I melted.

I stumbled backwards, clumsy in my heels, and he used his arm around my waist to guide me. My eyes closed. His tongue sought out mine and danced with it and I was panting, the blood thrumming in my ears as all the pent-up lust took hold. My bare ass brushed cool, painted wood: I was being pressed up against a door frame. His hands came up and took angry possession of my breasts, kneading and squeezing them. My nipples were already pebble hard, pushing through the thin silk, and he growled as he stroked them.

I was lost in the kiss, my hands roaming over the hard muscles of his back as I spiraled up, up, *up*. He crushed his lips against mine harder, as if he wanted to destroy me, and I pulled him in, needing to be destroyed. He pushed right up against me, and I had to step back with one foot to keep my balance. That opened my legs a little and suddenly he was between them, his hips spreading me, the hard, hot length of his cock scalding my inner thigh. He shifted, and I felt the head of his cock press up against the opening of my lips, the only barrier a few thin layers of fabric.

And then suddenly, I heard him ram his jockey shorts down around his thighs and there was only *one* layer of fabric, the gossamer-thin silk of my panties, already soaked through. I could feel the arrow-shaped head of his cock pressing my lips apart...

My eyes fluttered open. I was so lost in lust, it took me a few seconds to focus on the moving shapes behind him. They slowly formed into people. And most of them were watching us, waiting for us to—*Oh God are we going to do it right here?*

Radimir grabbed a condom from a side table, tore open the foil and rolled it on. I felt him wrench aside the silk of my panties, the cold shock of the air against my flesh and then his cock was spreading me...

My gaze locked with a dark-haired woman who was watching. She was vaguely familiar, but I didn't have time to think about it because at that second, I felt Radimir's cock push into me and my eyes widened in shock. *Oh Jesus yes, we're doing it right here!*

His cock surged up into me, gliding over every square millimeter of my aching, needy flesh, and my eyes closed. I suddenly didn't care who was watching. He pushed closer between my thighs and thrust again, filling me, and I moaned and grabbed for his shoulders. He pulled back, thrust a third time and I felt my mouth open as he slid into me to the hilt.

He broke the kiss. His lips brushed my ear. "I'm going to fuck you in front of all these people, *Krasavitsa*."

I wasn't capable of speech. "*Mmm,*" I nodded.

His hips drew back, a satiny *pull* that made me want to beg and claw at him, and then he slammed them forward and the wave of pleasure made my knees weaken. His hands came up under my ass, grabbing me and then lifting me. My legs came up around his waist and I caught my breath as his cock shifted inside me. He held me there, pinned between his body and the doorframe, and began to fuck me with fast, hard strokes. *Oh God.* I was skyrocketing, helpless, each thrust pushing me higher. The heated pressure of his body against mine, my nipples stroking his pecs as my breasts bounced, the steady pumping of his thick cock into my depths... His fingers dug into my ass cheeks as if he wanted to leave marks, wanted to mark me as *his,* and I went weak at the thought. I tried to imagine what we must look like to the people watching and it made it even better: it was like I was experiencing everything twice, once as me and once through their eyes.

His thrusts got faster and I moaned. I was getting close, already, and I could feel he was, too.

"*The men are all wishing they were me,*" he hissed in my ear.

My eyes fluttered open for a second. As Radimir's cock slammed into me again and again, I glimpsed the men all standing there, watching. And, God, the feeling of them all wanting me was amazing. I felt myself soar even higher, shooting towards my peak. But then I closed my eyes again and everything narrowed down to just *him,* and that was better still. Because—

I found his ear and whispered in it. "*But only you get to have me.*"

And that sent both of us over the edge. He kissed me deep and hard, rammed into me one more time, and wrapped his arms tight around me as we both came together. The room faded away as the orgasm roared through me, making me arch and tremble, but I could feel Radimir's arms around me, holding me securely until I'd finished.

Radimir gently withdrew and set me down. I stood there for a moment panting, eyes still closed. By the time I'd opened them, he was pulling up his jockey shorts. I looked around at the crowd, my face heating...but no one looked shocked or judgey. They were all smiling and I felt...oddly proud. I slumped against Radimir, happy and drunk on endorphins. I felt closer to him than ever.

Then, over Radimir's shoulder, I saw her: the dark-haired woman I'd locked eyes with just as Radimir entered me. This time, I recognized her. My eyes snapped wide. If *she* was here, then—

"You're a long way from Chicago, Radimir," said Konstantin from right beside me.

55

RADIMIR

SHIT. I saw Bronwyn redden and she looked at the floor as if she wanted to drop right through it. My face heated, too: this wasn't how I'd imagined us meeting. I took Bronwyn's hand, straightened up and turned around. "Konstantin," I said politely, looking him right in the eye.

He stared at me, inscrutable for a moment. The people around us had gone silent, peasants in the presence of the king. Even in just a pair of boxer shorts, the raw power rolled off the man. Then he inclined his head in a tiny nod and a smile tugged at his lips. Apparently, my lack of embarrassment had impressed him.

"We need to talk to you," I began.

Konstantin frowned in confusion. "You came here to..." His frown turned into a full-on scowl. "Maybe things are different in Chicago. But in New York, we don't do business in a place like this." He took his girlfriend's hand, turned and started to walk away.

"We didn't have a choice," I said, marching after him. "Everyone's cut us off."

"You broke one of The Eight's truces," snapped Konstantin without turning around. "What did you expect to happen?"

Desperate, I grabbed his arm and spun him around. But

something went wrong: Konstantin's face twisted in sudden pain, and he staggered, clutching at his arm. *Shit!* Apparently he had an old injury there. I quickly released him. "Sorry. We need your help."

But the damage was done: Konstantin had been riled but now he was *furious.* "You come into my city," Konstantin told us coldly. "Interrupt my time with the woman I love," he squeezed his girlfriend's hand. "All to ask for help you know I couldn't give you if I wanted to. And *I'm not inclined to want to!*"

The guilt and frustration that had been building inside me for weeks, ever since I messed up Borislav's killing, finally broke free. My family was going to be killed, our empire wiped out, Bronwyn was in danger, and it was *all my fault!* Our only chance of putting things right lay in this man, and he was refusing to help—

I stepped forward, my fists coming up. Konstantin stepped protectively in front of his girlfriend and raised his hands, too—

Bronwyn jumped between us and put a hand on each of our bare, heaving chests. *"Stop!* Just *stop!"* She looked at Konstantin, panting. "Mr. Gulyev, there are things you don't know. We didn't break the truce. We were tricked into killing Spartak's brother. Someone deepfaked a phone call from The Eight, to make us think it was them!"

But Konstantin just glared and pushed her aside to get to me. That made me growl protectively and muscle my way forward again. Bronwyn put both hands on my chest in an effort to hold me back. But now Konstantin was storming forward, fists raised—

Konstantin's girlfriend, looking stunning in black corset, black stockings and a black leather collar, squeezed between us and put her hands on Konstantin's chest. "Both of you just *calm down!"* She spoke into Konstantin's ear. "Someone deepfaking phone calls? That's new. Dangerous. We should at least listen."

Konstantin glared at me...but then he glanced at his girlfriend and the aggression seemed to go out of him. His eyes softened. "*Chyort,*" he cursed. And, reluctantly, he stepped back. Bronwyn pressed on my chest and I stepped back, too, and Konstantin and I looked at each other, scowling but subdued.

"Sorry," I muttered, pointing to Konstantin's arm. Konstantin grunted but nodded.

I took a deep breath and Bronwyn and I explained what had happened. How we were losing the war with Spartak. How we needed help. "We have an offer we'd like to make you," Bronwyn said.

Konstantin glowered at us for a long, stomach-clenching moment. Then: "Very well. Come to my house tomorrow morning at nine." And he gave us the address. "Now go." He turned to his girlfriend, hooked his finger in the silver ring that dangled from her collar and pulled her closer. His eyes narrowed and he gave her a look of such melting lust that I saw her swallow and flush. "You two have already had your fun. Now we need to have ours." And they walked away.

I let out a long breath. Then I put my hands on Bronwyn's shoulders and gently turned her to face me. I gazed down at her, slowly shaking my head in amazement. "What?" she asked, worried.

"I'm trying to work out what I did, before you were my wife," I told her. I cupped her face and ran my thumb lovingly along her cheekbone. "You are..."

"Acceptable?" she interrupted, in a bad Russian accent.

I pouted. "*Exceptional,*" I told her. And I leaned down and kissed her, softly and tenderly. She'd changed so much... God, just weeks ago, she'd hated the Bratva. Now she was helping me save my empire. She was exactly the woman I needed at my side.

I took her hand and squeezed it and the swell of emotion made it impossible to speak. I wanted this marriage to work. Wanted it more than I'd ever wanted anything. I owed her the truth about my past, I had to...*open up,* like the Americans always talk about. But Vladivostok was a place I only went to in my nightmares. I wasn't sure I could tell her.

"Let's get out of here," I managed, and led her towards the stairs.

As we descended, I saw Bronwyn give a worried glance over her shoulder to where we'd last seen Konstantin. I understood her nerves. We'd gotten our meeting, but tomorrow, we had to convince Konstantin that her plan would work.

56

BRONWYN

WE CHECKED into a hotel under fake names, paying cash. I insisted on being the one to go up to the reception desk because my face was less well known, but my heart was racing so fast I thought I was going to have a heart attack. There are plenty of Russian mafia families in New York, many of them with connections to Spartak. After our loud confrontation with Konstantin at the club, there was a good chance people knew we were in the city. It would only take one waiter or valet parking attendant to recognize us and make a phone call, and we were dead. We spent the night in our room with the door bolted, tensing every time we heard footsteps in the hallway. By morning, we were frazzled wrecks.

Konstantin's mansion was amazing, three stories high and built of huge slabs of cold gray stone, its doors flanked by massive pillars. We pulled up outside and got out, blinking in the sunlight. It was a beautifully clear morning, the sun sparkling off the snow. I'd put on the crisscross black dress and white jacket Rachel had given me, along with the emergency heels, even though they were hell on my legs: I needed every bit of confidence I could muster.

A bodyguard led us around to the back of the mansion and through a garden that wasn't so much overgrown as taken over by nature. Trees had twisted together like battling serpents, plants climbed over crumbling brick walls and a huge, ivy-covered oak loomed over everything like a benevolent monster. In summer, it must have been alive with wildflowers, butterflies, maybe even rabbits. Even now, in winter, it was beautiful in a spooky kind of way.

The bodyguard led us to a Victorian glasshouse, the one part of the garden that had been restored, with fresh white paint and sparkling panes of glass. Inside, a wood-burning stove made it comfortably warm. A ginger cat was sprawled on the floor, bathing in the stove's warmth and it gave us a glare for letting a draft in. Konstantin and his girlfriend were sitting at a circular, wrought-iron table and rose to greet us. "Hailey," the girlfriend told me, shaking my hand. That confused me because her name on social media was Christina. *Unless that crazy story Radimir told me is true?*

We sat down. "Last night," said Konstantin, "I neglected to congratulate you on your wedding." He looked at me, then at Radimir. "You've clearly found someone very special."

Radimir squeezed my hand. "I have."

"You've given me something to think about." Konstantin turned and looked at Hailey. She cocked her head and stared at him, but his face was inscrutable. Did he mean *marriage?* Was he serious, or just teasing her?

At that moment, one of Konstantin's servants appeared with a tray of coffee and pastries. Konstantin looked up...but not before giving Hailey a tiny smile, as if to say, *we'll talk later.* I poured myself a cup of coffee and just the smell of it was enough to kickstart my tired brain.

"Tell me what you need," said Konstantin.

"Men," said Radimir immediately. "At least thirty good men, with guns, to defend our territory and let us hit back. We didn't want this war," he leaned closer. "But with your manpower, we can win it."

Konstantin poured himself a cup of coffee, then sat back in his chair, thinking. "If I help you, I'm going against The Eight."

"You're not known for following the rules," pointed out Radimir.

"True. But there must be something in it for me. Something big. What are you offering?"

Radimir nodded. And then, to my horror, he turned to *me.* I'd just lifted my coffee cup to my mouth, and I stared at everyone, wide-eyed, over the rim. Yes, it was my plan, but... I stared at Konstantin. He was worth *billions,* he was one of the most powerful men in America. I was a bookworm who couldn't even get her store to turn a profit. *I can't do this!*

Radimir took my hand and squeezed again. I looked up, panicked...but when my gaze settled on those frozen-sky eyes, I went still. I'd never seen him looking more confident, more sure. He believed in me.

I glanced down at myself, at my new dress, shoes and purse. And made a decision. I glugged down about half my cup of coffee and the caffeine rose up to my brain and bellowed at it like a drill sergeant.

"Radimir explained your operations to me," I began. "And it turns out, the needs of our families are almost exactly opposite. You import massive quantities of merchandise through the port here in New York. But you've saturated the market here. Meanwhile, we have a massive market, but we don't have the same port access you do." I leaned closer. "We can open up Chicago for you...and from there, the whole Midwest."

Konstantin wrinkled his nose. "I admire your vision, but as an outsider, you don't understand how we do things. A deal on that scale would make us too reliant on you. Every family must be able to stand on its own, it's...tradition." He shook his head and put his hands on the table, ready to stand.

"Actually," I said, "I *do* understand. *Because* I'm an outsider. This tradition that's so important to you, the blind obedience to The Eight, the deals done on trust...that's exactly what got us into this mess." I stabbed a finger on the table. "That phone call blindsided us because the Bratva don't use technology in that way. The next generation of criminals are coming up and they're lean and they're hungry and they don't care about family or truces or *how you do things.* If the Bratva wants to survive, it's going to have to adapt!"

It went very quiet. I could hear myself panting. *I'm standing up. When did I stand up?* I stared at Konstantin, who was doing his inscrutable thing again. My stomach dropped. *Did I just*...lecture *Konstantin Gulyev?*

I held my breath.

"Good speech," said Konstantin at last. He looked thoughtfully at me and then at Radimir, stroking his chin. At last, he said, "Maybe it *is* time to shake things up a little."

Radimir and I let out silent sighs of relief. And for the next two hours, we thrashed out details and figures, with Radimir and Konstantin like two huge, heavy cogs that only grudgingly wanted to work together and Hailey and me subtle drops of soothing oil that helped them mesh. I caught Hailey's eye a few times during the negotiations, and she nodded silently to me. It slowly dawned on me that *maybe this is part of our job.* Female cooperation to counteract all the male machismo. We went through two more pots of coffee and I wound up eating three of the pastries: in my defense, I hadn't eaten the night before and the pastries were melt-in-your-mouth, buttery perfection topped with caramelized nuts.

When we were done, we walked out to our car, drunk on success and buzzing with caffeine. For the first time since our honeymoon, it felt like there was hope. Konstantin said he'd organize an escort for us to the airport and he and Radimir went to talk to Konstantin's chief of security. That left Hailey and me alone for a moment.

"You know, you did really well in there," Hailey told me softly. A cold breeze blew across us and she snugged her coat tighter around her shoulders.

I nodded in thanks, then looked around at the mansion. "I'm not sure I'm ever going to get used to this."

Hailey smiled. "I remember that feeling."

I looked sideways at her. Started to ask...and then bit my tongue. And then thought *screw it* and asked anyway. "I heard this story...about you and Konstantin." I stared at her. Did she really used to look like someone else? *Be* someone else? "Is it true?"

Hailey opened her mouth to speak but at that moment, Radimir and Konstantin returned, followed by six of Konstantin's security team. Hailey gave me a teasing smile, then hugged me goodbye. *"Next time,"* she promised. I hugged her back, grinning. I felt like I'd made a friend.

Radimir and I climbed into our hire car. Konstantin's security guys got into a big black SUV that would follow behind us. I suddenly felt a lot better about the drive back to the airport. I pried the five-inch heels off my feet and stretched my throbbing, aching legs. The confidence boost had been worth it, but *oww.*

I looked up and found Radimir looking at me. "Thank you," he said solemnly.

I eyed the heels ruefully. "Yeah, well, don't expect me to wear those except for emergencies. And maybe in the bedroom."

His eyes flared with lust. Then, "Not just for putting yourself through pain. For everything. For the plan. We have a chance, now." He shook his head, gazing at me in wonder. "I used to think doing this job meant being on my own. I was wrong: I needed *you* by my side. And I used to think it was weak to feel things. Now, I can't imagine *not* feeling the things I feel for you."

That flame at the center of me, the one Nathan had snuffed out so completely? It flared and swelled, back to its full size, lighting me up from the inside. I bit my lip, feeling the emotion well up and choke any words. I threw my arms around him and kissed him instead.

Halfway to the airport, we stopped at an intersection. I saw a sign and suddenly put my hand on Radimir's on the steering wheel. "Queens," I said, pointing.

Radimir looked at me blankly. "So?"

"If we turn off now, we could be there in a few minutes. We have Konstantin's men with us, we'll be safe enough." Radimir still looked blank. "Isn't Queens where your old friend lives? Alexei?"

Radimir looked away. Then he looked at the sign. I waited, praying...

But he shook his head and turned towards the airport. "I told you. People like me don't get to have friends."

I watched him sadly. He'd changed so much since I met him, he'd let *me* get close to him, but he wouldn't let anyone else. Why? Because of what happened to him and his brothers in Vladivostok, whatever that was? I wanted to help him, but I couldn't unless he let me. And I wasn't sure he ever would.

57

BRONWYN

BACK IN CHICAGO, Gennadiy couldn't decide whether he was overjoyed to see us safe or pissed at us for running off and making deals without telling him. He settled for a sort of grumpy relief. "Konstantin," he muttered, walking out from behind his desk. "I wouldn't have thought of that. Or offering him a pipeline into Chicago."

"It was Bronwyn's idea," Radimir told him.

Gennadiy turned to me, and I inwardly winced. I'd been hoping Radimir would miss out that part. I'd happily have skipped taking the credit if it meant my new brother-in-law wouldn't hate me.

But to my shock, Gennadiy stepped forward and embraced me, one of those full-on bear hugs Russians seemed to be so fond of. When he stepped back, he looked me in the eye. "Perhaps," he said solemnly, "I underestimated you. Welcome to the family."

I stared at him for a second, overcome. Then I pulled *him* into a hug and stared at Radimir over his shoulder, elated and almost teary. I felt part of something, in a way I hadn't done in years.

"Konstantin's men should be here late tonight," said Radimir as I stepped back. "They have to drive: they couldn't bring guns on a plane."

"Just in time," said Gennadiy. "Spartak took out three bars last night and..." He sat down on the edge of his desk and hung his head. "You haven't seen the news yet, have you? Spartak burned the stables." He glanced at me. "We own a few racehorses. Train them." He looked at Gennadiy. "Josiah, the trainer, did his best to get them all out. He has pretty bad burns to his face." His voice went tight. "Two horses are dead, and Heaven's Tears will never race again."

Radimir squeezed his brother's shoulder and Gennadiy put his hand gratefully on top. As Radimir led me out of the room, he whispered sadly "Gennadiy would never admit it, but he likes the horses."

I nodded and looked back through the doorway. Gennadiy had stood up and was busying himself making phone calls. It was worse, somehow, than if he'd just been sitting there sadly. Like Radimir, he wouldn't let himself show weakness. Radimir still wouldn't—couldn't—share his past with me but at least he had me and could sometimes let me see him vulnerable. Gennadiy didn't have *anyone. We need to find him someone.*

"Let's stop by the penthouse," Radimir suggested. "I need to pick up some paperwork. We'll take a couple of guys with us, just to be safe."

We walked towards the main doors, holding hands. I'd noticed we were doing that a lot, now. When we got outside, a viciously cold wind was sweeping across the driveway and it felt like it cut straight through my coat, clothes and flesh and whistled right over my bones. I winced, sucking in my breath.

"*Chyort*," muttered Radimir. "I forgot my phone."

"Keys!" I said quickly, before he disappeared. "I'll get the heater on."

He passed me the keys and hurried back inside the house. I unlocked the car and swung myself into the driver's seat so I could start the engine. My butt sank into the soft leather seat and—

There was a *click.*

The door thumped shut: I'd hauled on the handle as I swung myself into the seat because I'd wanted to stop the wind. The noise of the outside world disappeared. My finger was resting on the *Start* button, but I didn't push it. My whole body was taut, frozen.

That *click*...

I'd been in Radimir's car a million times by now and it had never made that sound when one of us sat down.

The car had been sitting here in the driveway the whole time we'd been in New York. What if someone had...

I'm being paranoid.

What if I'm not? Cold began to creep down my spine, soaking outwards as sweat.

I looked down into the footwell: nothing but expensive carpet and the Mercedes logo. I couldn't lean forward to look under the seat because that would mean lifting my weight off it.

I sat there thinking furiously for a moment. Then I took out my phone, turned on the selfie camera, and dangled it by my fingertips until the camera was pointing under my seat. Dark metal. The mechanism that adjusted the seat. *See, there's nothing—*

A boxy shape wrapped in duct tape. And a circuit board with a glowing red LED.

I was sitting on a car bomb.

58

BRONWYN

I DROPPED MY PHONE. It fell into the footwell and lay there with the selfie cam still on and my own terrified face staring back at me. I couldn't reach down to get it, to take another look under my seat. But I knew what I'd seen. I sat there with my breath coming faster and faster, trying to figure out what to do.

At that moment, Radimir emerged from the mansion and jogged towards the car. He headed straight for the driver's side because he always insisted on driving. He was going to open the door and—

"*Don't open the door!*" I screamed frantically. Who knew what the bomb was hooked up to, and now I'd armed it by sitting down... "*Don't open the door!*"

My voice was muffled by the thick glass and at first he thought I was joking, not wanting him to open the door and let the cold air in. He reached the car, put his hand on the door handle—

Then he saw the fear in my eyes and stopped, his face falling.

"*There's a bomb! There's a bomb under my seat!*" I took another panic breath, and my stomach suddenly heaved: I was actually going to throw up from fear. "It's under my seat I don't know what to do," I sobbed.

Radimir fell to his knees, his eyes darting around the car, frantic. Then he planted his palm firmly against the glass. I reached up and pressed my hand to his.

"Help me," I choked. Tears were running down my face.

He nodded hard. "I won't leave you." Then he turned and bellowed for Gennadiy.

First, the police showed up, four officers in two cruisers who had no idea what to do except cordon off the area and tell everyone to get back. When they approached Radimir, he turned from me just long enough to snap, "*I'm not moving!*" and they backed away.

Next the FBI showed up, alerted by the police. They tried to question everybody, including Radimir, but Mikhail took charge, batting their questions away with the skill of a politician.

Meanwhile, I sat alone in the cold, quiet car, slowly going insane. It's amazing how hard it is to just *sit still.* First, my legs started to cramp, and I didn't dare stretch them because that meant shifting my ass on the seat. Next, my ass started to go numb. And then the fear sent my mind spiraling down into *what ifs,* like when you're standing on a cliff edge and you worry you might just involuntarily jump. What if I just *got up?* It would only take one rogue command from my brain, one quick push with my feet and—

Radimir pressed closer to the glass. "*Miss Hanford!*" he said firmly.

I looked up, panting. He hadn't called me that in weeks.

"Listen to me," he ordered. "*I will get you out of this*. I promise."

I jerkily nodded. But my breathing had gone so tight, it felt like there was a metal band wrapped around my chest.

With a wail of sirens, the bomb squad arrived: two cars and a huge black truck. More cordons were set up, arguments broke out between the bomb squad and the FBI and Radimir was told to move again.

"I'm not leaving her," he snarled.

The chief of the bomb squad, an overweight guy in his fifties, looked at me and his face softened. "You can stay for now," he said at last. And he waved his team into position.

They didn't dare open the doors so a hole was drilled through the door and a long, snake-like thing with a camera on the end was threaded through it to look under my seat. "Make sure they're not looking up my skirt," I told Radimir, trying to lighten things. But my voice came out as a dry croak and Radimir just looked at me with such deep, heartbreaking worry, that my smile crumbled.

The bomb technicians gathered around a laptop, watching what the camera saw. *This might still be nothing. Maybe Radimir dropped something under the seat. Maybe it's part of the car. God, what if that's it, what if it's just part of the heater for the heated car seat and all of this is for nothing, and I feel like a complete idiot.*

Please please God let me be a complete idiot.

The chief of the bomb squad came over. "We can see explosives under your seat," he said gently.

Radimir cursed in Russian. I closed my eyes and counted to three, trying not to throw up. "Can you unwire it—break it—" *Jesus I've forgotten how to speak. "Defuse* it?" I managed at last.

He inhaled, a doctor telling the patient it's stage four. "We're not sure how to proceed. We don't know which of the car's sensors the bomb's wired into so we can't open a door or a window." He leaned closer. He had a reassuring manner: with his big, wide face and mostly bald head, he reminded me of an earnest little league coach. "But I've got a specialist coming in to take a look."

I nodded weakly and leaned my head back against the headrest, trying to force the panic down inside me. All I could think about was that little red light under my seat, and what it meant. A device primed to kill me, just waiting for one signal. *What happens when the battery runs out? What if it shorts? What if there's someone watching with a remote control and they can just press a button and—* I started to huff air through my nostrils, faster and faster—

"Hey!" said Radimir sharply.

I looked around at him.

"It's going to be okay." He pressed his palm harder against the glass. "I'm right here with you."

I nodded and tried to breathe. The minutes ticked past like centuries. I'd never gone so long without moving. With all the doors and windows closed, the air in the cabin was getting stale. I knew that there were vents but it felt like I was running out. And the walls of the car seemed to be creeping closer and closer, squeezing me into a tiny box. The fear took hold. *Oh Jesus Jesus God, I don't want to die—*

"Talk to me," said Radimir. "Tell me about..." —he thought desperately—"books."

"Books?" I tried to laugh but the fear made it come out kind of hysterical.

"What happened to Kurt the cowboy? Did he get together with Christa?"

I stared. I recognized the names, but they made no sense, coming out of a Russian mobster's mouth. *The book he read to me when I was ill.* "You still remember that?!"

He nodded. "I never got to find out what happened."

My mouth opened and closed a few times. "I never did either. I stopped reading it, after I got well."

"You didn't like it?"

"I loved it, but...it wasn't the same without you reading it."

There were people listening, police and the bomb squad and his brothers, but he didn't seem to care. "You hold on," he told me, "And I'll read the rest of that book to you." His eyes...were his eyes glistening? "Any book. I'll read all the books. Whenever you like."

I nodded, feeling my own eyes go hot. We sat there staring into each other's eyes...

"Hey," said a female voice right in front of me.

I jerked: but luckily went *back* into my seat. I panted, blinked...and focused on the woman who was standing in front of the car.

She was about my age, with blonde hair tied in a ponytail. She was wearing a death metal t-shirt, black jeans and a bright orange puffa jacket. And now she was...*climbing onto the hood. "Don't!"* I yelled, panicked, but she ignored me, too focused on balancing.

"Goddammit, Boxley, get off of there!" yelled the chief of the bomb squad. "What if it's hooked up to the suspension?!"

Radimir and I stared at the two of them, then looked at each other. This *is the specialist?!*

"It's not hooked up to the suspension," mumbled Boxley. "Because that would be stupid. It would make no sense to hook it to the suspension *and* the seat sensors." She stood up on the hood and then stepped onto the roof. *Oh my God she's crazy.* "I'm going to need an angle grinder."

"You can't *cut through the roof!"* roared the chief, going red in the face. *"Get off of there!"*

"The doors and the windows all have sensors, so the car knows if they're open," said Boxley calmly. "But the car won't know if there's a hole in its roof. I looked at the schematics on my way over. Right here," —she rapped her knuckles on the roof, over the backseat, "there are no wires at all. Just metal."

The chief's face slowly returned to its normal color. He looked at the car, thinking. "Okay," he muttered. "Okay, you might be onto something." He turned and yelled. "Someone get me the angle grinder!"

A few moments later, I was hunkered down in my seat, trying not to flinch as the metal blade of an angle grinder sliced open the roof. The noise was terrifying, and sparks kept arcing down into the car. I winced as one of them singed my white jacket. *Sorry, Rachel.* Radimir was wincing and cursing, too, worried about my safety. The only person who seemed completely relaxed was Boxley.

Boxley finished cutting and suddenly the car was filled with light as she lifted a rectangle of metal away. It was like she'd cut a sunroof over the back seat. The next thing I knew, she'd shed her puffa jacket and was slithering headfirst onto the backseat. She slid between the front seats and then into my footwell, squeezing herself in by my feet. Fortunately, Radimir is much taller than me and the seat was adjusted for him. She didn't seem afraid at all, despite putting herself within inches of a bomb. The woman was beyond brave.

"Open your legs, please?" she asked. She reminded me of my friend Luna, quiet and studious: she sounded like she should have glasses to push up her nose. I shuffled my feet apart. She clamped a flashlight in her teeth and peered between my ankles. There was silence for a few minutes. "Okay," she said at last.

"Okay?" I repeated hopefully. She didn't respond. She rolled onto her back and took a roll of tools from her belt. "Okay...you can defuse it?"

She stared at two screwdrivers as if she was trying to choose between them. Then she looked up and seemed to remember my question. "Yes."

It was like she wasn't used to dealing with people at all. I glanced through the window and caught the chief's eye. He gave me a firm nod, like, *I know, I know...but you can trust her.* I swallowed and nodded back.

Boxley went to work under my seat. "It's a good thing you didn't move," she muttered. "Or start the car."

"Oh?" I managed. My heart was racing so fast, I felt woozy.

"You know the sensor that detects when someone's sitting in the seat but hasn't fastened their seatbelt yet and it...*bong*s? The bomb's wired into that." She sounded fascinated: the bomb was just a crossword puzzle she had to solve. "But not under the passenger seat, only this one." She gave a little shrug. "Sometimes, they want to make sure there are two people in the car before the bomb goes off. But this time, they were only worried about killing the driver."

Outside, Radimir dropped his gaze and stared at the ground. I felt a fist clench tight around my heart. *He thinks this is his fault, because the bomb was meant for him.* "This isn't on you!" I told him desperately. But he just shook his head, and I could see the pain and self-hate in his eyes. Boxley looked up at me, worried and confused: *did I say something wrong?* It was a good job she wasn't a doctor because she had the worst bedside manner in the world.

"I'm going to defuse it now," Boxley announced.

A ripple passed through the crowd of people watching. Gennadiy and Valentin looked ill. Mikhail crossed himself. I felt my stomach drop.

The chief put a hand on Radimir's shoulder. "Sorry, pal. You're gonna have to move back now."

"I'm not going," Radimir told him.

"It's the rules, buddy, I'm sorry."

Radimir turned to him. *"I'm not. Leaving. My wife!"*

A big, warm swell of emotion overwhelmed me. I didn't want him to be in danger. I'd have told him to go if I'd thought there was a chance he'd listen. But he wouldn't. Nathan had left me as soon as it wasn't smooth sailing, but Radimir would be there, no matter what.

The chief sighed and ran a hand through his hair. "Okay," he said at last.

Radimir turned back to me...and I caught my breath. It was like the ice in his eyes had suddenly fractured and I could see something inside him I'd never seen before. A different *him,* younger, vulnerable. "If—" he began, but then he couldn't get the words out. "I—"

I put a hand to my mouth, my eyes prickling with tears again. *He thinks he's about to lose me.*

"I'm sorry," he blurted. "I'm sorry I couldn't—Just get out of this, *please,* and there won't be any more secrets."

It was like he'd forgotten that if I died, he was going to die too: he was crouching right beside the car. Then I realized that wasn't it. He just didn't care about himself, only me. I nodded tearfully.

In my peripheral vision, I saw Boxley shuffle forward. I looked down and then couldn't look away: she had tweezers and wire cutters in her hands and *Oh God* this was it: one slip, one mistake and all three of us were dead. I swallowed hard.

But it turned out that what she lacked in people skills, Boxley made up for in raw skill. My phone was still down in the footwell with the selfie camera still on, and I could see Boxley's hands moving, quick and confident as a master pianist's, tracing circuits to figure out where the power flowed, attaching tiny crocodile clips to terminals to reroute it and, finally, bringing in the wire cutters to snip the wires. She was so *confident,* so unafraid, like this was just a game, to her.

Every time the blades closed on a wire, I dug my nails into my palms and braced myself against the seat, as if that could make a difference. *If she gets it wrong, will I know or will I just be...gone? Will there be a flash of white light?* Then the wire cutters would snip through and I'd sag in my seat, a fresh wave of sweat drenching me.

"Last one," said Boxley calmly.

I couldn't look. I found Radimir's eyes and stared right into them. *He'll be the last thing I ever see.*

There was a snipping sound.

Nothing happened.

Seconds ticked by. I slowly turned my head and looked down at Boxley. She was meticulously putting her tools back into their tool roll. "Did you do it?" I croaked.

"Mm-hmm," she said, distracted.

"It's *safe?!*"

She blinked at me, then nodded.

I let out a wail of relief and pulled the door release. I tried to climb out of the car but after close to an hour of sitting perfectly still, my legs were completely numb, and they folded under me like paper. It didn't matter, though, because Radimir was already grabbing me and pulling me into his arms. I distantly heard everyone cheering as we went full-length on the ground, rolling and hugging, and then he was kissing me, over and over, as if checking I was really there. I went limp in his arms as all the tension drained out of me. Then I started kissing him back just as hard as he was kissing me, panting and drunk on the feeling of being alive.

Remembering something, I broke the kiss and turned back towards the car. Boxley was still in the footwell and while everyone else was celebrating, she was just...packing up her tools. I gestured to Radimir to give me a second, crawled over to the car and threw my arms around Boxley, pulling her close. *"Thank you!"* I croaked. "*Thank you!"*

She just knelt there stiffly for a moment. Then I felt her body slowly, cautiously, relax. My heart cracked. *Doesn't anyone ever hug her?*

She packed the last of her tools, then climbed past me out of the car. She didn't join the other police and bomb technicians, just walked off down the drive. The chief was the only person who even acknowledged her. "Great work, Boxley!"

Boxley just nodded. As she reached the street, she turned and glanced back. I saw her look at the people celebrating: at Valentin and Gennadiy; at Mikhail and his dogs, who he'd now let free from the house and who were jumping around us and woofing excitedly; at Radimir as he came up behind me and gently put his hands on my shoulders.

Just for a second, I thought I saw longing in her eyes, like she didn't want to be so alone.

And then she turned and was gone.

I turned back to Radimir, and he wrapped me up in his arms and squeezed me like he never wanted to let me go. He kissed the top of my head...and then I felt a hot drop of something splash on my scalp, and then another. Radimir squeezed me even tighter, so tight it was almost painful, but I didn't mind at all because I was hugging him back even harder.

"I love you," he said in a ragged whisper. "I love you, I love you."

He held me so tight that there wasn't room to speak, so I just nodded really hard. And then shivered. The cold was creeping into me and the aftershocks of what had just happened had started to roll through my body, ghosts of alternate realities where I hadn't heard that *click,* and had pushed the Start button—

I was suddenly lifted into the air. My legs went either side of Radimir's body and I clung to his shoulders as he marched towards the house.

"We still have some questions..." said one of the FBI agents.

"You can ask them tomorrow," Radimir told him. He stalked indoors, pushing past any agents who got in his way. He didn't stop until we reached our bedroom. Then he set me down by the bed. "Undress," he commanded, and went into the bathroom.

"What are you doing?" I asked.

I heard the faucets start. "Running you a bath. You're going to lie in it and relax."

I didn't argue because actually, a steaming hot bath sounded like exactly what my stiff, sweaty, cold body needed. "But what are *you* going to do?"

He came out of the bathroom and looked me right in the eye. "I'm going to tell you what happened to my family."

59

RADIMIR

BRONWYN STARED at me in shock, but I just nodded firmly. Watching her in that car, knowing how close to death she was, knowing that at any second, that could be *it*...something had cracked inside me, thick layers of ice that had been there for decades. I'd thought that ice was protecting me, and keeping us apart was the price I paid. But almost losing her had switched everything around. I couldn't let anything come between us ever again. And if the cost was pain, then I'd pay it.

There was a little bottle of bubble bath beside the tub, and I poured the whole thing in. Thick foam started to spread over the surface. By the time the water was deep enough, Bronwyn was naked. I pointed at the bath. "In."

She climbed in, still looking a little shell-shocked. As soon as her legs hit the water, her expression dissolved into bliss, and she slid down into the tub.

I wanted to tell her, but I needed to make sure she was okay, first. I waited until the heat had soaked into her bones and chased the cold away, and she stopped shivering. Then I scooped up some steaming water and began to rub her shoulder.

"What are you doing?" she asked, startled.

"Washing you," I told her firmly.

I worked my way over her body, soaping her skin and then sluicing the suds away, washing all the stress of the last few hours out of her until I felt her muscles unknot. We didn't speak a word the entire time. Eventually, her breathing had slowed, and her body was relaxed, and I knelt beside the bath, my big, suited form hulking over her naked one, stroking her back over and over like a cat's.

God, I loved this woman. Needed her like I'd never needed anyone. I could have gone on stroking her like that forever...but it was time.

I began, keeping one hand on her body to help me get through it. "The Aristovs weren't always criminals," I said slowly. "My father was a good man. He worked for the government. My mother was a dance teacher." I met her eyes for a second. "I was going to be a businessman. Valentin wanted to be an actor. Gennadiy, a doctor. What I turned us into...it wasn't what I intended. Wasn't even what I wanted. It was what was...*necessary.*"

I swallowed. It felt like I was standing at the top of some stairs leading down into a pitch-black basement. I hadn't ventured down into it for years and I was scared. Not because I didn't know what was down there but because I did.

But I'd promised.

"One night when I was fifteen, my father came home and told my mother that he'd stumbled on something at work. Corruption, on a massive scale. Hundreds of millions being secretly siphoned off. She begged him not to talk to anyone because she was afraid of what might happen to him. But he couldn't let them get away with it. He was that sort of man. They argued about it for hours: that's how my brothers and I found out about it, listening from the next room. A few days later, he reported what he'd found. But he'd underestimated how far the corruption had spread. A man called Olenev, a man my father thought was his friend, came to our house...and stabbed my father to death, right in front of us."

The pain began, a jagged tear, deep in my chest. "Seconds later, the police burst through the door: Olenev had friends in the force." I sighed and closed my eyes. "And they arrested us. Valentin, Gennadiy, and me."

I heard the water slosh as Bronwyn twisted around in the bath. I could imagine her leaning close to me, her eyes wide. "*What?!*"

"It wasn't enough to kill my father. Olenev knew that he'd probably told my mother about the corruption, and maybe us, too. But he couldn't kill the whole family, that would look too suspicious. So, he invented a story about the three of us killing our father. He said our father had found out we were selling drugs and confronted us, and we'd killed him in a drug-fueled rage. It didn't matter that we'd never touched drugs. It didn't matter that Gennadiy was only fourteen and Valentin only twelve. Olenev had sway with the prosecutor and the press. They painted us as feral kids who rebelled against their good, honest father. The three of us were sent to a youth detention center, and not in Moscow, where we lived. A particularly brutal one, for violent youths...in Vladivostok." Even now, I have trouble saying the name. The pain in my chest grew, the wound ripping wider.

I opened my eyes. "Olenev was clever. We were out of the way, no one would ever believe us, and he could use us as leverage to make sure our mother stayed quiet: he told her that if she went to the press, he'd arrange for us to be killed while we were behind bars."

Bronwyn was staring at me, her mouth open in a silent O of horror. I focused on the droplets of water on her bare shoulders, on the bubbles that clung to her red hair like snowflakes. I was descending fast, now, into that dark basement and I needed to be able to climb back out.

"We were three pampered city boys from a good family. Every other boy there had been into gangs and drugs for years. We were soft." I said it without emotion. "Easy pickings. And Olenev, he knew the warden. That's why he had us sent there. The warden and his guards tried to break us." It was getting harder, now. I could smell the place, bleach and piss and fear. I could see the cold tiled walls and my blood splattered on them under the flickering fluorescent lights.

"They'd withhold food for days, until we were too weak to fight.

Or beat us with rubber hoses. And it went on week after week, month after month." My voice slowed. I was unleashing memories I'd kept locked down under layers of ice for decades, and it felt like they were going to suffocate me. I remembered seeing Gennadiy being kicked to the ground and then pissed on, while I was held down, unable to help. I remembered seeing Valentin, my baby brother, howling and sobbing, as they burned the soles of his feet with cigarettes. I remembered the pain of being kicked in the ribs when they were already fractured, bruises layered on bruises, cuts reopened before they had a chance to heal. "They had different ways of torturing each of us. With me, their favorite thing was to make me stand outside, naked, in the snow." I looked down at my shoes, then met Bronwyn's eyes. "That's how I lost some of my toes. Frostbite."

Bronwyn put a wet hand on my cheek, and I closed my eyes again and sank into the softness. It would have been so easy to just nestle there, retreating back to safety. But there was more, and she needed to hear all of it to understand. I just wasn't sure I could make myself tell her.

"At first, we got visitors. Our mother came each month, to catch us up on news and tell us to be strong. But then the warden found out and...." My hands curled into fists. "He strip-searched her. And then...he raped her. In front of the other guards. After that, we told everyone not to visit, and we were completely on our own." I inhaled, but the air came in shakily. I hadn't realized how hard this would be, but I had to get through it.

"About a year into our eight-year sentence, our mother got cancer. The warden wouldn't let us visit. Not when she was in the hospital, not when she was in a hospice..." My voice went tight. That had been one of the worst parts. I remember sitting on my scratchy wool blanket, tears rolling down my cheeks, knowing she was in agony, alone, and not being able to reach her...it felt like it happened yesterday. I inhaled the sweet, damp air of the bathroom, trying to remind myself I was *here*, with *her*. But the pain was so bad now, it was hard to breathe. I wasn't sure I was going to be able to go on. "The warden wouldn't even let us go to the funeral." My voice was ragged. "We'd lost both our parents, and we didn't get to say goodbye to either of them. That nearly destroyed us."

Bronwyn threw her arms around me and pulled me against the bath, her wet arms and breasts soaking my shirt, her breathing ragged in my ear. "This is what you have nightmares about," she whispered.

I nodded. Then I closed my eyes and just held her close, and the warmth of her and the scent of her made the pain retreat a little. I took three long breaths, then pulled gently back so I could look her in the eye.

"It's okay," she said softly. "You don't have to tell me any more."

But I shook my head. "Yes I do." She needed to hear the best part. Which was also the worst part. I stared at her and let the sight of her give me the strength to continue.

"You see...they'd made a mistake, with the three of us." My voice turned bitter and savage. "They thought that they could break us, grind us down. But there was something inside us. When they had me outside, naked, and the wind was so cold it felt like it was tearing the flesh right off me, the only way I could survive was to stop feeling. To get through the pain and humiliation, we became like ice. The beatings they gave us...they forced us to build our bodies and become stronger. And the way they isolated the three of us made us stick together, until we were so close nothing could break us apart. The warden thought he was breaking us, Bronwyn. But he was creating monsters." I felt the grim satisfaction I'd felt back then: knowing that we were changing, that we'd have our revenge someday. And I felt the sickness, too, at what we were becoming.

I rested my forearms on the edge of the tub, wetness soaking through my shirt. "We'd seen for ourselves that the official system—government, police, courts—was corrupt. So we decided to build our own system. We were surrounded by criminals: everyone there had been in a gang. We learned everything we could: how to steal, how to smuggle, how to kill." I rolled up my shirt sleeve and showed her a tattoo on my right bicep, rough and blurry. "We got our first tattoos in that place, done with soot and a needle made from the straightened-out spring from a pen. For three years, we grew, we hardened...and we *planned.*"

"There was a small metalworking shop, and we made a key to our cells. When it was dark, we slipped out and crept to the warden's office, where I strangled the bastard with a phone cable. Then we ran into the night: no money, no food, nothing but the clothes on our backs. It took us months just to get back to Moscow, stealing so we could eat. From there, we bought passage on a cargo ship going to the US. But not before I'd visited Olenev, the man who killed our father, and cut his throat." I paused for a second to let that sink in. I needed her to know the worst of it, the worst of *me:* I'd said *no secrets.* "We went to New York, worked our way up through the street gangs and after a few years, we went to work for a Bratva boss called Luka Malakov. There was a guy there about the same age as me, who'd done some time in the army: Alexei. He taught me how to be a hitman and we became friends. We all worked together, gradually gaining status and respect. And eventually, after years, my brothers and I moved to Chicago to start up on our own. Mikhail joined us soon after: he has...his own story."

I looked down at myself. There was almost nothing left of the innocent boy who'd gone to Vladivostok.. My shirt was soaked through, almost transparent, and we could see the muscle I'd built through years of fighting, the scars I'd gotten and every dark line of my tattoos. "That's what happened in Vladivostok, Bronwyn. We went through hell, and we became what we needed to, to survive. But what we became were *monsters.*"

I let out a long, shaky breath. I'd never thought I'd tell another living soul. Reliving it had left me worn out and broken, but...now that it was out, there was a clean edge to the pain, like when a bullet is pulled out of you. Maybe now, it could start to heal. At the same time, another emotion rose, filling me like ice water.

I'd thought it was just the pain that had kept me from telling her. But I was *afraid.* Afraid to meet her eyes because what if that fear was back, the fear I'd seen the night I killed Spartak's brother? What if she told me to *stay away from me!* I was afraid of losing her.

I slowly lifted my eyes to look at her.

Her eyes were swimming with tears, but it wasn't fear and disgust in her face...it was love and acceptance.

And some part of me that I didn't think could ever feel complete again was suddenly whole.

We both dived forward and slammed together, water flying from her soaking body, arms locking around each other's backs. "I love you," I told her. "I love you, I love you."

"I love you too," she told me firmly. "And I'm proud to be your wife."

We crushed together even more tightly, but the wall of the tub was still between our lower bodies, and I needed to feel her against me completely, *now*. So, I pulled her right out of the bath, naked and slippery as a mermaid, and fell back full-length on the floor with her on top of me.

I ran my hands up and down her warm, wet back. Her damp hair fell around my face, and I inhaled her scent. Then I put my hand on the back of her neck and pulled her lips down to mine.

60

BRONWYN

I MOANED as he tugged my head down and crushed his lips to mine. I wanted him to be rough, wanted to feel every inch of my softness brutally mashed against that hard body: whatever would give my beautiful monster comfort. My chest was aching for him. Even though he was so much bigger than me, I felt protective, determined that no one was even going to cause him that sort of pain again.

I'd meant what I said. I knew everything now, there were no more secrets and nothing holding us apart. And I was proud to be his wife.

We kissed deep and hard, the roll of his lips and the darting of his tongue sending me tumbling down into a hot blackness so exquisite I didn't want to come up to breathe.

I shifted position and my wet breasts rolled against his chest, making him groan. Between us, the layers of his suit and shirt were soaked through and I could feel the hard ridges of his abs stroking my stomach. Lower down, his cock was hardening, the shaft rising, the sopping fabric of his pants clinging to it as it pressed against my naked pussy.

The mood changed.

His big hands slid further down my back and grabbed my glistening ass, squeezing the cheeks and grinding me more firmly against his cock. My thighs slid either side of his legs and I felt my pussy lips open just a little, letting me feel the heat and slick wetness inside. I broke the kiss for a second to pant. He took my lower lip between his teeth, and I lost the capacity to think.

His hands went to my shoulders, then slid down the entire length of me to my ass, his strong fingers molding me to him. My wet skin was cooling, and I knew I should be getting cold. But I was lying on the world's best heated bed, a deliciously contoured maleness that throbbed warmth up into me. And every time my back started to get cold, his big hands would slide all the way down it again, soaking heat into my skin and then squeezing my ass and sending a deeper heat trembling inwards to my core.

But he must have been worried about me because he suddenly scrambled up, lifting me with him, and set me down on my feet. Then he grabbed one of the thick white bathrobes that hung on the back of the bathroom door and pulled it onto me, dressing me like a doll. It was sized for a man, so it hung down over my hands and reached down past my knees. He pulled it closed around me, then picked me up and carried me in his arms to the bed.

I could feel the robe soaking all the water from my skin and when he dropped me on my back on the bed, I was mostly dry. The robe flopped open a little, revealing my bare legs, my bare pussy and a narrow slice of my upper body, just the sides of my breasts visible. I lay there with my hair a damp halo around my head, staring up at him. I felt...different. Dreamy and relaxed and hornier than I'd ever been. There was a connection that hadn't been there before, a closeness that came from knowing the worst of him and the best of him. It was like a current that flowed between us: from the look in his eyes, he could feel it, too. He gazed down at me and, without words, began very slowly and deliberately undressing.

First his shining leather shoes and socks came off. Then he unbuckled his leather belt and pulled it through the belt loops.

I could feel my hand wandering. Without conscious thought, it moved down between my thighs.

His chest filled as he inhaled. He stared at my fingers as I began to tease my lips. Then he locked eyes with me and started to pop the buttons of his shirt one by one.

My fingertips stroked down the join of my lips and then glided back up, already sticky, and I caught my breath as I circled my clit. It was almost as if it was someone else doing it. I didn't feel like I was teasing or performing, I was just responding to the look he was giving me, out of control.

He opened his soaked shirt and tugged it down his arms and off. I swallowed as those glorious, hard pecs came into view, shining wetly. My fingers traced down my lips again and I felt them part.

He unfastened his pants and let them fall. He stepped out of them and now I could see the jutting outline of his cock as it stretched out the fabric of his soaking, black jockey shorts. I inhaled, my breath trembling, my fingertips easing between my lips, feeling my wetness.

He stripped off the jockey shorts and stood naked. He took his cock in one hand and began to stroke the hard shaft, and even though I wanted to stare at the swelling, purple-pink head, I couldn't look away from his eyes. We were joined, the two of us locked together in a feedback loop: what he was doing to me and what I was doing to him. The room fell silent, the only sound was our breathing and the slow movement of our hands. The tension built and built. I could feel my fingers getting wetter, could hear his breathing hitch as his cock strained in his hand—

A breathy moan escaped me, and I shifted my feet on the bed, opening them just a little to give myself better access. That pushed him past breaking point. He grabbed a condom off the dresser and rolled it on as he marched towards the bed. He slid his hands between my thighs and shoved them roughly apart, sending the robe flying open and baring me. His gaze raked down my body and stopped on my pussy. He positioned himself, the head of his cock just breaching my entrance, and I gasped. Then he thrust up into me and I groaned and rolled my head back on the bed at the silken stretch of him, the hot throb of him inside me.

I lifted my knees just as he thrust again, sinking deeper, gliding on my wetness, and I bit my lip and thrashed my head. He pulled back and I grabbed at his shoulders, his arms, already aching for him. He slammed forward and this time buried himself completely inside me, little droplets of water shaking loose from his chest and tumbling down as his groin met mine. A wave of pleasure washed through me, leaving me gasping, and I trembled, my toes tapping the bed, heady at the feel of him so deep.

He lowered himself, taking his weight on his elbows, and cupped my breasts in his hands. My skin was super sensitive from the bath, and I caught my breath as he stroked me. Then he pressed my breasts together, dipped his head and licked across both my nipples, and I twisted and circled my hips, pushing my breasts up to meet him. Radimir groaned as my walls caressed his shaft. "*God!*" He looked down at me in wonder. I panted and did it again, a giggle escaping me, and his eyes widened.

It had never felt like this before. I felt happy and... *free.* Him opening up to me had changed everything. *This is what it's like,* I realized, *when you're with someone you trust completely.* I loved it. But a little part of me wondered if this meant we'd lost something, too, that dark edge of danger. I circled my hips one more time, teasing him—

He mock-scowled, grabbed my wrists and pulled them up above my head, then trapped them there with one powerful hand. He shifted his body, using his muscled weight and *Oh God,* suddenly my hips were pinned to the bed, too, and I got that roller coaster *drop* of helplessness.

No. We hadn't lost it.

With his free hand, he reached down and rolled my nipple between finger and thumb. He drew the stiffening bud up to hardness and then pinched with just the right amount of roughness. The pleasure expanded and turned silver-edged, and I moaned into his kiss, his lips spreading mine and his tongue plundering me. He didn't give me a chance to recover: he began fucking me with long, hard strokes, rolling my breast in his hand and pinching my nipple on each thrust. The waves of pleasure began to come faster, a new one washing through me before the last one had drained away, and with his lips on mine I couldn't gasp or moan, I had to *kiss* it out, my lips frantic on his, our tongues dancing. As the pleasure built, I tried pushing upwards just a little with my wrists and went heady when he didn't let them lift *at all.*

He began to fondle and pinch my other breast, leaving the first one to bounce, super-sensitive, against his chest as he fucked me. His thrusts sped up, becoming fast, brutal pumps, and the pleasure expanded, a pink cloud that filled every inch of me, shot through with silver crackles of lightning every time he pinched my nipple. God, I'd never felt so ruthlessly *taken:* the weight of his body, holding me down, the hard fingers tight on my wrists, his girthy cock pistoning inside me and that brutal kiss, his stubble scraping me as his lips made me his. I had a sudden flash of what we must look like, with his muscled hips spreading my thighs apart and his tanned ass rising and falling between them. The pleasure tightened and heated, a scalding storm ready to explode.

He broke the kiss for a moment. Licked at my aching, straining nipples. "You drive me insane," he told me in a throaty, Russian growl. "I'm never going to stop fucking you."

I was getting close and the words pushed me closer still. The feeling that he was right at the edge of control, and that it was *me* that was doing that to him...it made me buck my hips, grinding my pelvis up to meet him on every thrust. The waves of pleasure were slamming through me, now, filling me faster than I could control. I felt myself start to tremble—

"Come for me," he said. "Let me feel you go crazy around me. *Wife.*"

My legs came up and scissored around his ass, pulling him into me, and then I arched my back and began to spasm around him. He gave two more hard thrusts and then buried himself, kissing me deep as he came in long, shuddering streams inside me.

61

BRONWYN

We lay naked and entangled for a long time, even when we started to get cold, because neither of us wanted to move. But Gennadiy, despite all his money, didn't seem to believe in heating his house *at all* and we both started to shiver. Radimir stripped the bathrobe off my arms and pulled me naked under the covers and that was much better.

Outside, we heard the FBI and police finally leave. A freezing gray rain began, hammering the windows until the outside world was just a distant blur.

"Alexei," I said. It was the first time either of us had spoken in a while.

Radimir reached down and stroked my hair. I was lying on my side with my head resting on his chest so I couldn't see his face. "What about him?" he asked guardedly.

"Why won't you get back in touch with him?"

A sigh from above me. "I already told you."

"You explained who he was," I said gently. "You told me why you broke apart. But you never explained why you can't reconnect."

"It's been ten years. Why would I want to reconnect?"

I blinked, then craned my head back to look up at him. "Because he was your *friend*. Your only friend!"

He smoothed my hair again, but I could feel the tension in his hand. "I have my brothers. That's enough. I told you in New York: people like me don't get to have friends."

I raised myself up on one arm so I could look at him properly. "*Everybody* needs friends." I searched his face. Reran his words in my head. "You think you don't deserve friends?" I said quietly. "Because of what you've done?"

He looked away.

"Radimir..." He glared stubbornly at the window. "Radimir, look at me."

He reluctantly turned to me.

"You think you don't deserve friends, like they're a reward the universe drops in your lap? That's not how it *works!* Having friends isn't easy, it's *hard.* Asking for help is *hard.* Admitting you're wrong when you've argued is *hard.* Being there for someone is *hard.* And it's okay that it's hard, that's what makes it worthwhile. Do you know what I think?"

He scowled. "I rarely know what you think."

"I think you're scared. You've lost so much. I think it would hurt if you reached out and he rejected you. And instead of facing that, you isolate yourself."

Radimir crossed his arms. "You think I'm a screw-up. You think I'm *povrezhdennyy*. Damaged."

I looked him right in the eye. "No," I said gently. "I think you're a man."

He glared at me, but I refused to drop my gaze. And eventually, those frozen sky eyes softened, and he rubbed at his face and cursed in Russian—

There was a knock at the door. Radimir looked up but I leaned in front of him and gave him an imploring look.

He sighed. "I'll think about it." Then he turned to the door and raised his voice. "What?"

"It's Valentin. We need you."

We dressed and went downstairs. Gennadiy was leaning over the dining table looking at a huge map of Chicago with our areas of control marked in red. “Sorry, brother,” he said when he saw us. “You both deserve a rest. But Spartak’s men are attacking all over the city.” He shook his head grimly. “We’re not going to be able to hold onto everything. We have to save what we can.”

The rest of that day was brutal. Radimir and I spent most of it driving, racing from one emergency to another. A bar that had been smashed up. A crane destroyed at a construction project, setting it back months. A politician who’d suddenly switched allegiances to Spartak and now wouldn’t sign off on a new casino. And of course, the police noticed the upswell in violence and demanded to know what was going on, so we had to work with the cops we had on our payroll to calm things down.

We did our best to cling onto territory but just as Gennadiy said, we couldn’t save everything. We had to choose where to send the small number of men we had: which communities to protect and which to let fall to Spartak’s control. At one point, Radimir had to choose to let a commercial street on the south side go in order to reinforce a street packed with families in the north. Later, we had to drive through that same street and saw cars burning and stores with their windows smashed in. I saw Radimir’s knuckles whiten on the steering wheel: his empire was falling.

The only good moment all day was when, that evening, I realized that we’d been working side by side this whole time. Radimir was a master of intimidation and scaring people into submission and I found I was good at reassuring people and smoothing things over. I was becoming the Bratva wife I never thought I could be.

When we regrouped at Gennadiy’s mansion, half of the red, Aristov territory on the map had turned to black. Spartak had swept like a wave through the city: it didn’t feel like a war, it felt like a coup. “We’re not going to last until Konstantin’s men get here,” muttered Gennadiy. “Another couple of hours and they’ll have taken everything. And then they’ll come for us.”

“How did Spartak plan this so well in just a few days?” I asked. Radimir, Valentin, Gennadiy and Mikhail shook their heads despondently. We could all feel us losing. Even Mikhail's dogs had sensed the mood and were lying quietly, their heads on their paws.

A roar of engines made us all look up. Headlights blasted through the cracks in the drapes, lighting the room up. Valentin peeked outside. "Cars," he told us. "A *lot* of cars."

Spartak. He was coming for us *now.*

Radimir grabbed my hand and pulled me behind him, then picked up a gun. Valentin turned off the lights and we all moved back from the windows.

I could hear footsteps outside, scrunching through the gravel to the front door. We all exchanged looks. *Fuck.* We'd misjudged things. Most of our men were out fighting in the city, we only had a handful of guards.

Someone banged on the front door. Gennadiy pointed his gun at it, ready to fire as soon as they broke it down. "Go upstairs," Radimir ordered, his voice tight. "Hide. They might not find you."

I shook my head and squeezed his hand. "I'm not leaving you." I tried to sound strong, but my voice was shaky with fear.

Another bang on the door. Everyone tensed, ready...

"*Konstantin sent us!*" yelled a voice.

We all looked at each other. *It's a trick.* It was a twelve-hour drive from New York. Konstantin's men wouldn't be here for at least another few hours, however fast they drove. Radimir shook his head. Valentin cocked a shotgun and pointed it at the door...

"I come with a gift," yelled the man. "A box of the pastries Mrs. Aristov liked so much?"

My eyes widened. No one else would know about me snarfling the pastries. "It *is* them!" Before anyone could stop me, I ran to the door and pulled it wide.

The man on the doorstep was craggy and good looking, in an older man sort of way, his hair streaked with silver. He was dressed in a black suit and tie, and he presented a bakery carton to me with a flourish. "Courtesy of Mr Gulyev's girlfriend," he told me with a smile. "I am Grigory, Mr. Gulyev's head of security." I could hear the pride in his voice as he said the last part. Behind him, car after car was pulling up, filling the driveway.

Radimir and the others crowded into the doorway around me. "How did..." asked Gennadiy, looking at his watch. "How did you get here so fast? It's impossible!"

"We didn't drive," Grigory told him. "Mr. Gulyev was concerned about your situation, so he had us use his private jet." He smiled and glanced over his shoulder. "And he sent a few extra men, just to be sure..."

We all stared. Men were climbing from the cars, all carrying stubby sub-machine guns. But there weren't thirty, like we'd asked for. There were closer to—

"Sixty-three," Grigory deadpanned. "It was a little crowded, on board."

It was a long night. We had to coordinate Konstantin's men and our men and push back Spartak while also defending the territory we still held. It was slow work, but numbers were on our side, now, and Spartak was caught off guard: he'd thought we were finished. By morning, we'd taken back what was ours and actually started taking over Spartak's territory. Exhausted and running on nothing but coffee, we started to give each other cautious, hopeful glances. Finally, Valentin said what we'd all been thinking. "We might actually win this. If things keep going our way..."

Gennadiy rubbed his cheek, a full night of stubble rasping. "Even if we win, I don't know if we'll ever get back the power we had. Not as long as we're cut off from The Eight."

"One thing at a time, brother," Radimir told him, patting his shoulder.

"I need to go check on the store," I told Radimir.

A quick shake of his head. "Out of the question!"

I pointed to the map. "Spartak's never even come close to

threatening that neighborhood. It's deep, deep in our territory. The fighting's on the other side of the city."

He frowned and opened his mouth to argue. "Just for a few hours!" I said quickly. "Come on, Jen's been covering for me ever since the wedding. I can't leave her on her own anymore."

He glared for a moment and the protective need in his eyes made me weak. Then his face softened, and he sighed. "Just a few hours," he warned. "And I'll come with you, to make sure it's safe."

When we arrived, the store was already open. The freezing rain was still hammering down but the warm light from the store's windows was like a beacon, welcoming people inside. Walking in felt like coming home: I was never normally away from the store for more than a day at a time, and so much had happened since the wedding that it felt like I'd been gone for a month. *God, I missed this place!* I was buzzing, and not just from all the coffee I'd drunk to work through the night. Things were looking up: the war was going our way and the meeting with Konstantin had sparked an idea. I had a plan that maybe, just maybe, could save the bookstore.

I'd brought Jen a takeout cup of coffee and the box of pastries Hailey had sent over: it was the least I could do. As soon as I saw her, I pulled her into a hug. "*Thank you,*" I told her. "I don't know what I'd have done without you."

She hugged me back but without much strength and when I moved back, she looked pale and skittish. "You okay?" I asked.

She nodded quickly. "Just tired."

I gave her another hug, then turned to Radimir, who was standing in the doorway. His phone bleeped with another message: the war was going our way, but he was still needed. "Go," I told him. "Everything's fine here, I'll help Jen for a few hours: you know where I am if you need me." Radimir looked uncertain. "Leave someone here to guard the place, if you're worried," I told him.

He grudgingly nodded but insisted on leaving *four* of Konstantin's heavily-armed men in a car right outside the store. I made a mental note to take some coffee out to them. Radimir pulled me to him and kissed me. "*Be careful,*" he told me. His hands stubbornly gripped my shoulders, unwilling to let me go.

I nodded meekly. "You too." I looked towards the door. "Go," I said softly. "I'll be fine."

He sighed and released me. When I watched him drive away, there was an ache in my chest: it was the first time we'd been apart since we left for New York.

"Okay," I said, turning to Jen. "Tell me what's been happening."

"A delivery came," she said, and pointed. "It's in the back."

I followed her into the back room. "I can unpack it," I told her. "You sit down, eat one of those pastries and get some coffee inside you, you look—"

I stopped in shock. Jen had moved aside, and I could see Baba sitting in an armchair. "What—"

The door slammed closed behind me and I spun around.

"Hello, Mrs. Aristov," said Spartak Nazarov.

62

BRONWYN

I FROZE, staring, while my stomach plummeted. Spartak had a gun pointed right at me but it was *him,* the huge, muscled mass of him, so close, that terrified me. His hands looked as if they could crush my neck like a soda can.

"I'm *sorry!*" croaked Jen. Now I knew why she'd looked so pale. "Baba came to visit, she was going to surprise you. Then he walked in. He said he'd kill her, if I let you know he was here!"

I nodded quickly. "It's okay. You didn't do anything wrong." I looked between Jen and Baba. "Are you both okay?"

"Don't worry about me," said Baba. Her voice was weak, but she was glaring at Spartak, her eyes diamond-hard.

Spartak motioned with his gun. "Take out your phone," he told me. "Unlock it and give it to your friend." I did it and passed it to Jen, my hands shaking. "When we're gone, call Radimir," Spartak told Jen. "Tell him to call me. He has my number."

Oh Jesus. I was so scared I thought I was going to throw up. Spartak knew he was going to lose the war, and this was his last-ditch attempt to turn things around. He was going to use me as bait and kill Radimir when he came to rescue me.

Spartak pushed me towards the rear door that led out to the alley.

My mind was spinning. *Run?* He was right behind me. *Scream, and hope the men at the front of the store hear me?* Spartak could kill all three of us before they reached us. *Fight?* I had the switchblade Radimir gave me, but it was no match for a gun.

I opened the rear door. A car was parked in the alley, with two of Spartak's men keeping watch. Spartak opened the trunk and then gestured to it mockingly.

I looked around frantically but there was no one passing by the alley, no one looking out of a window. No one to see what was happening. *Fuck! What should I do?*

Spartak leaned close. "In," he rasped, his lips almost touching my ear. "*Now.*"

Heart racing, I climbed into the trunk. He smirked, staring at my thighs where my skirt had ridden up. I tugged it down, shuddering.

The trunk slammed shut, trapping me in a black, airless box. Then the engine started, and we roared away.

63

RADIMIR

I GOT the call when I was in a meeting with a city councilman. Bronwyn's number, but it was her friend's voice. *"He took her! Come to the bookstore, quick!"*

I didn't have to ask who *he* was. I stood up and walked out of the meeting, leaving the councilman staring. I was only a block away and the traffic was barely moving: it would be quicker on foot. The instant the elevator hit the lobby, I ran.

The rain was pounding the streets, and I was soaked before I'd gone ten feet, but I barely noticed. *Chyort! You fucking idiot! How could you leave her, even for a few hours? Where is he taking her? What is he doing to her, right now?*

When I marched into the store, the guards I'd left were waiting for me, their heads hung. "He was already inside when we got here," one of them told me. "He took her out the back, we never even saw them. I'm sorry."

I stalked over and stood chest-to-chest with him, my breath coming in huge, shuddering pants. I wanted to smash something, wanted to *hurt* someone, and he stood there stoically, waiting for his punishment. But hitting him wouldn't solve anything. And this was on me, not him. *I was here! I was right here, all I had to do was check the fucking back room!*

I looked around at the bookstore—*her* bookstore. A wonderful, magical place that was nothing without her in it. She was gone because I failed utterly to protect her, I let him just walk in here and *take* her—

I roared and upended a table of books, sending it crashing to the floor and scattering paperbacks everywhere.

Baba walked over, careful and shaky on her twin walking sticks, but determined. "Not your fault," she wheezed. She looked me right in the eye. "Just get her back."

I panted, the rage still pounding through me. Then I nodded and pulled out my phone.

As soon as Spartak picked up, the words spilled out of me. "If you hurt her, if you *touch* her, I will hunt you down and break your fucking neck. I don't care if you run back to Russia, I don't care if it takes me my entire fucking life, I will find you and I will *cut. Your. Fucking. Throat.*"

"Your life for hers," said Spartak coldly. "Tonight. Midnight. At my club. Come alone and unarmed." And he hung up.

My life for hers. It wasn't even a decision. Of course I'd take that deal. And of course Spartak wouldn't let her go. But it was my only chance of maybe getting her out of this alive.

I'd be walking into *his* building, filled with *his* men, unarmed. I needed some way to even the odds. I couldn't just show up with an army, or Spartak would just kill her. I needed one person, someone who could sneak in undetected. My brothers couldn't do it: their faces were known; they'd never get into the club. And there was only one other person I'd trust with something like this.

I stared at my phone. It had been so long...and I was the one who'd ended our friendship. He might not want to know me anymore...

I sighed. *That woman knows me better than I know myself.* I *was* scared. But that didn't matter, not now.

It's been years. His number will have changed. I called Konstantin. "I need you to put me in touch with a guy who used to work for Luka Malakov. His name is Alexei."

64

ALEXEI

I WAS STRETCHED out on my back in the kitchen with my head and shoulders in the cupboard under the sink. A flashlight clamped between my teeth was shining up at a leaking U-bend. The apartment was almost silent, only the quiet little skitters and pecks of Gabriella's fingers on her keyboard, down the hall and the splatting of drips on my forehead. So, when my phone rang, a few feet from my head, it was *loud.* Anyone else would have banged their head but years of lying in wait for my targets, sometimes for hours or days, have given me superb self control. I groped for the phone and brought it to my ear, feeling smug. "Yes?"

Two shaky breaths. Then, "Alexei, it's Radimir."

I sat bolt upright. My forehead slammed into the U-bend, and I fell back down again, the world spinning. Suddenly, it was seventeen years ago, and I was a green young thing, not long out of the Russian army and still finding my feet in the Bratva. And *he'd* been green, too, him and his brothers, brand new to Luka's organization. They'd clearly been through hell. But they had a sophistication I never did: it was Radimir who got me into wearing suits. He'd always been cold but, when we got close, I'd found he had a softer side. Between jobs for Luka, Radimir and I used to go see movies, or go to upmarket bars where he'd coach me on how to talk to women. I remembered helping them all move into their first, tiny apartment, trying to maneuver a mattress for the youngest, Valentin, up four flights of stairs.

And I remembered how he'd changed. I'd always been happy to be a soldier, killing who they told me to kill and not asking questions. But Radimir was always ambitious and the higher he climbed, the colder he became. He laughed less, scowled more. When he and his brothers broke off from Luka to go and make their way in Chicago, we'd almost lost touch. But there'd been one more chance: after I saved Gabriella. I'd called Radimir to tell him I was out of the Bratva and...he'd been *angry.* Like I'd betrayed him, somehow, by getting out...or by falling in love. At the time, I'd been shaky and uncertain: I was high on love but I was also *lost:* I'd walked away from the Bratva and that meant leaving everyone I knew. I'd reached out to my one friend and his rejection had hurt...more than I wanted to admit. That had been ten years ago, and we hadn't spoken since.

My head was throbbing. I closed my eyes. "What do you—" I didn't even know what to say. And then it bubbled up from inside. "Are you okay?" I still cared.

A pause. "No," he croaked.

My eyes opened. Radimir admitting weakness? That never happened, not when I knew him. But I could hear the pain, even in that one syllable. The man was hurting. "What's wrong?"

A deep, shuddering breath, like he was fighting to control himself. "He took her."

I snaked my body out of the cupboard and slowly stood up. *Radimir...fell in love?* "Your girlfriend?"

"My wife."

His wife?! I frowned at the floor as I carefully picked my way through all the junk I'd had to clear out of the cupboard.

"I was wrong, Alexei," said Radimir. "I'm sorry."

I stopped. *Sorry?* Radimir would never be this...open. Not the Radimir who'd left for Chicago, coldly ambitious. But not even the Radimir I'd first met, when he'd come to work for Luka. He sounded more vulnerable, more humble. And I felt the apology slide down deep and lock into place, healing something I hadn't realized had still hurt, after all these years.

"Is okay," I grunted.

"I need your help to get her back," said Radimir. "You're the only one I trust." And he told me about meeting Bronwyn, about Spartak's nightclub and the exchange at midnight. "I'd need you on the next plane," he said, then took a deep breath. "Will you help?"

Back in with the Bratva. Walking into a trap. A good chance I'd be killed. Of course I wouldn't do it.

Except for a friend. "Yes," I told him.

I'd wandered down the hall to Gabriella's study. She was sitting in the dark, as she always did, but her keyboard and mouse pulsed scarlet and she had the text on the bank of monitors in front of her set to amber so she looked like some sorceress, bathed in light from a river of lava and fire. I leaned against the wall for a second and just gazed at her. She'd never looked more beautiful. Then she saw me out of the corner of her eye and looked curiously at my phone. *Who is it?* She mouthed.

"And your hacker girlfriend, Gabriella," asked Radimir. "We could use her help. Could she come along, too?"

"She's my wife, now," I told him, gazing into Gabriella's eyes. "And if I know Gabriella, she'll *insist.*"

65

BRONWYN

THE CAR PULLED up to the curb and stopped next to a long line of people. The temperature was well below zero and it had started snowing again: I could see women in short skirts pulling their coats tight around them as they waited to get into the club.

Beside me, Spartak leaned close. "We're going in, now. Walk right in front of me. Try to run and I'll snap your neck."

I nodded mutely. I'd spent the afternoon locked in a side room at some sort of warehouse. When I'd tried to make a break for it, he'd hit me so hard I saw stars. I'd managed to slip the switchblade into my bra, but it wasn't much use now: they'd handcuffed my wrists behind my back.

Spartak and his two bodyguards climbed out of the car and then hauled me out, Spartak pulling me back against his chest so that no one could see my cuffed hands. They walked me straight past the line and up to the door, where the bouncers nodded respectfully and waved us in. I saw now why Spartak had wanted to do the exchange here: everyone but us had to walk through a metal detector to get in. When Radimir came, he'd be unarmed and defenseless. And he *would* come. I'd heard Spartak's phone call, and I knew Radimir would make the trade: his life for mine. Then Spartak would kill us both.

One of Spartak's bodyguards opened a set of heavy doors ahead of us and a wall of sound slammed into us, pummeling my ear drums. The bass was making the floor jump and tremble under my shoes and all I could see ahead of us was a claustrophobic crush of bodies, silhouetted by sweeping lasers and smoke.

Spartak pushed me forward, into the crowd and across the huge room. For a moment, I thought I might be able to slip away into the crowd, but he killed that hope instantly, gripping the chain of my handcuffs and twisting it in his fist so that my wrists ground painfully together. We were so close, I could feel his breath on my neck. He used me as an icebreaker, pushing me through the sea of people ahead of him, and it was terrifying: when you're pushing through a crowd, you naturally use your hands to pry people apart and make a path. But my hands were trapped behind me, so it was my face and chest that touched people first. I got elbowed in the face three times, and two guys took the opportunity to "accidentally" brush against my breasts.

I tried to get my bearings. The club was huge, with one massive, hexagonal dance floor downstairs and at least three floors of balconies and smaller VIP rooms looking down over it. Right at the top of the building, I could see a glass-walled room that overlooked everything. The place had a run-down, seedy feel: the carpets were sticky from spilled beer and the place stank of weed. I could see people openly popping pills and it felt like there were way too many people there for it to be safe: every balcony and bit of floor was crammed. The worst thing, though, was the atmosphere. In some clubs, everyone's caught up in the music, riding the same natural high as the DJ plays the crowd like an instrument. Even around strangers, it feels like you're part of something. But here, there was an undercurrent of nervous, twitchy energy. Women moved around in groups, thumbs over the mouths of their beer bottles. Men leaned against pillars and walls, watching, waiting, moving in when they saw a woman on her own. The place felt *unsafe.*

We finally reached the stairs and began climbing, spiraling our way up around the edge of the club. The stairs were slippery with spilled drinks and cluttered with people sitting on them: security would pass by and make everyone get up and as soon as they were gone, everyone would sit back down again. The club was just too full, there was nowhere else to sit. And some of the people on the stairs weren't capable of standing anyway, either drunk or drugged. It was slow going and the stairs seemed to go on forever: by the time we got to the final flight, my joints felt like they'd been packed with salt. Then I tripped over someone's handbag strap and went down face-first. Spartak caught my handcuff chain just in time, and I snapped to a stop with my face an inch from the stairs. "Say thank you," he told me as he hauled me upright.

I stood there panting and shaken, looking up at him. He was intimidatingly big and with my hands trapped behind me, I felt completely defenseless. "Thank you," I managed.

He leered at my breasts, and we moved on, the panic notching higher and higher in my chest.

At last, we reached the glass-walled room at the top. A blond-haired guy in a blue suit who I assumed ran the club lounged in a chair, using a gold credit card to chop a line of coke. He scrambled to stand up when Spartak walked in. I recognized Liliya, Spartak's wife, effortlessly graceful in a white dress that looked like it was made of leather. When she saw me, being pushed along in front of Spartak, her face softened for a second. Then she quickly looked away. Her lower lip was swollen and puffy on one side, as if she'd been punched, and I felt the anger flare in my chest.

Spartak strolled in behind me, then gave me a push that sent me stumbling into a corner. "Radimir will be here soon," he announced. He pointed to the guy in the blue suit. "Make sure he's searched. *Twice.* Then have your men bring him up here."

Spartak's bodyguards took out their guns and checked them. I stared at them, my heart slamming harder and harder against my chest. *They're going to execute him right here.* He'd walk in and Spartak would give the order and he'd be *dead—*

Unless I did something. I looked across at Spartak, who'd pulled Liliya to him and was kissing her hard, which must have been agony with her bruised mouth. She was standing there passively, letting him maul her, but behind her back I could see her digging her fingernails into her palms.

I swallowed. I could feel the instinctual dread I always got around Spartak twisting in my stomach, telling me to stay right where I was. He could hurt me. Or worse. But I had to do this.

I summoned up every bit of Bratva Queen energy I could muster...and marched over there, head high. "Mr. Nazarov, listen to me, please," I said desperately. I figured he'd like being called *Mr. Nazarov.*

Spartak broke the kiss and looked at me. I tried to ignore the way his eyes roamed over my breasts.

"There's something you don't know," I told him. "When...Radimir killed your brother, it was because he'd been ordered to. Someone fooled us, they pretended to be one of The Eight and told us to kill Borislav." I looked up at him imploringly. "They did it so that *exactly this* would happen, we'd wind up in a war with you. *We are not your enemy!* Whoever fooled us, *they're* the ones you should be mad at." Spartak was glaring down at me, furious, and all I wanted to do was slink away, but I kept my eyes on his. "You should *join* us, not fight us! Help us figure out who did this! Look...I know you're hurting because of your brother." I shook my head gently. "I can't even imagine what that must be like. But please...help us find out who's really responsible. And you can have your revenge against the *right* person."

I stared up at him breathlessly, tears in my eyes. I searched his face for any sign it had worked...

And then he burst out laughing. A great big belly laugh that smelled of vodka and cigars. I stood there staring, completely thrown.

"Look at you!" he spluttered. He fisted my hair and yanked my head back painfully. "The brave little bookseller. Gets some fancy clothes and thinks she's Bratva. Giving *speeches!* I heard it was even you who talked Konstantin around: on your knees, I assume."

I stared up at him. My face had gone scalding hot. All the

insecurities I'd fought my way through were suddenly back. *Of course you're not a fucking Bratva Queen.* Spartak's bodyguards were laughing at me, too. I wanted the ground to swallow me up. Only Liliya was looking on in sympathy.

"You're a woman," spat Spartak. "And your only place in the Bratva is on your back with your legs open." He put his face close to mine. "You think you're so fucking smart. But you're a stupid little *shlyukha.*"

He's right. I was too big, too uncool, with a body that couldn't even handle fucking *walking* some of the time and a bookstore I couldn't make profitable: my big new idea, that had seemed so great that morning, was probably another failure waiting to happen. I stared up at him through eyes swimming with hot tears.

Spartak sneered at me and turned to one of his men. "*Ona yeshche boleye zhalkaya, chem moy brat.*" And after all that time with the language app and watching Russian movies, my brain automatically translated: *She's even more pathetic than my brother.*

I stared at him in shock as the meaning sank in. *It was an act.* All of his grieving and raging for his beloved, dead brother. *He hated him. But he kept up the act because...* My mind spun. *Because...*

"You had him killed," I thought out loud. "It was *you. You* made the deep fake phone call."

He blinked at me, shocked that I'd understood the Russian. But he couldn't stop himself grinning in pride.

"You *wanted* a war," I said, stunned. Now I knew why the attacks over the last few days had been so perfectly thought out. This whole thing had been planned from the beginning, so that Spartak could wipe us out. "That video from the hidden camera in your brother's apartment: you had it from the start! *You put the camera there!* You were hoping the police would point the finger at Radimir on their own, but they didn't get there, even after you pressed them to re-examine the scene. The video was your backup plan." I stared at him. The funeral. All that time he'd played the grieving sibling, desperate for vengeance. "You tricked us into killing your own *brother,*" I whispered. "Just so you'd have an excuse to go to war with us."

"Borislav was getting ideas," Spartak told me. "Just like you've been getting ideas. He thought *he* should be running things."

I felt my jaw fall open. His plan let him eliminate his brother *and* the Aristovs.

Spartak smiled at my expression. "You see how things work now. You don't belong in our world. You never did."

He gave me a savage shove. I went stumbling backwards, tripped over my own feet and went down hard on my ass. Without my hands to catch me, I couldn't control my fall, and I rocked back and cracked my head against the wall. Fresh tears sprang to my eyes, and I lay there, head throbbing, utterly defeated.

66

ALEXEI

THE DOORMAN STARED SUSPICIOUSLY at me. I lifted an eyebrow and stared back at him. Maybe he thought—correctly—that I looked Russian. But there were lots of Russians in this part of Chicago. And my clothes matched all the other guys in the line: shirt and jeans. Plus, a drunk blonde in a tight red dress who'd lost her friends and kept calling me *Boris* had surgically attached herself to me in the line and was doing a good job of distracting him. Eventually he sighed and waved both of us forward. He made sure I went through the metal detector *and* gave me a pat down, just to be sure, but he didn't find anything because I was unarmed. He gave me a last frown and nodded for us to go in.

Inside, I made sure the blonde found the friends she'd lost and then made an excuse and slipped away.

I made my way up to the men's bathroom on the third floor, which I figured would be the quietest, and into the last stall on the right. The extractor fan was right where it had been on the blueprint, a big ugly white box built into the center of a windowpane.

I climbed up onto the toilet and then put my hands on the tops of the stall walls and heaved myself up like a gymnast on the parallel bars. I bent my legs and kicked the fan as hard as I could. Nothing happened. I kicked it again. Again. *This better work.* Because otherwise I was unarmed and not much good to anyone. I grunted and kicked again—

There was a cracking sound and the sealant holding the fan in place gave way. The extractor fan disappeared into the darkness and a few seconds later there was a distant crash as it hit the ground three floors below, barely audible over the thumping music.

Panting, I lowered myself down until I was standing on the toilet. Then I took off my bracelet: one of those outdoorsy, survival ones, fifty feet or so of parachute cord woven into a thick band. I unraveled it and dropped the end out of the hole in the window.

A moment later, I felt a tug on the cord. That meant Gabriella, who'd been waiting in the alley, had done her job. I hauled the cord all the way back up. Tied to the end was a black bag of guns.

I jumped down into the stall and started hiding the guns under my jacket. When I was done, I threw the bag and cord out of the window and stepped out of the stall. I caught my reflection in the mirror and stopped for a second, straightening my collar. "*Vse yeshche ponyal*," I muttered with pride. *Still got it.*

Then I went to find a place to hide.

67

RADIMIR

MIDNIGHT.

I pulled up right outside Spartak's club, in the middle of a no parking zone. If by some miracle I survived the night, I'd happily pay for the parking ticket.

Spartak's men were waiting for me and pounced immediately, dragging me over to the metal detector and pushing me through it. They seemed a little disappointed that I wasn't trying to smuggle a gun or a knife in, and patted me down twice just to be sure. Then they walked me inside. Two of them had their hands on my shoulders, each with a gun pressed into my back. They weren't taking any chances.

My eyes swept the crowd as they walked. Had Alexei made it in? For all I knew, he was still stuck in the line outside. And if that was the case, we were screwed.

We wound our way up through the club until we came to a glass-walled room right in the rafters. Spartak was waiting for us, along with four of his men. Liliya, Spartak's wife, was standing nervously next to him. But where was—

Then I saw her, lying on the floor, a sticky, glossy patch of blood next to her head. For a second, I thought she was dead and I just... *collapsed* inside. I wanted to fall to my knees and sob.

Then she moved and my heart started beating again. She lifted her head and looked at me, her eyes red from crying, and struggled to get to her feet. I started forward but Spartak's men blocked me. "Are you okay?" I asked Bronwyn.

She nodded bravely.

"She's fiiine," Spartak drawled. "A cryer, though." He scowled. "I don't know how you have the patience."

I turned and fixed him with a glare but said nothing. There were four of his men in front of me plus the two who'd walked me up here, plus Spartak himself. Seven against one and they were all armed, and I wasn't.

I'd decided how I was going to handle this. If it looked like Spartak would keep his word and let Bronwyn go, I'd go through with the trade: my life for hers. It was the best way of keeping her safe. I'd made Gennadiy promise that he'd look after her, afterwards. He, Valentin and Mikhail had tried to talk me out of coming alone, but I'd been firm. *If all of us show up, guns blazing, Spartak will kill her.*

Besides, I wasn't alone. I had my backup plan, waiting in the darkness. I hoped.

"I'm here," I told Spartak. "Let her go."

Spartak grinned and walked over to me. He nodded to the two guys behind me, and they grabbed me, wrenching my arms back behind me. Spartak put down the drink he was holding, stretched his shoulders, limbering up...and then he drove his fist into my stomach with every ounce of his strength.

I doubled over, pain radiating out in shuddering waves. It was a strange, silent kind of agony: all the air had been forced out of my lungs and they hurt too much to draw a breath. As I choked and wheezed, Spartak grabbed Bronwyn's hand and pulled her over to us. "I'm a man of my word," he told me. "I *will* let her go...once every one of my men has had a turn at her."

The rage exploded in my chest. *You're not fit to touch her.* So, it was the backup plan, then.

"It was him," Bronwyn said quickly. "*He* faked the phone call."

I stared at her, still struggling to breathe. Suddenly, it all made sense. And now I knew there was no way Spartak would let her go. He'd kill her...or keep her forever.

The two men behind me forced me to my knees. Spartak took out his gun, then checked around. We were in the center of the room, which meant even with the glass walls, we were hidden from everyone below. He pressed the muzzle to my forehead.

I imagined Alexei, lying full length on a gantry somewhere, up in the lighting rig above us, watching for my signal through his sniper scope.

I imagined Gabriella, sitting in a car out in the alley, her face lit by the glow of her laptop screen, waiting for the radio message from Alexei. Her finger hovering over the key that would change one digit in one database and make the power company think the club hadn't paid its power bill in over a decade.

I nodded twice.

And every light in the club went out.

68

BRONWYN

SOMETHING you never really think about: there are no windows in a nightclub.

When the lights went out, it didn't go dark, it went *black*. And for a second, it went silent: everyone in the glass-walled room froze in shock. The music had stopped, too, and my ears throbbed from the sudden quiet. Then the crowd downstairs began to scream and panic.

And then the shooting started.

It didn't *sound* like shooting. More like a hard thud, and the sound of glass breaking, and a man crying out, all at the same time. I heard a body slump to the floor, somewhere behind Radimir. Then it happened again. And again. And again.

Spartak still had hold of me. He gripped my wrist so hard, I thought the bones were going to snap. I could hear him fumbling frantically with something and then suddenly there was light: he'd turned on the flashlight on his phone and was shining it around—

The light found a body lying on the floor. One of Spartak's men, his chest ruined and bloody. A second body. A third. And then Radimir, rising from his knees, his face like thunder.

Spartak went sheet white. He hooked an arm around my neck and pulled me back against him, using me as a shield. There was another shot and another of Spartak's men fell. This one toppled forward and fell through the glass wall, smashing a huge hole and then tumbling into the darkness. A few seconds later, the screams from the people three floors below turned full-on hysterical as he landed in the crowd.

I saw Spartak look around in terror: he only had one man left, now, and Radimir was marching towards him. He put his gun to my head, and I froze as the cold metal kissed my temple. Radimir froze, too.

Spartak looked around, then began dragging me backwards, towards the wall. *Where's he taking me? There's nothing there!* The only door was on the far side of the room.

But then Spartak pushed on one of the wall panels and it swung aside: a secret door. He pulled me into a cramped, dark stairwell leading down. He snapped his fingers at Liliya, ordering her the way you would an animal, and she hurried in after us.

"Kill him!" Spartak yelled at his last surviving bodyguard. Then he pulled the door shut and shot a heavy metal bolt across, locking Radimir out.

69

RADIMIR

THE PANEL CLOSED and I was in blackness again. I wasted precious seconds getting my phone out and turning on the flashlight, then ran to the wall and felt the wall panel. It was smooth, painted metal like all the others: if I hadn't seen it open for Spartak, I wouldn't have even known it *was* a door. I pushed on it like he did, but it refused to open: he must have locked it from the other side. My plan was falling apart: I hadn't bet on him having a secret escape route. I'd glimpsed stairs behind the door, leading down. I had to get downstairs and find Bronwyn, *now,* or he'd escape with her and—my stomach flipped. I didn't want to think about what he and his men would do to her.

First, though, I had another problem. The last of Spartak's bodyguards had been fumbling with his phone, trying to get his flashlight on so he could see. But now I'd turned *mine* on, he was going for his gun instead—

There was no time to turn my flashlight off. I dodged, and covered my phone with my jacket, and we were in darkness again. A shot rang out and I felt a bullet hiss past me, horribly close.

I ran for where I thought the noise had come from, hoping to shoulder-charge him. But instead of whacking into him, I stumbled on and on...and then suddenly had to pull up short, arms windmilling, when I felt a breeze in front of me: I'd very nearly run straight out of the hole in the glass wall and gone plunging to my death. I stood there shaking and sweating for a second, trying to figure out where the bodyguard was. Then he slammed into my side, and we crashed to the floor together, rolling and struggling in total darkness.

Broken glass crunched under me. Then he punched me in the face, and I reeled, dazed. Another punch from the other side and now I was barely conscious: I couldn't avoid them, couldn't even see where they were coming from...

Bright white light suddenly washed across us. I could see the man straddling me as he looked up in surprise...and then there was a shot, and he fell backwards off me. Alexei stepped into view, just as coolly professional as I remembered him all those years ago.

I nodded my thanks, and something passed between us. My throat tightened, thinking of all the times I should have called him, over the last decade, all the times I could have made things right, and didn't.

He reached down and offered his hand, and I took it gratefully. "He took her," I told him as he hauled me to my feet. "Downstairs somewhere."

Alexei stepped over to the hole in the glass wall and looked down at the scene below, shining the flashlight on his gun so we could see. It was total panic down there, hundreds of people, mostly drunk or on drugs, crushed together in total darkness. The stairs and balconies would be even worse. And Spartak's men would be everywhere, looking for us. "Is not good," Alexei summarized.

"I know," I said softly. The plan had been to grab Bronwyn and run: we should be gone by now. "But we've got to find her."

Alexei nodded and handed me a gun: a pistol with a flashlight attached, the same as his. I took a deep breath...and we set off into the darkness.

70

BRONWYN

THE STAIRS WERE METAL, like a fire escape, and only big enough for one person at a time. They were incredibly steep, too, almost a ladder. There was a handrail but with my hands cuffed behind my back, I couldn't use it. One slip and I was going straight to the bottom, however far down that was. It was terrifying: I tried to go slow so I could keep my balance, but Spartak kept getting impatient and pushing me from behind, making my heart jump into my mouth as I stumbled and teetered. My legs were already worn out from climbing up to the top of the nightclub and after a few minutes of the downward climb, my joints were screaming. *We have to reach the first floor soon.* But we didn't. The stairs went on and on until I could barely stand.

We finally emerged through a steel door...but not into the nightclub. I stopped and stared.

It was a hallway, the walls were bare brick and the floor concrete. There were lights overhead, but they were all off: the power was out down here, too. And for some reason, no one was using the flashlights on their phones. The only light came from a few security guys who were running around with flashlights. In the beams I saw people wearing one-piece disposable coveralls, hairnets and masks. Through a doorway, I could see what looked like a massive chemistry lab, with glass flasks bubbling over blue flames. And through other doorways I could see people standing at long conveyor belts scooping tiny *somethings* into bags. For one crazy moment, I thought we'd come out in a candy factory.

Then one of the workers pushed a trolley past me loaded with bags and I saw what they were full of: pills. *Spartak's drug factory.* It was hidden beneath his nightclub: that's why no one had ever found it. But...wait, Spartak had been dealing drugs for years. There were dozens of workers here: not one of them, in all that time, had ever let slip that this place existed?

A security guard ran past me and his flashlight lit up another room, just for a second. I saw bunk beds. And then it sank in that all the workers I was seeing were women, and they all looked terrified. *They're trafficked!* Probably from Russia. *That's why they don't have phones.* I looked around in horror: we were in a cellar, no windows. *Jesus Christ, how long is it since some of these women saw sunlight?*

While I'd been gazing around, Spartak had been busy. He was rounding up the security guards, making sure they had guns and leading them towards a door. He'd looked terrified upstairs, when he'd faced Radimir one-on-one. But now he was surrounded by soldiers, he was back to his arrogant self. "You all come with me," he told them.

"What about her?" one of the guards asked, nodding at me.

Spartak grabbed my wrist and pulled me down the hall to a storeroom full of barrels of chemicals. He opened my handcuffs for a second, then recuffed me with the chain around a pipe. "You stay down here," he told Liliya, giving her a flashlight. "Keep an eye on her." He turned to the posse of guards he'd assembled. "Tell the door staff not to let anyone leave. He can't get out of the club. We'll hunt him down!" And they set off down the hall.

Fuck. I wrenched at the handcuffs, but they didn't give at all. My heart was hammering. Radimir would be searching for me, but he'd never find me, not down here. Spartak and his men would find him and then...

I pulled at the handcuffs again. "Come on," I begged, my voice tight with panic. "*Please!*"

71

RADIMIR

"I DON'T SEE HER," muttered Alexei.

We were on the second-floor balcony and it was a horror movie. The dark was making some people panic and they were running, tripping on the stairs and going down, and other people were tripping over *them.* Then there were the people who thought the best idea was to sit down and huddle until the lights came back on. They blocked the balconies and caused more accidents. The nightclub had already been over-full when the lights went out and now everyone was trying to get downstairs, creating a crush. Alexei and I were having to shove our way through and use our guns to scare people back.

I looked down onto the first floor, sweeping my flashlight over the crowd. *Jesus.* It was a heaving, claustrophobic sea of scared people. The panic was spreading and any minute now, it would turn into a stampede. Plus, the first floor would be full of Spartak's men. We'd managed to avoid them in the dark until now but that wouldn't last.

"I'm not leaving without her," I told Alexei. "We have to go down there."

Alexei nodded grimly. I knew he'd do the same, if it was

Gabriella. *And I'd be right by his side.* I grabbed his shoulder and squeezed it. And we headed down into the crush of the dance floor. *Bronwyn,* I pleaded silently, *where are you?*

72

BRONWYN

I GAVE one last tug on the handcuffs and slumped, exhausted and defeated. I'd tried both breaking the chain and wrenching the pipe off the wall but all I had to show for it was scraped, bleeding wrists. I could *feel* Radimir looking for me upstairs in the club. He was going to wander right into Spartak's posse and get killed and it was all because of me, letting myself get kidnapped like an idiot. *All I need is a freakin' tool or something. If only I wasn't alone...* I let out a long string of curses and kicked the pipe. It clanged and Liliya jumped back, startled.

And that's when I remembered I wasn't alone.

"Liliya," I said, twisting around to look at her. "I can get you out."

She blinked at me, then quickly shook her head and looked away. But I'd seen that millisecond of hope in her eyes, before she'd shut it down.

"I *can!*" I insisted. "Look, the Aristovs can win this thing. They can wipe Spartak out. You can be free of him." I looked up at the ceiling, towards where I knew Radimir must be. "But they need their *Pakhan* to do it!"

She shook her head again and stepped back, crossing her arms protectively. "I guard you," she said firmly. Her English was surprisingly bad, for someone who'd lived in America for years. Then my stomach churned: Spartak probably never let her go out on her own or make American friends. He kept her isolated and stopped her learning English to make it harder for her to run away. "I've seen how he treats you," I said softly. "I know he hits you."

She stared at the floor.

"I can get you out," I said. "Liliya, look at me."

She wouldn't.

"*Look at me!*"

She finally lifted her eyes, and I saw something like shame there.

"It's not your fault!" I told her firmly. "It's not! Look, I can get you out. Liliya, if you help me, I *promise* you I will get you out. You'll be safe."

There were tears in her eyes. She stared at me, wanting to believe me but terrified.

"We can get you a new name, a new identity. You can go wherever you want."

She bit her lip then shook her head. *Shit.* I was losing her. I stepped towards her, stretching out as far as the handcuffs would allow. "Liliya, *please!* Help me escape and *you never have to see that bastard again!*"

She stared at me, blinking back tears...and then shook her head again and ran. Since she'd been the one with the flashlight, that left me in darkness.

I sighed and rested my head against the cool metal of the pipe. That was it, then. Spartak would hunt down Radimir and kill him. And then he'd come back for me and...my stomach heaved as I thought about being used by him and his men. And then I'd be dumped in a shallow grave somewhere when he got tired of me.

Minutes passed. Then I heard footsteps and an approaching flashlight. I looked up hopefully, then sighed as Liliya shuffled back into the room. *My guard is back.*

But something was different. Her hands were behind her back, and she was looking at me with huge, guilty eyes, a child who knows she's done something bad.

She brought her hands out from behind her back and showed me what she'd been hiding there. Bolt cutters. I drew in a strangled gasp of hope.

"You *promise!*" she hissed. "You promise I get out?"

"*Yes!*" I nodded frantically. "Yes, I promise."

Liliya looked at me for three more heartbeats, debating. Then she leaned forward and cut the chain on my handcuffs. I grabbed her hand and crept with her to the doorway. "How do we get out of here?" I asked.

She pointed down the hallway. At the very end, there was a heavy metal door with a guard standing in front of it. We weren't getting out that way.

There had to be some other exit. I crept with her down the pitch-black hallway. I found the door to the secret stairway Spartak had brought us down, but it was locked. Liliya and I searched the rooms one by one. The guards were stretched thin, now that Spartak had taken so many of them, and in the darkness, we could sneak past them if we were careful. The workers ignored us, too scared of the guards to so much as look up from their work. But there were no more doors and the only air vents were far too small to fit through. The place was a prison.

We were creeping through what I was calling the chemistry lab when our luck ran out. A guard saw us and grabbed me, trying to wrestle me to the ground. Liliya hooked an arm around his neck and pulled him off me and the two of them staggered through the middle of the lab. One of Liliya's elbows caught a complex web of glass tubing and it went crashing over, spilling chemicals everywhere. Then the guard knocked against a gas burner, and it tipped and—

The dark room suddenly lit up orange as flames licked across an entire tabletop. *Shit!* The chemicals must have been flammable. Fire was dripping down onto the floor, spreading to other tables. The workers began to scream and run and choking gray smoke began to fill the air.

The workers spilled out into the hallway. It was chaos, now: the whole place was still dark, with only flames and a few flashlight beams to light it up, and already the air was becoming hazy. My lungs were burning and like everyone else, I followed instinct. *Get out, get out!*

But as we reached the end of the hallway, the guard at the door raised his gun and yelled at us in Russian. The workers ducked in fear and retreated.

Oh fuck. Spartak couldn't let the police find out about this place. The guard would be under orders: don't let anyone out, no matter what.

They'd let us all die down here.

73

RADIMIR

WE'D CIRCLED RIGHT around the dance floor and there was no sign of Bronwyn or Spartak. *Where the hell are they?!* I tried to push towards the center again, but the crowd was packed so tight I could barely move. I couldn't even scare a path by waving my gun because there was nowhere for people to move *to.*

And then it got worse. My nose wrinkled and I whipped my head around to stare at Alexei. He nodded, looking worried. *Smoke.*

You could see the realization spread through the crowd. Then someone started to cough, and the panic began, people's fears kicking in even before the smoke was really visible. The crowd surged towards the doors. But the guards at the doors wouldn't open them: they were under orders because Spartak knew I was here. I ground my teeth. *This is on me. People are going to die because I came here.*

And I *still* couldn't find Bronwyn. The smoke seemed to be drifting up from somewhere below. Was there another floor? I couldn't find any stairs leading down and we'd tried every door. *Where the hell is she?*

There was a gunshot and Alexei shoved me aside. I heard a bullet pass between us. As the screaming started, I grabbed Alexei's shoulder and ran with him to the bar that lay along one side of the hexagonal club. We dived over the bar and crashed head-first to the floor behind it. I got my foot trapped between two mini-fridges and twisted it trying to get it free. Pain blossomed in my ankle, and I cursed and finally got it loose. As more bullets passed over our heads, we knelt and peeked over the top of the bar.

Spartak and a handful of men were firing at us from across the club, not caring who they hit. The gunfire finally cleared some space on the dance floor, with people retreating to the edges and up onto the balconies, but that only made the crushes there worse. And the smoke was thickening: it was getting difficult to breathe and it was getting hotter, too: there was a full-on fire happening somewhere.

More bullets hit the bar. Alexei and I shot back, but we were hopelessly outnumbered. If we didn't get out of here, we were dead. I saw Alexei's jaw tighten and knew that he was thinking about *his* wife, out in the alley. The guilt crushed my heart in a fist. He'd been out of the Bratva, he'd been safe, and I'd dragged him back into it. Now he might never see his wife again. And I might never see mine.

74

BRONWYN

I DOUBLED OVER, coughing. The smoke was so thick, now, that we could barely see. The room where the fire had started was an inferno and the flames were spreading down the hallway. The workers were screaming, hysterical. But there was still no way out. The guard at the door had tied a cloth over his mouth to help him breathe through the smoke and even though he was clearly panicked, he wasn't moving. He probably knew Spartak would execute him if he let us escape. It actually made a grim kind of sense: Spartak could buy more trafficked women to work in the drug factory, rebuild what the fire damaged...but he couldn't recover if the police found the place and arrested him. *He'll let us all die.*

And it was my fault: before I'd come along, these women were prisoners but at least they were alive. I leaned back against the wall, my eyes streaming from the smoke, my joints burning so much from all the stair climbing and running around that I could barely stay standing.

I was dimly aware that Liliya was speaking in Russian to two of the workers, trying to reassure them. She pointed in my direction. And then, to my horror, all three of them turned to me.

I blinked at them. *Oh shit.* They expected *me* to think of something.

One of the workers grabbed my sleeve. "*Please!* I have child!"

I stared at her, frozen in fear. Now they were *all* looking at me. *What do I do? I don't know what to do!* I remembered Spartak's words. I wasn't a leader. I wasn't *anything.*

But as more and more women clustered around me, I felt something shift inside. It didn't matter that I wasn't a leader. It didn't matter that I ran a freakin' bookstore. It didn't matter if I was scared. They needed me.

I took a shaky breath and thought. "Okay," I said at last, my voice croaky from the smoke. "This is what we're going to do."

I laid it out and then Liliya translated my plan into Russian for the workers who didn't speak English. As it spread through the crowd of workers, I slipped a hand down my dress and pulled out the switchblade. I pressed the button, and the blade shot out. I swallowed...and stepped out into the hallway, keeping the knife hidden behind my back.

Down at the far end, the guard was still trying to keep order. He was panicking and choking on smoke himself, the sweat running down his face as he swung his gun left and right, warning everyone to keep back.

I started to run. I heard footsteps following and checked over my shoulder: Liliya was following behind me. She gave me a nervous thumbs up and I nodded.

At first, the guard didn't notice me: lots of people were running back and forth, trying to get away from the flames, and he was more worried about what was happening down at *his* end of the hallway. When I was halfway to him, he seemed to see me...but he still wasn't too concerned. A whole crowd of frantic workers were between me and him.

I pushed myself to go faster. My only chance was to reach him before he realized I was a threat. My knees felt as if bone was grinding on bone, sending white-hot pain shooting up my body, but I kept going.

The crowd magically opened up as I reached it, the workers dodging back out of the way at the last second as we'd planned. *Now* the guard paid attention. He swung his gun up, faster than I'd anticipated. *Shit!* I was still a few steps away—

There was a bang, almost in my face, and I tensed and waited for the pain, but it didn't come. Then I was on him, bringing the switchblade forward and slamming it into his stomach. The knife went in so easily, I thought I'd done it wrong. Then I felt hot wetness against my fingers and *Oh Jesus, I stabbed him.* I knew I was meant to twist but the guard was already stumbling sideways, the gun dropping from his fingers, and I jumped back, panting in shock.

The workers surrounded me and pulled open the heavy metal door. Stone steps led up. The workers flooded past me and up the stairs. Next to me, the guard rolled on the floor, clutching his wound, sobbing but alive.

I slumped in relief for a second. Then I turned to Liliya. "C'mon, let's—"

I froze. Liliya was leaning against the wall, her face white, and she was holding her stomach like it ached. Then I saw the blood oozing between her fingers. *The shot the guard fired...* "No," I said, shaking my head. "No. *No!*"

Liliya started to slide down the wall, her legs collapsing under her. I ran over and supported her as she slumped to her knees. "Help!" I screamed. "Somebody help!"

75

RADIMIR

I DUCKED back behind the bar again, panting, as more bullets took chunks out of the bar top. Spartak and his men were coming, creeping towards us through the smoke, and we couldn't hold them, not with just two of us. I exchanged a look with Alexei. *It's over.*

And then suddenly there was shouting from the other end of the club, behind Spartak. Clouds of smoke were billowing from behind the DJ booth and then...people started emerging from up out of the floor. People dressed in laboratory coveralls. *What the hell?*

I had no idea what was going on. All that mattered was that they were coming *up* from some sort of basement. I was betting that was where Bronwyn was. And it was definitely where the fire was: the smoke was getting thicker and thicker, lit up by orange flames. *Chyort, I have to get down there.*

But between us and the hole were Spartak and his men. They were distracted, trying to grab the people and corral them back downstairs...*maybe we can take them.* We had to, or Bronwyn was going to die down there. I nodded to Alexei, and we ran.

For the first few seconds, it looked like we had a chance. Some of the guards were looking the other way, focused on the escaping lab workers. But then they looked around and saw us and the bullets started flying, catching us out in the open. I felt one tug at the fabric of my jacket, inches from my chest. Alexei stumbled as a bullet clipped his leg. We couldn't fire back, not without hitting all the panicked people running back and forth. One of the guards lifted his gun and aimed right at me and I grimaced, bracing myself...

The guard suddenly flew sideways as a man in a suit rammed into him. *Gennadiy!*

Another guard fell, the handle of a knife sticking from his chest, and I saw Valentin standing in the shadows. A third doubled over as Mikhail swung a baseball bat into his stomach. And Mikhail's dogs were there, too, two of them latching on to a guard's arms and pulling him down while a third put his jaws warningly around his throat. I blinked: daylight was flooding into the club through the front door: my brothers must have fought their way in past the bouncers. And now the door was being held open by a flood of panicked people trying to get outside. For the first time since Gabriella killed the power, I could see beyond the reach of my flashlight. *Where's Spartak?* I'd lost sight of him.

I ran over to the fight and staggered to a stop. "What are you doing here?" I yelled at Gennadiy. "I told you to stay away!"

Gennadiy punched the guard in the face. "And I told you, you're my brother." Another guard ran towards us. "Go and find your wife!" Gennadiy told me. "We've got this!"

Alexei nodded to me and joined my brothers. I ran to where the people were emerging from behind the DJ booth. As I got closer, I saw a square hatch had opened in the floor. A stream of people, all women, were emerging. But Bronwyn wasn't among them. And I could see tongues of orange flickering down there. I raced forward—

A bottle shattered against the back of my head, and I went down hard in a shower of glittering glass fragments. My neck and back were soaked and I smelled vodka. Pain detonated in the center of my brain and throbbed outwards like a nuclear blast cloud, pushing out everything else. I couldn't think, couldn't function. I lay there for a few seconds and then tried to stand, but my feet just scrabbled at the floor uselessly. It slowly sank in that I was hurt. Hurt *bad.*

Spartak's shoes appeared in front of my face, glass crunching under his shoes like a fresh winter frost. "Oh Radimir," he chided. "Look what's become of you."

I knew I needed to get up, but my brain wouldn't issue any orders. The pain was so bad it vaporized all thought.

"I'm going to kill you," Spartak told me coldly. "Then I'll deal with your brothers and your uncle. When Konstantin hears the Aristovs are gone, he'll pull his men out." He placed his shoe on my cheek and pressed. The side of my face started to press into the broken glass on the floor, but I couldn't move: every time I tried to do something, the pain annihilated the thought, a blast cloud turning houses to matchwood. I was *done.*

"You make me sick," said Spartak, pushing a little harder. "You used to be one of us. No one was more ruthless than Radimir Aristov. And now you give yourself up *for a woman!*"

I'd had to close one eye because it was millimeters away from touching the glass. Through the other, I could see my brothers, Mikhail and Alexei still fighting the guards. I was on my own.

I looked at the hatch. It was blurry...in fact, *everything* was blurry. I must have a concussion. But I could see that women had stopped coming out of the hole, and flames were leaping up into the club, spreading the fire.

Spartak saw me looking. "Oh, she's down there," he confirmed. "I left her down there."

Fear clawed at my throat. I stared at the hatch, unable to take my eyes off it.

"Look at me!" roared Spartak, and he kicked me in the kidneys, rolling me onto my back. That's when I heard it in his voice: the same anger that I'd felt all those years ago, when I'd cut Alexei out of my life. When I'd been angry with him for falling in love.

"You're pathetic!" yelled Spartak, kicking me again. "You die for a *woman!*"

Except it wasn't anger in his voice: it was fear. He had Liliya but she was a possession, not someone who loved him. He feared, he *knew,* that he'd never have what I had.

I still had it. I still had her.

I just had to...*get the fuck up.*

The pain in my head didn't diminish. But now there was something in the firestorm, something made of diamond, indestructible. I focused on it.

Spartak yelled and swung back his foot for another kick, this one aimed at my head. But at the last second, I reached up and caught his ankle, the tip of his polished shoe an inch from my face.

She needs me.

I rolled onto my side and braced my hands on the floor. As I pushed, I felt shards of glass lancing into my palms, but I ignored it. I groaned. Grunted.

And *got the fuck up.*

Spartak stared at me in disbelief as I slowly rose to my feet. I could feel something warm dripping down my neck and wondered how badly my head was bleeding. One side of my face was bleeding, too, and my hands were a chewed-up mess.

I gripped my waistcoat, leaving bloody handprints, and tugged it straight.

Spartak ran at me, swinging wildly. I stepped forward and punched him in the jaw, ignoring the pain from the glass in my hands. The blow took him right off his feet and he went crashing down on his back. I followed him down, hitting him again and again, until finally he lay still.

Then I heaved myself to my feet again and stumbled down the stairs into the fire. My vodka-soaked jacket caught fire immediately and I ripped it off me just before the flames reached my face. I couldn't see anything but smoke. "Bronwyn!" I yelled. My voice sounded slurred and slow. There was no reply, and I yelled again, fear crushing my heart. "*Bronwyn!*"

The flames were roaring so loud I wasn't sure I'd be able to hear her even if she answered. I pushed on down the hallway, skirting around fires that seared my face. Something crunched under my feet and I looked down to see pills: thousands of pills, strewn across the floor. Blood was dripping down onto them...God,

I was leaving a *trail*, and I was lightheaded, too. How badly was I bleeding?!

It didn't matter. I'd search every inch of this place if I had to. "Bronwyn! Bron—" The smoke got in my throat, and I started coughing, then couldn't stop. I doubled over and went down on my knees.

"*Radimir!*"

Her voice, somewhere over to my left. I crawled through the smoke, still coughing. And then I saw her, and it was like my heart started beating again. She was on her knees next to Liliya, pressing on a wound in the woman's stomach. "I'm pressing on it!" she told me, tears running down her cheeks. "That's what you have to do, right?"

I threw my arms around her and hugged her tight, nodding weakly, still coughing. Liliya opened her eyes and looked up at me, her face deathly white.

"She can't walk," Bronwyn told me desperately. "I tried but I couldn't get her up the stairs."

An explosion shook the hallway and a fresh, choking cloud of black smoke swallowed us up, burning our eyes and forcing its way down into our lungs. I laid a bloody hand on Bronwyn's shoulder. She glared at me. "I'm *not leaving her!* I *promised!*"

My chest went tight. My little librarian was so brave...but the flames were spreading fast. We couldn't stay, and I couldn't carry Liliya, not in the state I was in. My jaw set and I gripped Bronwyn's shoulders: I'd drag her away, if I had to.

And then out of the smoke came a big, gloriously familiar figure. Alexei scowled down at me: *what have you gotten yourself into now?* Then he bent down, scooped Liliya up into his arms and turned towards the hatch. "We go now," he told me.

I didn't argue. I clambered to my feet and Bronwyn and I supported each other as we staggered down the hallway and back to the stairs.

When we got back up to the club, we found things had gotten worse, fast. The fire had really taken hold, spreading across carpets and up walls that Spartak had been too cheap to fireproof. The entire place was ablaze. But at least with the door open, the people had finally been able to get out. The club was empty.

Almost empty. My brothers intercepted us as we moved across the dance floor. "*Chyort*, brother," said Gennadiy, staring at my wounds, my singed, bloody shirt and my missing jacket.

"I'm okay," I wheezed. And I pulled Bronwyn tighter to my side. *Better than okay.* Together, we all headed for the door.

"Wait," croaked Bronwyn. "Spartak."

Everyone looked at her in confusion. "He's back there, out cold," I told her, pointing.

"Let him burn," said Gennadiy viciously.

Bronwyn shook her head. "He's the one who faked the phone call! If we get him out, he can tell The Eight what he did!"

I stared at her. *She's right.* I would have left him there and lost our only chance at clearing our name. *Whatever did I do without her?*

I showed Valentin and Gennadiy where I'd left Spartak's unconscious body—none of his men had tried to save him, they must have all fled when the club caught fire. My brothers picked up Spartak and a few moments later we emerged into blissfully cold, clean night air. We were coughing, our lungs raw from the smoke, our skin was singed, and I was bleeding everywhere and couldn't really see straight. But we were alive.

The street was filling up with fire trucks and paramedics and I could hear police sirens approaching, too. We took Liliya straight to one of the ambulances. Gennadiy, Valentin and Mikhail quickly put Spartak in their car so that they could spirit him away before the cops got him. A rental car came screeching around the corner and Gabriella stuck her head out of the window. "Get in!"

Alexei, Bronwyn and I climbed into the back. As the first police cars turned into the street, Gabriella roared away. She twisted around to look at us. "Hospital?"

I looked around. Spartak was gone. Everyone was okay. And I had my wife back.

"Hospital," I agreed. And passed out.

EPILOGUE

Two Weeks Later

Radimir

"HARD HATS FOR EVERYONE," the foreman told us, handing them out. "Please be careful, we've made sure the structure's safe, but I don't want anyone getting hurt."

I put a hard hat on Bronwyn's head, which made her look so adorable my chest went tight. I laced my fingers together with hers and squeezed her hand, then put a hard hat on myself. My head had taken enough knocks for a while.

I'd come out of the fire at Spartak's nightclub with smoke inhalation, a concussion, serious blood loss and enough shards of glass in my hands that it had taken a doctor a full hour to remove it all. Bronwyn had slightly worse smoke inhalation and some cuts and bruises, and was under orders to use her crutches until her arthritis had calmed down. But the worst casualty had been the club itself. Thanks to Spartak's lax safety measures and the chemicals stored in the basement, the fire had raged for hours and by the time the fire department got it under control, the club had been gutted. The damage did provide an opportunity for a fresh start, though, and that was important...because the club was now ours.

"This wall will be coming down," the foreman was telling Gennadiy. "All of this has to go..."

When the police had rolled up to the club, the first thing they'd found were about thirty trafficked women, some of whom had been in the basement for years. The second thing they found was the drug factory. They rounded up Spartak's surviving men—Bronwyn was relieved to learn that the one she'd stabbed had lived—and it was clear Spartak was going to jail for a long, long time.

Except...no one could find Spartak. The police thought he'd fled the country but actually he spent the day following the fire in a lock-up garage just a few miles from the club. Also in the garage was one of The Eight. He was *very* interested in how Spartak had used them to nearly eliminate the Aristovs. By the end of the day, he had a full confession, and Spartak was dead. The Eight restored our family's standing: we were no longer cut off. And in restitution, they gave us all of Spartak's assets and territory, including his nightclub. The war was over...and we were more powerful than ever.

The plan was to completely remodel the nightclub and turn it from a seedy drug-front into a legitimate business that Gennadiy would run.

"Wider balconies," Gennadiy was telling an architect. "We need to get rid of the bottlenecks."

"And more fire exits," said Valentin. "What are we going to do with the basement?"

Mikhail smiled and put a friendly arm around the architect's shoulders. "I have some ideas..."

I watched my family as they talked and planned, thoughtful and a little sad. I could see so much of myself in them: Vladivostok had left its marks on Gennadiy and Valentin, too, just in different ways. And Mikhail, always so warm and lighthearted...but he never talked about why *he* was still single, too.

I'd never known what I was missing until I met Bronwyn. Now I wanted them to find someone, too.

I looked across at Bronwyn, who was telling the architect how there should be more bathrooms, because there were never enough in nightclubs. *My wife.* She'd sensibly foregone the designer clothes and heels for this site visit and was in jeans and an old pair of hiking boots...and she'd never looked more beautiful. I drank her in: the soft waves of copper hair that brushed her neck, the gorgeous curves of her hips and ass, the tight denim... I listened as she talked through some ideas with the architect about how to lay out the club, so it felt safer for women, and a glow of pride filled my chest. I'd found the woman I needed by my side. Smart, beautiful, a demon between the sheets and not afraid to stand up to me when she needed to. My little librarian had become the perfect Bratva Queen.

Bronwyn

The next day, I was wearing a hard hat again. But this time, I was in Cassie's coffee shop, facing a wall with a big, red X spray-painted across it.

"I think you should do the honors," Cassie told me.

I shook my head, pressed the sledgehammer into her hands and picked up a second one. "We'll do it together. One, two, *three!*"

We both swung our hammers, awkwardly at first and then falling into a steady rhythm. The brickwork dented, then cracked. Then the first brick tumbled loose, and a rectangle of bookstore appeared. A whoop went up from Jen and the rest of my friends, who'd all come to watch. Baba was there, too: she still used a stick when she walked but she was getting stronger every day and was living in her apartment again. Radimir had paid a visit to her building's owner and within days, the elevator was working, the security cameras were fixed, and the graffiti was gone.

I'd been inspired by Konstantin and Radimir working together. If the Bratva could modernize and share resources...why couldn't we? My bookstore and Cassie's coffee shop both suffered from a lack of space and not being able to get enough customers through the door, but by knocking through the adjoining wall and forming one big space, we could solve both problems. Coffee drinkers could browse the shelves and book browsers could enjoy a coffee. It was more efficient for staffing, too: neither of us could afford to take on more help but we could pool our money and take Jen on full time. She could help serve lattes and muffins when the bookstore was quiet and restock shelves when the coffee shop was quiet. We'd have to wait to see if the change made us profitable, but I had a good feeling.

I walked to the subway that night tired but happy. My arthritis wasn't going anywhere, and my joints still throbbed and ached at the end of the day, but having Jen around in the store full time made things a lot easier and I was less self-conscious about using my crutches now. I'd started swimming and that seemed to help, too.

When the train arrived, I dropped into a seat, straightened my skirt and pulled a notepad and pen from the gorgeous, white leather purse Radimir had bought me. I was getting to like dressing like a mafia queen, even if I still preferred jeans and sneakers when we were around the penthouse.

I was so deep into planning where we could put extra tables in the cafe and how the book tables should be positioned, it took me a moment to notice what was going on at the end of the subway car. Three men were standing over a seated woman, blocking her in so she couldn't escape. She was pale and jumpy, on the edge of tears. They weren't touching her...yet. It was just that low-level harassment that gets written off as *harmless fun* when it isn't harmless or fun. But we have to put up with it.

Except I didn't. Not anymore.

Before I knew what I was doing, I'd marched down the aisle and pushed in front of the trio, so I was between them and the woman. "Leave her alone." I wasn't asking.

One of them opened his mouth to speak. I gave him a withering glance. "Do you know who I am?"

His brows knitted in confusion. Then one of his friends whispered in his ear and he paled.

"I ride this route a lot," I told them. "If I see you do this again, I will be *displeased.* Do you think that you want me displeased?"

He shook his head. All of them shook their heads.

What Radimir did—what *we* did—still bothered me. But if someone in this city had to have power, then better it was us. And if I had it, I was going to do some good with it. Spartak's territory had given us even more income and I'd made sure we spent some of it taking care of the women he'd trafficked and reuniting them with their families. Liliya was free now, too, and she was figuring out what she was going to do with her life. Part of me hoped she'd stay in Chicago: she was becoming a good friend.

I was getting to know Alexei and his wife Gabriella, too. They were in town for a few days, and it had been great seeing Alexei and Radimir reconnect. Last night, in a bar, Alexei had told us about what he'd been doing since he left the Bratva: helping Gabriella's all-female hacker group, the Sisters of Invidia. "Is good life," he told us firmly, squeezing Gabriella's hand. "Almost no one trying to kill me."

"I think you missed the action," Radimir had said playfully. "Just a little."

Alexei had shaken his head firmly. Then he'd exchanged a look with Gabriella, and she'd nodded to him, like, *it's okay.* And he'd squeezed her hand again and sheepishly nodded, a smile tugging at his lips. "Maybe just a little," he'd muttered. The two of them were spending the day sightseeing and then they were coming over for dinner tonight.

Life with Radimir was freakin' *idyllic.* With Spartak dead and the Armenians gone, things had gone quiet: I wasn't kidding myself that it would always be this peaceful, but I was going to enjoy it while it lasted. In the mornings, he'd cook breakfast and then drop me off at the bookstore, always giving me a lingering kiss outside the door. Evenings were for cuddly movie-watching under a blanket on the couch, or an elaborate function that involved him in a tux, me in a fancy dress and usually us creeping off to a quiet stairwell to fuck up against a wall shortly after the speeches started. On weekends, I'd spend all day stretched out on my stomach on one of the couches as I worked my way through a stack of books. I'd only stop to make one of my enormous sandwiches...and to make sure Radimir didn't work too hard, tempting him out of his home office with coffee, a glass of wine or, when necessary, by slinking around in nothing but some of Rachel's leather lingerie and lipstick.

Where I used to lie awake worrying, now I slept like a baby, wrapped in his protective arms. And where I used to be lonely, now I was so completely connected to another person, I could feel his mood from the next room, and he could tell as soon as I messaged him whether I was having a good or a bad day.

I knew that new enemies would come along, and that there were some big decisions we'd have to make: were we going to have kids? Would they be safe? Would they inherit this life? But we'd face those threats and make those decisions together.

When I got home to the penthouse, I dropped my purse on the counter. "Okay, we've got about ninety minutes 'till they arrive. Do you—"

I shrieked as a hand covered my eyes and another wrapped around my waist and pulled me back against a hard male body.

"Shh," whispered Radimir.

I slumped in relief as I recognized his voice. "What are you *doing?!*" I demanded.

"Surprising my wife." Even now, the sound of that word, carved by his Russian accent, sent a thrill through me. "Walk. No peeking."

He walked me across the living area to...wait, weren't we going to hit the wall soon? And why could I feel a breeze?

He stopped and removed his hand, and I gasped.

The glass doors onto the balcony were open and a line of candles led the way outside. And there, surrounded by more candles, was a hot tub. *Our own hot tub.* Just like the one in Cancún except this one had a view over half of Chicago.

"Do we have time to go in right now, before Alexei and Gabriella get here?" I asked.

"Yes, if you—" I was running to change before he could say *hurry*. "Wear the green swimsuit!" he growled.

Five minutes later, I was immersed up to my neck while jets pummeled my muscles. It was a cold night, the breeze icy against my face and that made the steaming water feel even more luxurious. I could feel my knots disappearing and my body melting into blissful taffy. "You're going to have to get a giant spoon and lift me out," I mumbled.

Radimir smirked and swam over, then slid in behind me so I could lean back and use him as a chair. Resting my head on his pec made it even better. I closed my eyes and sighed. Then opened them again when something soft touched my nose. A snowflake. It was snowing, silent and peaceful, and we had the best view in the city.

I snuggled in and for a few minutes we just watched in happy silence. Then Radimir leaned forward and kissed the back of my neck in the exact spot that always drives me crazy, and his hand began to slide upwards along my bare thigh.

"How long do we have before Alexei and Gabriella get here, again?" I mumbled.

Radimir gave a low, filthy chuckle. "Time enough."

I twisted around in his arms and kissed my husband.

The End

Thank you for reading! If you enjoyed *Frozen Heart,* please consider leaving a review, it really helps.

Alexei and Gabriella's story is *Kissing My Killer*. He's sent to kill her but when he looks into her eyes, he can't pull the trigger. Now they're on the run together and the man sent to kill her is the only one who can save her.

Hailey and Konstantin's story is *The Double.* Hailey's given plastic surgery by the FBI to make her into the exact double of Konstantin's evil girlfriend, Christina, and is inserted into his life. If he finds out who she really is, he'll kill her. And the feelings she's supposed to be faking are growing all too real...

For a full list of my books and to join my newsletter (you get two FREE ebooks!), visit helenanewbury.com